Home Sweet Home

Maree Rose

Home Sweet Home

by Maree Rose

Copyright © 2024 by Maree Rose

All rights reserved

First Edition: January 2024

Published by Maree Rose

All rights reserved, including the right to reproduce, distribute, or transmit in any form or by any means without prior permission of the author, except in cases of a reviewer quoting brief passages in review.

This book is a work of fiction. Names, characters, places and incidents (outside of those clearly in the public domain) are products of the author's imagination or are used fictitiously. Any resemblance to actual events, locales or persons, either living or dead, is entirely coincidental.

BLURB

When you're a teenager, life is usually simple and carefree. You could never imagine the evil that lurks in the shadows, waiting for a chance to steal your innocence. However, for Willow, that evil becomes a stark reality when she's abducted while walking home one night after spending the day with her best friends.

For 15 long years, Willow finds herself in the clutches of a sinister cult, her life dictated by the whims of those who seek to control and manipulate her. At the same moment that she tries to break free, she is finally saved, her life spared from what she considered a fate worse than death.

To reclaim the life she lost, she returns to her hometown, and the friends who never forgot her. But her life's not instantly filled with sunflowers. A lot has happened during the time she was gone, and people have changed, including her.

Willow's time in captivity has left scars on both her body and soul.

She wants to heal and move forward with her life. But will her past stay in her past? Has evil followed her home? Or was it there all along?

FOREWORD

Hello readers!

Thank you so much for picking up my book!

Please be aware that this book is a reverse harem, meaning our leading lady Willow will not have to choose between her men, because #whychoose.

There is explicit language and explicit sex scenes. This is absolutely an adult romance and is intended for readers 18+ due to the language and content.

Thank you and I hope that you enjoy Home Sweet Home.

PS. Okay mum... this one you can read...

For those who don't care about the content warning and like to live on the edge, skip the next page... for those who take the warning seriously, don't skip it... these ones are to be taken seriously...

CONTENT WARNINGS

Child abuse
Child abduction/Kidnapping
Prolonged physical and mental abuse
Religious trauma
Cult behavior and teachings
Attempted brainwashing
Sexual assault/Rape (including sodomy)
Body mutilation
Alcohol abuse
Death during childbirth
Forced betrothal
Stalking
Arson
Knife and gun violence
Intense PTSD depiction throughout (including panic attacks, flashbacks, nightmares, and misplaced guilt)

IMPORTANT NOTE: All reasonable efforts have been made to accurately reflect Willow's time within the cult and the resulting effects on her mental health. This story does delve deeply into PTSD symptoms and emotional and mental trauma from 'Willow's' perspective. Not everyone experiences trauma and PTSD symptoms the same way, or has the same thoughts.

These characters are fictional and although I have had assistance from those who have experienced this sort of trauma, creative freedom has still been used in writing this story, including the timeframe for Willow's recovery, as that has and will always be at your own pace.

Mental Health matters and is very important, if you or someone you know may be in crisis, or struggling with suicidal thoughts, you can use the following numbers to contact 24/7 assistance and confidential support:

USA and Canada: 988 (Suicide & Crisis Lifeline)

UK: 166 123 (Samaritans)

Australia: 13 11 14 (Lifeline Australia)

New Zealand: 1737 (National Mental Health Helpline)

Please check your local national lifeline number if not in the above countries.

For those who fought hard to escape
the chains that bound you,
I'm so proud of you.
And for those still fighting,
I believe in you, keep fighting.

PROLOGUE

Screams, fire and the loud, sharp sounds of gunshots surround me. Panicked people run in all directions. It was chaos in an environment that had been strictly built to ensure structure and compliance.

However, instead of feeling panicked or scared, I only feel immense relief. The happiness bubbles from deep inside me, escaping my lips and tugging them into my first smile in years.

I kneel on the dirt in front of the large compound, men dressed in tactical gear holding heavy weaponry moving forward toward the building at my back. Most of them continue on while the man closest to me comes to a standstill, only a step in front of me.

I bring my hands up to prove they are empty before lacing them behind my head. The movement makes my long honey blond waves move, brushing against my ass.

The man crouches down in front of me, reaching up to pull down the mask from his face and takes off the glasses revealing his whole face. After years of looking into the faces of evil men, it isn't hard for me to see that this man isn't one.

He has kind eyes, clear and blue. High cheekbones and a dusting of dark stubble across his angular jaw.

"Hey honey, you're safe now. My name is Easton. Can you tell me your name?"

It's odd to feel wetness on my face; I didn't even realize that I started crying. I'm sure I must look crazy, this smiling woman kneeling in the dirt with tears on her face.

"They called me Grace," I reply softly. A shiver runs down my spine as I momentarily think back on the common phrase whispered to me, *"By the grace of god."* Words that will now haunt me forever.

He slings the weapon onto his back before reaching out to hesitantly touch my elbows, moving my arms down as he raises me slowly, helping me back to my feet. He briefly looks down at my bare feet before quickly returning his eyes to mine.

I know what he sees, and the fact that he didn't take the time to look at me more just proves the sort of person he is. The white nightgown that I was forced to wear is semi sheer and you could clearly see the curves of my hips and breasts through the thin material, my nipples dark against the light fabric.

They forced me into it after they 'scrubbed my body of any impurities'.

Because it was the night before my wedding, and I had been given no choice in that fact. When you're told that you're to be married in our community, you simply smile, lower your eyes and say thank you for the blessing.

It doesn't matter that the man I was to be married to was pure evil. All that mattered was that he was the eldest son of our leader. I was being afforded an honor and was supposed to be grateful.

When they left me alone in his room to await his arrival to test my virtue, as was custom, was the moment when I had been grateful. It was my first time I was left alone anywhere; I even shared a room to sleep with three other girls my age. I took the chance I had been waiting on for years, climbing out of his window and making a run for it.

As I started to make a dash across the land behind the compound, I triggered the giant flood lights above, temporarily blinding myself from the sudden brightness. I felt my heart freeze in my chest, while my body stumbled causing me to fall in the dirt on my knees. It took a moment for me to realize that the flood lights were not aimed at me but aimed towards the compound where I now saw a swarm of heavily armed men making their way inside.

Easton gently guides me toward where I now see a lot of military-like vehicles, some of the light coming from spotlights mounted on their roofs. A woman in the same tactical outfit as the man ran toward us, stopping our progress and then wrapping a blanket around me.

I mumble my thanks to her before she smiles in response and disappears again.

As I tighten my new covering around my body, Easton once again cups my elbow and starts moving me toward the vehicles again. I can see the concern in his eyes as he keeps looking between me and our obvious destination.

I still can't stop smiling, the relief inside of me is so palpable.

"You say they called you that, is that not your name?" His voice is soft, like he's trying to be gentle with me in all aspects.

I shake my head in a quick jerk, using the arm he isn't holding to wipe my face with the blanket. Maybe if I get rid of the tears I won't look quite so crazy. "No."

"What is your real name, do you know it?"

Of course I knew it, I made sure to repeat it to myself every day since they told me my name was now Grace. But I doubted that would actually make much difference.

"Willow Silva."

He stumbles, his hand tightening on my elbow sharply almost the point of pain. I don't make any sign that he hurt me; They trained me to take worse without a sound. But my eyes do widen slightly when I see him looking at me with a shocked look.

"Oh my god. I know you... well, I have studied everything there was to find about your disappearance." His mouth is hanging open and all I can do is blink wide eyes at him while he seems to struggle with whatever turmoil simply saying my real name has created. "You have been missing for fifteen years."

CHAPTER 1

Willow

15 years ago

As a child in a happy small town, you never imagine that anything can happen to you. Any Amber Alert that scrolled across the bottom of our television screens or took over our radios were simply an annoyance. Any whispers from our parents about them were simply ignored.

Fifteen years ago, I was twelve years old and all I wanted to do was spend time with my friends.

We thought we were invincible, and in the safest place in the world.

How very wrong we were.

That fateful day fifteen years prior felt like any other day. I walked over to the neighboring property to play with my best friends.

Wyatt snuck us into the barn to check out the new foal, I think more for my benefit than for Mason or Gage. After that we spent hours riding the trails and occasionally racing each other.

I ran back home as the sun started to set, but never made it there.

You wouldn't imagine that between the space of one property and the next that something could happen. But thinking back on it, it was as though they waited for me. I barely had a chance to scream before I was unconscious, the chemical smell on the rag they held to my face impossible to get away from.

When I finally woke again, I felt sick and so very tired, and I was nowhere near the place I called home. The struggles of a twelve-year-old girl were useless against the bigger adult bodies and the ropes that bound me.

They told me my name was now Grace. And despite me screaming that my name was Willow, they kept calling me Grace. They dressed me in a plain brown cotton gown and soft shoes. They took everything from me, my clothes, my earrings, even the braided bracelet to match the ones that I made for my friends. I was left with nothing from what they referred to as my life before they "saved" me.

It was made very clear to me from the moment they showed me my new home that it would be difficult for me to escape, though that didn't stop me from trying the very first moment I could. As a result, I was chained to my bed on a short leash for a week.

The very first time they struck me with a leather strap to the bare skin at the back of my neck was a shock. I was told that it was so that I could feel it close to the mouth that was telling lies when I insisted that my name was Willow and not

Grace. That when I opened my mouth to tell more lies, it would be a reminder not to do that.

I didn't learn my lesson the first time.

Eventually, I did learn to just repeat it to myself at night instead of the prayers they insisted on.

The room they put me into when I first arrived was what I imagined would be in a convent. Bare walls, bare floors, nothing but a small bed with a thin mattress in a small square room.

And no windows.

Even at twelve, I heard about solitary confinement in prison, and this is what I imagined.

The first week, I screamed and cried until I couldn't do more than surrender to the numb exhaustion that slid over me like a blanket. Before I woke and the process started again.

Eventually, I could not do anything more than stare blankly into nothingness.

When I called out for my mummy and daddy, *they* appeared. They weren't my parents, but they now claimed to be. They were who led the people I was now forced to live with. They insisted that I call them Mother and Father, as that was who they claimed they were to me now.

I was given scripture to read and learn to become a good disciple to the faith. And when I refused to read it, I was refused food in return. I was told that my soul needed sustenance before my body did.

I followed along simply so I could have food to take away the ache in my stomach.

Months passed like this with my resistance and struggles becoming less frequent and less severe. And therefore the punishment for my disobedience also became less frequent.

But still not a day passed where I didn't shed silent tears at the memories of my parents and friends at home. And every night I told myself my name is Willow, my family and friends miss me and I will get away one day to return to them.

I knew escape was almost impossible. But no matter how long it took, I would find an opportunity to leave.

When they felt I surrendered to their will and accepted my place among them, they bathed me and scrubbed at my skin. I went along when they baptized me in some attempt to cleanse me of the impurities of the world they saved me from. That was how they worded it.

I was thankful that the water disguised the tears on my face.

It was the final step to becoming part of the family.

But no matter how willing they thought I was at that point, they weren't my family. They had stolen me from my real family.

CHAPTER 2

Willow

10 YEARS AGO

The man known as Father is giving me to his son.

He has promised me in marriage and I have no say in it.

I'm not even an adult yet, but I have been told that once I have transitioned through all of my scripture levels and have reached what they call full enlightenment, that I will be taking my place by Jacob's side. And in his bed.

The lecherous looks that I receive from Jacob tell me that is all he cares about.

He is tall and slim, and three years older than me. I had read and watched Harry Potter before my abduction. The man looked like Lucius Malfoy and Voldemort had a love child. And he had the creepy vibes to go with it. His pale skin was even lighter than the blond hair he kept tied back at the base of his skull.

And from the moment his father announced our betrothal he called me his Angel.

I was thankful that they were so strict with their beliefs and that sex before marriage was a harshly punished offense, though I doubt if they would actually punish their own son. But I couldn't imagine them actually cutting into him and leaving him in the middle of nowhere with nothing to save him.

I swore to myself in those moments that I would take as long as I could to progress through their scriptures. Maybe he would get bored of waiting for me and ask his Father for someone else instead.

That may be naive of me to think, but I couldn't give up the small sparks of hope that still existed inside of me after so long.

The hope that I would be able to escape still simmered inside of me even though they never allowed anyone to be alone. I wasn't the last girl to appear against my will. In the early days I heard the screams and crying of others and my heart ached for them.

I was already scarred from my attempts to reach them and give them hope we would get away from here. The backs of my legs for walking too closely to areas I shouldn't be in, and the backs of my arms for wanting to comfort those who were not yet "clean."

It took years but once they were happy that we all surrendered to their way of life, we were moved into a room together. They made it very clear that they had eyes and ears in the room, however, because I earned another scar across my upper back for trying to speak to them negatively about The Family.

Outside of the room we slept in, we were always escorted to our chores, worship and scripture lessons. We had etiquette classes that I mentally called Stepford Wife lessons.

Our commitment to God and The Family was always at the forefront of everything we were taught. On the inside, I was screaming, tearing at the walls of my own mind in protest of the constant barrage of manipulation.

Every day, I missed my parents and my friends. And every night, I still silently recited to myself that my name is Willow.

CHAPTER 3

Willow

3 YEARS AGO

At twenty four any hopes I have of holding off my marriage to the son of Satan were rapidly dwindling.

The moment my twentieth birthday passed, or at least the birthday they gave me when I refused to answer their questions, Jacob made it clear he would no longer tolerate my delays.

He went to his father and requested betrothal "dates" so that he could spend time alone with me until our marriage. All under the guise of getting to know his future wife better.

I very quickly learned to dread those "dates."

For the first year after he requested them, they were every other month and chaperoned. When the chaperone disappeared, so did the mask he wore.

His fingers dug into my skin hard enough to leave bruises as he threw me to the floor that day. They dug into my jaw and my scalp as he pushed his dick into my mouth until I choked.

It was thankfully over quickly, his cum sliding down my throat and making me want to throw up. I couldn't bring myself to move from where I was silently crying on the floor.

I was told in no uncertain terms that his parents would never believe me over their God fearing son. He made it very clear that if I breathed a word to a single soul he would make hell look like paradise.

He then maneuvered me until he could bare my back to him. He took a knife and sliced into the skin behind my shoulder in a single line.

"This is how we will keep track of your defiance, my Angel. For each month you delay the inevitable I will keep a tally on your pretty skin."

I tolerated the initial months with silent tears and thoughts of home. But the longer I delayed, the more sadistic he became.

He progressed after six months from only putting his dick in my mouth. As he very bluntly put it since he couldn't put it in my cunt, he would put it in the only other hole I had available. The pain was the worst I had ever experienced. He took even greater pleasure from the fact that I was in pain.

It took months but eventually I forced myself to become numb to the pain and ignore the words. I became a blank canvas for the tally he was carving into the skin of my back and a rag doll for him to use while at the same time keeping me 'pure'.

And yet behind the walls in my mind, I still screamed. I still clutched with a tight grip to the memories of my friends and family.

And I still told myself every night that my name is Willow.

CHAPTER 4
Willow

Now

It's been over a week since I was rescued.

It still amazes me that I held on for as long as I did. That I didn't fold to Jacob's abuse and just did as I was told. But in my mind I knew that even if I did allow myself to submit to him like he wanted, the abuse wouldn't get better but worse.

The man who helped me, Easton, has been an almost constant presence by my side while the medical teams assessed me. Even being there as I then sat through hours and days of interviews with the FBI and law enforcement. He had a way of soothing my nerves at having so many people focused on me.

It was daunting that we made the news internationally. I didn't like the attention. When I was at the compound, any attention ended up being bad.

Even now, reporters camped outside the hotel that they housed those of us they rescued. Barricades had been erected to hold the swarm back so that we still had privacy. But I just wanted to return home.

Parents and family of some of the girls that had been rescued arrived quickly, wrapping them in warm loving embraces and showering them in affection. But no one had been able to get a hold of my family yet.

Standing in front of the floor to ceiling glass windows in the hotel room, I can't help but reach out and touch the glass. The view of the city from here was a thing of beauty. But I desperately missed the countryside I grew up in.

They placed guards outside of our hotel room doors, but all of us freaked out about the strange men stationed so close to us outside of locked doors we couldn't just escape from. It reminded us too much of the compound. So they changed the guards to an all female team and stationed them at elevator access instead. They even cleared out the rest of the hotel floor of all other occupants.

Even with those measures in place, I was thankful that Easton was sitting on my couch watching me in silence. He brought me some dinner and sat with me as we ate, lending me his strength.

Dinner itself was a bland affair, with the medical team advising me not to rush into anything exciting after years of eating the basic flavorless food they gave us. Still, the chicken and vegetables sat heavy.

Easton stood and approached me. "What's on your mind, little butterfly?"

My lips tugged slightly at the nickname. When I asked him about it the first time he said it, he explained that it's what I reminded him of the first time he saw me. I was trying to fly away from my cocoon, the bad place that had smothered me and kept me caged until I was ready to spread my wings.

Glancing at him I let my fingers fall away from the glass. "It's pretty here. But I miss my home."

He nodded, glancing down. "I know the feeling, ummm about that–"

A knock on the door to my room interrupts what he is about to say, and with a sigh he moves over to see who it is. It only takes a few moments before he is leading others back into the living room.

I recognize two of the three people that follow him as FBI agents that have been assigned to our case, but I don't recognise the third. He is older, a distinguished gentleman in a suit with a briefcase in his hand.

Agents Mills and Walker are dressed in the stereotypical suit that makes me think of the movie Men in Black every time I see them. Even with Mills being a woman. Both of them have brown hair styled back, almost matching, but Mills' hair is longer and tied at the nape of her neck.

A flutter of nerves moves through me; not only is it late, but normally they don't come to the hotel room itself. It was always me going to them at their offices. It was odd for them to pay a personal visit.

Concern pulled at Easton's features but he didn't voice it.

Mills smiled at me as she reached the living area of the room. "Good evening, Miss Silva, we're sorry for the late visit."

Nodding slowly, I make my way to the couch where Easton has sat back down, taking a seat beside him. "That's okay Agents, it's not like I have any plans or anything."

The look of concern clears from Easton's face as he struggles not to give in to his laughter. It goes completely over the agents' heads and they just continue to nod in agreement with my statement.

"I'm sure you're wondering why we needed to visit at this time, but unfortunately we thought it best to speak to you in private," Agent Walker says, his face a mask of seriousness.

"We hadn't wanted to bring this up earlier, but as all of your interviews with us are coming to a close we thought it best to broach this subject. During your statement of events and interviews with us, you discussed another member of the cult that was abusing you, a man you called Jacob," Agent Mills continues.

I nod in response, a frown pulling at my face. I don't want to think about Jacob, and I certainly don't want to talk about him ever again.

Walker glances at Mills and my heart starts to race. "I'm sorry to let you know this, but we haven't identified the man you described among the prisoners or the dead."

I blink at them slowly, my mind racing to make sense of what he is trying to tell me.

"We believe that he somehow escaped along with several others in the chaos of the raid," he continues, unaware of the slow building turmoil taking over my body.

It feels like everything inside me drops suddenly through the pretty beige carpet of the hotel room. I almost don't reach the closest waste bin before my very bland chicken and vegetable dinner makes its way back out of my body.

A hand brushes my hair and I startle, falling to my side beside the bin. Easton holds his hands in front of him in a gesture reminiscent of when he rescued me and I allow him to slowly brush the strands of hair away from my face.

When I'm having to once again lean over the bin, I don't startle this time when he gathers my hair at the back of my head and rubs a hand against my back. He isn't aware that all that does is remind me of Jacob, his hand brushing over the scars that Jacob left on my body.

My breathing is rapid, my stomach now empty, and all I can do is dry heave a few more times. I slump back down onto the ground again to get away from Easton's hand on my back.

The struggle to draw in a breath is clamoring in my mind as Easton turns me physically to face him, his face taking over my entire vision.

"Look at me, Willow, focus on me. Focus on my voice," he says. The look on his face is one I haven't seen before. He takes both of my hands and rests the palms against his chest before he takes a deep breath. I can feel it all the way up my arms. "Feel my breathing. Breathe with me, Willow. That's it, deep breath in and out."

I struggle, but my body responds to his instinctively, matching him as he continues to take deep resounding breaths. It doesn't take too long before he has my panic subsiding and my mind clearing again.

A glass of water suddenly appears next to Easton's head and I flick my eyes to it and then at the older stranger holding it out toward me.

"Just take sips only, Miss Silva." Even his voice sounds distinguished and kind. I move one of my hands from Easton's chest and reach for the glass, bringing it to my lips to take tiny sips like he said.

It's soothing to my sore throat and I'm grateful to him even though I have no idea who he is.

I take a few more moments to slowly gather myself again, taking more sips as I continue to match my breathing to what I feel under my other hand. Easton helps move me back to the couch, taking the glass from me before sitting at my side once again.

Glancing once again at the stranger, I nod in thanks. "Thank you. I'm sorry, I don't know your name."

He gives me a sad smile. "That's okay, Miss Silva. I know you don't know me. I actually feel terrible to be here bearing more bad news for you on top of what you have already received."

I can't bring myself to respond as I mentally prepare myself for however else Jacob may be about to fuck up my life.

As though he understands this, he just continues. "My name is Bennett Green. You might not remember me, but I'm pretty much the only lawyer in your hometown. You might have been too young to know about me before… well, before what happened."

I frown, searching my memory and coming up blank.

He nods silently, as though understanding whatever he must see on my face. "It's completely understandable. You were just a child, after all. But the reason I'm here, and I'm so very sorry to be the one to have to tell you this, but unfortunately your parents were taken from us in an accident two years ago."

Again, I feel like my mind is struggling to process the words that left his lips. Because they make no sense to me. My parents were meant to be here, wrapping me up in their warm arms. I would breathe in my mother's floral smell and bury my face into her neck where she can tell me that I'm safe now.

"They never stopped looking for you, Miss Silva. I have a letter here for you that they left for you in my care, but everything they owned is now yours."

The buzzing in my ears is getting louder with every second that passes and I watch numbly as he places a folder on the low table a short distance from me. I can't bring myself to respond, the buzzing is becoming too loud.

I'm not even paying attention to what is being said anymore, until I hear the agents talking about putting me in witness protection.

"No." I say abruptly and they stop talking amongst themselves to focus on me again. I look at each of them, I'm not going to hide, I didn't before and I won't start now. "I'm going home."

Agent Mills frowns at me. "You can't just disregard the protection we are offering you. The man you said abused you is still out there. You can't just go home alone."

"She isn't going alone."

Everyone focuses on Easton at his words.

"And you can't just drop everything just to return to her home because that's where she wants to go. You have a job on the tactical team." Agent Walker scowls in frustration.

Easton is already shaking his head before Agent Walker finishes speaking. "I have already requested and been approved for a leave of absence. And you forget, that's my home too."

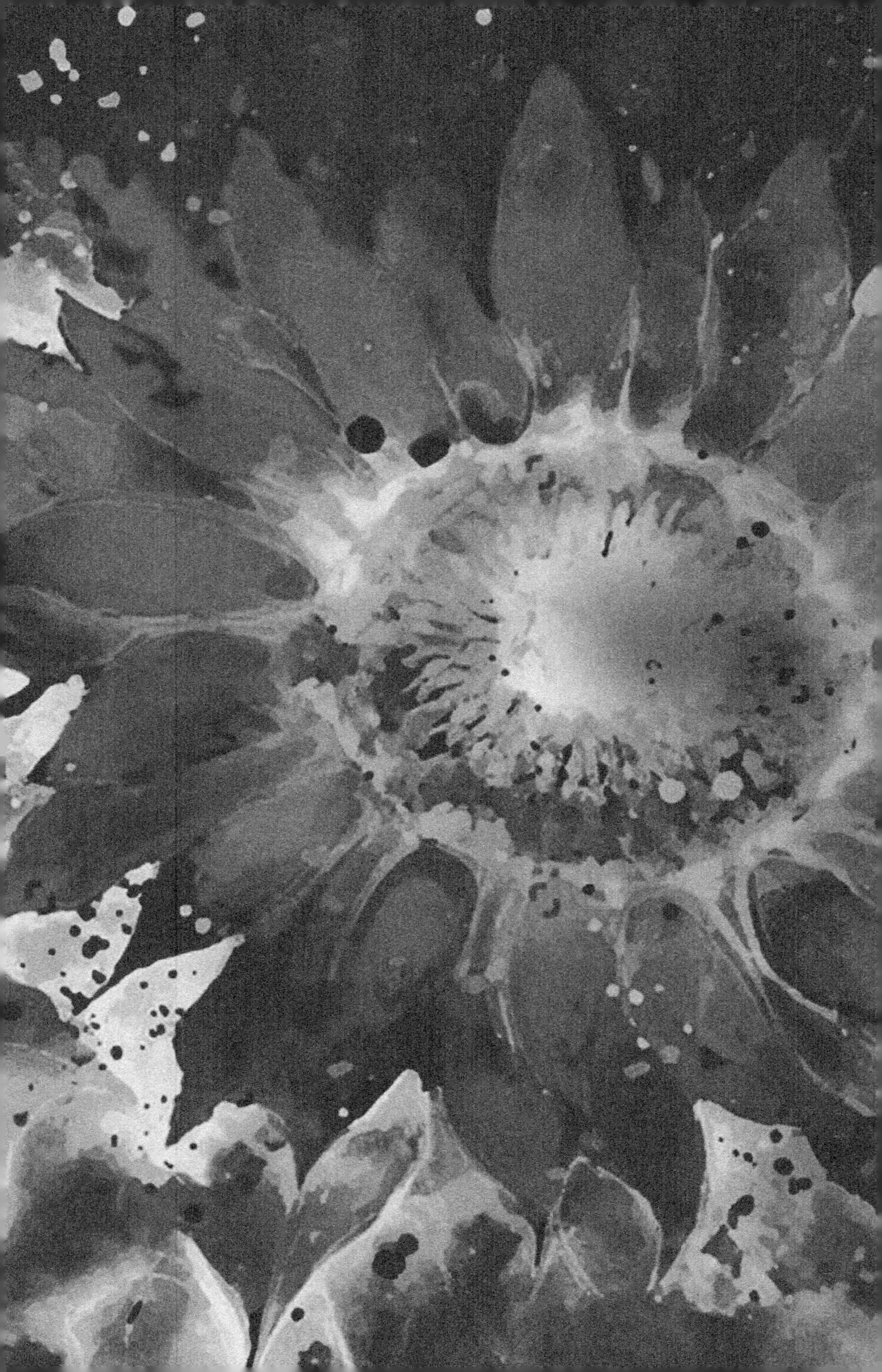

CHAPTER 5

Willow

I retreated to the bathroom and left them bickering in the living area after Easton's revelation. I am in a daze as I look at my own reflection. I may have been looking at myself, but that isn't what I see.

After everything I learned tonight, I'm even more desperate to return home. I want something familiar in my life again. I want the last place I felt truly safe.

Everything is bearing down on me, drowning me in the small enclosed space. All I can do is continue to stare at my own reflection as the image causes Jacob's voice to haunt me.

"*You're mine, Grace, my own living angel. That virgin cunt is going to bleed so prettily on my dick.*"

I struggle to blink away the tears and shake away his voice.

"*My angel, with her long golden hair. I can't wait to see it spread out beneath you on our wedding night. Will you scream and cry for me like a good little angel when I rip that cunt apart finally?*"

A loud sob escapes me, my tears now flowing freely as I tear my eyes away from the mirror. But looking down isn't any better, my hair falls forward and creates a golden curtain around my body.

My body shakes as the sobs consume me. I will never escape him. Not only is he out there somewhere, he is also in my mind.

A pair of scissors on the bathroom counter catches my attention. I left them here days before, after cutting the tags off the new clothes they gave me.

My hand shakes as I reach toward them. The sound of a knock on the door pauses me for a second as Easton's voice comes through from the other side of it.

"Willow, are you okay? Can I come in?"

I can't bring myself to answer him as I continue to sob, my fingers wrapping around the handle of the scissors and opening the blades.

Grabbing a fistful of the golden strands, I bring the scissors to it, trying to close the blades at a random spot somewhere above my shoulders. They struggle through the amount of hair in my hand and I continue to sob as I hack away at my hair.

Not a single strand in my head had been cut more than an inch or two in the last fifteen years.

Letting the strands in my hand fall to the ground, it almost feels like a small portion of my fear and the panic and desperation clawing at my chest falls with it.

I'm hacking into the hair on the other side of my head when Easton knocks again, his voice a mixture of fear and concern.

"Willow, please answer me, I'm going to come in there if you don't respond in the next five seconds."

But I can't respond. I can barely breathe through the deep heart wrenching sobs that shake my body as the strands of hair continue to fall to the floor.

I'm trying to cut into the last section of hair at the back of my neck when my legs decide they don't want to hold me anymore. They give out from under me and the scissors make a harsh sound on the floor when I put my hands out to stop myself from collapsing completely.

It's at that moment that Easton must finish counting. The door bangs against the wall as he forces it open. It takes him only a second to take it all in before he is rushing to my side, pulling the scissors from my numb fingers and wrapping his arms around me.

I can't stop myself from leaning into him, my face pressed to his chest as he starts rocking me. His hands set a soothing rhythm against my back as he whispers to me.

It takes a moment for his words to even register, my mind and heart still racing with emotional turmoil.

"It's all going to be okay, little butterfly. I have you now. He won't ever touch you again." His voice is soft and soothing against my chaotic mind. He keeps rocking me, repeating himself, until my sobs have died down to the occasional hiccup and sniffle.

Finally leaning away from me, he reaches up to tentatively touch the hair that I hacked into. "I'm sure we can work with this. Will you let me tidy it up a little?"

I hesitate a moment but the turmoil inside of me has calmed again and I can only imagine how it must look. The bathroom floor is now littered with a mess of long golden strands. That knowledge still has a small amount of anxiety gnawing at me but I push it aside, I will not let him control my actions anymore.

Giving a small nod, I allow Easton to lift me back onto my feet and when I hold out a hand to help him up, he just chuckles at me and is on his feet in seconds with no effort at all.

I don't dare to look in the mirror again, and I suddenly feel a small amount of embarrassment at Easton seeing the mess that I try to always keep hidden inside. Looking down at the bathroom sink in front of me, I see the long golden strands that fell there when I started to cut into my hair. They are long, the length of my back, and look like strands of sunshine glittering under the light in the bathroom.

I'm so mesmerized looking at them that I don't realize that Easton has come up behind me again, his tentative touch on my shoulders jolting me from my thoughts until his hands sooth down my upper arms. "You ready?"

Pushing the strands of hair off the counter, I nod my head again, still looking down.

"Hey," his voice comes softly before I feel his fingers on my jaw, turning me toward him. The concern written across his face softens into a gentle smile as our eyes meet. His thumb brushes away a new stray tear that I hadn't even noticed escaped.

"You're strong, Willow," he says, his voice filled with sincerity. "Stronger than you give yourself credit for. And I'm here for you, every step of the way."

I manage a small, appreciative smile, grateful for his presence. Easton reaches for a towel on the rack, dampening it under the sink before carefully wiping away the loose hairs clinging to my neck and shoulders. His touch is tender, a stark contrast to the violence of my memories.

"Are we wanting a complete change or just the length? If you want, I can go out and get something to change the color," he murmurs as he puts the towel aside and starts to tidy up my uneven strands.

A color change hadn't even occurred to me in the heat of the moment, and now that he mentioned the option, it feels like the right thing to do. "Yes please," I respond.

As he works, a comfortable silence settles between us, broken only by the soft hum of the bathroom fan and the clicking of the scissors in my hair. The tiny glances I steal of Easton's reflection in the mirror show nothing except his focused expression as he tidies up the uneven strands of my hair. It surprises me that someone on a law enforcement team would look so professional when cutting hair.

"Have you done this before?" I ask, stealing another glance at where his fingers are holding the ends of my hair in place. I don't miss the twitch of his lips at my question.

"Do you mean comforting someone? Or cutting hair?"

I can't fight the smile in response. "Cutting hair."

He hums as he parts another section of my hair and starts on that. "My mom was a hairdresser. When we moved to Sierra Valley it was so that my dad could take on a contract as a horsebreaker, so mom just started going to the different properties to cut hair for convenience. For a while I went along with her to help her since I didn't know anyone and she taught me the basics."

"That sounds like it was fun."

He smiles, but he pauses. "You're not going to ask?"

I know he means the revelation he dropped earlier as this was just another reminder. "It's not my place to ask questions."

He turns me towards him with a frown. "That's that hell talking, you aren't there anymore. It is your place to ask questions. You have a right to do and say whatever you want to without fear."

Emotions surge within me again. A mix of fear and hope colliding.

"When I was going to those properties with my mother, I made friends with the boys at one of the ranches. We were fifteen and you had been missing for a year and a half, but still you were all they talked about. Your case was the entire reason I joined law enforcement, Willow."

It feels like my heart stopped beating. My family and friends were all I thought of each night for the last fifteen years. And somehow this man who knew them had been there to rescue me.

"Did you know about my parents?" I finally ask after a minute of silence.

A sadness enters his eyes and a sigh leaves his lips before he shakes his head. "No, little butterfly, or I would have been the one to let you know." He turns me back around and gets back to my hair. "When I went home to visit after I finished at the academy, some stuff went down. My parents had retired to Florida, so I haven't been back."

There is a lot in that one statement that tells me so much, yet has so many more questions rising to the surface. "But you said you would go back with me?"

"I said I would be with you every step of the way, remember? Even if that means returning too."

I chew on my lip for a moment. "Is there something I need to know about why you left to begin with?"

He doesn't respond for a while, and for a moment I don't think he will. The scissors stop clipping at my hair and he puts them back on the bathroom counter, taking the towel to brush away the new strands on my neck and shoulders. "It's not really my place to talk about it, little butterfly. And it's probably not the right time to either."

Turning me back toward him, he offers me another smile that I can see doesn't quite reach his eyes this time.

"How about we promise each other to face our pasts together. However hard it may be." Not waiting for my response he tugs on my now much shorter hair. "Now, how about I go see what I can find this late at night to get this color changed?"

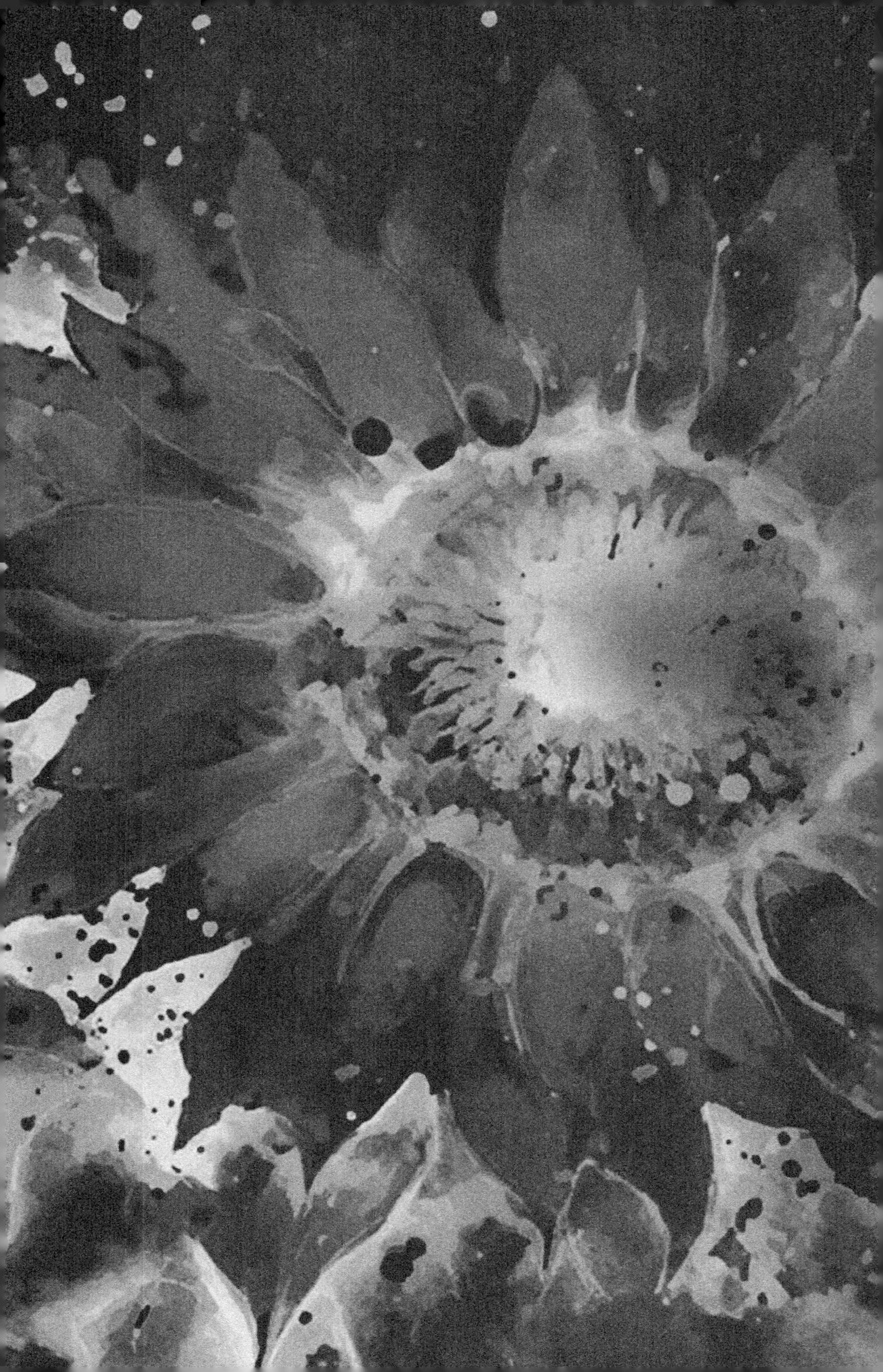

CHAPTER 6
Willow

The scenery beyond my window looks familiar, yet unfamiliar at the same time.

The roads appear to have had an upgrade. The houses look older for the most part, but I also see new houses in places that I recall had clear land.

We drove for hours, mostly in silence, but with music playing low through the speakers of the large SUV. Easton regularly asks if I need him to stop for any reason, but I've been happy just watching the view. It seems so odd to appreciate simply looking outside at the new scenery after not seeing anything but the inside of the compound for so long and then the view of the city from the hotel.

Once again, I glance over at Easton in the driver's seat. It surprised me that it was only us, but he explained that because I had declined the witness protection, the FBI wasn't inclined to just have their agents accompany me. Which is why Easton was now officially on leave.

They were still going to look for Jacob, and the other few members that had escaped with him, but that was the extent of their involvement with me now.

The vehicle we were in was Easton's, and from the look of it, he enjoyed driving what in my mind equated to a tank. A luxury tank, but still bigger than I had expected. The movement of my head as I turned it in his direction flared my newly dyed hair, the now dark auburn locks trimmed neatly and barely brushing against my shoulders.

Easton made good on his word and managed to find a late night drug store for a box of dye, using it the moment he returned. He spent another good hour on that and a final tidy before he camped on the couch in my hotel. The knowledge that he was there inexplicably calmed me enough to sleep.

We spoke to Mr. Greene, who had been happy to arrange for my parents' home, now my home, to be prepared for our arrival. Though he did admit he hadn't touched any of the contents, so it may be hard for me to see.

But then, when has life been simple and easy for me?

As we approach my childhood home, a flood of memories and emotions rush through me. The familiarity of the surroundings, combined with the anticipation of seeing my parents' house after so long, create a deep anxiety within me.

I am thankful that we don't have to drive through the town in order to get to the house. Already the passage of time is so evident and only adds to my anxiety. All too soon, we pass the still vacant land leading to our destination.

Turning the vehicle in the driveway, Easton pulls to a stop beside another car in front of the house. After he lets me sit for a moment to take it in, he mirrors me when I step out of the vehicle. The air seems different here, the scent of the trees tugging at my memories. I take a deep breath, and with it a feeling of comfort settles on me.

There were no words for the intensity of the homesickness that I experienced. A part of me was heartsick and devastated that even now that I was free, I would not get to see my parents. But the feeling of finally being home is like the sun filtering through the clouds on a miserable day.

A warmth touches my heart as I look at the house in front of me. All of my good memories are tied to this town and mostly to this house. There is nothing that could have stopped me returning; not even the thought of Jacob still out there was going to stand in my way of coming home.

The front door opens, startling me slightly, before Mr. Greene walks out toward us with an older lady that I would estimate to be around the same age as him. She instantly gives off a grandmotherly vibe, her gray hair up in a bun and a gentle smile on her face making the signs of her age more prominent.

They come to a stop in front of us and Mr. Greene indicates to the woman. "Miss Silva, this is my wife Estelle. She has been trying to make the house a little more homely for your return."

I reach forward to shake her hand and let out a startled squeak when she used the hand to pull me towards her. I can hear Easton give a slight protest before her voice is all I hear.

"Oh hush, come here, sweet child." Her voice is soft and kind but yet still has that edge of a worried parent. "Grandma Esse has you now."

I freeze for a moment as her arms wrap around me but then I melt into her embrace, my body instantly letting go of the edge of weariness that has been resting on my shoulders. She has a floral scent, like jasmine and lavender. Her touch doesn't cause panic in my mind or body; it actually gives me comfort and I realize how much I missed simply touching or being touched by another person.

The times that I had been comforted by Easton, I had already been deep into a panicked state, so I never took a moment to assess how it made me feel. Apart from him, Mrs. Greene is the first to touch me in an affectionate way since I had been abducted fifteen years before.

She eventually lets me go and I almost feel reluctant to step back to Easton's side. Not because I don't want to be there, but because of how a simple hug from Mrs. Greene makes me feel.

Continuing to smile at me, she continued. "I hope you brought your appetite, I've stocked up all of your fridge and pantry with food and everything you may need so you didn't have to go traipsing into town until you're ready. I even brought some of my famous apple pie and blueberry muffins, and don't you let young Easton steal them all, I know for a fact he has a sweet tooth."

I glance wide eyed in Easton's direction to see him with his head ducked down, kicking his toe into the driveway like a child in trouble. A soft laugh escapes my lips and Easton looks at me, startled, his eyes widening and I realize it's the first time I've really laughed.

"Come on inside and we will get you settled in," Mr. Greene says before turning back toward the door with us trailing behind.

The house is large but stepping through the front door it seems smaller than my memories. The timber floors and white walls seem worn in a way I don't recall from childhood. The entryway has a small table and Mrs. Greene put some fresh, cheerful flowers into a vase to brighten it up. Moving further inside the door, the living room is to the left and the same dark brown couches my parents had still sit in the same places. The stairs on the right I knew would lead up to the bedrooms that once belonged to my parents and myself.

Alongside the stairs was a hallway that I knew led to a spare bedroom and office. Instead of going up the stairs or down the hall, we continue toward the back of the house. The door at the end of the entryway leads straight into a dining area with an old round wooden table and chairs, and directly to the left is the kitchen where I remember my mother always cooking.

Memories wash over me and I have to force the emotions down, the grief wanting to drown me again.

Mrs. Greene pushes me toward the table as her husband takes a seat. "Sit, sit, I'll make you a nice cup of tea while you talk business."

I take a seat automatically. There is something about this woman that seems to speak to my soul like the symbolic grandmother that she told me to call her. My own grandparents passed away when I was very young and I couldn't recall being around anyone before with the same energy as she had.

I turn back to Mr. Greene who smiles at me as though he knows the affect his wife has on those around her. "She will treat you like her own grandbaby if you let her. She has a kind soul and means no harm, but I can limit her henpecking if you need me to," he whispers.

"I heard that, Mr. Greene!"

"Your hearing aids must be getting cross signals, Mrs. Greene!"

I don't even try to stop the laughter this time, the happy emotion bubbling up inside of me at their playfulness. He just smiles and winks at me before becoming serious again.

"Now we have been maintaining the house and had regular cleaners and gardeners sent over per the instructions that were left. Everything is tidy and clean, but everything is still the same as it was. We haven't touched anything which means that you will need to, at some point, sort through it all. While you were gone, your parents refused to change anything about your room, so apart from us cleaning it, it's also still the same. I'm going to leave it up to you if you want to be the one to do that, but if you want, I can organize for people to do it for you so you don't have to touch it. The offer is there, but take your time to think about it."

It's a kind offer. Just the thought of going to those rooms hurts my heart, and for a moment I wonder if I made the right decision to return.

He points to a folder on the table. "This folder has all the banking information. You obviously have no identification at the moment, but everything is in there so you can go do that and then go to the bank to get a card to the account. You should be able to withdraw over the counter until that comes through, but I've also taken it upon myself to draw some for you to use until you feel ready."

I look at the folder on the table. I'm not sure what he expected to be my response but I'm sure he doesn't expect the amount of panic that creeps into my mind. I have no idea what I'm meant to do with the information he hands me. I don't even know where to start. I had gone from being a child that had no responsibilities to being held against my will where all of my choices had been taken away from me.

The weight of responsibility, decisions to be made, and even the prospect of facing the untouched rooms of my childhood home all flood my mind. It's overwhelming, and for a moment, I feel like I'm drowning in the sea of expectations.

Mrs. Greene walks back toward us with a cup in one hand and a plate in the other, placing them both gently in front of me. She rests a soft hand against my shoulder and it helps calm me and push the panic aside. I can smell the hot tea in the cup, the scent of English Breakfast is strong. On the plate is a blueberry muffin that she has cut into quarters and warmed up and added butter to. I focus on those details instead, allowing them to ground me. It looks divine and my stomach grumbles at the sight.

"The doctor said she has to be careful with her food and start slowly." I hear Easton say softly as I decide which I want to taste first.

"Oh pshht, I haven't ever seen anyone have a bad reaction to my treats. Let the girl be." Mrs. Greene almost growls, but her voice is full of humor as she places a soft hand on my shoulder. "Now young lady, anytime you need anything, day or night you come find me. We live just down the hill closer to town, just past the Colter property."

My stomach drops. The Colter property. Wyatt's family home.

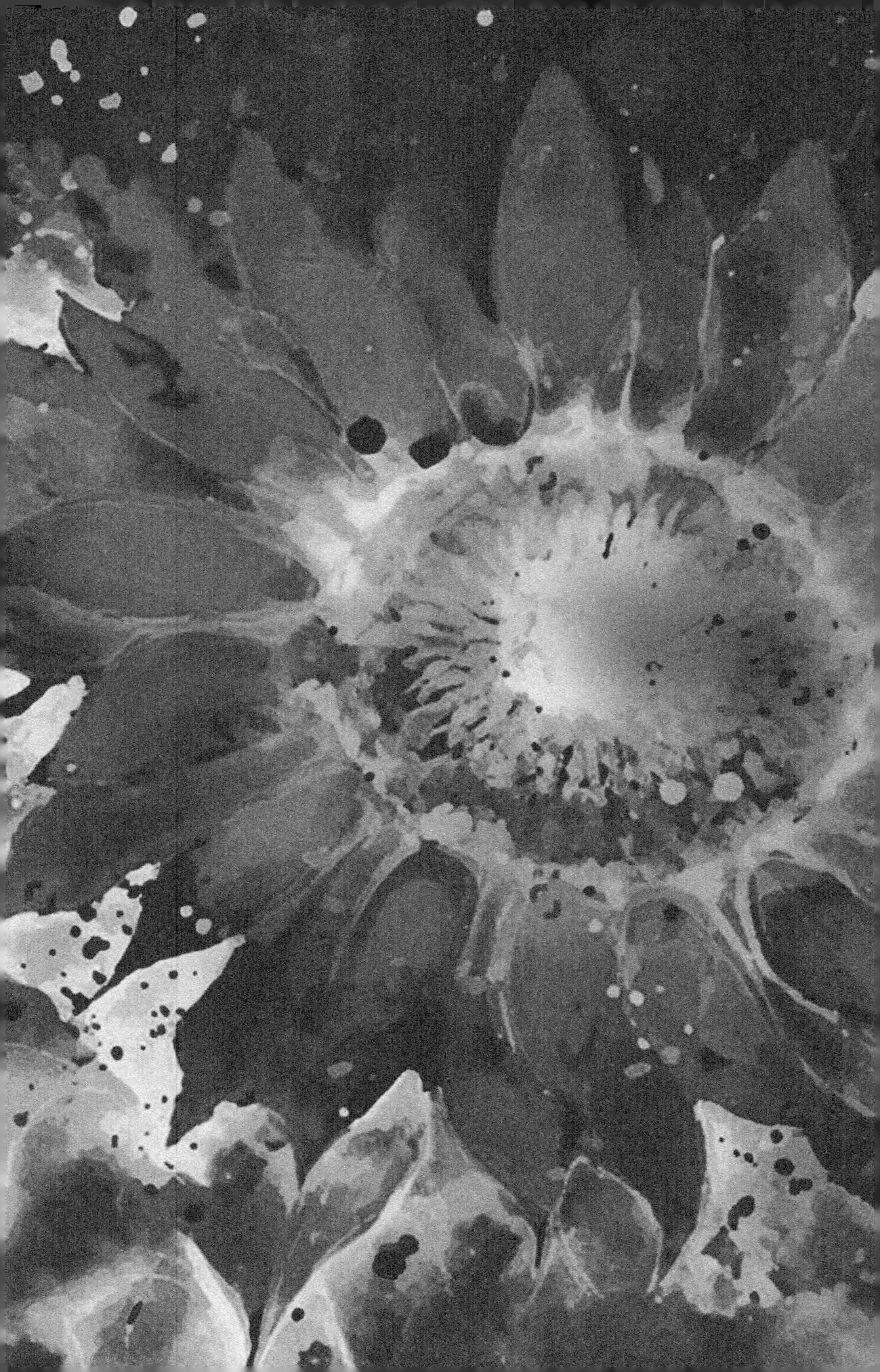

CHAPTER 7

Willow

I'm still frowning down at the muffin when Easton returns from showing the Greene's out and saying farewell. I should have felt bad for zoning out on the lovely older couple but the mention of Wyatt's family home had my stomach and mind in knots.

"I can eat that if you don't feel up to it, little butterfly."

Blinking up at him, he smiles at me softly and indicates the muffin in front of me.

I shake my head, realizing that I do want to eat it. Not just because it looks delicious, but because I want to reclaim some sense of normalcy, starting with enjoying a simple treat like a blueberry muffin. I pick up a piece and take a bite, savoring the burst of flavors. Mrs. Greene was right; it's delicious.

Easton pulls out a chair and sits across from me. "What's on your mind?"

I sigh, setting the muffin down. "I don't even know where to start. There's so much to process, so many emotions. It all feels like too much."

He reaches across the table, his hand covering mine. "Take your time. We're not in a rush, and I'm here for you, whatever you need."

I nod appreciatively. "It's just... being here, it's overwhelming. I thought coming back would be this magical, healing experience, but it's not that simple."

Easton squeezes my hand gently. "It's okay not to have all the answers right now. We'll figure it out together. And if you need to talk or if there's anything specific you want to do, just let me know."

I manage a small smile. "Thank you, Easton. I appreciate you being here for me."

He returns the smile. "Always, Willow. Now, about the guys, do you want me to try to reach out to them?"

I hesitate, uncertainty clouding my expression. "I... I want to see them, but I'm scared. What if they don't want to see me?"

Easton's gaze is steady. "They have been missing you for fifteen years. Why wouldn't they want to see you? You aren't going to know until you go and see them."

I sigh and look down at the muffin in front of me again. "I'm not the same person I was. A lot has happened and a lot of time has passed. A lot of damage has been done."

"Explain what happened to the best of your ability. You can't control how they'll react, but you can be honest with them. True friends will understand."

Taking a deep breath, I nod. "You're right. I need to see them, I can't keep being afraid of everything. I want my life back."

"That's the spirit," he encourages. "And if it gets too overwhelming, I'm right here."

As I finish the muffin, I feel a mixture of emotions. There's a long journey ahead, but for the first time, I feel like I have someone by my side who genuinely cares. With Easton's support, I'm determined to rebuild my life and reconnect with those I care about.

Easton takes my empty plate over to the sink, his movements thoughtful and silent. He glances back at me with a gentle smile before turning his attention to the dishes.

"Would you like to walk over to the Colter property?" he asks, breaking the silence. "I thought it might be a good way for you to reconnect with the familiar surroundings."

His suggestion sends a shiver down my spine, and I feel a sudden new panic welling up inside me. The memories of the last time I walked between the properties flood my mind, and my breath catches in my throat.

Easton notices the change in my demeanor immediately. He abandons the dishes and rushes back to my side, concern etched on his face. "Willow, I'm so sorry. I shouldn't have suggested that without thinking. I should have known better."

His apology catches me off guard, and I find my panic calming at the stress and worry on his own face. "It's okay," I manage to say, my voice a whisper. "I just... I'm not ready for that yet."

He nods understandingly. "I should have been more mindful. I'm here to support you, not make things harder."

A small smile tugs at the corners of my lips. "Thank you. I think, for now, driving might be the best option. It's still a bit overwhelming for me to navigate through the memories."

Easton nods, his expression still carrying a tinge of guilt. "Of course. We'll take it slow, do whatever feels right for you."

As he continues with the dishes, he glances up at me, concern etched in his eyes. "Are you sure you're okay, Willow?"

I manage a reassuring smile. "I'm fine, really."

He nods, accepting my words, though his worry doesn't completely fade. "Do you want to take the paperwork with us in case we have time and you feel up to going into town?"

I consider the idea, I know I need to deal with it. It's a good place to start reclaiming the life I lost, even if it is daunting. "Yeah, let's take it."

While Easton gathers the paperwork, I decide to freshen up in the small bathroom downstairs. The cool water on my face helps, but as I catch my reflection in the mirror, I can't help but feel like I'm looking at a stranger. My skin is pale, making my blue eyes look larger than usual.

I take a deep breath, reminding myself that I've faced worse and survived. I can do this.

After repeating those words like a mantra, I leave the bathroom to find Easton waiting in the hall. "Ready?" he asks, his eyes filled with understanding. At my nod, he places a gentle hand against my lower back, thankfully not touching the scars that serve as a reminder of Jacob.

He leads me out to his SUV and helps me into the passenger side, making sure I'm comfortable before closing the door. I watch him go around to his side, getting behind the wheel, and soon, we're back on the road.

The drive is quiet, the hum of the engine providing a steady backdrop to my racing thoughts. It doesn't take long before we turn onto the long, winding drive that leads to the Colter property. The scenery shifts to open fields and scattered trees, and my nerves kick in. Should I have asked Easton to call ahead? The worry nags at me, but it's too late now.

As we approach, I notice people moving around, but it's not the bustling activity that once filled my memories.

When we finally pull up to the main ranch area, Easton shuts off the engine, allowing me a moment to gather the courage I need to step out of the vehicle. I stare at the ranch buildings, memories flooding back.

Easton senses my hesitation and staying true to his word, he doesn't rush me. After a deep breath, I open the car door and step out onto the dusty ground. Easton immediately makes his way around the car to stand beside me.

Taking in the surroundings, I see someone walking toward us, wiping his hands on a cloth. Involuntarily, I step behind Easton, using him as a shield, my nerves getting the better of me. Easton, sensing my unease, turns to face the approaching figure.

"Mason," he calls out, and I can hear the smile in his voice.

The man approaching us fits the image of a rancher, dressed in typical country style—blue jeans, brown cowboy boots, a white shirt, and a Stetson shading his features.

He certainly doesn't look like the Mason from my memories, the once lanky teenager now all adult cowboy. A wide grin spreads across his face as he recognizes Easton. "Easton! Well, I'll be damned. When did you get back? What brings you out here?"

"Someone wanted to see you." Easton gestures toward me, and I step out from behind him, trying to muster a smile.

Mason's eyes focus on me for a moment, and then his expression shifts. The grin fades from his face as though he's seen a ghost. "Willow?" he gasps, dropping the cloth he was holding. His long legs eat up the distance between us in seconds, and Easton raises a hand to stop him from overwhelming me.

Mason freezes, looking at Easton, then back at me, his eyes wide with shock. Easton, sensing the tension, remains a steady presence, silently communicating that I need space.

"Willow?" Mason repeats, this time his voice softer, filled with disbelief. It's as if he's trying to reconcile the person standing before him with the memories he holds.

I manage a small nod, my throat feeling tight. "Hey, Mason."

He continues to stare, his eyes flickering over my face, as if searching for familiar features. "I... I can't believe it. It's really you, you're really here."

The weight of his gaze is heavy, filled with a mix of emotions I can't quite decipher. I take a cautious step forward, closing the gap between us. "It's really me. It's been a long time, Mason."

He finally seems to snap out of his shock, and a frown crosses his face. "Long time? That's an understatement. We thought we'd never see you again. Where the hell have you been?"

My heart thuds in my chest and my stomach does a backflip as the memories start to creep into my mind. Before I can speak, Easton steps forward with a concerned frown. "Mason, have you not been watching the news at all?"

Mason's frown deepens, and he dismissively waves a hand. "You know we don't have time for that shit, Easton. Been too busy keeping this place running."

Easton hesitates before continuing, his tone more cautious. "That means Wyatt wouldn't have seen..."

Before he can finish his sentence, a high-pitched voice interrupts from behind. "Uncle Easton!"

We all turn to see a little boy, around six years old, running toward us.

He looks like he is dressed as a miniature version of Mason and a mischievous grin that mirrors his excitement. Easton's face lights up, and he crouches down, ready to catch the approaching bundle of energy.

The boy crashes into Easton's open arms, and Easton lifts him up, spinning him around. "Hey, buddy! How's my favorite little man doing?"

The boy giggles, clinging to Easton. "Good! Dadda didn't say you'd be visiting. Who's that?" he asks, pointing at me with curiosity.

Easton glances at me, gauging my comfort level, and then smiles at the boy. "This is Willow. She's an old friend of your dads. Can you say hello to Willow, Bryce?"

Bryce gives me an enthusiastic wave. "Hi, Willow! Are you here to help me and Uncle Mason with the horses?"

My heart races at the uncanny resemblance between Bryce and the image of Wyatt that lingers in my memories. I manage to say softly, "Hello, Bryce. Maybe some other time. I'm not much of a horse expert."

Easton gently puts Bryce back onto his feet, and the little boy starts running around us, pretending to ride an imaginary horse. His laughter fills the air, momentarily lifting the heavy atmosphere.

Easton leans in, speaking quietly to Mason, "Surprised he recognized me, considering he hasn't seen me in so long. He's grown so much."

Mason smirks, glancing at Bryce with affection. "It's not like you don't talk to him on the phone every month, and we always show him your picture. He knows Uncle Easton well enough."

I take the opportunity to study Mason again. He's different from the boy I remember—more rugged, with lines on his face that tell stories of the years that have passed. There's a warmth in his eyes, as he looks at both Bryce and Easton, that reminds me of the boy I knew but also that I missed so much of their lives here.

As Bryce continues his playful antics, we're interrupted again, a loud voice cutting across the ranch. "Bryce! There you are!"

We turn to see Wyatt striding toward us, a scowl on his face. If I had been surprised by the transformation from boy to man with Mason then the change in Wyatt was more so. He was dressed similar to Mason but with a black shirt stretched across broad muscles, where Mason chose to be clean shaven, Wyatt had what looked like several days' growth.

Bryce, oblivious to the tension, runs toward Wyatt. "Dadda, look! Uncle Easton and Willow are here!"

Wyatt's eyes shift from Bryce to Easton and finally land on me. His eyes widen as they meet mine, and for a moment, he freezes in his tracks. The recognition hits him, and his expression transforms from confusion to disbelief. "Willow?" he says, his voice barely a whisper.

The air becomes charged with an unspoken tension as Wyatt's gaze remains locked on me. I muster a small smile, uncertainty clawing at my insides. "Hi, Wyatt."

For a moment, the world seems to hold its breath. Then, anger flashes across Wyatt's face, a storm brewing in his eyes. His jaw tightens, and his fists clench at his sides. I feel a chill down my spine at the look in his eyes.

Wyatt abruptly scoops Bryce into his arms, the little boy looking confused by the sudden change in his father's demeanor. "Easton, get her off my property," Wyatt orders, his voice low and edged with anger.

Easton, caught off guard, stammers, "Wyatt, you need to listen. You don't know—"

"I don't care, Easton. Get her out of here," Wyatt interrupts, his gaze never leaving me. The warmth in his eyes from earlier is replaced by a cold, distant stare.

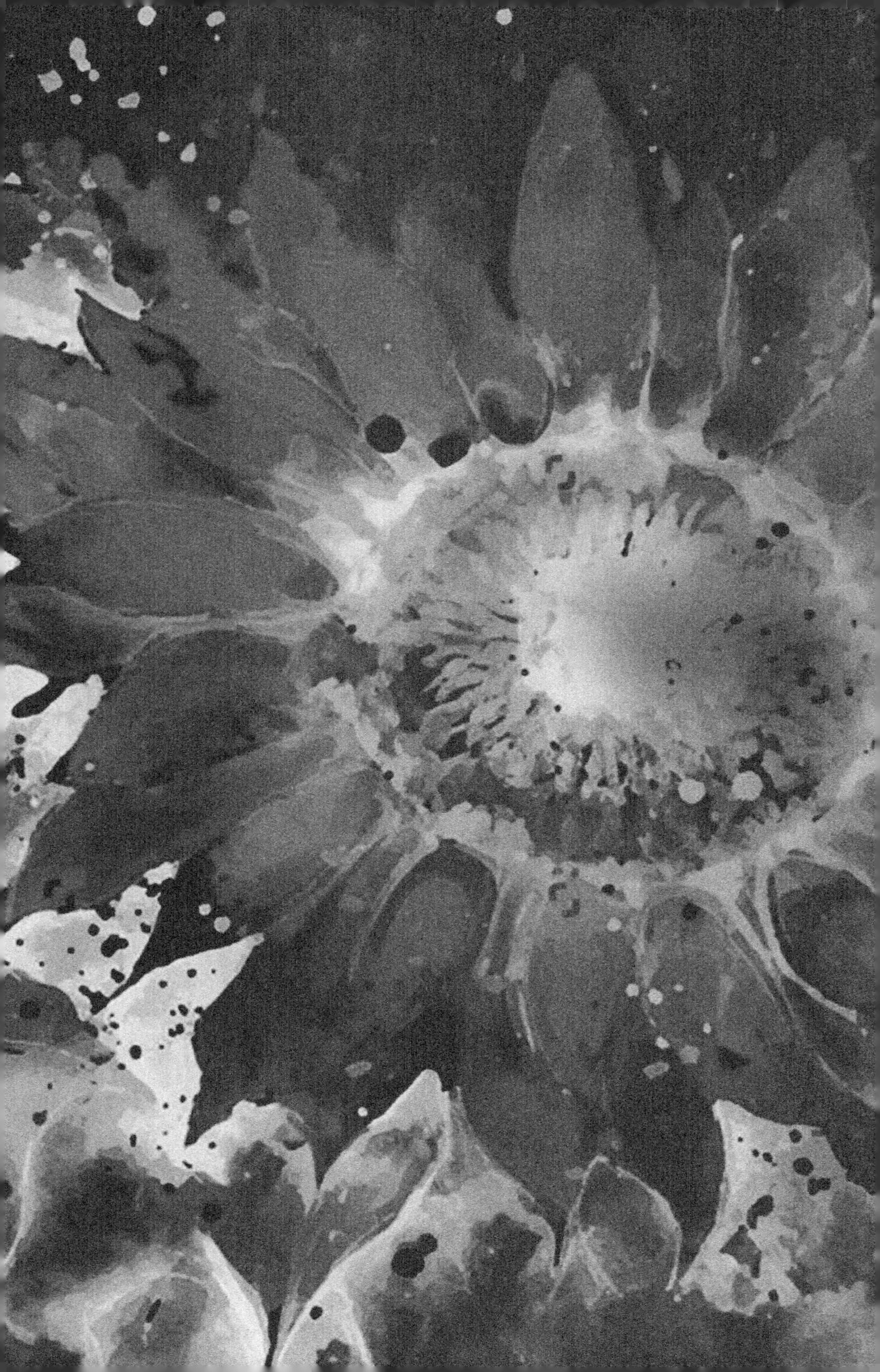

CHAPTER 8
Willow

I stand frozen, the weight of Wyatt's anger pressing down on me. Panic starts to take hold of me as memories of Jacob's anger at my delays flash through my mind with each second that passes. I want to speak but the years of conditioning to remain silent in the face of anger and danger grip me tightly. My breathing stutters in my chest and I feel the urge to claw at my own skin, but I force my hands to remain by my sides.

Easton shoots me an apologetic look but doesn't protest. He moves to guide me back toward the car, understanding the need to defuse the situation.

As we start walking away, I steal a glance back at Wyatt. His jaw is still tight, his gaze unwavering. The connection we once shared feels like a fragile thread that has just snapped.

When we reach the car, Easton helps me in, his expression torn between concern and frustration. As he closes the door, he mutters, "I'm sorry, Willow. I didn't think it would go like this. I thought he would have at least seen the news."

I manage a weak smile, my mind racing with confusion and hurt. "It's not your fault, Easton. I just... I don't understand..."

Easton sighs heavily, the weight of the situation evident in his tired eyes. "As much as I want to explain Willow, that's not my story to tell. Wyatt has his reasons, as much as I don't agree with them at all, it's still for him to deal with. Maybe, given time, he'll be ready to hear the truth."

I nod, though the ache in my chest persists. Easton starts the car, but before pulling away, he glances toward Mason, who stands at a distance, his eyes reflecting a mix of sadness and apology. Easton rolls down the window and calls out to him.

"Mason, I'll catch up with you later. We'll figure something out," Easton says, a solemn promise in his voice.

Mason nods, his expression regretful. "I'm sorry, Willow. We'll organize to catch up away from the ranch, alright?"

I manage a small, appreciative smile. "Thank you, Mason. I'll be looking forward to that."

He turns away and starts walking back toward the paddocks after Wyatt, but before he gets far Easton calls out, "Where's Gage?"

Mason pauses and turns back toward us. "Gage is at the bar. He bought it off old man Darby when he wanted to retire. He's been busy with renovations the last few months and now swamped with reopening week. If you're looking for him, that's where you'll find him."

As Easton starts driving down the driveway of the Colter property, I gaze out of the window, the passing scenery a blur. The heaviness in the air persists, but I find myself clinging to a small hope that Gage might offer a different reception than Wyatt.

Easton breaks the silence, his voice gentle. "We can go to the bar now if you want, or we can go back to the house. It's entirely up to you, little butterfly."

Quietly, I ask, "Do you think Gage will react the same way Wyatt did?"

Easton hesitates before responding, his eyes focused on the road. "No, Willow. The issue with Wyatt is Wyatt's alone. It's not you that Gage would have an issue with."

I contemplate the idea, unsure of what awaits me there. "Yes, let's go," I respond quietly.

The drive into town is both familiar and strange. The mix of old and new buildings, some worn by time, others bearing the marks of recent renovations, paints a picture of a town that has evolved in my absence. As we pull into the parking lot of the bar, the late afternoon sun casts a warm glow and I feel a knot tightening in my stomach.

Easton turns off the engine and looks at me with concern. "Are you sure about this, Willow? We can turn back if you're not ready."

I take a deep breath, steeling myself for what lies ahead. "No, let's do it. I need to get this over with if I have any hope of moving past the last fifteen years and reclaiming my life. That cult already stole enough time away from me, that stops now."

Easton nods, his support unwavering. "I'll be with you every step of the way. Just let me know if you want to stop."

Leaving the safety of the car behind, we make our way to the entrance of the bar. Pushing through the front door, the atmosphere shifts from the tranquility of the outside world to the lively hum of the patrons inside. The interior surprises me with its beautiful modern yet rustic industrial design, a far cry from the small-town simplicity I remember when I came here with my parents.

It's not a huge crowd inside but there is still a reasonable amount of people that we have to navigate through, I catch snippets of conversations and laughter. I feel a sense of anxiety building within me, but I remind myself that this is a necessary step in reclaiming my life.

Approaching the counter, there is already a man in front of us, engrossed in conversation with a pretty female bartender. He has short sandy brown hair and from what I can see of his face, it is covered in stubble. Heavily tattooed arms are braced against the bar while the rest of his muscles are hidden beneath a short sleeved dark green shirt, black jeans, and the typical cowboy boots. His laughter echoes in the air as he turns away from the bar, his expression carefree. However, as his familiar green eyes meet Easton's, his carefree demeanor vanishes, replaced by a scowl.

This time, it's Gage who looks angry, and I almost regret my choice to come back to the town. He stops moving, his eyes locked onto Easton. Just as he opens his mouth to speak, the anger etched on his face, Easton turns, putting an arm around me and guiding me out from behind him.

"I'm not here for me, Gage," Easton says firmly, "I'm here for her."

Gage's focus shifts to me, confusion crossing his face before recognition and shock take over. His eyes widen, and he croaks out the question, "Willow?"

As he starts to advance on me, mirroring Mason's earlier reaction, Easton steps in again, holding a hand up to stop him.

Gage snaps at Easton, his voice edged with irritation, "The fuck, Easton? Are you her guard dog now?"

I push past my fear and summon the strength to step back up beside Easton, facing Gage. "No," I say, my voice steadier than I expected, "but he was the one who rescued me."

Gage's eyes narrow, confusion mixing with skepticism. "Rescued you? What the hell are you talking about, Willow?"

Easton lets out a heavy sigh, the tension heavy in the air. "Gage, have you watched the news lately?" He gestures subtly toward me, and I can see the anger radiating from Gage just in response to Easton talking to him. I remain silent, they obviously have history that I'm unaware of and I don't really want to be in the middle of it.

Gage responds curtly, "No, I've been too damn busy with the reopening."

I step forward, nerves and anxiety pushing through again. "Can we please go somewhere less crowded?" I ask, directing my plea more to Easton than Gage. The atmosphere in the bar feels suffocating

Gage's attention shifts to me, and for a moment, he seems to soften as he looks at my face. Reluctantly, he agrees, "Fine. Follow me." Without waiting for a response, he turns and leads us through the crowd toward a set of stairs at the back of the bar. We follow him up the stairs and into a dimly lit office.

The room is small, with a desk cluttered with papers and a worn-out leather chair. Gage gestures for us to sit, and he takes a seat in the chair behind the desk, crossing his arms across his chest.

Easton glances at me, silently asking if I'm okay. I manage a nod, but my nerves are still on edge. Gage looks between us, waiting for an explanation.

Without much preamble, Easton pulls his cell phone from his pocket and after a moment of scrolling, slides it over to Gage. Gage frowns at the device for a second before touching the screen. Suddenly, sound fills the room, and I hear the now very familiar news reports of the raid on the Church of Enlightenment, otherwise known as the cult of Stolen Souls. Gage's face goes blank with shock again as I hear the actual footage of the raid being played over from the phone's speaker. The news person explains that several girls who had been missing for years were rescued, including Willow Silva from Sierra Valley, who they abducted from outside of her home fifteen years ago.

Gage's eyes widen, and the anger that had been etched on his face is replaced by disbelief. He listens intently as the news report unfolds, detailing the horrors of the cult and the brave rescue mission that finally brought it down.

As the news segment comes to an end, Gage's gaze shifts between Easton and me, a mixture of shock and confusion on his face. The silence in the room is heavy, and I can feel the weight of the past fifteen years lingering between us.

Gage looks visibly ill, his face turning a shade paler as the reality of the news sinks in. He rests his elbows on the desk in front of him, burying his hands in his short brown hair. The room is filled with a heavy silence, broken only by the muffled sounds of the bar below.

Tears glisten in Gage's eyes as he struggles to find the right words. Finally, he speaks, his voice hoarse with emotion. "Willow, I... I'm so sorry. I didn't know. We all looked for you for years but as each year passed we just lost hope. The one person who hadn't given up was the only one of us who hadn't even known you when you disappeared."

His admission is raw, and I can see the pain etched across his face. The weight of the years of uncertainty and guilt seems to crush him in that moment. He suddenly looks like the boy that I remember. There's something inside of me that wants to reach out, to comfort him, but I remain in my seat with my own emotions and fear like a lead weight.

Gage glances at Easton, his expression a mix of confusion and accusation. "The tactical team that we fought about, the one you left us for?" There's bitterness in his voice.

"That's the one that found her, Gage." Easton glances at me, a look of guilt and shame crossing his own face. When he looks back at Gage, his voice carries a weight of regret. "By the time I went on that mission even I had lost hope. When I approached the girl kneeling in the dirt outside the compound, I never even considered that it was Willow until she said her name."

Gage's eyes widen in disbelief. "You found her?"

Easton nods solemnly. "I found her. But I didn't recognize her at first. She was just another victim of that cult, just another broken soul we had gone there to rescue."

Gage runs a hand through his hair, frustration evident in his voice. "Why didn't you call the moment you knew she was alive?"

Easton's response is immediate and filled with annoyance, "I tried, Gage. You didn't answer my call."

Gage's expression shifts from confusion to shame. He looks away, unable to meet Easton's gaze.

I interject, "It's all in the past now. We can't change what happened, but we can decide what to do from here on out. I need to feel like I have control over my life again, to move forward."

Gage stands up and comes around the desk and stands in front of me, a hesitant expression on his face. "Willow, can I... can I touch you?"

I take a moment to consider, then nod. His hands hover uncertainly for a moment before gently cupping my face. "I missed you so fucking much," he whispers, his voice filled with a mix of emotions. "No one will ever take you away from us again."

He pulls me from the chair and into his arms, and as he holds me, I feel the warmth of his embrace. The past may have been painful, but in this moment, there's a chance for healing and rebuilding. I can't stop the tears from escaping. Closing my eyes, for a moment I simply try to allow the comfort of his embrace to wash away the years of isolation and fear.

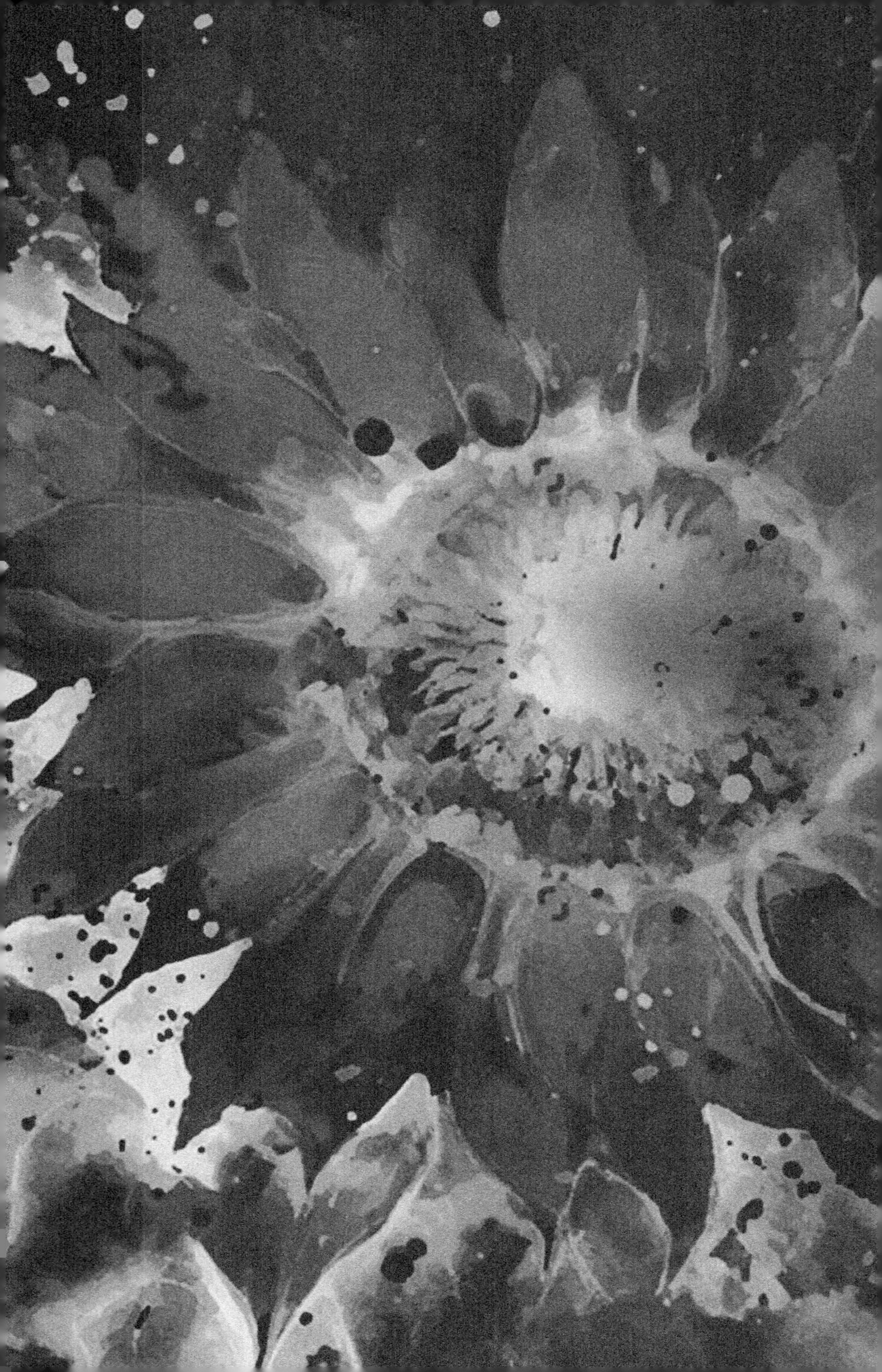

CHAPTER 9

WILLOW

Moments after Gage's arms encircle me, anxiety and panic start to claw at my insides. His touch, once a source of comfort, now feels like a heavy weight pressing down on me. The memories of captivity, the fear that had been ingrained in me, resurface with a vengeance.

My breath quickens, and I feel a knot tightening in my chest. The dimly lit office suddenly feels too small, and I'm acutely aware of the walls closing in. It's as if the past has reached out to grab me, refusing to let go.

Gage senses my discomfort and pulls back, concern etched across his face. "Willow, are you okay?" he asks, his eyes searching mine.

I manage a nod, but my hands tremble at my sides. "I... I just need a moment," I stammer, my voice betraying the turmoil within.

Gage steps back, giving me space, and Easton shoots him a warning look. The atmosphere in the room shifts, becoming charged with unspoken tension. Gage, seemingly caught between guilt and confusion, rubs the back of his neck nervously.

"I didn't mean to overwhelm you," he says, his voice softer now, filled with regret.

"It's not your fault," I murmur, attempting to steady my breathing. "It's just a lot to process, and I thought I was ready, but..."

Easton interrupts, his tone firm. "Give her time, Gage. She's been through more than any of us can imagine. We need to respect her space."

Gage nods, a mix of regret and understanding in his eyes. "Yeah, of course. I just... I need you to know how much having you back means to me."

I manage a weak smile. "Let's just take it one step at a time."

Easton breaks the tense silence. "Maybe we should head back to the house for now. Willow needs some time to process everything, and we can talk more when she's ready."

As Gage and Easton escort me out of the office, I can feel the weight of their concern lingering in the air. The cool night breeze hits my face as we step into the darkness outside. My mind races with conflicting emotions, but amidst the turmoil, a newfound determination takes root.

"I'm not letting my trauma win," I whisper to myself, as if reaffirming a promise. I steal a glance at Gage, who's walking a step behind me, and then at Easton, whose presence is surprisingly reassuring. The idea of reclaiming control over my life becomes a beacon of hope.

As we reach the car, I turn to Gage, my eyes locking onto his. With a deep breath, I decide to take a leap. "How about you join us for breakfast together tomorrow? Somewhere quiet, just to catch up without the walls closing in."

Gage's eyes brighten with a spark of hope. "Yeah, I'd like that. Where do you want to meet?"

"I need to come back into town to take care of all the legal bank stuff," I explained. "So, let's sit and talk. But maybe somewhere with outdoor seating? I don't want to feel so closed in."

"Magda's Diner has a nice outdoor area, they do a good breakfast there" Gage suggests.

Easton nods in agreement. "Magda's it is, then. Let's meet at 9. That should give Willow enough time to handle the legal matters."

As Gage helps me into the car, he squeezes my hand briefly before stepping back and closing the car door for me. There's a brief moment of quiet acknowledgment between Easton and him. It's clear there's more on Gage's mind.

As Easton turns to move around the car Gage grabs his arm. "Easton, wait. Has Wyatt seen the videos?" Gage asks. Although they are on the outside of the car, I can still hear them clearly.

Easton's jaw tightens, frustration evident on his face. "He kicked us off his property before I could even show him the video. Didn't give me a chance. And he obviously hasn't been watching the news either."

Gage frowns, looking down momentarily. He looks back up at Easton and starts to say something, regret crossing his face, but before he can get the words out, Easton squeezes his shoulder and cuts him off. "It's fine, Gage. It's in the past."

The tension in the air seems to subside, at least for the moment. Easton makes his way around to his side of the car, sliding in and closing the car door. Gage gives us both one last look before he takes a step back, allowing the car to pull away out of the parking lot.

As we head back toward the house, I find myself silent, gazing out of the window at nothing in particular. The passing scenery blurs into a mix of shadows and streetlights, mirroring the whirlwind of emotions inside me. Easton breaks the silence, his voice filled with regret.

"Sorry about how the day has turned out, little butterfly," he says, his eyes focused on the road ahead.

I turn to him, offering a small, genuine smile. "Easton, it's in no way your fault at all. A lot has happened, and a lot of years have come between us. All I can ask for is to eventually find some way to earn my happiness and their friendships again."

Easton nods, his expression filled with empathy. "You didn't deserve to have any of this bad shit happen to you."

The weight of his words hangs in the air, and I appreciate the sincerity behind them. As we pull into the driveway of my home, Easton guides the car to a stop before turning it off.

Easton opens his door and steps out. He circles around the car to my side, offering a hand to help me out. I take it gratefully, feeling the steadying support of his touch. Together, we make our way inside the house.

Coming back home is another reminder that there are rooms upstairs filled with my life before the cult, and the lives of my parents who are no longer here. I still don't want to deal with them, so for now, I push those thoughts aside.

Once inside, Easton turns to me with a genuine expression of concern. "Are you hungry? I can make you some dinner."

The offer is kind, and I appreciate the gesture. "Yeah, that sounds good. But I want to help," I say, feeling a sudden need to assert some control over my surroundings. As we make our way to the kitchen, I add, "It's meant to be my place as a woman to cook."

Easton stops suddenly and I almost run into him as he turns to look at me with a serious look on his face. He's closer than normal when he responds, "I'm more than happy for you to help me, Willow. But don't ever think that it's solely your job or responsibility to cook. We're in this together, and we share the load."

I nod in appreciation before we make our way to the kitchen. Together, we prepare a simple meal, the rhythm of chopping and sizzling providing a comforting backdrop to the evening. As the aroma of food fills the air, it feels like a small victory to me—a step toward reclaiming normalcy.

Easton turns toward me, a thoughtful expression on his face. "The hospital suggested that you perhaps connect with someone for therapy to help. If you want, I can get that organized for you."

His offer is genuine, and I consider it for a moment. Therapy might be a step toward healing, a way to untangle the knots in my mind.

"Yeah, I think that could be a good idea," I respond, my voice steady. "Thank you, Easton."

He smiles softly at me. "Of course, little butterfly. I just want what's best for you."

We finish preparing the meal, and as we sit down to eat, the conversation takes a softer turn. We talk softly about our lives growing up before everything turned into a nightmare.

Easton shares stories of his childhood, and I find comfort in the sound of his voice. The tales of simpler times, filled with laughter and mundane struggles, provide a welcome distraction from the shadows that linger in the corners of my mind.

However, as the night wears on, a yawn escapes me, prompting Easton to notice.

"You look tired, Willow. If you want to head up to bed, you can," Easton suggests, his eyes filled with concern.

I consider his offer but then admit, "I don't want to go upstairs. There are too many memories, and I just don't feel up to it right now."

Understanding flickers in Easton's gaze, and he nods. "That's okay. You can take the guest room on the ground floor for now. We'll take things at your pace."

"That was meant to be where you were going to sleep," I point out, feeling a twinge of guilt for displacing him.

Easton shakes his head, a reassuring smile on his face. "No worries. I'll take the couch. It's not a problem. And we will repeat this process every day until you're ready."

Tears well up in my eyes, and I feel a lump forming in my throat. His kindness, his understanding, it's overwhelming in the best way possible. I never expected to find this level of support, especially after everything I've been through.

"Thank you, Easton," I whisper, my voice catching with emotion. "I don't know how to express my gratitude for everything you have done for me since we met."

He reaches out, his fingers brushing softly against my cheek as he gently wipes away a tear that escapes my eye.

"You don't have to, Willow. Just focus on you. Your healing is what matters most."

As I settle into the guest room, I can't help but feel a sense of warmth and safety, something I haven't experienced in a long time.

Closing my eyes, I take a deep breath, allowing the weight of the day to settle. And for the first time in a long while, I feel a glimmer of hope flickering in the darkness. But with sleep comes a nightmare.

In the quiet of the night, I find myself caught in the clutches of the dark memories of Jacob. The walls of the guest room seem to close in on me, and the air becomes thick with the echoes of fear.

A bead of sweat forms on my forehead as I jolt awake, gasping for air. The darkness of the room feels suffocating, and for a moment, I'm disoriented, struggling to distinguish between the dream and reality.

Suddenly, a gentle knock on the door startles me. "Willow, are you okay?" Easton's voice, filled with concern, seeps through the cracks in the door.

I take a moment to compose myself, wiping away the lingering traces of tears from my face. "Yeah, just a bad dream," I responded, my voice betraying the effect it had on me.

The door creaks open, and Easton steps into the room, his eyes scanning mine with worry. "Nightmares are a common part of the healing process. It's your mind's way of processing the trauma," he explains, his tone soothing.

I nod, appreciating the reassurance. "I know, but it doesn't make it any easier."

Easton takes a seat on the edge of the bed, his presence comforting. "Do you want to talk about it?"

I hesitate for a moment, grappling with the vulnerability of exposing the raw edges of my nightmares. "It's just... the memories, the fear. It's like I'm still there, like he's still hurting me."

Easton's gaze softens, and he reaches out to gently grasp my hand. "Willow, you're safe now. Jacob can't hurt you anymore. You're here with me, and I won't let anything happen to you."

I take a shaky breath, allowing his words to anchor me in the present. "I know, but it's hard to shake off the feeling, you know? That he's still lurking in the shadows."

Easton nods in understanding, his thumb tracing soothing circles on the back of my hand. "You're not alone in this, Willow. I'm here for you, no matter what. And I'll keep reminding you that you're safe until you believe it with all your heart."

As he starts to withdraw his hand, an unexpected surge of panic sweeps over me, and I instinctively tighten my grip on his. "Easton, would you... stay with me until I fall asleep? Just for tonight?"

His eyes reflect understanding, and without a word, he shifts to a more comfortable position on the bed. I scoot over, making room for him beside me. The bed creaks slightly as he settles in, and his mere presence brings a sense of solace.

"Of course, Willow," he says softly, his voice a calming melody. "I'll be right here until you feel at ease."

Easton starts to hum a melody, a tune unfamiliar but soothing. His soft hums become a lullaby, and gradually, the fear and tension ease. As he continues his comforting hums, I find sleep embracing me, letting go of the day's struggles.

I drift into a peaceful sleep, and as it claims me I hear Easton's soft words, "I'll be here for you forever if you want, my little butterfly."

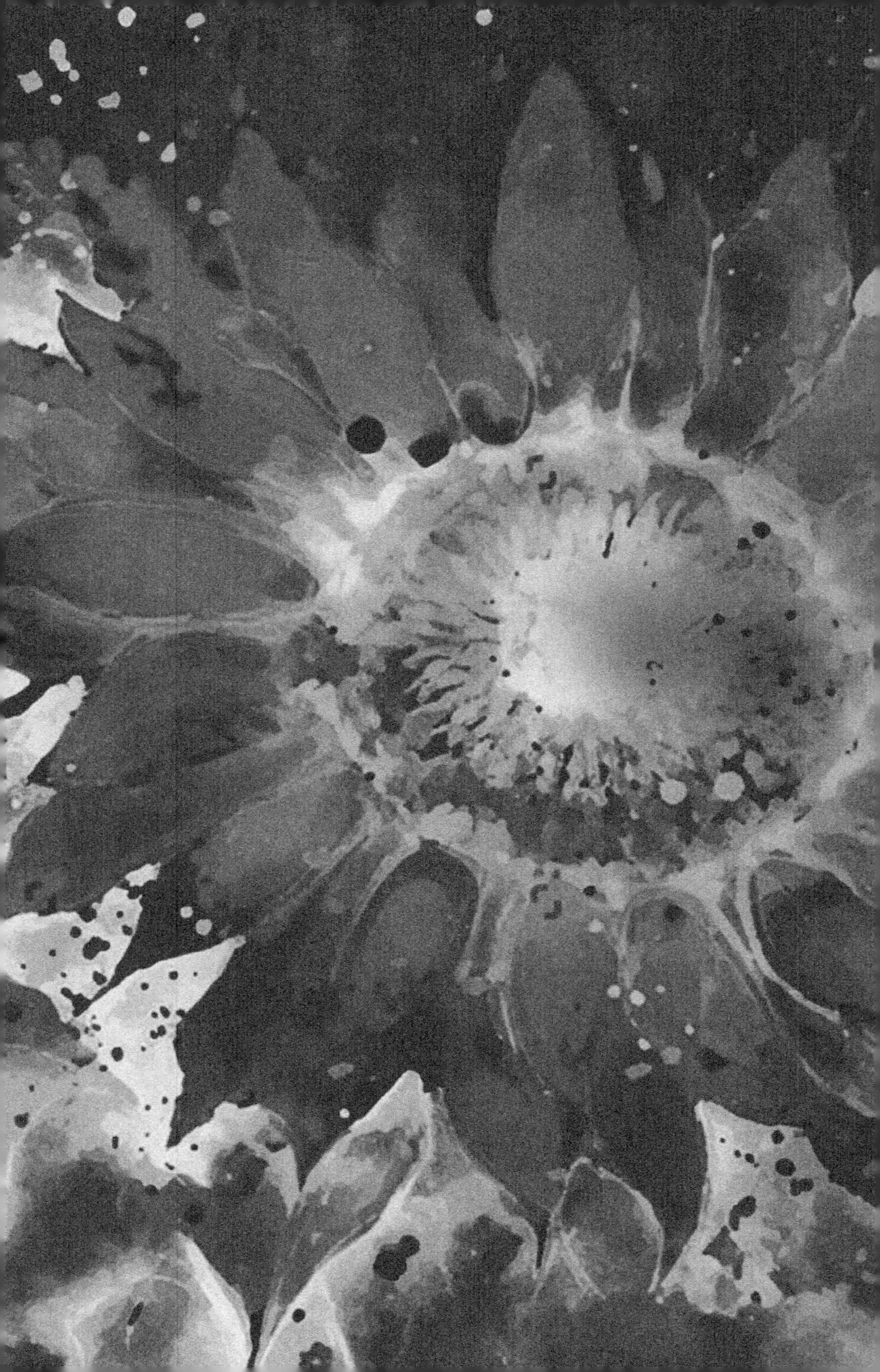

CHAPTER 10

Willow

The next morning, Easton and I arrive at Magda's Diner. The sun bathes the outdoor seating area in a warm glow, and there aren't many people around. We choose a table in the open air, and as we settle in, Magda herself approaches, her eyes widening in surprise.

I can only vaguely remember her from before. She has a friendly approachable air, her loose bun shows that her brown hair is starting to turn gray, so I imagine her to be the same age my mother was. She accentuates her curvy figure with what looks like a flared swing dress and her brown eyes are framed by winged glasses.

Her name is done in glittery writing where you would normally see a name badge.

"Bless my heart, little Willow Silva. How are you doing, sweetheart?" she exclaims, drawing the attention of a few other patrons. For a moment, I feel the urge to hide, but I push past it, smiling at her.

"Stepping one foot in front of the other," I reply, a saying my mother always used. Magda's face softens with understanding as she reaches out to pat my hand.

"I saw all those God-awful news reports. It was just terrible. If you ever need anything, you come see me, alright?" she says warmly. Easton orders a coffee, and I opt for tea as Magda leaves menus with us.

I glance down at the menu, feeling a little overwhelmed with the choices. Magda's Diner seems to offer a variety of options that I'm not accustomed to. My eyes scan over the vibrant descriptions of dishes that range from exotic to comforting, and I can't help but feel a bit out of my depth. The doctor's words echo in my mind, reminding me to stick with plain foods and gradually introduce more variety.

As I contemplate my limited options, the chair to my right suddenly pulls out, and Gage sits down with a warm smile. Before I can fully process his arrival, the chair on my left is pulled out and when I look in that direction Mason is standing by it, looking at me with a half smile.

"Do you mind if I join you? Gage told me he was meeting you here."

I look at Mason, genuinely surprised by his presence. It takes a moment for me to register his question, and then I softly say, "Yes, that's fine."

Once Mason takes a seat, he looks at me, and I see a mixture of sadness and shame briefly crossing his face. He takes a deep breath, breaking the silence, "Willow, I want to say that I'm sorry for how everything went down at the ranch. After you left, and after I spoke to Gage, I looked at the news reports myself. I'm so sorry for my ignorance. I had no idea what you went through."

His words carry a genuine sincerity, and I find myself appreciating his honesty.

Easton, however, scoffs slightly and directs a pointed question at Mason, "What does Wyatt think of you being here and not on the ranch working?"

Mason's expression turns serious, and he frowns. "Give Wyatt time. I tried to talk to him last night, but he's not ready to hear it."

Easton crosses his arms. "Someone needs to figure out how to fix this, Mason. Willow doesn't need more complications right now."

Mason narrows his eyes at Easton, a tension building between them. "Because you're already so aware of what Willow needs," he retorts, his voice edged with frustration.

My anxiety starts to claw at me, and I interject softly, "What Willow needs is for you all to not fight, please, and for someone to help me choose some food that won't be too much too soon."

The table falls into an uneasy silence, and they all look a little guilty. Magda, who seems to sense the tension, comes back over and asks, "Is everything alright over here?"

Gage beams a smile at her that has her blushing a little. "Everything's fine, Magda. Just catching up." He then orders a coffee, and Mason mumbles a request for the same.

Magda nods and heads back into the diner, leaving the four of us with the menus. Gage leans back in his chair, his eyes lingering on me. "Willow, we're here for you. Let us know how we can make things easier."

I appreciate Gage's sentiment, but the reality of navigating these men and my own emotions is daunting. Taking a deep breath, I focus on the menu, hoping to find something that won't overwhelm my senses.

Mason glances at the menu too and then at me. "I suggest something light. Maybe toast or eggs?"

Easton adds, "And avoid anything too spicy or rich. We don't want to push your stomach too hard."

I nod, grateful for their suggestions. "That sounds good. I'll go for eggs, then."

Magda returns with our drinks, delivering a steaming pot of tea for me with a delicate china cup. She takes our breakfast orders, jotting them down on her notepad with a smile. The atmosphere lightens a bit as she engages in small talk, asking about our preferences and making suggestions.

Magda then takes the menus away, leaving us to enjoy our drinks and ease into the conversation. Sipping at my tea, I find the warmth soothing. The gentle breeze carries snippets of conversation from other patrons, and the soft hum of morning activity creates a backdrop of white noise.

Gage breaks the silence by steering the conversation toward safer topics. "So, Willow, what's on your schedule for today?"

I appreciate the shift to something more neutral. "I need to go to the bank and start taking care of some of the legal requirements to reclaim my life," I reply, my gaze focused on the swirling patterns in my teacup.

Gage nods thoughtfully. "That's a great place to start. Sorting out the legalities will give you a sense of control over your life again."

Mason chimes in, genuinely interested, "After that, do you have any plans?"

I hesitate for a moment, realizing that I haven't fully thought about what comes next. "I'm not sure. I thought maybe I might have a look at some clothing stores. The FBI provided me with these," I gesture down at my plain long black pants and blue shirt, "and they aren't exactly the most flattering or comfortable."

Mason nods, understanding. "That sounds like a good idea. A bit of normalcy and self-care could go a long way."

Easton leans back in his chair, a thoughtful look on his face. "It's important to reclaim some sense of identity. Choosing your own clothes might be a small but significant step."

Gage finally speaks up, smiling hopefully, "We can help you with that, Willow. If you want, we could accompany you, make it less overwhelming."

I see Easton trying to suppress a smile as he leans forward to pick up his coffee but I don't question it. I appreciate their willingness to support me in the simplest of tasks. "Thank you, all of you. It means a lot."

Magda returns with our food, setting a plate of eggs and buttered toast in front of me. My stomach rumbles in anticipation, and I feel a twinge of excitement at the prospect of eating something different than plain toast or porridge. Magda smiles warmly before leaving us to enjoy our meal.

Once she's out of earshot, Easton raises an eyebrow at Gage and Mason, a hint of humor in his tone. "Don't you two have your own jobs and responsibilities?"

Both of them stutter a little but Gage recovers first, flashing a charming smile. "I have management staff that are trained for moments like this. They can handle things in my absence."

Mason looks down at his own breakfast and simply states, "Wyatt can cope without me. I've already informed the foreman about taking a personal day."

Easton raises an eyebrow, seemingly skeptical. "And you're okay with leaving the ranch during this time?"

Mason shrugs before responding. "Wyatt's got a good team in place. They can manage without me for a day."

Easton looks mildly humored by their responses, shaking his head with a smile. As we all start eating the meals in front of us, the conversation gradually shifts to lighter topics.

Gage shares details about the opening week at his bar, describing the lively atmosphere and the positive response from the community. Mason talks about a new horse he's been working with, expressing his hopes of taking it on the rodeo circuit. I find myself falling into easier conversation with all of them, and even Easton joins in, sharing anecdotes from his own recent experiences while he was away. Before he rescued me.

As we talk, I realize how much I've missed this camaraderie. The laughter and teasing remind me of the times when we were young, carefree, and unburdened by the challenges that life would later throw at us.

When we're finished eating, Magda returns with another girl to help clear away our plates and drinks. We all get up to move to our next destination, and I hesitate for a moment, realizing we need to pay for our meals. I mention it, and Mason flashes a grin while holding a hand out, allowing me to decide if I want to put my hand in his.

"After yesterday, Wyatt deserves a hit to the bank account," he jokes, his eyes sparkling with a mischievous glint. I chuckle softly and place my hand in his, feeling a sense of familiarity and comfort in the gesture.

Mason tucks my arm into his elbow, and together we follow the others out of the diner. The morning sun casts a warm glow on the sidewalk as we step into the day, and the prospect of facing the challenges ahead seems a bit more manageable with their support.

They lead me down the road to the bank, and surprisingly, that part of my day doesn't take as long as I expected. The bank manager, an older gentleman with a kind smile and a calm demeanor, had already been warned to expect my arrival by Mr. Greene. He guides me through the necessary steps, explaining the paperwork and legalities involved in getting control of all the finances. The process feels empowering, a step toward independence that I desperately need.

Once I'm done at the bank, the guys lead me to a small clothing boutique a few stores down. It's a modern yet casual place, and as we enter, I catch a glimpse of the name – "Loretta's Threads." The name sparks a memory from my childhood. Loretta, the owner, is someone I recognize from when I was young.

The bell above the door jingles as we enter, and Loretta looks up from behind the counter. Her eyes meet mine, and she puts on a fake smile, her demeanor instantly changing. But I can see the strain in her smile and the coldness of her eyes. I can see that she doesn't want me there, and the memory of her not liking me, even back before I was abducted, surfaces.

"Willow Silva," she greets me, the feigned warmth in her tone belying her true feelings. "What brings you to my store?"

Gage steps forward with a grin, seemingly oblivious to any tension, and answers for me, "We're here to help Willow get a few outfits, Loretta. She doesn't have any clothes of her own and we thought this would be a nice way to boost her spirits."

Loretta's smile tightens, but she nods and gestures towards the racks of clothes. "Well, feel free to browse. I'm sure we can find something suitable."

As we start looking through the clothes, Loretta joins us, attempting to play the helpful store owner. However, it becomes evident that her idea of 'helpful' is subjective. She suggests outfits that wouldn't suit me at all, either too trashy or too conservative.

Easton, Gage, and Mason, unaware of the underlying tension, try to be helpful in their own way. Easton suggests a casual yet stylish outfit, and surprisingly, I find myself liking it. As I step out of the changing room to show the guys, Loretta's disapproving gaze follows me.

Gage gives an approving nod, "Looks great, Willow. That style suits you."

As they return to browsing the racks, Loretta seizes an opportunity. She discreetly steps forward into the changing area, out of earshot of the guys, and hands me a white dress that sends shivers down my spine. It's eerily similar to what I was found in—the dress I wore the night I ran from Jacob's room.

Loretta hisses at me, "You should return to your fiancé where you belong, Grace."

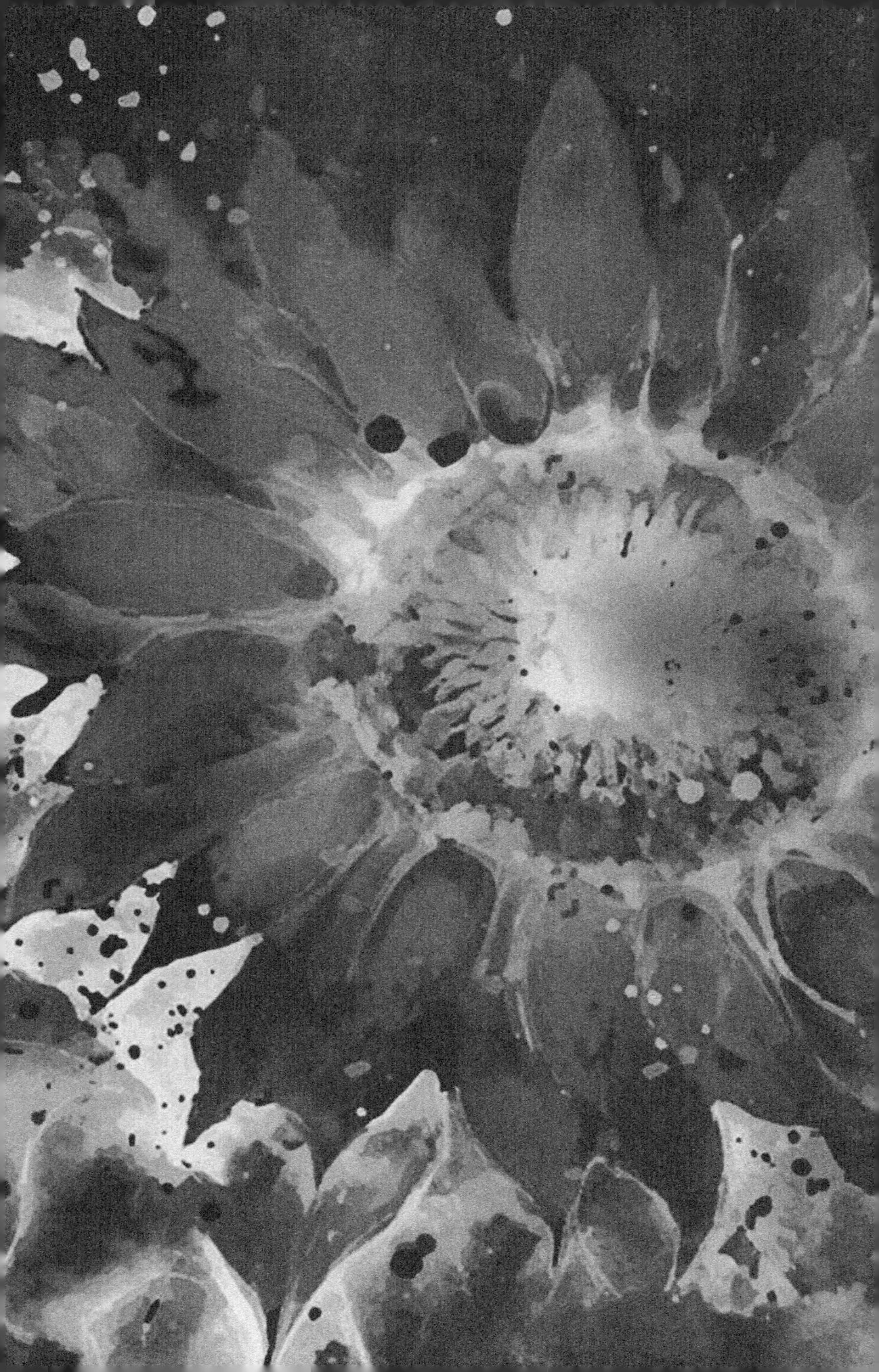

CHAPTER 11

Willow

The weight of her words crash over me like a tidal wave. Grace. The name that was forced upon me, a name that symbolizes a past I'm desperately trying to forget. It triggers a surge of memories—of abuse, of fear, of a life that wasn't mine.

Panic claws at my chest, and I feel a sudden tightness around my throat. The dressing area begins to spin, and I struggle to keep my composure. Without warning, the memories flood back, vivid and unrelenting. Kneeling on the hard floor repeating prayers. Jacob's knife cutting into my skin. The pain of being violated.

I stumble backward, desperately trying to escape the haunting images. Instinctively, I reach for the tiny waste bin in the corner of the dressing area, barely making it in time before I lose my breakfast. The nausea, the fear—it all rushes back, overwhelming my senses.

I can't stop until my stomach is empty and even then I continue to dry heave and gasp for breath that I can't take in. Easton, alerted by the commotion, rushes into the dressing area. His eyes widen as he sees me, pale and trembling, crouched over the bin. "Willow, what happened? Are you okay?" he asks, genuine concern etched on his face.

I can't find the words to respond. My mind is a chaotic swirl of emotions, and my throat feels constricted. Easton turns to Loretta, his expression fierce. "What did you do? What did you say to her?"

Loretta, feigning innocence, puts on a performance worthy of an award. "I don't know. She just started feeling sick. Maybe it's something she ate."

My hands clutch the sides of the waste bin, knuckles turning white as I try to ground myself in the present. The dressing room walls seem to close in, and the memories continue their relentless assault.

I find it hard to distinguish between the past and the present. Sweat beads form on my forehead, and my heart races, a cacophony in my ears that drowns out the concerned voices around me. Gasping for air, I struggle to maintain control, but it slips through my trembling fingers like sand.

She turns to Gage and Mason, her eyes widening in fake concern. "I hope she's not contagious. I can't afford to have anyone sick in my store."

Easton's voice, though muffled in my disoriented state, cuts through the chaos. "Willow, look at me," he pleads, crouching down beside me. His hands rest gently on my shoulders, attempting to anchor me in the here and now. "Breathe, okay? Just focus on your breath."

Gage and Mason, oblivious to the emotional turmoil that Loretta has just stirred, glance at each other with concern. I want to scream, to tell them the truth, to expose Loretta's cruel intentions, but my voice remains trapped within me.

Easton notices the white dress on the floor, and a flash of realization crosses his face. Anger tightens his jaw, and he snatches the dress from the ground. Without a word, he hurls it at Loretta, commanding, "Get this out of here."

Loretta scurries out with the dress, a triumphant glint in her eyes that she sends my way before disappearing from the dressing room. The weight of her manipulation settles heavily on my shoulders, and I struggle to find my voice.

Easton helps me back to my feet, his protective arm still wrapped around me. Gage quickly comes up on my other side, offering his support. The kindness and concern in their eyes provide a lifeline, grounding me in the present.

Mason's eyes narrow at Loretta's retreating back. "Let's get her out of here."

Easton guides me towards the exit, my legs still shaky from the emotional storm.

"We can go to my bar, it's not far," Gage suggests as he stays close behind us.

As we begin to exit Loretta's Threads, her voice rings out in protest, loudly demanding attention. "She can't leave in those clothes! She hasn't paid for them!"

Mason spins back to Loretta with a fierce expression. "Somehow you caused this. Send me the bill or suck it the fuck up."

He follows us out of the store, and as we move down the street, I can still hear Loretta's indignant complaints fading into the distance. As we step out into the daylight, the crisp air helps to clear my mind, even if only slightly.

Gage leads us towards his bar, but as we approach, he pauses, stopping our momentum. I can see his reason from here, there is a lunch crowd and the bar appears to be busy. He looks at me with concern, "Maybe it's not the best idea to go in there right now. We can find somewhere quieter."

I lean my head against Easton's shoulder, appreciating the support. The world seems a bit too overwhelming at the moment, and a moment of respite sounds like a welcome idea. Gage scans the surroundings, searching for an alternative.

Just then, Mr. Greene appears from the door of the building we've stopped in front of. His eyes narrow as he takes in the scene. "Is everything alright?" he asks, genuine concern etched on his face.

Easton, still supporting me, explains, "Willow had a bit of a... moment. We were looking for a quiet place."

Mr. Greene nods, understanding. "Come inside. My office is just up the stairs. It's quiet there."

As we enter the building, a woman who appears to be an assistant greets us, offering a kind smile. "Mr. Greene, is everything okay?" she asks.

He nods, gesturing towards the staircase. "Just a momentary situation. We need some quiet."

We climb the stairs, and Mr. Greene opens the door to his office, ushering us inside. The room is spacious, with large windows letting in soft natural light. He guides me to a comfortable couch as Easton helps me settle.

The woman suddenly reappears and hands me a glass of water. I take a few sips, feeling the cool liquid soothing my parched throat. As I glance at her, a spark of recognition flares in my mind. She was always nice to me in school.

"Kathryn? I'm so sorry for the trouble," I murmur, my voice shaky.

Kathryn offers a reassuring smile, "Don't worry about it, Willow. You've been through a lot. Trauma doesn't follow a schedule."

I take a closer look at Kathryn, realizing how much she's changed from the tall, lanky teenager I used to know. Now, she's stunning, with curves that put me to shame. Her long black hair is piled up in a bun, and her makeup only accentuates her hazel eyes and high cheekbones.

She crouches down in front of me, her professional demeanor taking over. "Can you give me your hand, Willow? We want to make sure you're okay."

I hold my hand out to her and instead of taking it she presses her fingers against my wrist while looking at the watch on her own, she explains, "I spent some time in the medical field before deciding I couldn't cope with it. Now, I work as a shared assistant to a few different businesses in the building. It's a bit of everything, but I like the variety. And by the way, you can call me Kat."

Her casual conversation helps distract me from the lingering unease. "Shared assistant? That sounds interesting."

Kat chuckles. "It is. I get to dabble in various tasks, from managing schedules to handling paperwork. It's less emotionally draining than nursing, that's for sure."

I nod, appreciating the change of topic. "I remember you from school. You were always nice to me."

She smiles warmly. "You were always easy to be nice to, Willow. Maybe we can have a drink together sometime soon, I could use a friend."

I manage a small, grateful smile. "I could use another friend too."

Kat gives a knowing look toward Gage and Mason, who are hovering nearby. "I'm sure you could definitely use a female friend with all that testosterone surrounding you." She gestures discreetly toward the two men, and I can't help but stifle a laugh.

It's then that I notice Easton has stepped away, though he hasn't gone far. He stands off to the side, still watching over me like he's afraid something might happen. His attention seems divided as he talks softly into the cell phone pressed to his ear.

Kat pats my hand gently, bringing my attention back to her as she moves to sit next to me on the couch. "How are you feeling now, Willow?"

I take a moment to assess myself. The dizziness has subsided, and the tightness in my chest has eased. "Better, thank you. Sorry for causing a scene."

Kat waves off my apology. "No need to apologize. Panic attacks can be unpredictable. I'm just glad I could help."

Easton finishes his call and joins us, crouching down on my other side. His worried eyes meet mine. "Do you remember what we spoke about last night?" he asks gently, his voice low.

It takes me a moment, but then I remember. "Yes, I remember," I reply softly.

He continues, "There's one in this building, and she has some time open. She's willing to see you if you want to talk to someone."

Kat, catching Easton's drift, adds, "She's lovely. You can't go wrong with going to see her. It can only help you."

I appreciate their concern, knowing that seeking professional help might be a step toward healing. "I... I think I'd like that," I admit, feeling both cautious and hopeful at the same time.

Easton nods, a reassuring smile on his face. "It's a positive step, Willow. I'll let her know."

He moves away, quietly murmuring to Gage and Mason before making another call. They exchange nods, and then Gage and Mason come over, tentatively brushing kisses against my cheek. "Take your time, Willow. We'll give you the space you need for your appointment and to recover," Gage says with genuine concern.

"We can try shopping for clothes again another time," Mason adds, his eyes showing understanding.

Kat looks at Gage and Mason. "Where did you take her to shop?"

Gage replies, "Loretta's Threads."

Kat scoffs, a look of disdain on her face. "No wonder she had a panic attack. Loretta is a nasty piece of work, always hated Willow. She probably did something on purpose to mess with her."

Now that my head is clearer than it was when confronted with Loretta, it does occur to me to wonder how she knew the details that she knew. What I was wearing that night may have been public information because of the news stories of our rescue, however the details of my name and Jacob were only spoken behind closed doors with law enforcement.

Kat turns toward me again with a look of determination. "You know what? Tomorrow is my day off, so I'm coming to your house, and we'll have the best kind of retail therapy there is—online retail therapy."

I can't stop the soft laugh that escapes me at the way she proposed her offer. "That sounds like a great idea, Kat."

It isn't long before Easton is returning and guiding me out of Mr. Greene's office and down the hallway to another office. He knocks on the door, and when it opens, I'm taken by surprise to see Gage's mother.

"Mrs. McMillian?" I ask, unable to hide my surprise.

She smiles warmly, her eyes holding a gentle understanding. "Yes, Willow. But please call me Margot. I hope you don't mind. I asked Easton not to say anything when we spoke earlier. If you'd prefer to see someone else or go to a different town, I can arrange that."

I shake my head, appreciating the sincerity in her voice. "No, it's fine. I didn't even know you were a therapist."

Margot nods, her expression kind. "I decided on a career change just after you were taken. Your mother and I were friends, and I wanted to find a way to help, even if indirectly."

A pang of sadness hits me at the mention of my mother. I try to distract myself from the emotions by saying, "I'm surprised Gage didn't come up with me to see you."

She shakes her head, laughing. "I'm not surprised at all, actually. Not just that he avoided me so well, but that he was in your company. But enough about that. Why don't you go in and take a seat." She glances at Easton. "Why don't you get yourself a coffee or something? Willow and I can have a private chat."

Easton hesitates, looking at me for confirmation. I manage a small smile. "I'll be okay. I'll see you in a bit."

He nods, pressing a gentle kiss to my forehead before walking away down the hallway. Margot closes the door behind herself and takes a seat across from me, her demeanor calm and reassuring. "How are you holding up, Willow?"

I take a deep breath, feeling a mix of emotions. "I've had better days. But I'm sure you already know by now that I've had a lot worse."

She nods, understanding. "Knowing you have had worse days doesn't mean you aren't still allowed to have tough days. We'll take it one step at a time. Whenever you're ready, we can start talking about whatever you feel comfortable sharing. Perhaps first let's talk about what you would like to get from our sessions."

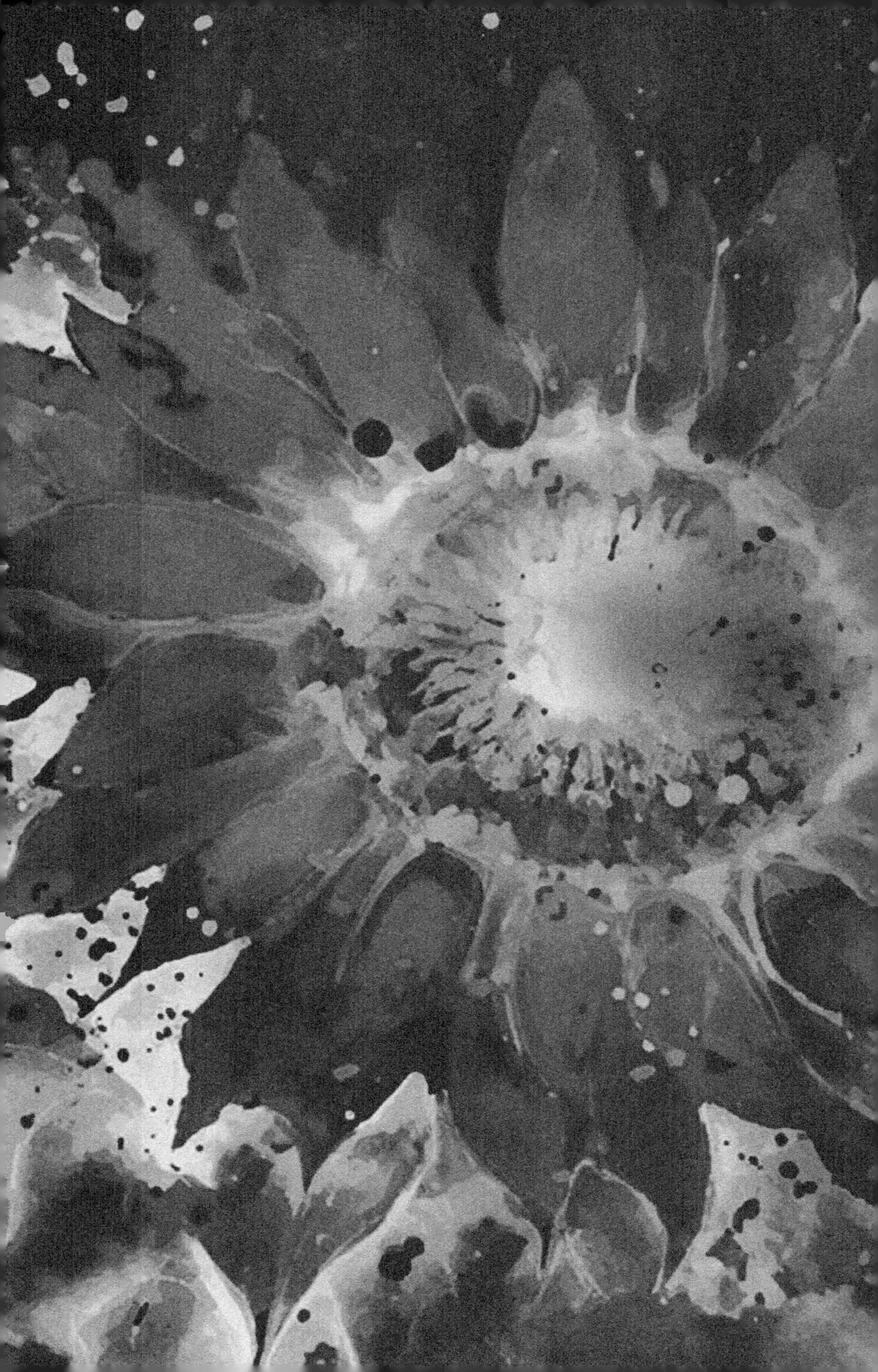

CHAPTER 12

Easton

I suddenly feel helpless. There haven't been many moments since I came upon the girl kneeling in the dirt outside that compound that I was away from her. But she needs this.

Walking out of the building and into the sunlight, it doesn't take me long until I'm walking into Gage's bar. I know I have at least an hour, though Margot cleared her schedule completely so Willow could stay as long as she needed.

Looking around, it doesn't take long to spot them at the back of the room, each with a beer in hand. Making my way over to them, I pull out one of the chairs at the table and slump down into it.

Gage looks at me, concern etched across his face. "Is she okay?" he asks, his voice worried.

I run a hand through my hair, my eyes flickering towards the entrance of the bar as if I could see through walls and check on Willow. "Really, I'm not sure if and when she will ever be okay," I admit with a heavy sigh. The events of the day have taken their toll, and the uncertainty surrounding Willow's healing process lingers like a shadow.

We sit in silence for a moment, each lost in our own thoughts. Mason breaks the quiet with a question that hangs heavy in the air. "I know we watched the news broadcasts and everything, but that doesn't obviously give all the details. How bad was it?"

I take a moment to reflect on everything I've learned about Willow's ordeal, my jaw tightening as I recall some of the details of what she endured. Closing my eyes briefly, I steady myself before looking at them again. "Very bad," I say simply, my voice holding a note of sadness and anger.

Gage takes a sip of his beer, his expression troubled. "She deserves some peace, man. What can we do to help?"

I appreciate the genuine concern he seems to have. "Right now, she needs time. And maybe a little normalcy, whatever that means for her."

Mason nods, his gaze distant. "So we got her back physically, but mentally... I guess that's a whole different battle."

I reach over and steal Gage's beer and take a sip, the cool liquid doing little to ease the heaviness in my chest. "She's strong. She survived that place. Now, we just need to help her survive the memories."

Gage leans forward to take back his beer and, after finishing it, he starts picking at the label. I can see that he is deep in thought and I know I just need to wait him out. "So, is there something more going on between you two?"

I can't decide if I want to scowl at him or simply slap him in the back of the head. "Really? I highly doubt she will be ready for whatever it is you are thinking for a long time."

He pauses and glances at Mason before returning his gaze to me with a raised eyebrow. "I was talking about your feelings for her, but I see where your mind went."

I let out a long exhale, my shoulders slumping as I lean back in the chair. The truth is, Gage hit a nerve, and his question brings to the forefront something I've been grappling with since the rescue—my developing feelings for my little butterfly. It's a complex tapestry of emotions that I hadn't fully unraveled.

Mason looks between Gage and me with a knowing expression. "We all have feelings for her, man. We have since we were kids. It's not a secret. But right now, that's not the priority. We need to help her heal."

Gage nods in agreement, but doesn't let the topic drop. "I get that, Mason. But it doesn't hurt to talk about it. Up until recently he only had feelings about the idea of her, but now he's currently sharing space with the living, breathing, albeit traumatized, woman."

I rub my temples, feeling the weight of the situation pressing on me. "It's not that simple. Yes, I care about her, but she's been through hell. I can't just throw my feelings into the mix, not to mention all of your feelings, like they are the solution to everything."

Mason leans back in his chair, crossing his arms. "We're not saying you should. But acknowledging your feelings is the first step. She's not fragile, Easton. She's strong. The other girls in this town wouldn't have survived half the shit I know she's been through, and I don't even know all of it. She deserves to know she's cared for in whatever way that manifests."

Gage adds, "We're not rushing her into anything. But we need to be honest with ourselves and, eventually, with her."

I run a hand through my hair, frustration and uncertainty swirling within me. "I just want her to be okay. I want us to be there for her without complicating things."

Mason smirks, a hint of mischief in his eyes. "Love is complicated, man. And I think you're in deeper than you realize."

Gage chuckles, lifting his empty beer bottle. "To love, the most complicated thing in the world."

I scowl at them, not in the mood for their teasing. "This is serious, guys."

Mason's expression softens, and he puts a hand on my shoulder. "We know, Easton. We just have to take it one step at a time. For now, let's focus on being there for Willow."

I shrug off Mason's hand, my gaze shifting between the two of them. "How the fuck can I even really believe you guys feel the same still when the person who spoke the most about her isn't even there for her anymore and won't even listen to the truth?" The frustration in my voice is palpable.

Mason frowns, his eyes lowering to his beer. "That was before. He chose his path, Easton. It's obviously not the same path as ours anymore."

I run a hand through my hair, frustration evident in my voice. "He just walked away, and we all know his reasons were bullshit. Willow needed him to keep looking, and he chose to abandon her."

Gage sighs, "We can't change his choices, Easton."

I lean forward, my frustration boiling over. "But you guys almost abandoned her too. I was the only one still searching for her, trying to find her and bring her back. You were ready to give up, and all the while, she needed us."

Mason's expression tightens, acknowledging the truth in my words. "We made a mistake, Easton. We let our own shit cloud our judgment. But we're here now, and we're not leaving her side again."

Gage's voice is calm but resolute. "Sometimes the pain of letting go is easier than the pain of holding on. I wish I could take back what we all said back then, but as you told me last night, it's in the past. What we can control now is our commitment to being there for Willow."

I let out a frustrated breath, my shoulders tense. "I get that, but it's hard not to be pissed off about it all. Especially with how Wyatt acted. Willow deserved better than that."

Mason nods, sympathy in his eyes. "She did, and we're going to give her better. We're not going to let her down."

Gage clears his throat. "Speaking of commitments, Mason, if you keep wanting to be there for Willow, how's Wyatt going to handle your mysterious disappearances from the ranch? You can't keep vanishing for entire days without consequences."

Mason chuckles, taking a sip of his beer. "Oh, you know Wyatt. He grumbles about it, threatens to replace me, but deep down, he knows he can't find someone as good as me to handle those horses."

I raise an eyebrow, skeptical. "You do realize that ranch life is full days and hard work, right? Realistically, you can't just abandon your responsibilities. You work for Wyatt, and you shouldn't push him too far."

Mason chuckles, "True, true. Maybe I should take up that offer Gage gave you a while back, managing the bar. You know, the one you turned down to join the tactical team."

Gage rolls his eyes at him. "Not funny, Mason. And no, you're not going to manage the bar."

He grins, undeterred. "Or, who knows, maybe I can frustrate Wyatt enough that he might actually pull his head out of his own ass and pay attention to the truth about Willow."

I scoff, "That's a terrible plan. Don't mess with Wyatt too much; when he isn't being a stubborn, immovable object, he's got a short fuse."

Mason winks, "Well, if he gets frustrated enough, maybe he'll start seeing things straight."

Gage interjects with a smirk, "Or maybe he'll just fire you, and then you won't have any responsibilities to keep you from helping Willow."

I shake my head, the corner of my mouth lifting despite the serious conversation. "You guys are ridiculous."

Mason raises his hands in mock surrender. "Alright, alright. Serious mode activated after one more question, was it you who did her hair?"

I know he intended it as a way to lighten the mood, but the memory of her breaking down in that bathroom has all the humor leaving my face.

I take a moment, my gaze falling to the table as I gather my thoughts. "Yeah, it was me," I reply, my voice more serious than before. "She had a breakdown at the hotel. She was in the bathroom, and I found her... she'd hacked off all her hair. It was just too much for her. The sight of her own hair pushed her over the edge."

There's a stunned silence between us as they process what I just revealed. The weight of the situation seems to settle in, and Mason and Gage exchange glances, the playful banter replaced by a somber acknowledgment of the depth of Willow's pain.

"I helped her tidy it up and dye it," I continue, my tone heavy. "It was the least I could do to offer some semblance of control and comfort. But she's hurting, guys. Badly. The attack you saw today wasn't her first, and it won't be her last. And before you both say you're going to be there for her, you need to make sure you care for her enough to be there even through those moments."

"We get it, Easton," Gage says quietly. "We're in this for the long haul. Whatever it takes."

Mason nods in agreement. "We might not fully comprehend what she's been through, but we're not backing down. We'll be there for her."

Their words give me a sense of comfort, that Willow will have as much support as possible. Still, a part of me wishes Wyatt could be here, sharing in this resolve. But deep down, I understand that may never happen.

"And I'm sure that will mean the world to her, guys," I say, my voice sincere. My gaze drifts to the entrance of the bar. The need to be with Willow pulls at me. I check my watch, realizing that time is ticking away, and the urge to return to her side intensifies.

When I look back toward them, Gage gives me a half smile as though he can read my thoughts. "Go. She should be finished with my mom soon and I'm sure she will need you there."

I duck my head gratefully. "Thanks, I'll probably see you tomorrow. Kat is coming over apparently, but I'm sure she would love it if you both visited too."

Mason salutes me with his almost empty beer. "Every day. Without fail. Until she gets sick of us."

The promise brings a smile to my face again. "Somehow, I don't think that will ever happen."

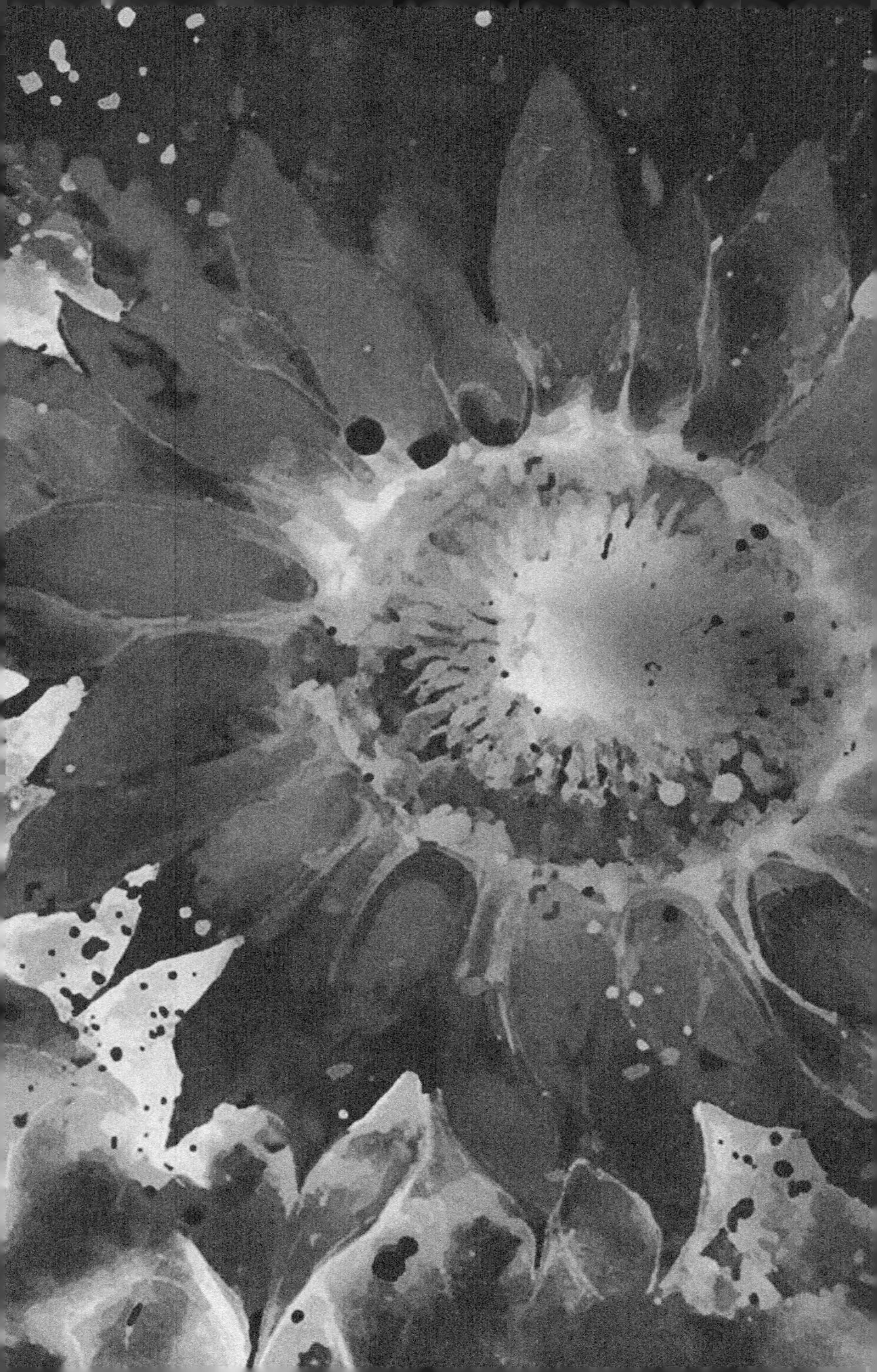

CHAPTER 13

Willow

I'm not sure if I have exceeded the time I am meant to be in here talking to Margot, but she doesn't mention it and just keeps talking to me.

I appreciate Margot's calm and understanding approach. Taking a moment to collect myself, I begin to share bits and pieces of my story. She listens attentively, asking questions when necessary but never pressuring me to reveal more than I'm comfortable with. The weight of my experiences feels a little lighter as I express my thoughts and feelings.

Margot guides the conversation, offering insights and gentle prompts to help me. She encourages me to explore both the pain and the resilience that allowed me to survive. It's an emotional process, but there's a sense of relief in sharing my story with someone who understands without judgment.

She nods along, acknowledging the weight of my experiences. "That must have been incredibly difficult for you. It takes strength to confront these memories, and I want you to know that it's okay to feel whatever emotions come up."

She suggests a grounding exercise, bringing my focus back to the present. She guides me through deep-breathing techniques, helping me regain a sense of control over my emotions. She also walks me through ways to ground myself during a panic attack. As the session comes to a close, we schedule initial appointments twice a week.

Walking me to the door of her office, her kind eyes reflect understanding. "Take your time, Willow. Remember, progress is progress, no matter how small. If you ever need to talk or if something comes up, don't hesitate to reach out. But I will see you in a few days for your next session."

I nod appreciatively, feeling a renewed sense of determination. "Thank you. I'll keep that in mind."

As I step out into the hallway, I notice Easton waiting for me. His eyes immediately lock onto mine, searching for any signs of distress. "Hey, how was it?" he asks, his concern palpable.

I offer him a small, reassuring smile. "It was good. Margot is helping me work through things. It's not easy, but I do think it will make a difference."

His expression softens, and he holds a hand out to me. "Let's go home, okay? You can relax while I make dinner for us."

I hesitate for a moment, the gesture has my heart fluttering slightly. I recognize that Easton's offer is genuine, a gesture of support and care. Still, an inexplicable flutter of nerves tickles at the edges of my consciousness. I take a moment to quell the reaction, reminding myself that this is simply Easton being the friend he's proven to be—nothing more, nothing less.

I consider the irrationality of my initial reaction and decide to push aside any unwarranted feelings. I nod appreciatively, accepting his hand.

"Sounds good," I reply, forcing a lightness into my voice. "Dinner sounds like a wonderful idea."

He intertwines his fingers with mine, a gesture that feels comforting. We walk out of the building together, and the cool afternoon air provides a welcome contrast to my slightly flushed skin.

As we approach Easton's car, he opens the door for me, helping me in and I slide into the passenger seat. The gentle hum of the engine surrounds us as he starts the car, and soon, we're on our way back to the house.

The drive is quiet, but not awkward. It's a companionable silence, allowing me the space to process the session while knowing that Easton is there if I choose to share my thoughts.

When we arrive at the house, Easton parks the car in front of it. The familiar sight of the place I once called home still feels strange, like I'm an intruder in a space that no longer belongs to me. The memories of my life before the cult flash through my mind, but they are distant, almost like a happier dream that came before the nightmare.

I glance at Easton, who wears a concerned expression. "You okay?" he asks, his eyes searching mine.

"Yeah," I respond, but the uncertainty lingers. "It's just... as much as I missed it, it's strange being back here. This wasn't really my home before. I spent more time at Wyatt's house growing up. And now, coming back to it, it still feels foreign."

Easton nods understandingly. "You don't have to force yourself to feel at home right away."

The concept of home is now feeling elusive, and I wonder if it is going to be something I can rebuild or if I need to find it elsewhere.

Opening the door I slide out of the car and close it behind me meeting a frowning Easton at the front of the vehicle. His concern is etched on his face. "I love that you're gaining some independence, little butterfly, but you're meant to wait until I come around to help you out."

I offer him a soft smile, appreciating his concern. "I'll keep that in mind." We make our way inside the house, and Mrs. Greene's cheerful flowers in the entryway brighten my mood a little more.

We walk straight back to the kitchen, and Easton glances at me. "How are you feeling? Is your stomach up to some not so bland food?"

I feel a small laugh escaping me at his tone, and Easton flashes a happy grin my way. "I'm happy to try anything you make," I reply, my eyes meeting his.

As Easton begins to prepare the meal, I notice a very slight blush to his cheeks. It's a subtle change, but it catches my attention. I wonder if I was wrong earlier, dismissing the notion that there might be something more than concern in his feelings. The thought lingers in my mind, creating a gentle curiosity that I choose to explore later.

I find myself observing him with a newfound curiosity.

He glances my way, catching my watchful eye. "What?" he asks, a playful smile tugging at his lips.

I shake my head, a small smile playing on my lips. "Nothing. Just appreciating the chef in action."

Easton chuckles, his blush deepening ever so slightly. "Well, I hope you appreciate the taste as much as the show." He reaches into his pocket, retrieving his phone and moments later music fills the room. It's cheerful and I can see the subtle shift in Easton's movements to match the beat, making my smile widen. I can definitely appreciate him trying to lighten the mood after the day I've had.

The savory aroma of cooking food fills the kitchen. Then finally he orchestrates the final touches with a flourish, presenting the finished dishes with a proud smile.

"Voilà," he declares, gesturing toward the plates. "Glazed chicken and roasted veggies, served with a side of charm and a sprinkle of culinary prowess."

I can't help but chuckle again at his dramatics. "Looks amazing. You might have missed your true calling as a chef," I tease, enjoying the effort he's put into making the meal special.

He feigns a modest bow. "Well, I do aim to impress. Bon appétit!"

He lowers the volume of the music but leaves it playing in the background as we settle in at the table, the warm glow of the kitchen lights casting a cozy ambiance.

The first bite of the glazed chicken bursts with flavor, and I must make some noise of appreciation as he startles and looks at me with wide eyes. Ducking my head I focus on the plate in front of me.

"I must say, you've outdone yourself," I remark after a few moments, glancing back up at him, savoring a bite of the glazed chicken. "I might become a food critic at this rate."

Easton grins, a mischievous glint in his eyes. "Well, I'm honored to have the first critique. Just be gentle with me, Chef Easton is still in training."

As we eat our meals, the conversation flows effortlessly. There's a lightness in the air, a nice reprieve from the emotions and turmoil that seems to be my life lately. Easton's playfulness is contagious, and I find myself laughing more freely than I have in forever. The laughter comes easily, and in that moment, I'm so grateful for Easton.

At one point, a piece of roasted vegetable escapes my fork and lands on the table. Easton eyes it with mock seriousness. "Ah, the great vegetable escape. A rebel in our midst."

I play along, trying very hard to suppress the smile spreading on my lips, adopting a faux scandalized tone. "Well, we can't have that. It's causing a stir at the dinner table."

He chuckles, reaching across the table to snag the rogue vegetable and hold it out towards my mouth. My breath stutters in my chest and I know my eyes have gone wide at his action, but I part my lips. His fingertips brush my lips as I close them around the piece of food and I can feel the heat on my cheeks at the same time I see color spread over his own.

He ducks his head as he presses his fingers against the cloth covering the table. "Crisis averted," he murmurs before picking his fork back up and starting to eat his meal again.

The moment, while innocent, leaves a subtle tension in the air. My heart beats a little faster, and I catch myself stealing glances at Easton, wondering if he felt the same charge in that small exchange. He continues to eat, his eyes focused on his plate, but there's a lingering awareness between us.

As we finish the meal, a sense of guilt begins to claw at me. I tell myself I shouldn't feel that way, that there's nothing to be guilty about. Yet, it persists, a nagging voice questioning my behavior and my actions. The teachings that the cult spent so long ingraining into our brains and enforcing begin to surface, whispering that simple, innocent moments like these are forbidden, that they carry a weight of wrongdoing. I push back against those thoughts, reminding myself that I'm free now, that I have the power to choose the life I want.

Easton starts clearing the table, and I watch him, the tension within me slowly giving way to a quieter, internal struggle. The music in the background shifts to a softer melody.

Finally, Easton breaks the silence, his voice carrying a genuine concern. "How are you feeling about venturing into anywhere else in the house yet?"

I take a deep breath, grappling with conflicting emotions. "I still don't think I'm ready to go upstairs," I confess, my voice quieter. "But maybe I could try the living room. Maybe we could, I don't know, sit and watch a movie or something. I haven't been able to do that for fifteen years. "

Easton nods with a soft smile. "That sounds like a good idea, little butterfly. We can see what movies are available. I'm sure there's a lot you've missed."

A small smile forms on my lips. "Yeah, a whole decade and a half worth of movies to catch up on. Where do we even begin?"

Easton joins in with a grin, and the tension between us eases. "Well, we'll figure that out. One movie at a time."

We move to the living room, and Easton sets up a cozy spot on the couch with blankets and cushions. He gestures towards the TV. "Alright, any genre preferences? Comedy, drama, action?"

I consider the question. "Anything that isn't about a cult kidnapping a girl would be great," I say with a half-smile.

"Comedy it is," Easton responds with a grin. "And how about we make our way through the years from oldest to newest? That way, you'll feel like you're catching up in the right order."

I chuckle, appreciating his thoughtful approach. "Sure, sounds like a plan. Let's start this movie marathon."

Easton navigates through the movie options, and we settle in to watch a comedy that was released just after I was abducted. The sound of laughter gradually fills the room, blending with the cozy atmosphere. As the movie progresses, I find myself genuinely enjoying the simple pleasure of watching a film without the shadow of the past looming over me.

As the second movie begins, my blinks get longer, and the weight of the day coupled with the emotional session with Margot starts to take its toll. The laughter from the movie becomes a distant hum, and my eyelids begin to droop.

I fight against the pull of sleep, not wanting to miss a moment of this small feeling of newfound freedom. But eventually, I succumb, my eyes closing for longer intervals until the darkness of sleep envelops me.

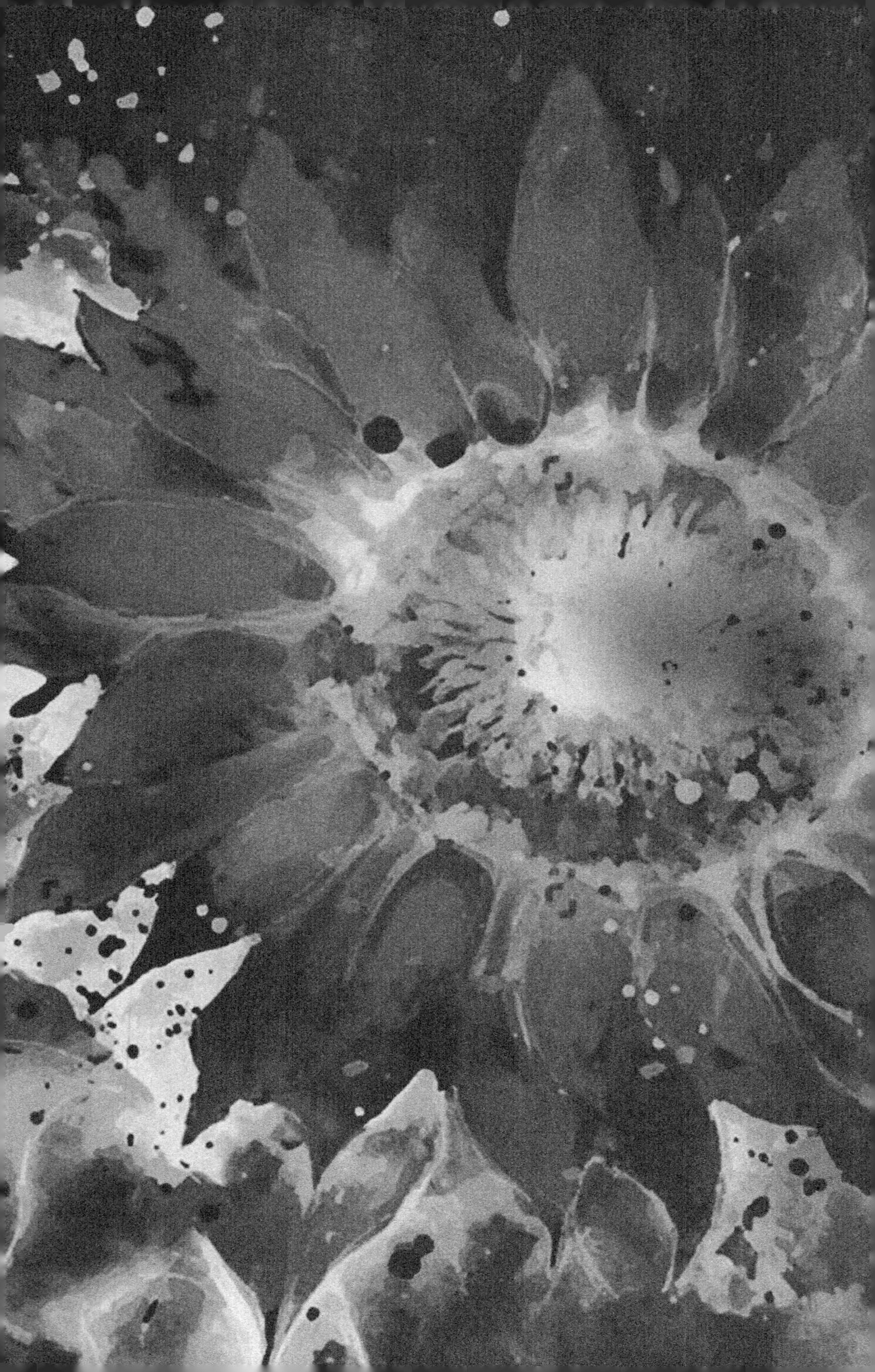

Chapter 14

Unknown

I should have known she would return to Sierra Valley.

She might think she can slip back into her old life, into their lives, but she underestimates me.

I look forward to making her regret it.

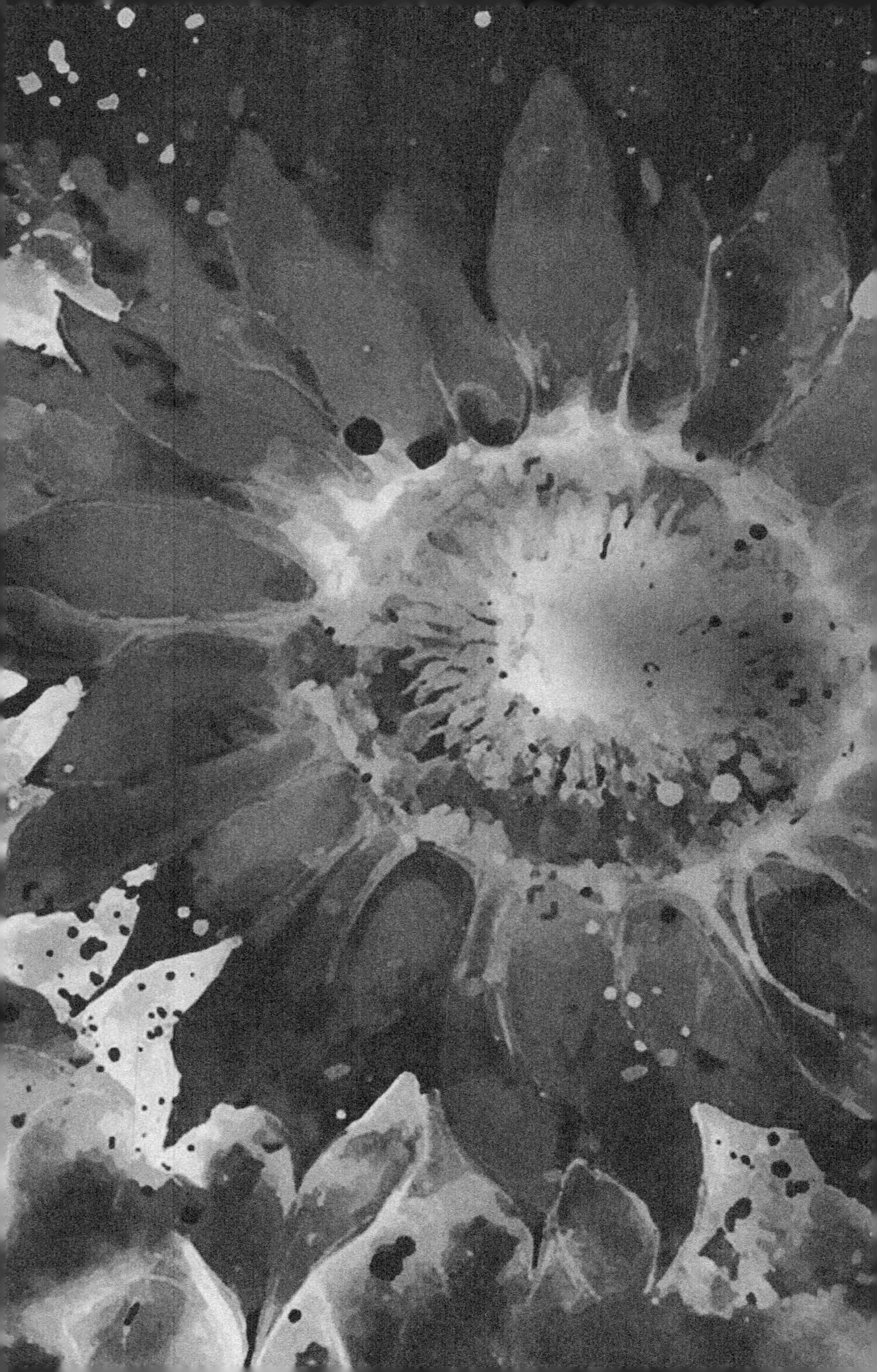

CHAPTER 15

Willow

I wasn't asleep long before the nightmares came.

They returned with a vengeance, dragging me back into the depths of the cult's darkness. The visions are vivid, haunting me with memories of the life I was forced to endure. The cruelty at Jacob's hands replays in agonizing detail, the bruises on my skin where it couldn't be seen by others.

I feel the weight of his hands, cold and unyielding, as they grasp the back of my neck, leaving invisible marks on my soul. The lashes for disobedience sting across my back, and the memory of the hunger that gnawed at my stomach during moments of stubborn defiance tightens its grip on me. The echoes of the cult's twisted teachings reverberate in my mind, their words haunting every corner of my dreams. All the while, the cult claimed it was for my own good, that their actions were driven by a twisted sense of love and protection.

The torment intensifies, each nightmarish scenario blending into the next. I find myself trapped in a cycle of fear and helplessness, reliving the moments I was powerless to stop.

I'm jolted awake, the echoes of the nightmares lingering as I gasp for breath. Easton must have moved me to the bedroom while I slept, and the room feels stifling. Panic sets in, and I stumble toward the bathroom, barely making it to the toilet before the contents of my stomach spill out in violent heaves.

The taste of bile is bitter, a harsh reminder of the nightmares that refuse to release their grip. I cling to the edge of the toilet, the cold porcelain a stark contrast to the feverish heat of my skin. Tears well up in my eyes, a mix of frustration, fear, and a profound sense of powerlessness.

I struggle to recall what Margot taught me only hours before, the exercises I had been happy to learn now just out of the reach of my panicked mind.

Moments later, I hear Easton's soothing hum, a melodic sound that pierces through the remnants of my nightmares. His presence is becoming like a balm, a lifeline grounding me in the reality of the present. Slowly, he approaches, his steps gentle, and I feel his hands pulling back my hair, a tender gesture that brings a sense of relief and gratitude flooding me.

The touch is gentle, so very different to the memories of harsh hands that linger in the recesses of my mind. Easton's fingers brush through my hair, and I can feel the genuine care in his actions. A soft sigh escapes me as the cool air kisses my forehead, a welcome change to the lingering heat of my distress.

With my hair pulled back, Easton's hand glides soothingly down my arm, a gesture that offers comfort. I'm grateful for him not touching my back, he must realize that at this time his touches there might be triggering, unwelcome reminders of a past I'm desperately trying to escape.

"Deep breaths, Willow," Easton murmurs, his voice gentle. "You're here, in the present. Those nightmares can't hurt you now."

I nod, grateful for his presence, for the soothing sounds and the comforting touch that bring me back to the safety of the bathroom. The tension in my shoulders begins to ease.

The techniques Margot imparted earlier now echo in my mind, urging me to ground myself in the present.

As Easton's touch continues to soothe, I follow the advice Margot shared. I focus on my breath, the rise and fall of my chest. I notice the coolness of the tile floor beneath my knees, the subtle scent of soap in the air. These tangible sensations become my liferaft, pulling me away from the haunting echoes of the nightmares.

With each intentional breath, I feel a sense of control returning. The fear loses its grip, replaced by the comforting reality that I'm no longer ensnared in the cult's darkness.

Easton gently helps me back to my feet, his arm supporting me as we move toward the sink. He turns on the faucet, and the sound of running water fills the small space as he reaches for a fresh towel. His actions are methodical, careful, and filled with a quiet understanding.

"Let's get your face washed," he says softly, guiding me closer to the sink. I lean against the edge, focusing on the water's rhythm and the familiar scent of soap.

With tenderness, Easton wets the towel and begins to gently clean my face. The cool water feels refreshing, and the soft touch of the towel wipes away the lingering sweat and tears. The mirror above the sink reflects my image, and I take a moment to look into my own eyes, searching for a glimmer of strength.

Easton's gaze on me is a silent source of support, his eyes filled with compassion and unwavering care. He hands me the towel, allowing me to continue at my own pace. The simple act of washing my face becomes cleansing, not just physically, but also symbolically, as if I can wash away the remnants of the past that cling to me.

As I finish, Easton takes the towel, disposing of it with a quiet efficiency. "You're doing great, little butterfly," he assures me, his voice a comforting murmur.

"Thank you, Easton," I whisper, my voice soft in the enclosed room. "I don't know how I would've managed without you."

He places a hand on my shoulder, his touch grounding as he turns me to face him. "Willow, I need you to know something," he says earnestly. "These moments don't make you weaker. They make you stronger. Each time you face these nightmares, each time you work through the pain, you show just how much fight is in you. You're the strongest person I've ever met."

His words resonate in the quiet space, and a swell of emotion threatens to overflow. Easton's encouragement is a reminder that strength isn't just measured in the absence of fear but in the ability to confront it and emerge resilient.

"We all have our battles, Willow," he continues, his voice a steady anchor. "And you're winning yours. Don't forget that. You're not defined by your past, but by the courage you show every day."

A tear escapes despite my efforts to contain the flood of emotions. It trickles down my cheek and without hesitation, Easton leans forward and kisses it away, his lips warm against my skin. When he pulls back, he meets my gaze with a sincerity that pierces through the shadows.

"Your tears are precious, Willow," he says softly. "They should only be shed for those who have earned them, for moments that truly matter."

His words are soothing, and I nod in gratitude. Easton's understanding touch and compassionate words are mending the fractures of my spirit, one piece at a time.

"Are you ready to go back to bed?" he asks gently, his concern evident.

I hesitate for a moment, uncertainty flickering through me. "Yes," I respond, my voice a fragile whisper, "if you can be there until I fall asleep again."

His response is a reassuring smile. "Of course, Willow. I'll be right there beside you."

We make our way back to the bedroom, the shadows retreating in the face of dim, soft lighting. Easton helps me settle into bed, and as he lays down beside me, a comforting warmth spreads through the room. In the semi-darkness, I sense his calming presence.

As we both find our places in the bed, his hand brushes against mine. It's a gentle, reassuring touch, and without hesitation, I take hold of his hand. His fingers intertwine with mine, creating a connection that speaks volumes in the quiet of the night.

Easton starts humming again, a melodic tune that wraps around me like a gentle lullaby. The vibrations of his humming resonate through our intertwined hands, creating a soothing rhythm that guides me toward sleep.

I close my eyes, letting the gentle hum and the reassuring grasp of Easton's hand cradle me. The nightmares, though still lingering at the edges of my consciousness, begin to fade. The darkness loses its grip as the hum becomes a guiding light, leading me away from the haunting memories.

The steady rise and fall of Easton's chest, the warmth of his presence, and the comforting melody guide me into a realm of peace. As I drift off to sleep, I carry with me the echoes of his words and the tenderness of his touch.

———--------------

We barely had breakfast the next morning before there was a brief knock at the front door, followed by the loud voice of Kat as she let herself inside.

"Morning, lovelies!" Kat's energetic voice echoes through the house, carrying an air of vivacity that instantly lifts the atmosphere. Her laptop is tucked under her arm as she strides into the room, a mischievous glint in her eyes.

I feel Easton's hand gently squeezing my shoulder in anticipation of the whirlwind that is Kat. She barely spares a moment before declaring, "Today is all about Willow! Are you ready? We're going shopping!"

Confusion crosses my face as I exchange a glance with Easton. Kat, noticing our bewilderment, grins widely and pats her laptop as if it holds the secret to the universe.

"I've got a whole online shopping spree planned. And don't you worry, Willow, it's all on me. Consider it a little welcome home gift," she says with a wink.

"But Kat, I..." I begin, attempting to voice my protests, but she cuts me off with a wave of her hand.

"Nope, no arguments," she declares, her determination leaving little room for negotiation. Grabbing my hand, she pulls me up from the breakfast table. "Easton, sweetie, I'm stealing your girl for some girl time. You go have fun elsewhere, and we'll see you back here later."

Easton chuckles, raising his hands in surrender. It seems futile to even try arguing with Kat. "Alright, alright. You ladies have fun. I'll find something to occupy myself with."

With that, Kat ushers me toward the living room, her infectious energy filling the space. "Now, Willow, we're going to pick out the most fabulous outfits, blast some empowering tunes, and have a grand ol' time. Trust me, you need this."

As she settles on the couch with her laptop, she gestures for me to join her. "And don't you worry 'bout a thing. This is a judgment-free zone. We're all about embracing the fabulousness that is you."

With a deep breath and a glance at Easton, who offers an encouraging smile as he passes on the way out of the house, I take a seat beside Kat.

Kat wastes no time, her fingers dancing across the keyboard as she navigates through online stores with lightning speed. "Alright, Willow, let's see... what's your style? Bold and daring or subtle and elegant? Or maybe a mix of both?"

I shrug, still unsure of how to define my style after so many years of having it dictated by the cult. Kat simply grins, undeterred. "No worries, we'll figure it out together. How about we start with something that makes you feel confident? We're going to build a whole new wardrobe, my friend."

As we browse through an array of options, Kat shares anecdotes of her own fashion adventures, transforming the task into something far less daunting than I had anticipated. At first I'm overwhelmed, stressed about the fact that I have never had the chance to really find my own identity and don't know what sort of clothes I even like. But Kat's enthusiasm is infectious, and slowly, I find myself getting into the spirit of the impromptu shopping spree. We scroll through pages of dresses, pants, tops, and accessories. Kat offers style suggestions knowing that I don't know what style I like yet, occasionally pausing to admire a particularly bold or elegant piece.

"Ooh, what about this one?" Kat points to a flowing dress in a vibrant shade of blue. "Imagine strutting into a room wearing this. Heads will turn!"

I can't help but smile at her excitement. "I don't really want heads to turn though."

Kat shoots me a sly look, her eyes narrowing with playful curiosity. "Not even Easton's?"

My cheeks heat up instantly, and I duck my head, attempting to hide my blush. When I woke up that morning, just like the prior morning, I had been alone in my bed. For the first time in the time since I had been rescued I wasn't sure how I felt about waking up alone. "Kat, it's not like that. Easton has been... he's just been really kind and supportive."

Her eyebrows raise, and she leans in, her expression teasing. "So, you're saying there's a chance?"

I stammer, "No, I mean, not like that. We're just friends. Really good friends."

Kat continues to look at me with an amused glint in her eyes. "And what about Mason and Gage? Any chance there?"

I blink in surprise, "Mason and Gage? No, Kat, they're just trying to be the friends they used to be before I was taken. I highly doubt Easton thinks of me like that, let alone Mason and Gage."

She sits back, still wearing that mischievous grin. "You know, Willow, sometimes friends can become something more. And it's clear those guys care about you. Besides, you deserve happiness after everything you've been through."

I shake my head. "Kat, it's not like that. I doubt Easton or anyone sees me that way. They're just trying to help me heal from the past."

Kat's gaze softens, and she places a supportive hand on my shoulder. "Willow, I get it. Healing takes time, and you've been through a lot. But don't close yourself off to the possibility of happiness. You deserve it."

"Thank you, Kat," I reply. Trying to escape the conversation, I turn my attention back to the laptop, scrolling through more clothing options. Kat continues to watch me, a knowing smile playing on her lips.

She leans in again, her tone playful. "Fine, I'll let it go. But, Willow, I don't think I'm imagining things. There's something there, I can sense it."

I blush again, a bit flustered. "Kat, really, there's nothing. We're friends, and that's it."

She winks at me. "Alright, alright. We'll see. I'm pretty good at reading these things, you know. In fact, I'm so confident, I'll bet you money that by lunchtime, all three of them will be in this house."

I look at her, incredulous. "All three? You mean Easton, Mason, and Gage? That's not going to happen."

Kat grins, clearly enjoying this. "Oh, it will. You'll see. And when it does, you owe me fifty bucks."

I laugh, thinking the idea is preposterous. "Okay, deal. But I'm telling you, you're going to lose that bet."

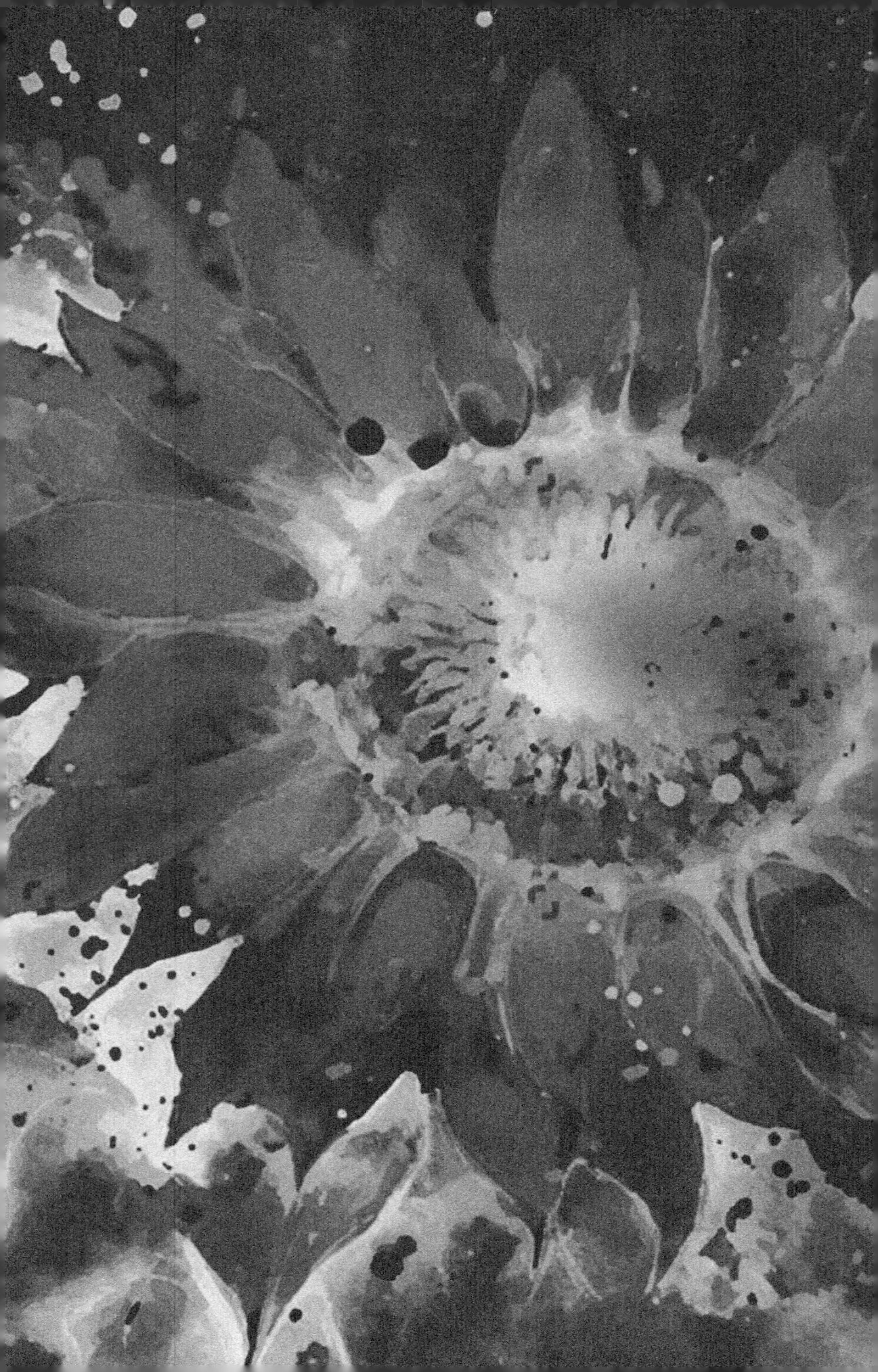

CHAPTER 16

Mason

I don't know why I'm nervous as I pull my truck up outside of her house. I had avoided this place for the last fifteen years. It hurt too much to be here, to feel the void she left in our lives.

But now that she is back, I couldn't imagine staying away.

I knew at some point soon I was going to have to look more closely at how I felt about one of my best friends when I was a teenager. There were a lot of things I knew I was going to have to confront in the near future. Like my feelings and now the fact that I'm avoiding one of my other best friends.

I pull the dirty gloves off my hands and throw them into the passenger side of the truck as I look down at myself. I'm covered in pieces of hay from feeding the animals before I left the ranch. I probably should have made myself more presentable but I didn't want to chance running into Wyatt. So far, I had succeeded in not seeing him since the day he sent Willow away from the ranch with no explanation.

Taking a deep breath, I push open the door of my truck and step onto the gravel driveway just as Easton's SUV pulls in. The engine rumbles to a stop, and Gage's car follows suit.

It seems like they were together, a realization that stings a little, but it makes sense. They had been close friends before Easton left, and after everything that happened with Wyatt and Willow, I doubt Easton would be in a hurry to visit him. Or me, since I live on the same ranch.

Even after being with both of them for so long yesterday, I still feel the distance between us because of Wyatt. I feel the guilt clawing inside of me that Willow still doesn't know the reason for Wyatt's actions. Admittedly, Gage and Easton don't know the full story, but I do. But it wasn't my story to tell. And I somehow doubt Wyatt would be telling that story anytime soon.

The moment Gage and Easton step out of their vehicles, Gage flashes me a friendly grin, and Easton nods in greeting.

"Mason," Gage greets with a casual yet warm tone, giving me a clap on the shoulder as he steps up to me.

"Hey, Mason," Easton adds, a small smile on his face.

I return their greetings as we approach the front door. The sound of music and laughter spills into the air, instantly lightening the atmosphere and bringing a smile to our faces.

Kat was in her element. As we reach the entrance of the living room, the scene unfolds before us, with Kat attempting to coax Willow into an impromptu dance session. Her animated gestures and lively movements have Willow reluctantly swaying to the beat in the open space in front of the couch.

Kat's eyes widen as she catches sight of us, and her attempt at coordination takes a comical turn. She teeters on the edge of balance, almost falling over in a fit of contagious laughter. Willow, her face flushing, presses her hands to her cheeks.

"Looks like the party just got better!" Kat exclaims, still chuckling, as she gestures at Willow with a dramatic flourish. "And, it looks like you owe me."

Easton, observing the scene with an arched eyebrow, glances between Kat and Willow, curiosity etched across his face. Kat, still caught up in her laughter, waves him off with a dismissive flick of her hand.

"Oh, Easton, don't mind us! Just a little spontaneous dance therapy. Willow here is a natural, aren't you?" Kat's mischievous grin widens as she playfully nudges Willow.

Willow, her embarrassment now a vivid shade of crimson, groans again, but her eyes sparkle with amusement. The blush paints her skin a delicate hue, and I push aside the instant reaction to the sight.

"How about I whip up some lunch for everyone?" Easton offers, attempting to shift the focus.

Gage, always ready for a good meal, chimes in, "I'll help. What do you say, Mason?"

I nod in agreement. "Sounds good. Lead the way."

As we move toward the kitchen and dining area, the lively atmosphere continues. The music plays loudly, blending with the occasional laughter. It creates a comforting and familiar ambiance. The unease I initially felt began to dissipate, replaced by a sense of camaraderie.

Once in the kitchen, Gage and Easton efficiently start preparing lunch. I lean against the counter, looking at Kat and Willow who join us. "So, how did the online shopping adventure go?"

Kat's eyes sparkle with mischief. "Oh, it was fantastic! Willow here is going to have the most fabulous wardrobe in no time."

Willow, her blush still lingering, adds with a smile, "Kat has a talent for convincing me to step out of my comfort zone."

Kat nudges her playfully. "And don't you forget it! Now, Mason, when are you going to let me give you a makeover?"

I chuckle. "What? You don't like ranch couture?"

Kat laughs, her eyes glinting with humor. "Oh, it goes perfectly with 'Eau de Horse.' Very rustic chic."

I grin, shaking my head. "I'll pass on the makeover, thanks. I'll stick to the classic ranch look."

Kat feigns disappointment. "But think about the untapped potential, Mason. We could turn you into the town's most eligible cowboy bachelor."

Gage, who was busy chopping salad, simply laughs and shoots me a look. I could never hide my feelings from my best friends, and he had always known how I felt back then and now.

As the banter continues, I find myself lost in the moment. Gage's knowing look brought a subtle reminder of the unspoken emotions that linger beneath the surface. The notion of being the town's most eligible cowboy bachelor felt like a distant concept. I didn't consider myself a bachelor in the true sense. I chuckle, brushing off the playful teasing. But deep down, I know my heart had been claimed a long time ago.

Easton and Gage skillfully finish preparing a chicken salad with fries; the aroma of the food fills the kitchen, adding to the already inviting atmosphere. The banter flows effortlessly as we all gather around the table, ready to enjoy the meal together.

Kat can't resist pushing the makeover idea a bit further. "Come on, Mason, just imagine the possibilities. You will have dates lining up in no time!"

I scoffed, shaking my head. "I'm not sure the town is ready for a revamped Mason. I'll stick to being the classic cowboy."

Willow, her embarrassment from earlier now transformed into amusement, joins in. "I think the rugged ranch look suits you just fine, Mason. No need for a makeover."

Willow's words bring a warmth to my chest, and her laughter echoes in the kitchen, creating a melody that resonates through all of us. As we settle around the table, the delicious aroma of the food filling the air, I can't help but steal glances at Willow. She already seems to be more at ease than the day before.

We sit down at the dining table and dig into the chicken salad and fries that Easton and Gage prepared for us. Between bites of salad and sips of drinks, we catch Willow up on the happenings in town—the new businesses, the latest scandals, and the comings and goings of familiar faces. It's a crash course in small-town life, and Willow absorbs it all with genuine interest.

As the plates empty, we share stories of our own adventures, the escapades we had navigated over the past fifteen years. Once the last bite is eaten and the dishes cleared away, we migrate to the cozy living room. Easton informs us that he and Willow are progressing through movies from oldest to newest.

We each find spots around the room, claiming the best seats for the movie marathon that awaits us. The comfortable atmosphere enveloped us as we settled in. Kat, armed with the remote control, takes her place as the self-appointed movie master.

I couldn't help but notice how naturally Willow gravitates toward Easton, choosing a spot next to him on the couch. It's a subtle gesture, but one that doesn't escape my attention. As the first movie begins, I observe the ease between them, the shared laughter, and the occasional exchange of glances. There's a connection there already and I hope deep down that it helps her be happy.

As we watch the movie, I find my eyes drawn back to Willow again and again. I love watching her reactions to the movie; the emotions that cross her face are so easy to read. Humor, surprise, even the occasional cringe that crosses her face has both happiness and affection bubbling inside of me.

But as much as I'm enjoying myself, I know that I have responsibilities to take care of. With a reluctant sigh, I stand up as the first movie finishes, drawing the attention of the group.

"Hey, sorry, I've got some things to take care of back at the ranch," I announce, offering a sheepish smile. "Enjoy the rest of the movies, though. Thanks for the great company."

Gage gives me an understanding nod, while Easton and Kat wave off my departure with casual reassurances. Willow, sitting next to Easton, looks my way with a genuine smile. "Thanks for joining us, Mason. It was great having you here."

I return the smile. "Anytime, Willow. Have a good evening, all of you."

Upon returning to the ranch, I walk into the quiet kitchen. I sigh before Wyatt's voice cuts through the stillness.

"Where the fuck have you been, Mason?"

His words hang in the air, a heavy tension settling over the room. I turn to see Wyatt standing there, his expression a mix of concern and frustration. It's a confrontation I had been avoiding—the reckoning looming over us since Willow's return.

I meet Wyatt's gaze. His eyes pierce through the silence, searching for answers. The weight of his question hangs in the air and I take a moment before responding, trying to keep my own frustration in check.

"Out with friends, catching up," I reply, my tone measured. "What's it to you?"

Wyatt's expression darkens, his frustration turning into anger. "You can't just disappear whenever you feel like it, Mason. We've got responsibilities here, things to take care of. You can't just run off to her house whenever you want."

I sigh, feeling the exhaustion of the last few days settle in. The tension in the room escalates, and I sense Wyatt's anger reaching a boiling point. As I look at him, I realize this confrontation is long overdue.

"I've supported you in everything for most of my life, but I can't support you in this. Willow is back, and you need to see the truth that's right in front of your face," I respond, my voice steady.

Wyatt's jaw tightens in frustration. "I don't need your judgment, Mason. My soulmate already left me once 15 years ago. That was made clear to me six years ago. And then the woman who was there for me when I found out how quickly she had moved on was taken away from me and left me a single father. So she's back now to what? Try to slide into some sort of place with us again now that something's obviously happened with whoever she was with? No, she can go back into whatever hole she ran away to."

My fist makes contact with his face before I even realize I moved in his direction. The punch lands with a resounding thud and Wyatt stumbles back, caught off guard by the sudden blow. Only his hand on the wall stops him from losing his balance. The room pauses with suspended stillness.

"You don't get to talk about her like that," I say, my voice low and controlled, my fists clenched at my sides. The anger simmering beneath the surface erupts, fueled by the frustration of years of silence and unresolved issues.

Wyatt, his hand against his jaw, glares at me. "You don't understand, Mason. You don't know what it was like."

"I know more than you think," I retort, my tone sharp. "But that doesn't give you the right to treat her this way. She deserves to know the truth, and you can't keep hiding behind your own pain."

The room crackles with tension, our eyes locked in a battle of wills. But I know the pain and vulnerability that he's concealed for far too long.

"She doesn't need to know anything," Wyatt spits, his voice edged with bitterness. "She made her choice, she moved on and I've moved on. We've all moved on."

I take a step closer, my gaze unwavering. "Moved on? Look around, Wyatt. Nothing's been the same since she left. You've built walls, pushed away the people who care about you. And for what? To protect yourself from getting hurt again?"

Wyatt's jaw clenches, and for a moment, I think he might retaliate. But instead, he lets out a heavy sigh, his shoulders slumping.

"You don't get it, Mason. You never did," he mutters, his tone weary.

I can't let it end there. Frustration and concern fuel my actions as I close the distance between us. Without hesitation, I grab Wyatt by the shoulders, shaking him with a firm grip.

"I do get it, Wyatt. But none of this adds up," I say, my voice intense. "It doesn't make sense, and I need to know why."

Wyatt frowns, confusion etching his features. It's a vulnerability I haven't seen in him for a long time. It only fuels my determination to break through the walls he erected. "What are you talking about?"

"Have you watched the news, Wyatt?" I demand, my grip on his shoulders tightening. "I left you a note, and if you haven't seen it, you need to. What's in the news is real, and it changes everything. It makes what happened six years ago not make any sense at all."

Wyatt stubbornly shakes his head. "I haven't watched the news, Mason. I've been dealing with things here while you ran off after her. Why the fuck are you even running after someone who left us?"

"Just watch the fucking news, Wyatt," I insist as I shake him again, my voice urgent.

Wyatt's eyes narrow with skepticism. "What are you talking about? What does the news have to do with any of this?"

I sigh, suddenly feeling tired, and I release my hold on him. "Because it's about Willow, you stubborn asshole. You need to know what's going on. There are things you don't know, things that will change everything."

Wyatt's expression shifts from confusion to frustration. "Fine, I'll watch your damn news. But I don't see how it's going to change anything."

"You'll see," I reply, my tone heavy with the weight of the unspoken truth. "You'll see, Wyatt, and then maybe you'll understand why you can't keep living in the past."

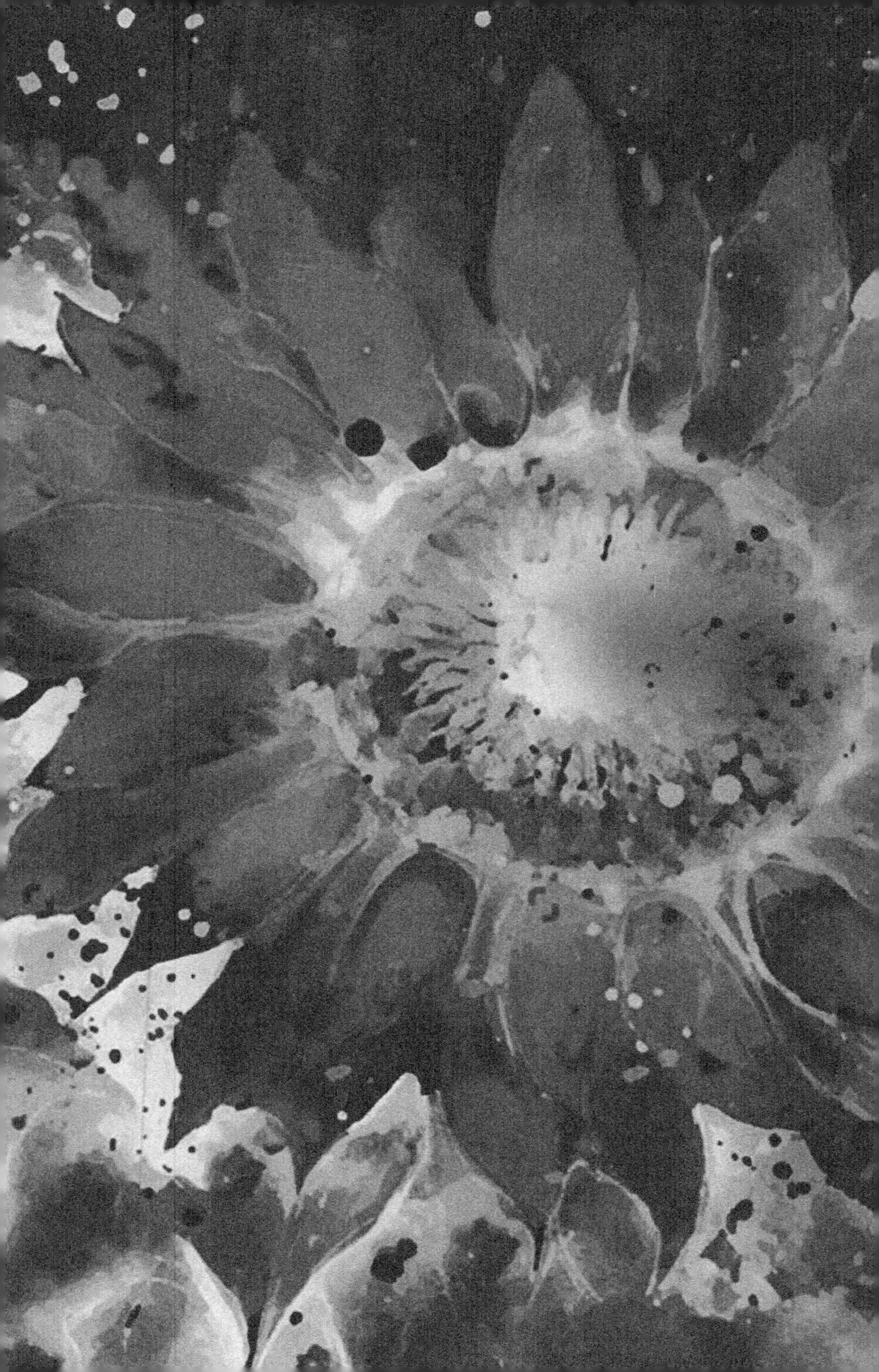

CHAPTER 17
Willow

"How are you feeling today, Willow?"

I raise my eyebrow in Margot's direction, but she just smiles calmly at me. Patiently waiting for me to respond. It's my second time sitting in this chair and even though I had a slightly better sleep the last two nights, I'm hesitating. How do I feel?

"I'm... a little better than last time," I admit, offering a small, tentative smile. "At least, I think I am."

Margot nods understandingly. "That's progress. Remember, it's okay to take your time, Willow. Healing doesn't happen overnight."

As I sit there, contemplating my own emotions, Margot breaks the silence. "Do you want to talk about what happened last time? About the panic attack?"

I take a deep breath, considering her question. After a few moments of internal debate, I decide it's time to share what triggered that overwhelming reaction. "It was Loretta," I start, my voice steady but carrying the weight of the memories. "When we were in her store, she... she tried to give me a dress. A dress similar to the one they made me wear that final night in the compound."

Margot's expression remains empathetic, encouraging me to continue. "And that dress triggered a panic attack?"

I nod, my gaze fixed on some point in the room as I recall the haunting memories. "Yes, but it was more than just the dress. She called me Grace."

Margot's brows furrow in concern. "Grace? Is that significant?"

I take another deep breath, trying to find the words to explain. "In the cult, that's what they called me—Grace. It was my name there. I don't know how she knew, but hearing her say it, combined with the dress... It was too much. It brought back everything—the fear, the lack of control. I felt trapped again."

Margot listens attentively, her supportive presence allowing me to open up. "It sounds incredibly difficult, Willow. I can't imagine how triggering that must have been. But you're safe now. You have people here who care about you and want to help you through this."

I nod, grateful for her understanding. "I know. It's just... sometimes the past feels so close, like it could swallow me whole."

Margot's gaze remains compassionate as she continues the conversation. "I'm here to support you every step of the way. Now, let's talk about your sleep. How have your nightmares been?"

I shift uncomfortably in my seat, the memories of the vivid dreams haunting my nights still fresh. "They've been bad, especially after our last session."

Margot nods, understandingly. "It's not uncommon for difficult discussions to stir up emotions that manifest in dreams. Can you tell me more about what you've been experiencing?"

Closing my eyes briefly, I try to summon the courage to articulate the haunting scenes that replay in my mind. "They're like flashes from the past—images of the compound, the people there, and the things they made me do. It's like I'm reliving those moments, and I wake up feeling trapped and scared."

Margot offers a supportive nod. "Nightmares can be powerful, but they're not a reflection of your current reality. It's your mind processing the trauma. We can work on strategies to manage them, perhaps grounding techniques to bring you back to the present when they occur. Would that be something you're open to exploring?"

I consider her suggestion, realizing that finding ways to cope with the nightmares might bring some relief. "Yes, I think that would be helpful. I'm willing to try anything."

Margot smiles reassuringly. "Good. We'll work together on developing coping mechanisms that suit you. Remember, it's okay to reach out when you need support, even outside our sessions. Now, let's explore some of the positive moments you've had recently. Have there been any situations or interactions that made you feel a sense of safety or joy?"

I take a moment to reflect on the positive moments that started to weave their way into my life. A genuine smile forms on my face as I recall the efforts of Easton and Kat to bring light into my days.

"Well, Easton has been helping me with something," I begin, the warmth of gratitude evident in my voice. "He came up with this plan to reintroduce me to movies, starting from the oldest ones. We've been watching them in order, and it's been surprisingly comforting. It's like he's creating a new set of memories for me."

Margot nods, encouraging me to share more. "That sounds like a thoughtful approach. How does it make you feel?"

"It's... nice," I admit, a genuine spark of joy lighting up my eyes. "It's a small escape, and it helps me focus on something other than the past. And when the nightmares hit, he's been there, offering reassurance. It's like he knows when I need someone around."

Margot smiles. "Supportive relationships can play a crucial role in the healing process. It's wonderful that you have someone like Easton by your side. And what about other moments? Anyone else you've connected with?"

My thoughts shift to Kat, the energetic and spirited friend who has been relentless in her efforts to bring joy back into my life. "Kat has been amazing too," I continue. "She came over for a virtual shopping spree. It was a bit overwhelming at first, but she has this way of making everything fun. She convinced me to try on some clothes, and we laughed a lot. It was... nice to feel normal for a little while."

Margot's eyes light up with encouragement. "It sounds like you're building a support system, creating positive moments to counterbalance the challenging ones. That's a significant step, Willow."

I nod. "Yes, it really is. And Gage and Mason have been visiting every day too," I add, feeling a slight blush creeping up my cheeks.

"Gage and Mason?" Margot repeats, her tone curious.

"Yeah, they've been checking in on me, making sure I'm doing okay. It means a lot," I explain, glancing down at my hands. "It's just... Gage is your son, and I didn't want it to be weird or anything."

Margot chuckles softly. "Willow, it's not weird at all. Gage is a caring person, and Mason has been a close friend for many years. They both care about your well-being. It's a positive sign that you have such a strong support system."

I nod at her reassurance. "Yeah, I guess I'm just not used to having so many people around who genuinely care."

Margot leans forward, her gaze steady. "You deserve that care and support, Willow. Surrounding yourself with people who genuinely care about your well-being is crucial in the healing process. And remember, it's okay to lean on them when you need to."

I continue to nod, taking in Margot's words. Her reassurance and understanding comfort me, making it easier to have these difficult conversations.

Margot gently redirects the focus. "Now, Willow, I'm glad to hear about these positive connections you're building. It's essential to acknowledge the progress you're making. I also want to explore your feelings about returning to activities you enjoyed before, or perhaps discovering new ones. Is there anything you'd like to try or revisit that brings a sense of fulfillment or joy?"

I ponder the question, considering the prospect of rediscovering parts of myself that were overshadowed by the trauma. "I used to love riding horses and also painting," I admit, a flicker of nostalgia crossing my mind. "It's been years since I've done either, but maybe it's worth a try."

Margot smiles at the mention of horse riding. "Horseback riding can be a therapeutic and fulfilling activity. It allows for a connection with nature and a sense of freedom. Do you have access to a stable or horses, or would you be interested in exploring that?"

I hesitate, a pang of sadness shadowing my expression. "I used to ride with Wyatt," I confess, "but he didn't want to see me. So, I don't think horse riding is an option, sadly."

Margot nods. "I see. What about painting, then? You mentioned it earlier."

A faint smile tugs at the corners of my lips. "I used to enjoy it a lot. It was a way to express myself without words."

"That's wonderful," Margot replies warmly. "Have you considered trying it again? Perhaps you have some art supplies at home?"

I pause, contemplating the idea. "I might have some supplies upstairs at the house, but I still haven't been able to bring myself to go up into that area. Everything is still there from my parents' lives and my life from before the abduction."

Margot nods in understanding. "It's completely normal to feel a range of emotions about revisiting those spaces. Going through personal belongings can be a delicate process. If and when you feel ready, exploring that part of your home could be a significant step in your healing journey. In the meantime, we can focus on other activities or find ways to bring art into your current space. How does that sound to you?"

I consider Margot's suggestion, deciding that taking small steps may be good for my recovery. "Yeah, maybe I can start with some basic supplies and see how it goes."

Margot smiles. "That sounds like a good plan, Willow. Starting with the basics can be a gentle way to reconnect with your artistic side. Maybe when you feel comfortable with it you could even try painting the things you see in your nightmares, it's another form of therapy that could help you. It's all about the act of getting those traumatic images out of your head and when you watch yourself moving them from your mind to the paper it can help your brain process those images and memories. Remember, the journey is about progress, not perfection."

I feel excited to reclaim parts of my life that once brought joy, and if it in any way helped me reduce my nightmares then I would give it a go. "Thank you, Margot. I'll give it a try."

She nods appreciatively. "You're welcome. Now, let's discuss your feelings about the house and those specific areas you've been hesitant to revisit. What thoughts come to mind when you think about going upstairs?"

I take a moment to gather my thoughts, tracing my fingers along the edge of the armrest. "It's just... that part of the house holds so many memories. It's like a time capsule of my life before everything changed. Going up there feels like confronting a version of myself that I've tried to forget."

Margot listens attentively, offering a compassionate nod. "It's completely normal to feel that way. The past can be a complex landscape to navigate, especially when it's tied to traumatic experiences. Would you be comfortable sharing what specific concerns or emotions arise when you think about revisiting those spaces?"

I take a deep breath, attempting to articulate the conflicting emotions within me. "I'm afraid of what I might find—the belongings of my parents, reminders of the life I had before the abduction. It's like opening a door to a time when everything was normal, and I was a different person. But at the same time, I'm scared that confronting those memories might make everything more real, more painful."

Margot nods. "It's understandable to have these concerns, Willow. Your feelings are valid, and we can explore ways to approach this gradually. Would you be open to creating a plan or setting specific goals for revisiting those areas, ensuring that you have the support you need along the way?"

I consider Margot's suggestion, realizing that breaking down this daunting task into smaller, manageable steps might make it more achievable. "Yes, I think that could help. Maybe starting with one room or even just sorting through a few items."

Margot smiles. "That's a great approach. We'll work together to set realistic goals, and I'll be here to guide you through the process. Remember, it's all about empowering you to take control of your healing journey."

As our conversation continues, Margot guides me through various topics, gently exploring areas of potential growth and self-discovery. We discuss strategies to manage anxiety, and she introduces mindfulness techniques that may help ground me during moments of distress. Margot consistently emphasizes the importance of self-compassion and taking things at my own pace.

As we near the end of the session, Margot offers some homework for the few days until our next session. "I'd like you to consider making a list of small, achievable goals related to the activities we discussed today. These goals should be tailored to your comfort level and designed to bring a sense of accomplishment and joy. It could be as simple as gathering a few art supplies or choosing a movie to watch with Easton. What do you think?"

I nod, these small steps giving me purpose. "Yeah, I think that would be a good way to focus on the positive things."

Margot smiles, her support evident. "Great. Remember, I'm here to support you between our sessions. And if anything feels overwhelming, don't hesitate to reach out. We're working together to create a path towards healing, one step at a time."

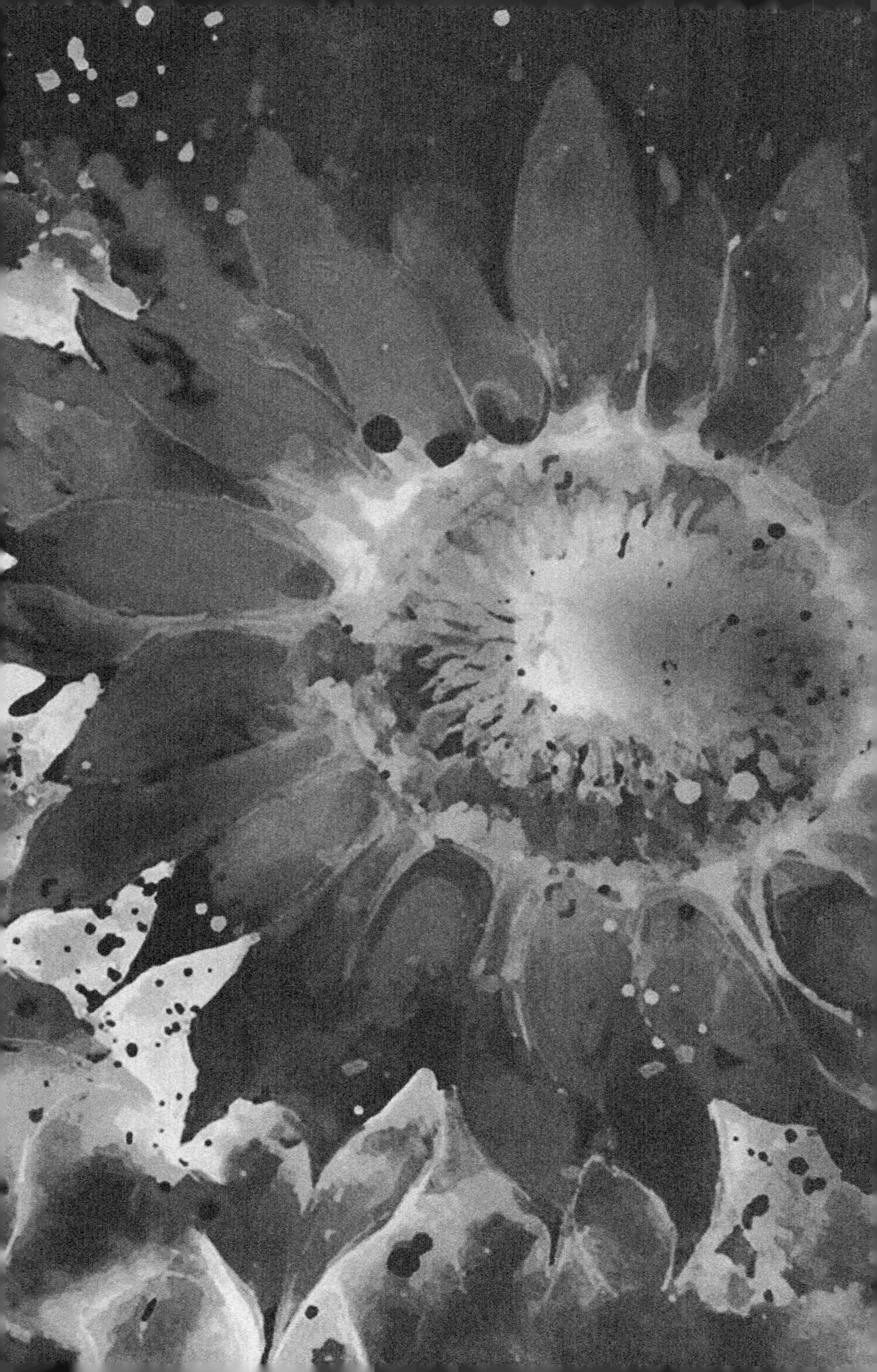

CHAPTER 18

Unknown

I hate that this is such a small fucking town. I would be too easily seen if I follow too closely.

It's forcing me to stay within the shadows. I loathe the familiarity of the streets and the way everyone knows everyone else's business. The close-knit nature of this community poses a challenge.

I've watched them from a distance, studying their every move like a predator eyeing its prey. If I get too close, the risk of exposure becomes too great.

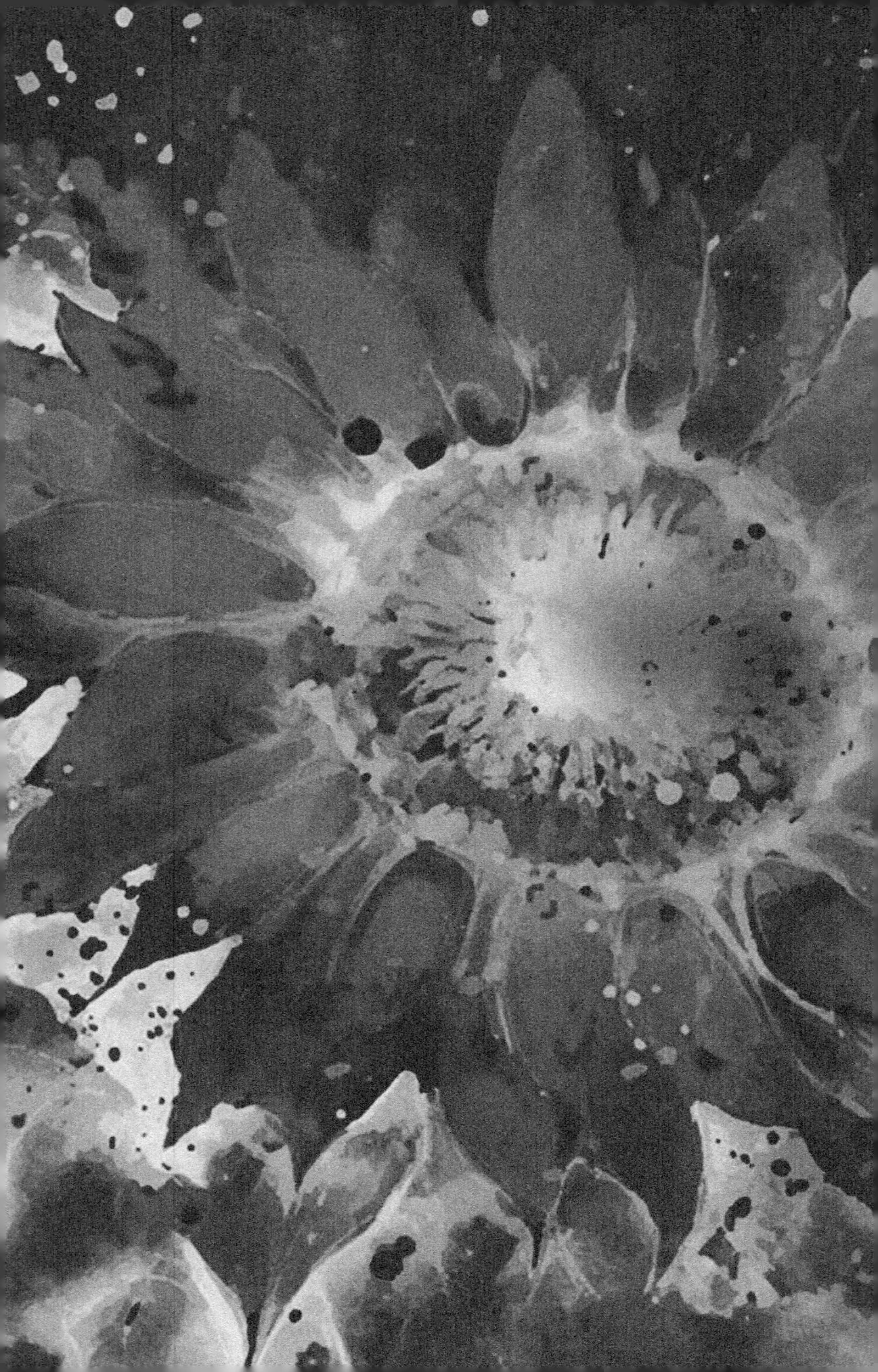

CHAPTER 19

Wyatt

Mason is right. I am a stubborn asshole. Which is why it's been forty eight hours since he left the angry bruise that I have on my jaw and I'm only now sitting down at the desk in my office.

I don't see how whatever he wants me to look at is going to change anything at all.

When I walked away from him the other night, I needed to bathe and put Bryce to bed. And then yesterday I had to go check the fence line.

Which are all just excuses for me being the way I'm acting. Even now I'm looking at the note he left me with the web address on it and trying to think of more excuses.

I know I'm being irrational. I spent a good part of fourteen years in love with my best friend and then another eight years pining after her memory. I thought we were soulmates.

The memories hit me like a freight train as I sit at the desk, staring at the note in my hands. Willow. The name itself carries a weight, a history I've tried desperately to bury.

Seeing her again stirred something in me—something I thought I buried deep within. The moment I laid eyes on her, my heart did that familiar dance, the one that used to happen whenever she entered the room. Time gave her a woman's body and etched lines in her face. She even changed the color of her hair. But there was no chance of me not recognizing her. She was imprinted in my soul, an indelible mark from the years we spent together.

But I can't let myself care for anyone again. Not after everything I've been through. Especially not for someone who ran away from us, from me. Who left me alone with questions and a pain I never thought I'd recover from. I was left to pick up the shattered pieces of a life that once felt whole.

Eight years I searched for her in whatever capacity I could. Eight years of chasing a ghost, clinging to the hope that I might find her, or at least some answers. When I got the letter, it was like the universe granted my desperate wish, and yet, the reality of it had been a bitter pill to swallow.

I hadn't shared the contents of that letter with the guys. I couldn't bring myself to do it, knowing it would devastate them as much as it devastated me. Instead, I retreated into a self-destructive pattern, seeking solace in the arms and beds of any woman who would have me. But even that temporary escape couldn't erase the pain, the void left by Willow's absence.

Then Callista entered my life. She refused to let me drown in my misery, and for a while, she became my lifeline. When she told me she was pregnant, I had considered it fate—a chance at a new beginning. But fate seemed to like fucking with me because, in giving me Bryce, it took Callista away.

Once again, I was left shattered. This time, however, I had a baby to look after. Bryce became my anchor, a reason to keep going even when everything else seemed to crumble around me. The responsibility of fatherhood forced me to put aside my own pain and focus on creating a stable life for him.

So, I built walls so high and so thick that nothing could get past them ever again.

Mason's words echo in my mind. "You're a stubborn asshole," he said, and he was right. The walls around me had been fortified with the pain of loss and betrayal. The anger and frustration were easier to carry than the vulnerability of caring for someone and risking that connection being severed again.

But Mason knew why. He found me one night shortly after Callista died, drowning myself in bourbon. He saw the wreckage of a man who lost too much, who gave up on the idea that happiness was something he deserved.

I confessed everything to him in that haze of alcohol-induced numbness, not caring that Mason loved Willow too.

The memories of that night flood back—the dimly lit room, the empty bottles strewn around, and Mason's unwavering presence. He didn't offer empty comforting words or condolences; instead, like only days ago, he punched me square in the jaw, snapping me out of my self-destructive stupor.

I look at the note in my hands, the web address mocking me. Mason wouldn't insist I look at whatever was there if he didn't believe it could make a difference. What could be so important that it required breaking through my carefully constructed walls?

With trembling hands, I open my laptop and force myself to type in the web address. The screen flickers to life, revealing a narrative—a narrative of pain, survival, and resilience.

The screen displays a series of articles, testimonials, and photos detailing the horrors Willow endured during those years of separation. Each word is a punch to the gut.

Those words on the screen cut through my defenses, breaking down the walls I thought were impenetrable. Willow's story unfolds before me, and with each sentence, I feel the weight of guilt intensify. Guilt for not being there, for not protecting her when she needed it the most.

The guilt that I felt when she first disappeared slams into me once more. The thought that if only I walked her home that night, she would have still been with us. Those feelings of it being my fault return with a vengeance, the pain once again clawing at my insides. That guilt that lived with me for eight years feels like a lead weight in the center of my heart.

The more I read, the clearer it becomes—she didn't run away. She fought. She endured. And she survived. Willow faced horrors that I can't even fathom, and all this time, I blamed her for leaving.

The realization hits me like a sledgehammer, and I feel the ground beneath me shifting. Nothing I believed makes any sense now. The anger and resentment I held against her, fueled by that letter, crumbled as I read the truth.

I clench my fists, the frustration building within me. The truth stands before me, stark and undeniable. Willow didn't abandon us; she fought tooth and nail for her survival.

I glance at the note Mason left me, and a wave of gratitude washes over me. He saw through the walls I erected, understanding that facing this truth was the only way forward.

As the web page scrolls with the harrowing details of Willow's journey, a mix of emotions swirl within me—guilt, regret, and a deep longing. The woman I loved suffered in silence.

I come upon a video and I'm almost afraid to click play, but I do. And the vision on my screen almost completely tears my heart out. There she is, kneeling in the dirt, the golden blond hair that I remember so long it is brushing against the ground. But what hurts the most are the tears on her cheeks and the look of utter relief that I can see clearly on her face.

Easton is in front of her, even with his tactical gear on I recognize him. All the anger and frustration I felt toward him for continuing to search for her is washed away at that moment. I'm beyond thankful that he chose someone he never met over his friends, as crazy as that seemed.

As the video ends, the weight of the past presses down on me, and the tears I've held back for so long threaten to spill over. It's not just Willow's story that I need to confront; it's my own story also.

And then, a tiny voice breaks through the chaos in my mind. "Dadda, why are you crying?"

I blink away the tears, realizing that Bryce entered the room. His innocent eyes meet mine, searching for an explanation. In that moment, I see Callista in him—the warmth, the love, and the reminder of a life I once had.

I quickly swipe at my cheeks, putting on a brave front. "Ah, it's nothing, buddy. Just something in my eye."

But Bryce is perceptive. He studies me, and he asks, "Did you read something sad, Dadda?"

I swallow hard, trying to find the right words. "Yeah, something like that. It's just... sometimes, grown-ups have feelings too, buddy."

He tilts his head, studying me with the curiosity only a child possesses. "Sad feelings?"

I manage a small nod, my voice catching in my throat. "Yeah, sad feelings."

Bryce takes a step closer, his small hand reaching out to touch my cheek. "It's okay, Dadda. Hugs make sad feelings better."

The simplicity of his gesture breaks down another layer of my defenses. I scoop him up in my arms, holding him close, letting more tears escape.

The warmth of Bryce's embrace and the sincerity in his words offer a comfort that transcends the complexities of adult emotions. I steal a moment to breathe in as I hold him close, to take in the fragrance that clings to him—the scent of childhood and untainted optimism.

"It will all be okay, Dadda," he says, his small arms wrapped around me.

I appreciate the profound wisdom in his simplicity. It may be a while before everything is truly okay, but in this embrace, I make a silent promise to myself. I would do everything I could to make it okay—for Bryce, for Willow, and for the fractured pieces of my own soul.

I gently pull away, wiping away the last traces of tears from my eyes. "Thank you, buddy," I say, mustering a small smile. "You're right. Hugs make sad feelings better."

Bryce returns the smile, his eyes filled with a purity that momentarily eases the weight on my shoulders. He climbs onto my lap, his small hands resting on my cheeks as if to assure himself that I'm okay now.

"Dadda," he begins with genuine concern, "can I help you? Like how you help me when I spill my juice?"

His innocent offer tugs at my heart. I ponder the question, realizing that in his simple yet profound way, Bryce might indeed be able to help me. However, I hesitate for a moment, contemplating the complexities of the emotions and revelations that surfaced tonight.

"Not tonight, buddy," I finally respond, brushing his soft hair with my fingers. "But you know what? I think you might be able to help me tomorrow."

Bryce's face lights up with anticipation, and he nods eagerly. "Tomorrow? How, Dadda?"

A small, genuine smile plays on my lips as I consider how Bryce might be my beacon of light in the darkness that has overshadowed my life. I take a deep breath before answering, "Well, tomorrow, I think you can help me by doing what you do best—making someone happier."

Bryce's eyes widen with curiosity. "Making someone happier? Like how?"

I chuckle at his eagerness. "You see, buddy, sometimes people carry a lot of sadness in their hearts. And you, with your laughter, your warmth, and your joy, have this amazing power to make people forget their troubles, even if just for a little while."

Bryce's face lights up with understanding, a radiant smile breaking across his features. "So, I can be a happiness superhero?"

I nod, genuinely touched by his enthusiasm. "Exactly, Bryce. Tomorrow, you and I are going to be a team of happiness superheroes. We'll spread joy, laughter, and maybe, just maybe, we'll make someone's day a little brighter."

He claps his hands in excitement, fully embracing the idea. "Team happiness superheroes! I'm ready, Dadda!"

I gently ruffle Bryce's hair and say, "But before we become superheroes, my little sidekick, you need to get a good night's rest. Tomorrow will be here before you know it."

Bryce pouts playfully, "Aw, Dadda, can't we start now?"

I chuckle, but I stand firm. "Tomorrow, buddy. Right now, it's time for bed. Superheroes need their rest to have enough energy for all the happiness they're going to spread."

Bryce seems to consider this for a moment, then nods in agreement. "Okay, Dadda, but promise we'll start as soon as I wake up?"

I smile and playfully salute him. "Promise. Now, off to bed, little hero."

With a reluctant nod, Bryce slides down from my lap, but not before giving me a tight hug. "Goodnight, Dadda. Love you."

"Goodnight, Bryce. Love you too," I reply, savoring the warmth of his hug.

As Bryce heads off to bed, I find myself alone in the quiet of the room once again. I take a moment to center myself, knowing I needed to follow Bryce to read him a bedtime story. The laptop screen, still displaying Willow's journey, serves as a silent reminder of the path that lies ahead.

I close the laptop and follow after Bryce, feeling a storm of emotions. The weight of the past, the guilt, and the revelation of the truth linger.

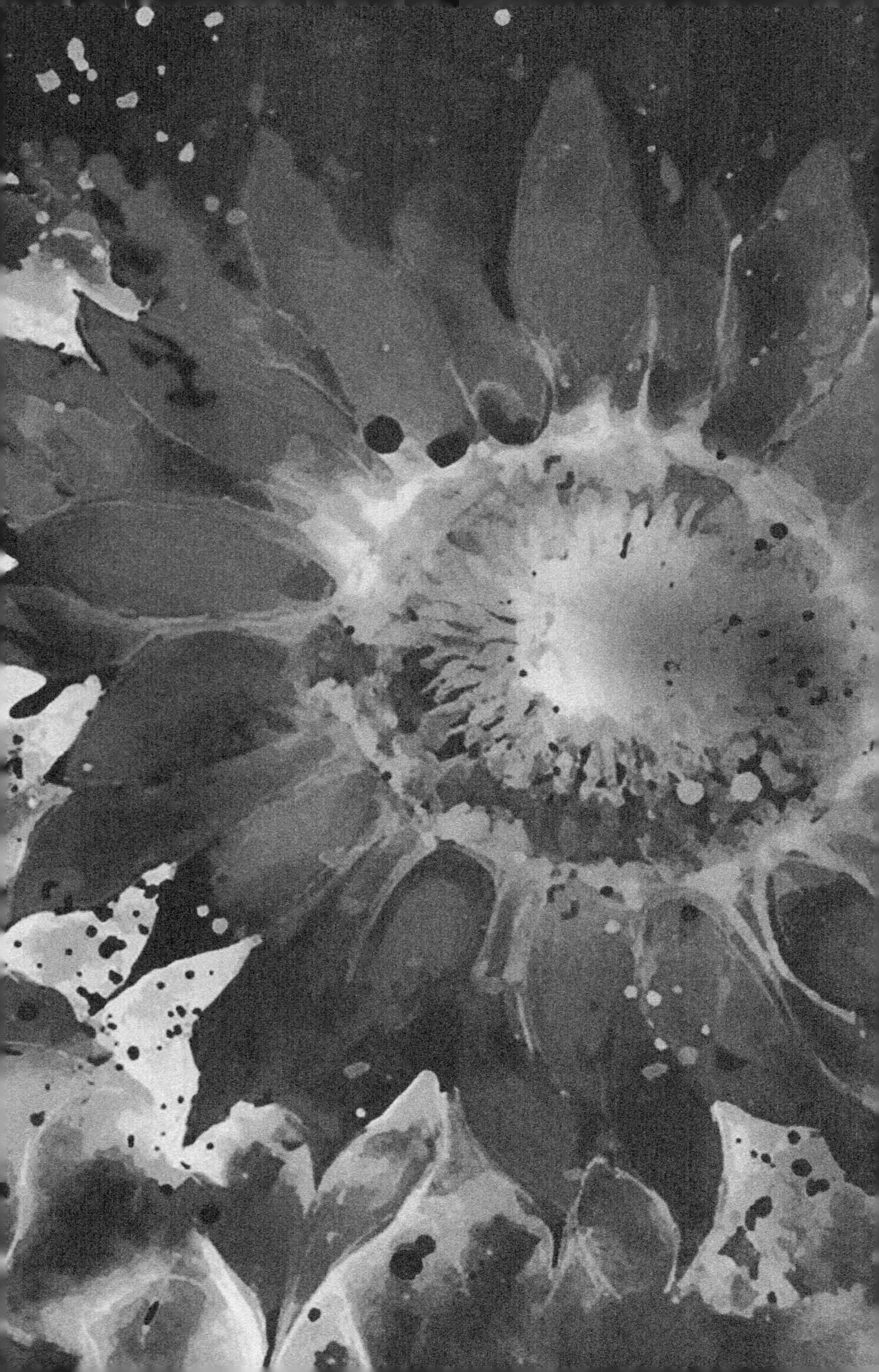

CHAPTER 20

Willow

When the doorbell rings after breakfast the next morning I almost giggle thinking that Kat has decided to make sure she visits me the day after every therapy session. But I don't hear her automatically barging into the house with her bright and bubbly personality.

Frowning, Easton makes his way toward the front door and after a few moments of quiet murmuring he walks back toward the dining area with a smiling Mrs Greene. Just her presence brings a matching smile to my face.

"Good morning, dear! I made some pumpkin pie and thought you might like one."

"Good morning, Mrs. Greene. That sounds amazing, thank you," I reply, genuinely touched by her thoughtfulness.

She places the pumpkin pie on the dining table, and the aroma of cinnamon and nutmeg fills the room. It's a warm and comforting scent. Mrs. Greene takes a seat, and Easton joins us, the frown from earlier replaced by a more relaxed expression.

"You're too kind, Mrs. Greene. Thank you for the pie," Easton says, offering his gratitude.

Mrs. Greene waves it off with a smile. "Nonsense, dear. And I told you both to call me Grandma Esse! Now, how are you holding up, sweetheart?" She directs her caring gaze toward me.

I take a moment to consider her question. "I... I'm doing better, Mrs. Greene. Thank you. It's been challenging, but I'm taking things one step at a time."

She reaches across the table, patting my hand reassuringly. "That's the spirit, dear. I find that having good company and some delicious pie always helps."

A soft laugh escapes my lips, and the atmosphere at the table seems to lighten. "Well, if delicious pie is the key to healing, then I'm already ready for seconds."

Mrs. Greene chuckles warmly. "Oh, you're a gem, dear. Now, how about we enjoy a cup of tea? It's the perfect follow-up to pie."

I nod in agreement, appreciating the idea of a comforting cup of tea. "That sounds lovely, Grandma Esse. Let me make it this time. It's the least I can do."

She gives me an approving nod, and I make my way to the kitchen, determined to take charge of a small task. As I prepare the tea, the rhythmic sounds of boiling water and clinking cups become a soothing background to our conversation.

Returning to the table with a tray of tea, I distribute the cups, and we settle into a comfortable silence, sipping the warm beverage.

Only seconds pass before the doorbell rings again. Easton furrows his brow and heads to the door again. The muffled voices rise briefly, and I strain to catch any indication of who might be there, but the words remain indistinct.

A hush falls over the entryway for a few moments, leaving me in suspense. Then, as though carried by a gentle breeze, the silence gives way to the sight of a bunch of vibrant, large sunflowers floating toward me. It takes a moment for the details to register, but soon I notice the tiny face peeking around the sunflowers. Instantly, I recognize Bryce.

A soft gasp escapes my lips, and a smile spreads across my face as Bryce appears, carrying the sunflowers like a little floral guardian. His eyes light up with excitement as he approaches the table.

"Miss Willow! Look what I brought for you!" Bryce exclaims, presenting the sunflowers with all the pride and joy a child can muster.

Touched by Bryce's sweet gesture, I express my gratitude, "Oh, Bryce, these are beautiful! Thank you, buddy." I reach out to ruffle his hair, and he giggles with delight.

As I gently take the sunflowers from him and lay them on the table, Bryce announces with infectious enthusiasm, "Dadda and I are happiness superheroes!"

I glance up and notice a hesitant and serious-looking Wyatt hovering just inside the doorway to the room. Beside him stands Easton, wearing a scowl that hints at anger and frustration. His arms are crossed, and his gaze is fixed on Wyatt.

Turning my attention back to Bryce, I smile and say, "You sure are, Bryce."

Bryce beams with pride, seemingly unaware of the tension that lingers in the room. The contrasting emotions are palpable—the joy of Bryce's innocence and the unspoken weight carried by the adults.

Wyatt hesitates before greeting me, "Morning, Willow."

"Wyatt," I respond, keeping my tone neutral.

Wyatt winces, rubbing the back of his neck, a gesture I remember well from our past.

"Hey, um, do you think we could... talk? I mean, if you're up for it," Wyatt asks, his eyes showing a blend of sincerity and apprehension.

Before I can respond, Grandma Esse interjects with a kind smile, her focus on Byrce, "Hey, sweetie, how about you come with us to the store? We could use a superhero like you to help pick out some groceries," she suggests.

Bryce's eyes light up at the idea, and he nods enthusiastically. "Yes, I want to be a superhero helper!"

She chuckles warmly. "That's the spirit! Uncle Easton will even come along as your sidekick!" she continues, giving Easton a pointed look. When he opens his mouth to protest she just talks over him. "Off we go, then." With that, she gets up from the table and leads Bryce out of the room. She waves Easton in front of her so that he ends up leading the way out of the house, leaving Wyatt and me in a somewhat awkward silence.

Wyatt shifts uncomfortably, glancing at the retreating figures of Bryce, Grandma Esse, and Easton. The tension in the room is thick, and I can sense that Wyatt is struggling to find the right words. I hesitate but then decide to break the silence.

"If you want to talk, Wyatt, let's do it in the living room. We might as well be comfortable," I suggest softly, gesturing toward the adjacent room.

He nods in agreement, and we make our way to the living room. As we settle on the couch, Wyatt looks at me with regret and sadness, his eyes reflecting the turmoil within.

Wyatt frowns and leans forward, resting his elbows on his knees. I take a moment to reflect on how I have never seen him so hesitant to speak his mind, at least not since he was a teenager. Even in the few moments of seeing him since my return, he seemed self-assured and confident. The change in his demeanor is evident, and I can't help but wonder about the gravity of what he's about to share.

"Look," Wyatt begins, his voice heavy with sincerity, "I know I fucked up, and I'll admit that. But you need to understand everything the way I knew it."

I nod, signaling for him to continue. The weight of his words hangs in the air, and the living room seems to close in around us.

"Before you say anything," Wyatt says, his expression a mix of plea and determination, "just let me get everything off my chest. Please."

I nod silently, granting him the space to speak his truth. Wyatt takes a deep breath, his gaze fixed on some distant point as he begins to unravel the story of his past.

"When I was a kid, I had an amazing childhood," he starts, a nostalgic smile playing on his lips. "I had three best friends, and we were inseparable. We spent all our time together, doing everything kids do."

As he reminisces, Wyatt's eyes light up with the warmth of cherished memories. It's a side of him I haven't seen before, a vulnerability beneath the tough exterior.

"As we got older, I started noticing that one of my best friends was a girl," he continues, his tone shifting to a more thoughtful one. "I never really got the whole cooties thing, you know? I never felt that way about her."

He chuckles lightly, attempting to inject a bit of humor into the heavy conversation. "I guess I was a weird kid."

Wyatt's gaze meets mine, and he continues, "As we got older, things changed. We were still best friends, but I didn't feel the same way about my guy friends as I did about her. I just... I felt this need to always be near her, and I didn't understand what I was feeling."

I glance away, feeling a blush creeping up my cheeks. The atmosphere in the room shifts as Wyatt delves into the more intimate aspects of his past.

"And then," he says, his expression growing more somber, "I started to understand the... umm, physical feelings I was having."

I glance back at him, meeting his eyes for a moment before quickly looking away again. Wyatt frowns, his gaze softening with understanding.

"Sorry," he mutters, clearly realizing the awkwardness of the situation.

"No, it's okay," I reply, feeling a mix of embarrassment and understanding.

Wyatt continues, a heaviness returning to his voice, "I was trying to get the courage to ask her to the next school dance. I thought... I thought maybe we could be more than just friends. But then, one night, after we had spent the day together, the Sheriff came knocking on the door of the ranch."

His expression darkens, and I can sense the pain in his words. "He asked when the last time we had seen her was. She never made it home."

Wyatt's voice trembles with the weight of the memory, and I feel a lump forming in my throat. "My whole world just stopped spinning," he admits, his voice carrying the weight of regret. "Days later, all I could do was blame myself. Maybe if I had walked her home, she wouldn't have disappeared."

I open my mouth to say something, to tell Wyatt that it wasn't his fault, that he couldn't have known what would happen, but he raises his hand, gesturing for me to stop before I utter a word. His eyes plead with me to let him finish.

"I know my reaction may have seemed extreme and melodramatic," Wyatt continues, his gaze fixed on a distant point as he recalls the past. "But Willow, as a teenager, it just felt like I was missing a large part of my heart. It had disappeared along with you. For a while, I was oblivious to how much your disappearance affected not only me but our other best friends. They were hurting too, and we were all scared, just feeling like not only a piece of our hearts was gone but, for me, it felt like a piece of my soul was gone too."

He takes a moment, his eyes conveying the deep sense of loss that still echoes through the years. "We were constantly bugging the Sheriff for information and updates, doing everything we could to search ourselves. A couple of years later, we made a new friend who moved to town. He joined the search with us—it meant that much to us. As we got older, we searched harder and harder."

A flicker of confusion crosses Wyatt's face, as if he's processing something that doesn't quite add up. He frowns and takes a moment, his brow furrowing with a hint of uncertainty. Just when I think he might falter, he gathers himself and continues.

"And then, about six years ago," Wyatt continues, his voice now tinged with wariness, "I got home after yet another frustrating trip, chasing a false lead. I felt exhausted, defeated, like I was hitting dead ends at every turn. As I walked up the steps at the front of the ranch, I saw something on the stoop outside my front door. A letter."

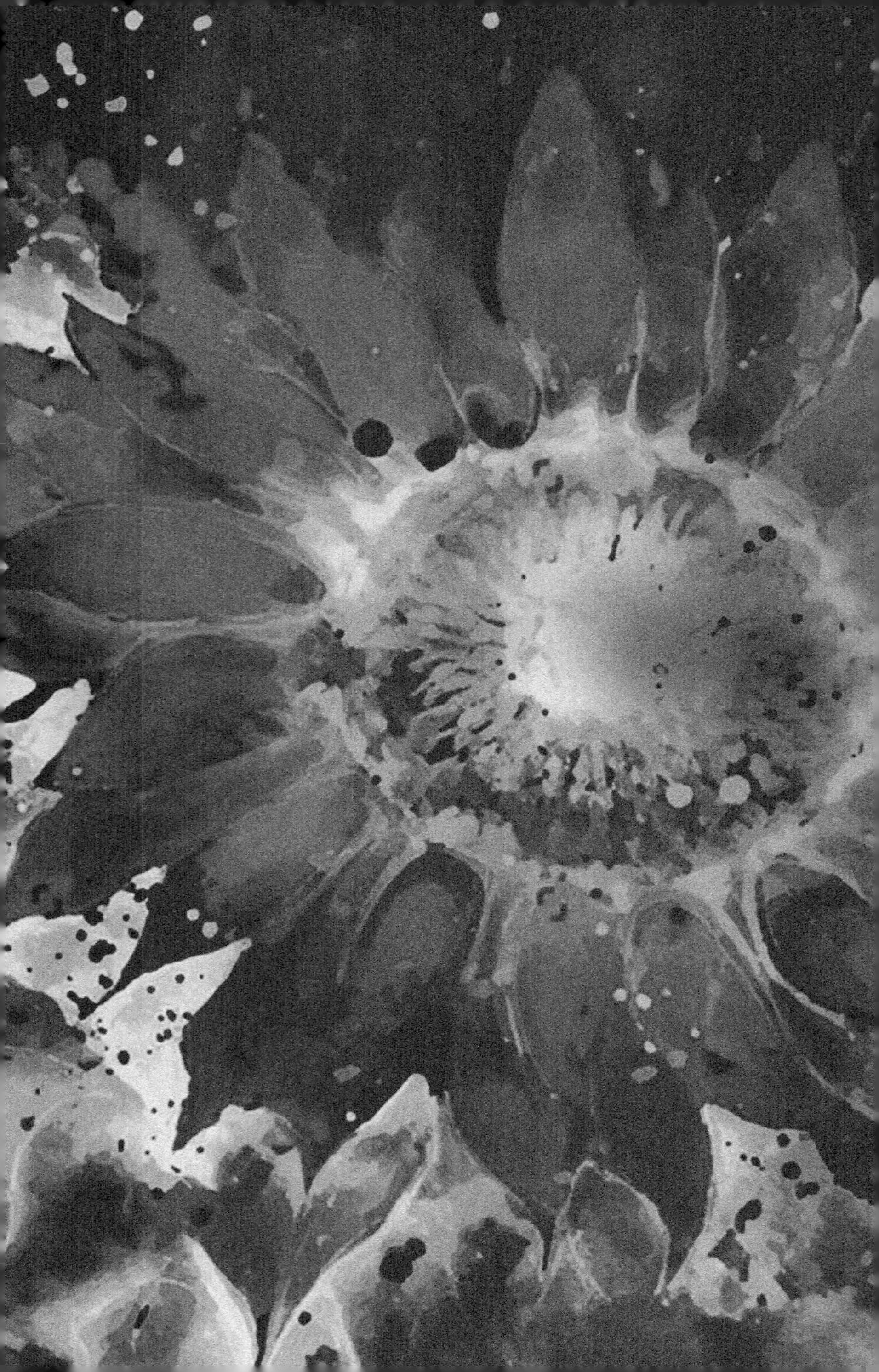

CHAPTER 21

Willow

Wyatt's voice grows quieter as he reaches into his pocket and pulls out his wallet. He carefully extracts a well-worn piece of paper, unfolding it with a practiced ease. The paper shows signs of having been folded and unfolded countless times.

"When I read this letter," Wyatt begins, his eyes fixed on the paper, "I should have doubted its contents, especially now after seeing exactly what had happened to you. But back then, I was at my most disheartened. It had been eight years of searching for you, Willow, with no leads, no hints of you anywhere. To me, it felt like you didn't want to be found."

He hesitates for a moment, and I seize the opportunity to ask the question burning in my mind. "Who sent the letter?"

Wyatt's frown deepens as he studies the paper. "It's not signed, and there was no postage stamp. It was just there, on my doorstep."

Suppressing my frustration, I press on. "What was in the letter, Wyatt?"

His gaze remains fixed on the paper, and he looks genuinely pained. "The letter said you hadn't simply disappeared. It claimed that you ran away, that you told the person who wrote it that there was nothing about your home that you liked, that I and the guys were just playthings to you. It said you didn't care about any of us."

A mix of disbelief and anger surges within me, but I manage to keep my emotions in check. "Why would I say something like that?"

Wyatt's expression becomes solemn, his eyes filled with sadness and guilt. "The letter went on to say that you'd already found your place with a man you were destined to marry. That I should stop looking for you because you had moved on."

He pauses, rolling his lips and closing his eyes for a moment. When he opens them again, a fire burns in his gaze, a fire I haven't seen since the day he threw me off his property.

"And there were pictures," Wyatt growls out, his voice laced with anger. "Pictures of you, and him. Intimate pictures."

I want to be sick. The realization hits me like a sledgehammer, and my stomach rolls with a sickening wave of nausea. Images of me and Jacob, intimate images of him sexually violating me, sent to Wyatt under the guise that it was something I had wanted. I feel the air escape my lungs, and I instinctively raise my hand to stop Wyatt from continuing. The room spins, and I focus on the breathing techniques Margot taught me to regain some semblance of composure.

In the momentary calm that follows, I lower my hand and look at Wyatt again. Tears stream down my face as I muster the strength to ask the unthinkable. "Can I see the pictures, Wyatt?"

He flinches, a visible shudder coursing through him. After a moment, he admits, "I burned them. Seeing them briefly once was already too much for me. But I should have looked at them. Studied them. I should have paid enough attention to see the truth in those photos, and for that, I am so fucking sorry."

The weight of his words settles in the room, and my heart aches. "You burned them?" I manage to whisper, a knot forming in my throat.

He nods, his own eyes reflecting the pain he carries. "I couldn't stand the thought of having them anywhere near me."

Taking a moment to gather myself, I inhale deeply and exhale slowly. "Okay, what happened then?"

Wyatt's eyes drop, and he admits with a sigh, "I was hurt, angry. It felt like my life had been shattered again, and any hope I had went up in smoke. I should have questioned it all, but instead, I went straight to Old Man Darby's bar. I picked up the first woman who looked at me sweetly. I stopped functioning unless it was to drink or pick up women."

He pauses, a pained expression on his face, and continues, "One night, not long after I started that cycle, I arrived at the bar, looking for my next conquest. Callista stepped in front of me and told me I needed to sober up and stop being a miserable asshole or I was going to run out of willing pussy pretty quickly."

A bitter smile plays on his lips as he recalls the moment. "She dragged me out of the bar, took me to a late-night cafe, and spent hours pouring coffee into me, talking to me. She came to the ranch every morning and made sure I didn't spiral again. And then, she just didn't leave."

A faint recollection of the name Callista tugs at the edges of my memory. I ask, my voice barely audible, "Callista... is that the same Callista we went to school with?"

Wyatt nods, a somber acknowledgment in his eyes. "Yeah, it is. Callista McKinley."

I try to remember her, but the details remain elusive. The image of a girl from our past is vague, like a faded photograph in the recesses of my mind.

Continuing Wyatt says, "It was only a couple of months after I received the letter that Callista came to me and told me she was pregnant. Everything felt like it was happening so fast. I wasn't sure how I felt about it. She had told me she was on birth control, but I vowed to do the right thing by her. I got her to move in with me. It seemed only natural that over the course of her pregnancy, she briefly became my new everything, my whole focus."

A deep sadness and hurt wells up within me, but I know I have no grounds to feel it. Wyatt's choices were made based on the cards dealt to him, none of which I could fault him for.

He stops for a few moments, a pained look crossing his face. When he starts again, I can feel the sadness radiating from him. "Even then I hadn't been paying enough attention. I wonder now if subconsciously I had been resentful of Callista for pushing into the space that you had left, as I had been thinking about you quite a bit at the time. And, also, I was so focused on breeding the new mare when Callista was eight months pregnant that when she asked me to hang the mobile in the nursery, I kept dismissing her. So she tried to hang it herself, but then she slipped and landed wrong on the crib."

His voice trembles with the weight of guilt, and I can sense the impending tragedy in his words. "I didn't even know anything until I saw the ambulance flying down the driveway. One of my staff had heard her scream and tried to reach me. When I got to the hospital, they told me that shards of the wooden crib had entered her body. It was a race against time, but they could only save one of them. Callista told them to save the baby."

The room tightens around us as Wyatt recounts the heartbreaking events. "That was the last coherent thing she said. After that, she just rambled and became delirious. The doctors did their best, but Callista didn't make it."

He pauses, a heavy silence filling the room. I can feel the weight of his grief and the tragic turn his life has taken. "I held my son for the first time, Willow, with the knowledge that his mother, the woman I had thought would be my new future, was gone. And I was responsible for it."

The air grows still as the magnitude of Wyatt's pain settles between us. I want to reach out to him, to offer comfort, but words fail me and my anxiety is in the way.

Wyatt continues, his voice strained with the weight of remorse. "Even with a small baby to take care of, I tried to escape into the bottom of a bourbon bottle each night. I slid back down into that hole that Callista had pulled me out of, but this time it was just booze. As the days turned into months and years, my guilt transformed into anger and resentment against women, against you in particular. It felt like everything bad that had happened to me led back to you."

He takes a deep breath, and the heaviness of his words hangs in the air. "I'm sorry, Willow. I won't ask for your forgiveness because I haven't earned it yet. But I need you to know my truth, even if it doesn't change anything. I need you to know what I've become, the person I allowed myself to be after losing you."

The vulnerability in his eyes reflects the pain he carries, and I find myself torn between the past and the present, between the person I once knew and the man standing before me now.

His eyes lock into mine, pleading for understanding. "When I saw you last week I had spent years hating myself, hating you, and I carried that hate for far too long. And the thing that made that hate fester like an open wound was that even after everything, the moment I saw you, I knew I still loved you."

Wyatt takes a moment, as if gathering his thoughts, and his gaze meets mine. "I thought I had moved on, built walls so high that no one could get through. But seeing you again, it all crumbled. The hate, the bitterness, the self-loathing—it all came rushing back. I stubbornly refused to listen to any of the guys for days. In my mind, there was nothing that would change it. I hated you so much that I wouldn't listen to anyone who tried to tell me I didn't know the truth."

"Even after Mason tried to knock some sense into me," he touches a bruise on his jaw briefly, "it took days for me to actually stop and pay attention. I was so entrenched in my own bitterness that I couldn't see beyond it. When I finally pulled my head out of my own ass and looked at the news and saw everything that had happened to you, I felt like such a fool. I failed you over and over again."

I sit there, absorbing Wyatt's words, pain and regret evident in his confession. It takes a moment for me to find my voice, to navigate the emotions swirling within me.

"I appreciate you telling me that, Wyatt," I finally said softly. "It's a lot to process, and I need time."

Wyatt nods, understanding. "As I said, I don't expect you to forgive me, Willow. I know I fucked up. I just want you to know that I'm willing to do whatever it takes to earn your forgiveness."

I take a deep breath, trying to steady my racing thoughts. "That's going to take time too, Wyatt."

Wyatt looks at me, his eyes searching for any sign of hope. "Please, Willow, just tell me I haven't ruined everything. That there's still a chance, however small, that we can find some connection, rebuild something."

I meet his gaze, seeing the desperation and sincerity in his eyes. "Wyatt, you haven't ruined everything. I need to understand who we are now though. We have both been through too much to just go back to what once was."

Wyatt nods as a look of relief crosses his face. "I can work with that, Willow. I can work with anything you're willing to give me. I just need to know that there's a chance, no matter how small, for us to find our way back to each other. However long that takes."

I frown at him as a thought occurs to me. "Wyatt, I need to be honest with you. It feels like you may have an unfair advantage in winning me over."

He looks at me curiously, a hint of confusion in his eyes. "Unfair advantage? What do you mean?"

I sigh, but it's exaggerated enough to see through it. "If you keep bringing that gorgeous boy around with sunflowers, it's going to be hard for me to resist. I mean, seriously, sunflowers? That's just playing dirty."

A small smile tugs at the corner of Wyatt's lips, and he chuckles, the tension in the room momentarily lifting. "So, you still like sunflowers, huh?"

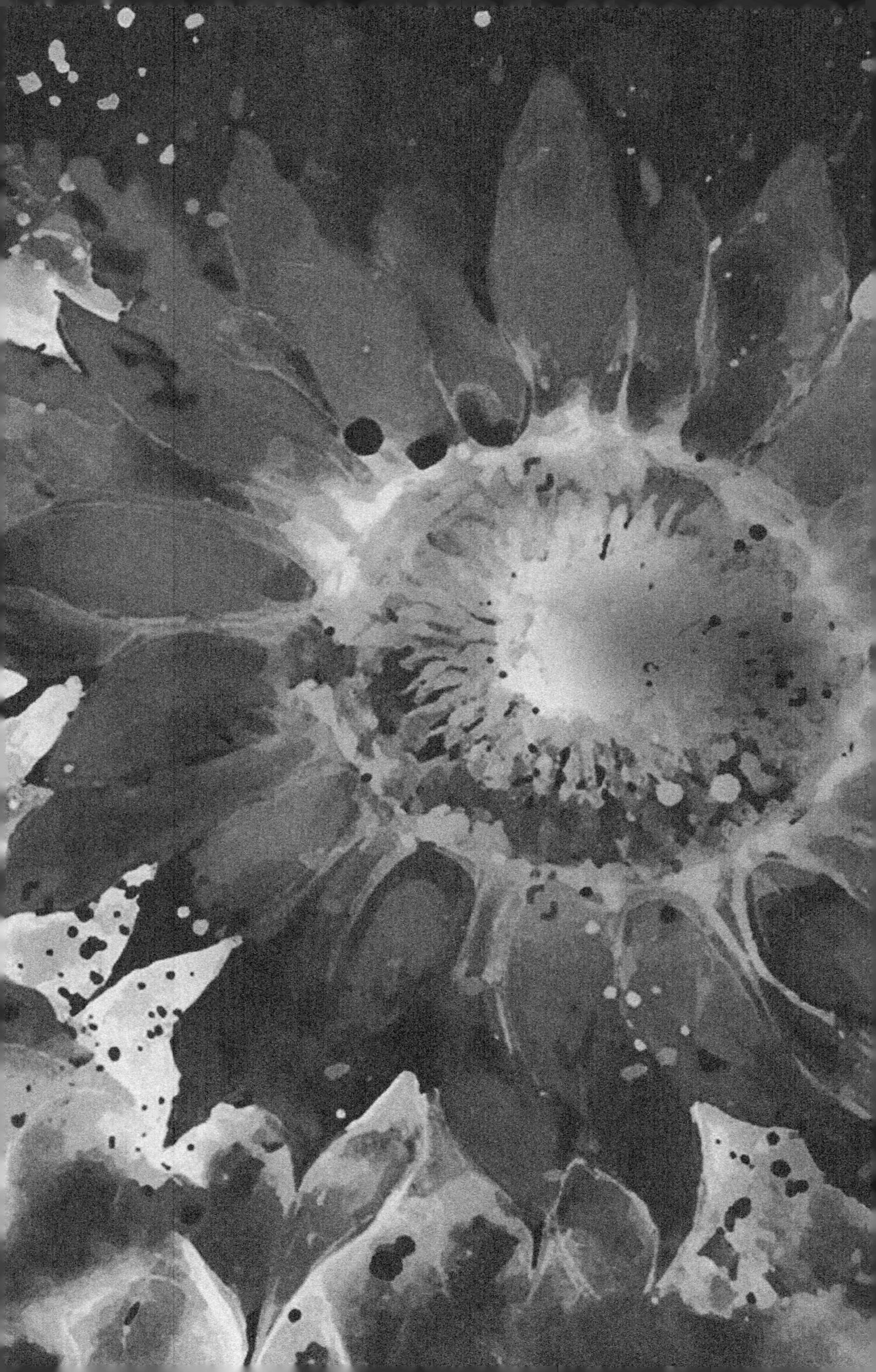

CHAPTER 22

Willow

"How are you feeling today, Willow?"

I smile softly as I look at Margot. This is my sixth session with her. I have officially been back in Sierra Valley for three weeks.

My life fell into a routine, but that routine still feels restrictive. I was starting to feel restless, and that was my response to Margot.

"Given you spent fifteen years confined within the cult compound, and following a strict routine day in and day out, that feeling is understandable. What are you doing that makes it feel routine?"

I take a moment to gather my thoughts before responding to Margot's question. "Well, I have therapy sessions twice a week. The mornings I have these sessions, I have breakfast with all the guys at Magda's. The day after my first session of the week, I spend with Kat just hanging out at the house. And tomorrow I know Wyatt will visit with Bryce. On the following days, Gage or Mason will visit in the afternoons and watch movies with us."

Margot listens attentively, nodding in understanding. "It's important to have a support system, especially during the early stages of your recovery. Having regular interactions with people who care about you can provide a sense of stability. However, I sense that you're starting to feel a bit confined by the predictability of your schedule. Is that accurate?"

I nod. "It's as if I've replaced one set of routines with another. While it's comforting, I can't shake the feeling that I'm stuck in a loop, reliving the same days over and over again."

Margot leans back in her chair, a contemplative expression on her face. "Variety and new experiences can be instrumental in breaking that monotony. It doesn't have to be drastic changes, but introducing small modifications to your routine might help. We spoke once about your art hobby, have you looked into that?"

After a moment I admit, "Actually, Easton and I started spending small amounts of time upstairs the week after we discussed it, he found my art supplies for me. I haven't really taken the time to sit and use them, though."

Margot's eyes light up with interest. "That's a significant step, Willow. Exploring the upper rooms and finding your art supplies shows progress. It's understandable that taking that next step, actually engaging in the creative process, might feel a bit daunting. What's been holding you back?"

I glance down, fidgeting with the edge of my sleeve. "I guess I'm afraid. Afraid that I won't remember how to draw, or that what I create won't live up to my own expectations. It's easier to keep the supplies as a comforting idea than face the uncertainty of whether I can still enjoy it like I used to."

Margot nods thoughtfully, her empathetic gaze reassuring. "It's completely normal to have those fears, Willow. Art is a personal expression, and it's okay if it takes time to reconnect with that part of yourself. The act of creating is more important than the end result. Perhaps you can start small, just doodling or experimenting without any pressure."

Feeling encouraged, I nod. "You're right. Maybe I'll set aside some time this week to give it a try."

Margot smiles warmly. "That sounds like a wonderful plan. I know you mentioned going to Magda's and to here but have you tried exploring anywhere else in town yet?"

I consider Margot's question, realizing that aside from Magda's and Margot's office, I haven't ventured much beyond the familiar spaces. A memory of a recent conversation with Kat surfaces.

"Well, actually," I begin, "Kat has been suggesting that we go to Gage's bar one night. She thinks it might be a good way for me to step out of my comfort zone and experience something different."

Margot's eyes light up with approval. "That's an excellent suggestion, Willow. Stepping outside your comfort zone, even in small ways, can be transformative. How do you feel about the idea of going to the bar?"

I can't help but feel nervous. "Honestly, it makes me a bit anxious. The idea of being in a crowded place, surrounded by people I don't know, is intimidating. But at the same time, I understand that facing these fears is part of my healing process."

Margot nods in understanding. "It's completely normal to feel a bit anxious about new social situations, especially after what you've been through. The key is to take it at your own pace."

I appreciate Margot's guidance and take a moment to reflect on the possibility. "You're right. Maybe I can give it a try with Kat by my side. It might be a good way to challenge myself."

Margot smiles warmly. "Remember, Willow, every small step you take is a victory in itself. Whether it's exploring the upper rooms, rediscovering art, or venturing out to new places, embrace the journey and the growth that comes with it. It's wonderful to see you approaching these challenges with such courage. Now, I also wanted to ask about your reconnection with your friends. How has that been for you?"

A small smile plays on my lips as I reflect on the positive aspects of reconnecting with my friends. "It's been great, actually. They've all been incredibly supportive. Spending time with Kat, Gage, Mason, and Easton has helped remind me of how important friends are. I'm slowly rebuilding what I had before."

Margot leans forward with a smile. "That's fantastic to hear. Reconnecting with friends can be a powerful source of healing. How about Wyatt? How has it been with him?"

I hesitate for a moment, my smile faltering. "It's been a little different with Wyatt. I can sense that he's trying, and we've had some good moments, but I think there's still a small part of him that's caught up with what happened during our time apart. It's like there's an unspoken tension, and I'm not sure how to address it."

Margot nods again. "Rebuilding trust can take time. Communication is key. Perhaps finding a quiet moment to talk openly with Wyatt about your feelings and concerns could help bridge any lingering gaps."

I take a moment to think on her advice, I know she is right and I need to be patient, but if talking to him can bridge the gap then I could try that. "You're right. I should talk to him. It's just that... I don't want to burden him with my own struggles. Everyone's been so supportive, and I don't want them to feel responsible for my healing."

Margot smiles gently. "It's commendable that you're considerate of their feelings, Willow. But remember, true friendships are built on openness and understanding. Sharing your thoughts can strengthen your connections and provide the support you need. Now, speaking of connections, how are you feeling about the guys? You mentioned spending time with them, and there was a look you got when you spoke that I think we should touch on—any particular thoughts or feelings you'd like to explore?"

I feel a subtle heat rising to my cheeks as I consider Margot's question. "Well," I admit, blushing again, "there have been a few moments where my thoughts about them... have taken on something a little more than platonic."

Margot raises an eyebrow, a knowing smile on her face. "Romantic feelings can be a natural part of human connections, Willow. It's important to explore and understand those emotions. Is there anyone in particular you find yourself thinking about more?"

I chuckle nervously, "It's not that simple, Margot. Each of them has qualities that draw me in—different aspects that I appreciate. I'm just not sure what to make of it all yet."

Margot leans back in her chair, her gaze thoughtful. "Feelings can be complex, especially when you're navigating the aftermath of such a challenging experience. It's okay not to have everything figured out right away. Take your time to understand your emotions and, when you're ready, consider sharing your thoughts with those involved. Have you been able to open up to the guys about what happened to you yet?"

I shift uncomfortably in my seat, a combination of fear and vulnerability welling up. "No, not really. I've thought about it, but the fear holds me back. I'm scared of how they'll react, scared of burdening them with the weight of what I've been through. It's like this wall, and I don't know how to break it down."

Margot listens attentively, her eyes filled with empathy. "Opening up can be one of the most challenging steps in the healing process. It requires vulnerability, and it's completely normal to feel scared. However, it's also an essential part of building trust and deepening connections. Have you considered what specific fears are holding you back from sharing your story with them?"

I take a deep breath, trying to put my swirling thoughts into words. "I guess I'm afraid of their reactions—of pity or judgment. And I'm afraid it might change how they see me, that they'll treat me differently. I want things to go back to normal, but I'm scared that sharing my truth will alter everything."

She tilts her head in contemplation. "Those are valid concerns, Willow. Opening up is a risk, but it's also an opportunity for true connection. It might help to remember that your friends care about you, and sharing your experiences can deepen your bond. You have control over when and how much you share. Take small steps, and if you feel overwhelmed, it's okay to pause and reassess."

I can't help but feel a twinge of frustration with myself. "I feel like fear is holding me back from everything. I want to move forward, but I'm stuck. It's like I'm paralyzed, and I don't know how to break free from it. I thought coming back here would be a fresh start, but I'm just carrying my fears with me, like I'm still in that place."

Margot offers a compassionate smile, her voice gentle and reassuring, "It's not uncommon to feel this way, Willow. Fear is a powerful emotion, especially after what you've been through. But the fact that you're able to identify these fears is already a significant step forward. Acknowledging your feelings and recognizing the barriers that are holding you back is a crucial part of the healing process. It takes time, Willow, and progress is often gradual. Remember, even in acknowledging these fears, you're making strides toward understanding and overcoming them."

I let Margot's words sink in. The frustration I felt a moment ago starts to give way. "I just... I want my life back, you know? I want to be able to live without constantly being held back by what happened to me."

Margot's gaze remains understanding, and she responds with empathy, "Willow, wanting your life back is a perfectly natural desire. But it's important to acknowledge that what you've experienced and lived through is unimaginable to most. You've already shown incredible strength in facing these challenges, and it's okay to recognize that progress might be a slow journey. Be patient with yourself and try not to be too hard on the person you are becoming in this process."

I take a deep breath, absorbing Margot's words. The weight on my shoulders feels a little lighter. "Thank you, Margot. Sometimes I forget that it's okay not to have everything figured out right away."

Margot smiles warmly. "Absolutely, Willow. Now, I'd like to touch on something you mentioned in our previous sessions. How have your nightmares been lately?"

I take a moment to gather my thoughts before responding. "They seem to be getting better, actually. There have been some nights recently where they haven't come, and when they do, they're not as intense."

Margot's smiles, I can see the pride in her eyes. "That's positive progress, Willow. Have you noticed any patterns in the frequency of your nightmares? Any specific triggers that seem to influence them?"

I furrow my brow, contemplating the question. "Well, I've noticed that they tend to be more prominent after a therapy session. It's like discussing my past brings those memories to the surface. Also, if I spend too much time thinking about or discussing my time in the cult, the nightmares tend to be stronger."

Margot nods thoughtfully. "It's not uncommon for discussions about traumatic experiences to impact one's dreams. It could be a way for your mind to process and make sense of the emotions stirred during those conversations. Are there other situations or thoughts that seem to trigger the nightmares?"

I ponder for a moment. "Sometimes, if I'm feeling particularly anxious during the day, it can carry over into the night. But it's not consistent. The therapy sessions and discussions about my past seem to be the most significant triggers."

Margot smiles. "Understanding these patterns is a crucial step in managing your nightmares. It might be helpful to explore strategies that can provide comfort and security after those triggering moments. Perhaps engaging in a calming activity or having a routine before bedtime could create a more peaceful transition."

I consider Margot's suggestion. "It might be worth trying. I'll explore some activities that help me unwind after sessions or discussions that bring up difficult memories."

Margot smiles encouragingly. "Remember, it's about finding what works best for you. Small adjustments can make a big difference over time. And if you ever find that the nightmares persist or become overwhelming, we can explore additional therapeutic approaches."

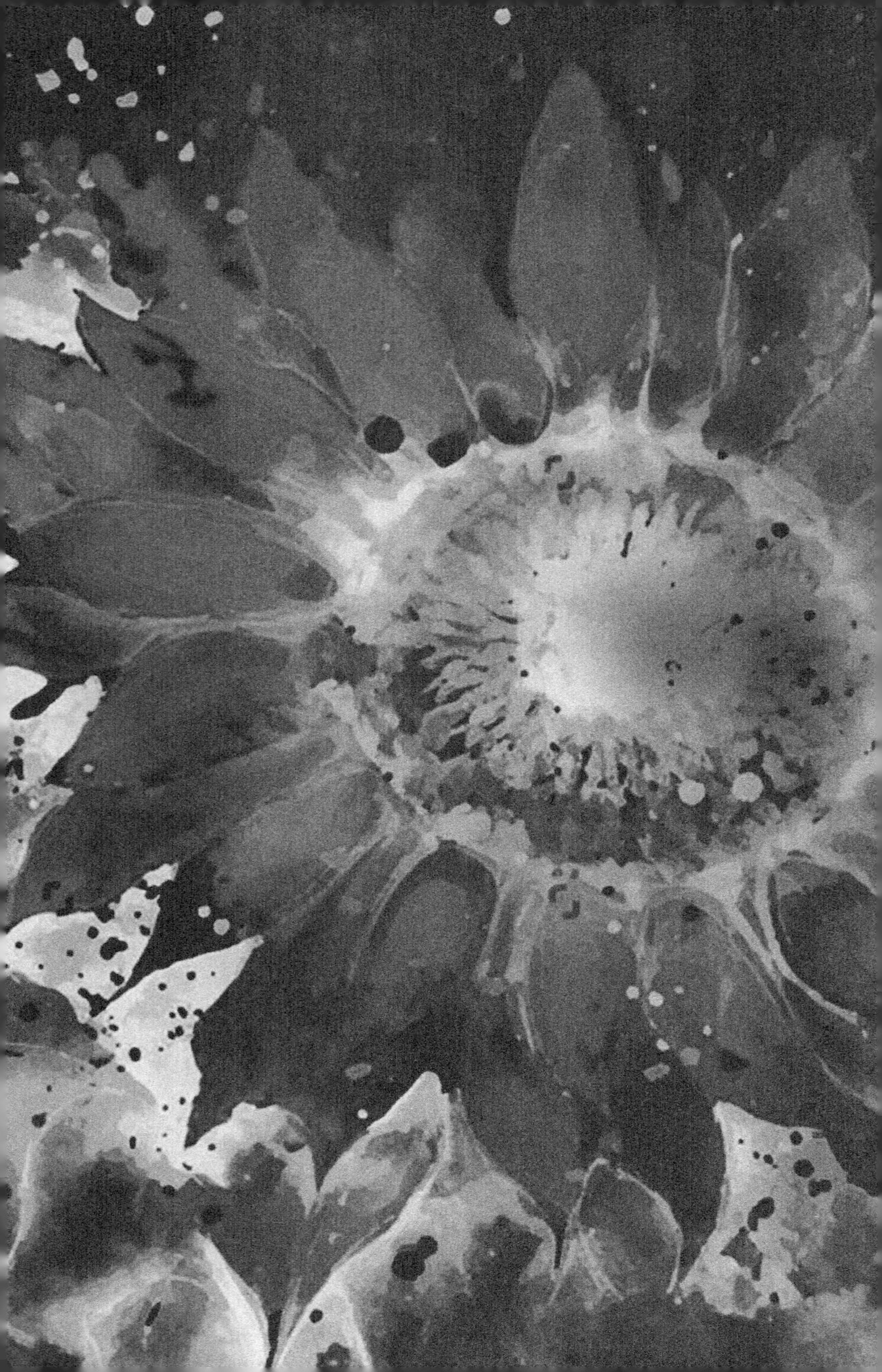

CHAPTER 23
Unknown

The frustration bubbles within me, a seething anger that threatens to consume every rational thought. I've observed them closely, their laughter echoing in my ears like a taunt. I want to dismantle their happiness. To break the bonds that have reformed that hold them together. But nothing has worked so far and my patience is wearing thin.

I watch them from the shadows, unseen and unheard. I can't fathom how they continue to elude my carefully laid traps as though they don't even notice them.

My mind races, contemplating darker and more sinister methods to shatter their happiness. I want to see them broken, it will make it easier to force them to obey.

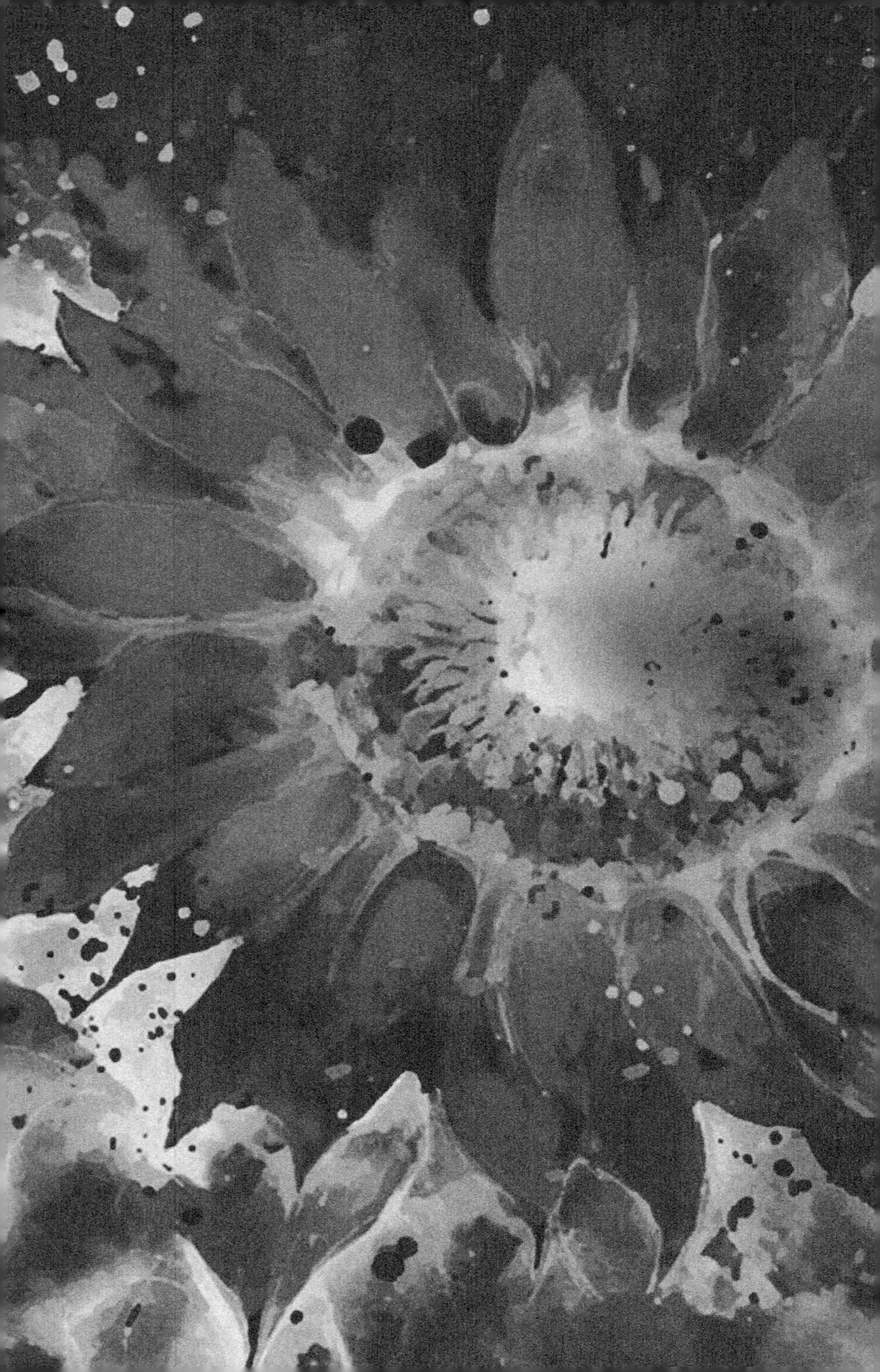

CHAPTER 24

Willow

I didn't really lie to Margot, the nightmares were getting better. But with how fuzzy my mind was this morning I wish they had gotten a lot better than they were.

Feeling groggy and disoriented, I stumble through the corridor, my single-minded focus on reaching the bathroom. The dim light filtering through the curtains adds to the haze in my mind.

I push open the door with the intention of splashing some water on my face to shake off the remnants of sleep. However, as the door swings open, my drowsiness is instantly replaced by a surge of awareness. The old house seems to have surprisingly good soundproofing between rooms, and the first indication of this is the sound of running water.

The sight before me unfolds like a scene from a dream, vivid and surreal. The shower is a cascade of steam, and within it, Easton stands with his back to me, his silhouette carved in the misty air. His forehead is pressed against his arm, which is casually propped against the tiled wall of the shower. The water flows over the contours of his muscles, tracing rivulets down his arm, the side of his chest, and his back.

In that frozen moment, my gaze inadvertently lowers, and my eyes widen at the unexpected sight. Easton's other hand is wrapped around his cock, his movements steady and deliberate. The realization hits me like a bolt of lightning, electrifying my senses and sending my heart into a rapid rhythm.

I should look away. I should leave. But my body seems to have a mind of its own, rooted in place, captivated by the scene before me. My eyes watching how his hand slides along the length over and over, squeezing tightly.

My cheeks flush with warmth, a mixture of embarrassment and an unexpected surge of arousal that I've never felt before. The internal conflict rages within me—part of me urging a swift retreat, and another inexplicably drawn to the mesmerizing image in front of me.

In the midst of this internal struggle my brain kicks in, and with a sharp inhale, I turn on my heel, leaving and closing the door behind me as softly as I can. My face is undoubtedly beet red as I retreat from the bathroom, my heart pounding in my chest.

As I stumble back into the corridor, my mind races with a mixture of embarrassment, confusion, and a newfound awareness that tingles beneath my skin. I lean against the hallway wall, trying to steady my breathing and make sense of the unexpected encounter that has left me feeling more awake and alive than any splash of cold water could ever achieve.

The realization of what I just witnessed crashes over me, and I lean more heavily against the wall, my breaths coming in short, uneven gasps. My face burns, and a sense of guilt gnaws at me for intruding on such an intimate moment.

I take a few moments to collect myself, closing my eyes and attempting to push the vivid image from my mind. The pulsing sensation that lingers in my pussy catches me off guard, a physical reaction I've never experienced to this degree before. Confusion and a sense of disorientation accompany the aftermath of that unexpected encounter.

The soundproofing that shielded me from the initial awareness of the shower now seems inadequate, failing to muffle the unmistakable moan that escapes Easton's lips. The sound of my name escaping as part of that moment sends another pulse of arousal through me.

As I stand there, grappling with the whirlwind of conflicting emotions, the realization hits me like a tidal wave. In all the times I suffered the abuse at Jacob's hands, not once did I feel even a tiny amount of arousal. Nothing he did ever elicited anything for me, and I knew that was his twisted aim—to break me down, to make me submissive. So, to feel this new and foreign sensation upon seeing and hearing Easton is both disorienting and confusing.

I'm not naive. I recognize the flush in my cheeks, the racing of my heart, and the strange pulsing sensation in my core. I'm aware of the arousal that courses through me. Even before I had been taken I had experienced the teenage version of these feelings, I had experienced sexual thoughts and fantasies, mainly for the boys who were my best friends. Though I would never have admitted it at the time.

Realizing I can't linger in the hall forever, I retreat to the bedroom and flop back onto the bed, my mind still reeling from the intensity of my reaction.

My body, however, seems to have its own agenda. The awareness and arousal continue to pulse through me, and without much thought, I find my hand slipping into my pants. Brushing my fingers against where my pussy is pulsing, a sharp bolt of pleasure has me whimpering. Guilt quickly follows, chasing the feeling, and I remove my hand as if burned. Curling onto my side on the bed, I try to push away the sensations, my mind a swirl of confusion and conflicting emotions.

The echoes of Easton's moans and the vivid imagery replay in my mind, making it challenging. As I lie on the bed, I grapple with the realization that something within me has shifted, awakening desires and responses I never anticipated.

The sound of the bathroom door opening snaps me out of my internal turmoil, and I quickly shift my gaze towards the doorway. When Easton appears, fully dressed and seemingly unaware of the storm of emotions within me, I'm momentarily relieved. However, my relief is replaced by a different kind of tension as he looks at my flushed face with genuine concern. His voice breaks through the swirling thoughts in my mind.

"Hey, Willow, you okay?" he asks, his voice gentle.

I swallow hard, attempting to dispel the tension that lingers in the air. "Yeah," I manage to reply, my voice a little hoarse. "I just... woke up feeling a bit disoriented."

Easton's expression softens, and he steps into the room. "I was actually coming to check on you. Was wondering if you're awake and if you'd like some breakfast."

The ordinary nature of his question contrasts sharply with the extraordinary circumstances of moments ago. The realization that Easton might be completely unaware of what I saw and the effect it had on me strikes me. "Breakfast sounds good," I reply, my cheeks still bearing the heat of embarrassment.

Easton takes me at my word, turning away to head toward the kitchen. After a moment, realizing that I still need time to gather myself, I call out to his retreating back, "I'll be there after I have a shower."

Once in the bathroom, I close the door behind me, the memory of what I witnessed coming back in vivid detail. The heat returns to my skin, and I feel a mixture of confusion, arousal, and guilt. Stripping down, I turn on the warm water, stepping into the shower, hoping it will clear my mind.

As the water rushes over me, I try to push aside the images and echoes of Easton. But the more I try to suppress them, the more they persist, vivid and intrusive. The steam swirls around me, creating an isolated space where my thoughts become a raging storm.

Frustration builds within me, and a sudden surge of anger takes over. I shouldn't feel guilty for how I feel or what I saw. I'm not in the cult anymore. I'm free to make my own choices, free to explore my desires, and, damn it, free to choose whoever I want.

I allow the memories of Easton pleasuring himself to resurface, and at the same time, my fingers instinctively move between my legs. The ache and throb that linger there become too insistent to ignore. The pulsing feeling intensifies, and I can't ignore the growing arousal that accompanies the memories. As I explore these newfound sensations, guilt attempts to creep in, but I push it aside.

The water rushes over me, both soothing and exhilarating. I give in to the impulses, allowing my fingers to trace the contours of the most intimate part of me. My fingers gliding through the slickness there that I knew was a response to my thoughts and not water.

The internal conflict persists, but a voice in my head grows louder, insisting that I deserve this, that I deserve to experience pleasure on my terms. The pulsing feeling intensifies, resonating with the echoes of Easton's moans, and I can't deny the raw desire that courses through me.

It's a moment of rebellion against the shackles of the past, a declaration that I am in control of my body and my desires. I let my fingers explore, finding the entrance to myself before moving back to the small bundle of nerves right at the top that is sending pulses through my body.

I let my fingers circle it tentatively before pressing my fingers directly to it. The result is electric, a burst of pleasure that surges through me. My breath catches in my throat as I continue to explore, an experience I denied myself for far too long.

As I continue, my mind momentarily clears, focusing solely on the waves of pleasure building within me. Easton's moans transform into a melody in my mind, harmonizing with the pulsing rhythm of my own need. I feel a strange tightening in my pussy as the pleasure that builds inside of me starts to send a tingling feeling into my limbs.

The intensity almost has me stopping but I want to know what I have been deprived of for so long. I want to know the pleasure that Easton felt when he moaned so deeply I could hear it on the other side of the door. With a gasp, I allow myself to tumble over the edge, succumbing to the climax that crashes over me like a tidal wave. It's a release of pent-up tension, a catharsis that leaves me breathless and vulnerable. The steam in the shower swirls around me, embracing me in its warmth as I ride the aftershocks of pleasure.

As the pleasure gradually subsides, I stand there for a moment, supported by the tiled walls, the water now a gentle caress.

Guilt attempts to rear its head again, and although I try to swat it away like an annoying insect, it isn't so easily dismissed now. I remind myself that I am no longer captive to the horrors of my past, that I am free to define my own boundaries and embrace the pleasure that was rightfully mine. It's a brief cathartic moment, a rebellion against the indoctrination that sought to suppress my autonomy.

With trembling hands, I scrub myself clean, trying to erase the moment from my body and mind. The steam in the shower seems to close in on me, turning from a comforting embrace to a stifling confinement.

As I stand under the water, I can't shake the feeling that I've betrayed some unspoken law. The guilt increases with every pass of the soap, each drop of water attempting to cleanse not just my body but the perceived sin of self-indulgence.

Exiting the shower, I wrap myself in a towel, but the vulnerability I feel has transformed into a raw exposure. The bathroom mirror reflects a face still flushed, not just from the heat of the shower. My own eyes betray me, reflecting a turmoil that wasn't there before.

Once I'm dressed and composed, I step out of the bathroom, but the weight of guilt follows me like a shadow. I find myself questioning the choices I made in that shower, questioning whether I'm truly free from the chains of my past.

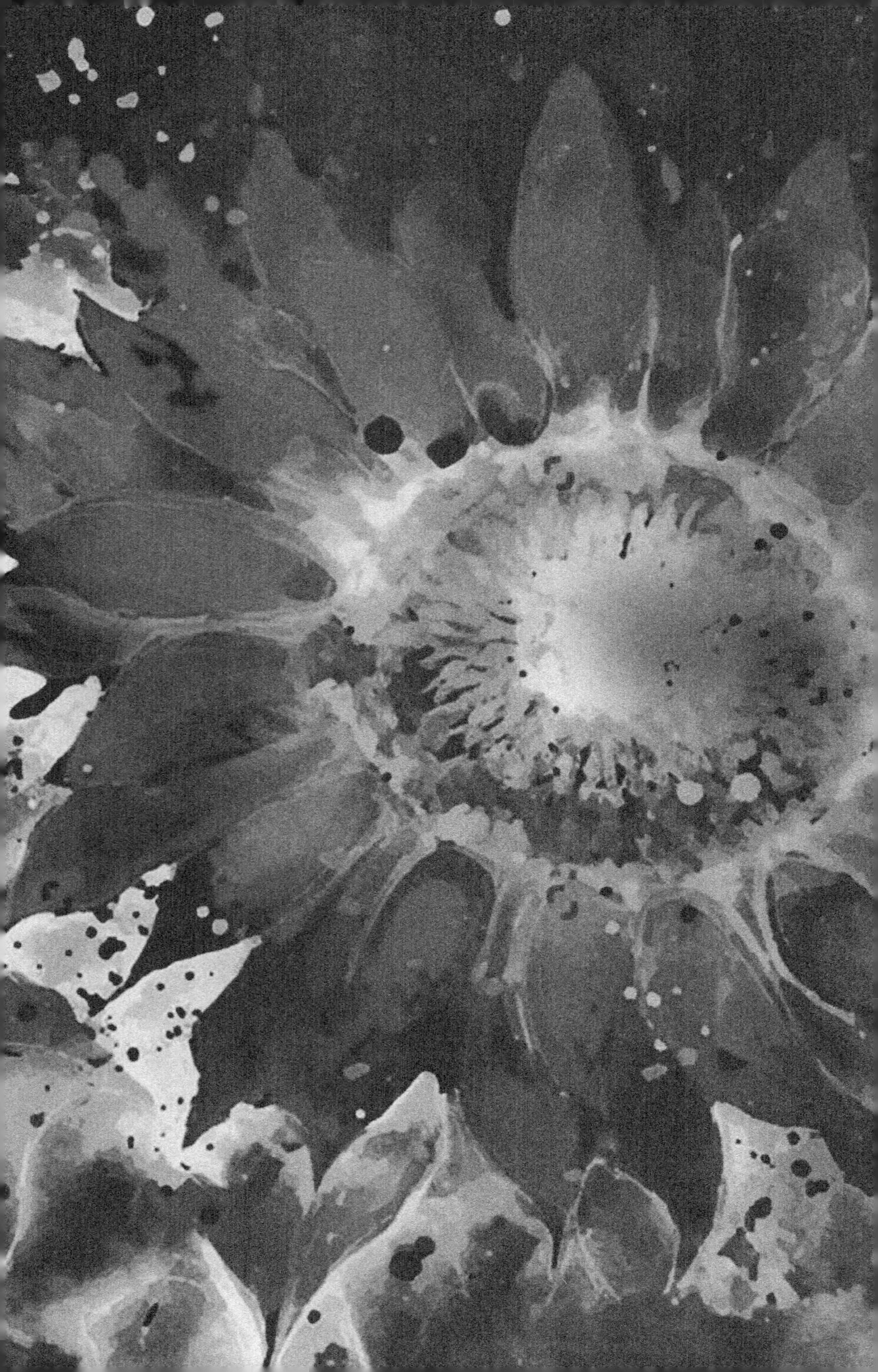

CHAPTER 25

Easton

I don't know what came over me. Actually I do; Willow.

The nightmare she had the previous night hadn't been as bad as I had seen before but it was still not gentle. I had heard the sounds of her whimpers and gone to her as quickly as I could.

I found her tangled in her sheets, a sheen of sweat on her forehead. Gently, I brushed a hand down her arm, making soothing noises until she calmed down in her sleep. It's become a routine—a quiet dance in the night, an unspoken promise that I'll be there to chase away the shadows that linger in her dreams.

As she slept, I couldn't help but marvel at the strength she displayed. Brushing her hair away from her face, I marveled at her beauty, undiminished even after the ordeal of a nightmare. The blonde is starting to regrow in her hair and I made a mental note to ask if she wanted me to dye it again. It's a simple gesture, yet in these moments, it feels like a profound connection—a testament to the bond we've formed over the past month.

Reflecting on the time spent with her, I can't help but acknowledge how close we've become. Willow, my little butterfly, emerging from the cocoon of her past. There are moments when accidental touches linger longer than intended, and in those instances, I catch a glimpse of something in her eyes—a longing, a desire.

I've resisted the temptation to let my eyes stray to the rest of her body, as much as I would have loved to explore every inch of her. She's fragile, learning to live again, and I've been careful not to push her boundaries. In her, I've found a companion, a confidante, and the gravity of my feelings for her can't be ignored.

I savor the quiet moments while I sit with her for a couple hours. The vulnerability she shows in her sleep is a stark contrast to the strength she exudes during the day. As dawn approaches, I slid my hand out of hers with utmost care, not wanting to disturb her rest.

I retreat to the shower thinking the steam and water might wash away the thoughts that cling to my mind. Yet, the echo of Willow's presence lingers, an ethereal thread that's wound its way through my thoughts.

As the water cascades over me, I can't shake the magnetic pull she has on me. My body responds to the thoughts, my cock growing hard and throbbing. The pulsing sensation intensifies, and I can't resist the temptation any longer.

My hand moves instinctively, finding its way to my aching length. I can't deny the surge of pleasure that courses through me as I imagine Willow's touch, her presence in the most intimate of moments. I close my eyes and rest my forehead against my arm, her face filling my thoughts.

Imagining her hand wrapped around my cock or her body pressed against mine.

The shower may be loud but it isn't so loud that I don't hear the moment she opens the door to the bathroom. My heart races when I realize she's there witnessing me. The pleasure thrumming through my body only intensifies. I know I should stop but her presence clouds my judgment.

The sound of the shower provides a thin veil of privacy, yet the awareness that she's looking at me only makes my desire more prominent. Even after she quietly backs out of the room, her presence lingers so physically that the tingling sensation of my climax races down my spine until I'm groaning out my release in the confines of the now empty bathroom.

The realization of what just happened hits me in a wave of guilt and confusion. I hadn't meant for Willow to see me like that, and I question the consequences of my actions on the delicate bond we formed. The boundaries I tried to uphold seemed to blur in that moment.

When I check on Willow after the shower, her own embarrassment is evident in the subtle shift of her gaze and the faint flush on her cheeks. I decide to swallow down my own feelings, maintaining a facade of nonchalance, as if nothing out of the ordinary occurred. I want to respect her privacy and not add another layer of awkwardness to the situation.

As she goes to have her own shower, I find myself lingering outside the bathroom, my mind in turmoil. Then, I hear the telltale sounds of her own pursuit of pleasure, and a genuine smile tugs at the corners of my lips. Despite the complex emotions swirling within me, I feel happy that she feels comfortable enough to explore her desires, especially after everything she's been through. It's a small victory, a sign that she's reclaiming ownership of her body and her pleasure.

Quickly retreating to the kitchen, I focus on preparing breakfast. The sound of sizzling bacon and brewing coffee provides a comforting backdrop, grounding me in the familiar routine.

When she emerges from the shower, I greet her with a casual smile, acting as if the morning unfolded just like any other. The unspoken tension between us hangs in the air, but I choose not to address it directly. Instead, we sit down to breakfast, exchanging light conversation as if the events of the morning were nothing more than a fleeting dream.

As we share the meal, I can't help but marvel at the resilience in Willow's eyes. Despite the challenges she faced, she continues to navigate through the complexities of her past and the uncertainties of the present. Our connection, though, is now tinged with a new awareness.

WYATT

I can tell something is off the moment I guide Bryce into the dining room. Once again I gave my little boy a bunch of sunflowers to give to Willow and I watch the smile spread across her beautiful face at the sight of them.

But there's tension in the air. I feel it. But I don't want to upset Willow unnecessarily.

Willow, her eyes sparkling, leans in and whispers to Bryce. "I've got this itch to paint something beautiful, and these sunflowers are just the thing to make it happen. How about you help me?"

Bryce's face lights up, his excitement bubbling over. "Really? Can I do art too?" he asks eagerly.

Willow chuckles at his enthusiasm. "Of course, sweetie! I'd be honored to create art with such a talented artist like you. Let's make something magical together."

As Willow gracefully rises from the dining table, I catch Bryce's eye, "Be on your best behavior for Miss Willow, alright?" He grins and nods, making my heart ache for a moment as he reaches out and takes Willow's hand.

With Bryce and the sunflowers in tow, Willow leads the way into the living room, giving me a soft smile on her way past and leaving me alone with Easton. The air crackles with unspoken tension, and I can't let it linger any longer.

I turn to Easton, a furrow in my brow, and ask quietly, "What the fuck has happened, Easton?"

Easton's gaze hardens and he responds with a defensive edge, "What's between Willow and me is our business, just like what is between you and her is yours. I never told her the reason behind your behavior, because it's your relationship, so don't go interfering with mine."

I narrow my eyes at Easton, his words sinking in like a weight on my chest. "You knew?" I grit out, a mixture of disbelief and frustration coloring my tone.

Easton meets my gaze unflinchingly, his expression defiant. "Of course, I knew," he says, his voice carrying an undercurrent of irritation. "Like I wasn't about to question why one of my best friends suddenly stopped searching for the girl he loves and went on a bender and started shacking up with someone else."

I grumble, frustration building within me as I mutter, "Fucking Mason."

Easton's gaze doesn't waver, and he responds with a stern tone, "You shouldn't have left that burden on Mason's shoulders. We all had a right to hear it from you, especially since we were your best friends."

The weight of his words hit me, and a pang of shame creeps in. I cut off my best friends during a difficult time, and now the consequences are surfacing. I sigh, realizing the magnitude of my actions.

Looking out of the back windows of the house, we let the silence linger for a moment before Easton speaks again, his voice more measured this time. "The fact that you believed it without question means you have a long way to go with Willow. But," he adds, "it's still between you and Willow. Whatever relationship any of us develop with her is our own, I won't interfere in anyone else's. All I want is for her to be loved like she deserves."

A combination of relief and apprehension wash over me. Easton's words, though stern, carry a hint of understanding. I nod, acknowledging his point. The living room echoes with the sounds of laughter. Whatever Willow and Bryce are doing kept them blissfully unaware of the conversation unfolding in the dining area. I can't help but smile at the beautiful sound.

"I get it," I finally admit. "I messed up, and I need to make things right. Not just with Willow but with everyone."

Easton's expression softens. "Start with Willow. The rest will follow."

Taking a deep breath, I look directly at Easton and ask with a touch of vulnerability, "Are we gonna be okay, Easton?"

He regards me for a moment, the sternness in his gaze softening. "We've weathered storms before. Just handle your business and be there for Willow, and we'll see where things go."

I nod, a mix of gratitude and regret settling in. "I'm sorry for how I let everything play out, for shutting you guys out. I messed up, and I should have trusted you all more."

Easton's response surprises me as he offers a small smile, "Apology accepted. We're not perfect, none of us. Just make things right with Willow. That's what matters now."

As the tension eases between us, Easton's demeanor shifts, and he leans back in his chair. There's a moment of silence before he breaks it with a more contemplative tone. "Do you have any idea who even sent that letter?" he asks, his eyes probing.

I shake my head, still grappling with the fallout of recent events. "No, still no clue. I wish I did. It just came out of nowhere."

He sighs. "Based on what I know now, the person they said she was with was obviously Jacob."

My brow furrows at the mention of Jacob. "Jacob? He's the guy from the cult? What do you know about him and her time there?"

Easton's gaze turns distant, as if recalling memories he'd rather forget. "Not much more than what was in all the news articles. Willow hasn't spoken about it to me, and I'm not even sure she's told everything to her therapist. I'm not going to push her. She'll tell us when she's ready."

I nod. "Has she given you any hints, though, about what she experienced?"

Easton takes a moment, inhaling deeply before exhaling. A flash of anger, so unlike him, flickers across his face. "I've seen things," he finally admits. "Scars on her skin that she doesn't realize I've noticed. But it's not just the physical wounds; it's the scars on her mind and soul. The nightmares that wake her during the night, how her PTSD can grip her so quickly."

I sit in stunned silence, absorbing the weight of his words. "Scars?" I murmur, my voice barely above a whisper.

"Yeah," Easton continues, his gaze distant. "She will forever carry the aftermath of that time with her, and neither the physical nor emotional scars are something that will just fade away. It's etched into who she is."

A heavy silence envelopes us and I feel a surge of guilt for not being there for her when she needed support the most.

"What can we do?" I finally ask, helplessness washing over me.

Easton's gaze meets mine, filled with a mixture of understanding and empathy. "Be patient. Be there for her when she needs it. But don't push. She'll share what she's comfortable sharing when she's ready. She's only been free for a month and already I can see she's trying to shed her past and move on with her life."

A strange smile crosses Easton's face, and for a moment, I am tempted to question the tension I walked in on earlier. However, he continues, "When she's ready for more, she'll let us know. And you know what? I know of four men who will treat her like a queen, make her forget ever experiencing an ounce of pain at Jacob's hands."

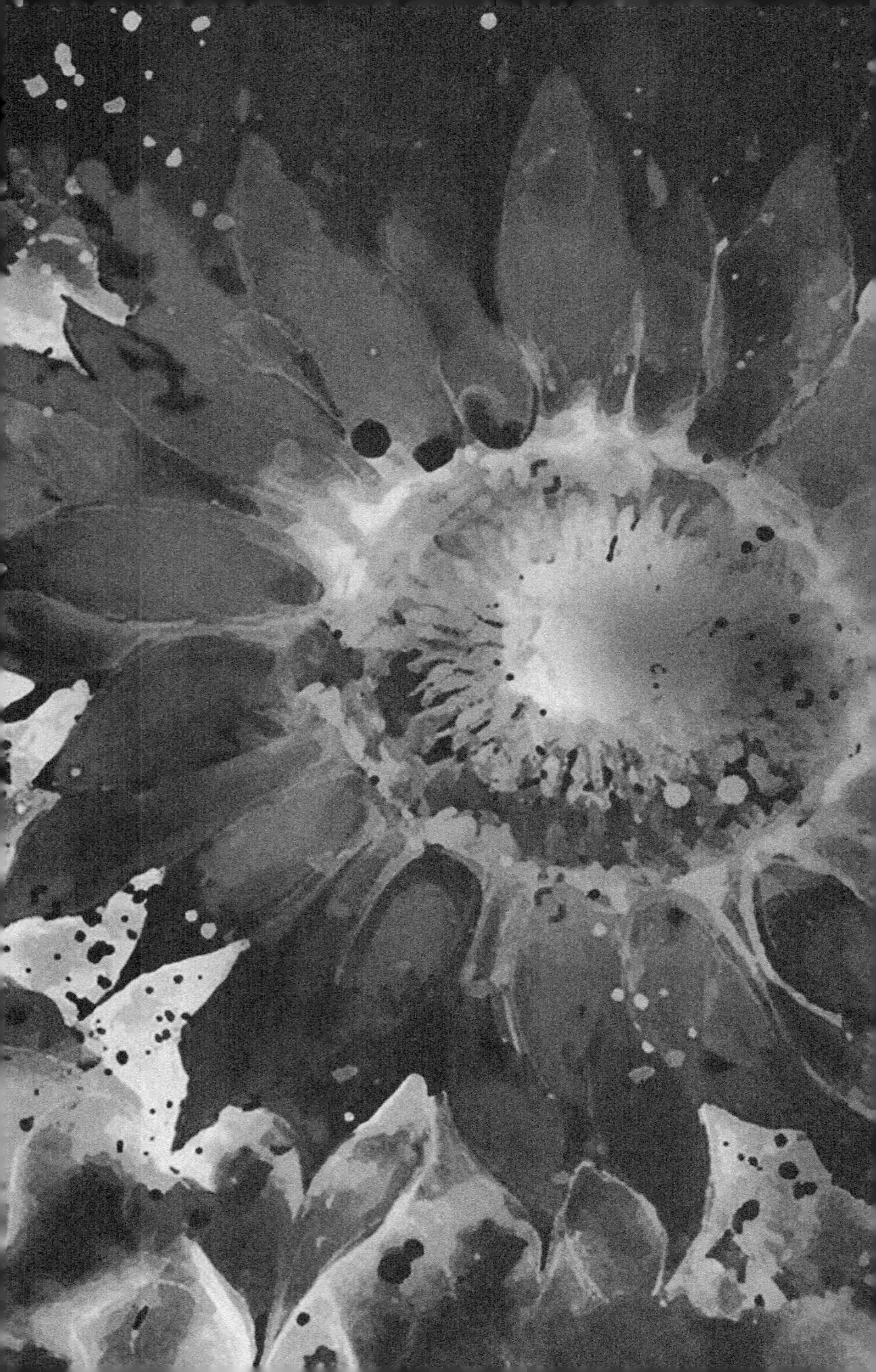

CHAPTER 26
Willow

After Wyatt's visit the day before we spent the night watching movies again. I couldn't help but grin every time I caught sight of the two masterpieces drying to the side of the room. Pretty yellow and orange sunflowers fill the paper. Admittedly, it was easier to tell the sunflowers in the larger image while the smaller piece was a chaos of paint in the same colors. But both warmed my heart at the sight.

This morning Easton took a trip into town to get a new hair dye so he could fix the blonde that was growing out in my hair. I hadn't brought it up to him even though every time I saw it, it made my heart race a little bit faster.

It isn't long after I let Kat know that I want to take her up on the offer of going to the bar together that she is on my doorstep with a bag of makeup and a grin.

The bedroom floor is a chaotic mess of clothes, evidence of my attempt at finding the perfect outfit for the night. Kat insisted on a fashion show to some upbeat music, turning the decision-making process into a spectacle. After parading numerous options, from dresses to skirts, she finally settles on a simple blue sundress. She also insists on a pair of cream wedges that look like a precarious choice for someone with my coordination—or lack thereof. I could already envision myself breaking an ankle by the end of the night.

With my outfit selected Kat maneuvers me into a dining chair and starts applying makeup to my face. At which point Easton sits in another dining chair interrogating Kat.

As Kat works her magic, she explains the plan for the night, responding to Easton's inquiries. "Yes, we're only going to Gage's bar. And yes, Gage said he'd be there. No, Easton, you can't come. It's a girls' night out, and the only reason Gage is allowed is because he owns the damn place."

Easton's attempts to negotiate were met with a firm refusal from Kat, who seems to revel in the challenge of holding her ground.

"For fucks sake, East, stop hovering! I'm perfectly capable of taking care of her," Kat snaps, and I couldn't help but giggle in response. Her tone is filled with playful annoyance as she expertly blends eyeshadow.

"Yeah, but—"

"No 'buts,' Easton. You can find something else to do tonight."

Easton feigns a wounded expression. "I'm hurt. Rejected from a girls' night. What has the world come to?"

Kat rolls her eyes, not missing a beat with the makeup application. "The world is just fine. Willow needs a night out, and I promised her a good time. No distractions, no testosterone, just fun. Got it?"

Easton raises his hands in surrender. "Fine, fine. I'll find something else to occupy myself tonight. But you better take good care of her, Kat."

Kat shoots him a mock salute. "You got it, Captain Obvious. Now shoo!"

With that, Easton chuckles and leaves the room, leaving Kat and me laughing at his retreating back. Kat puts the finishing touches on my makeup and steps back to admire her work. "There you go. Ready to turn heads and have a great night."

I glance in the mirror she holds up, surprised by the transformation. Kat worked her magic, enhancing my features without masking them. It's subtle and I like the natural look as well as the slight shimmer to my cheeks. I smile in appreciation.

With a final check in the mirror herself and a last touch of lipstick, Kat declares her mission accomplished. "All set. Now, let's go paint the town, or at least Gage's bar, red!"

Kat and I head toward the front door, where Easton is already waiting to give us a ride to Gage's bar. The evening air is cool as we climb into Easton's car, and I can't help but feel excited.

Once we're in the door of Gage's bar, I feel a twinge of anxiety clawing at the edges of my newfound excitement. The confined and noisy atmosphere already has me edgy and uncomfortable. Still, I force those feelings aside, determined to embrace the experience.

Kat links her arm with mine and leads me toward the bar. The lively chatter and clinking glasses surrounds us, and I couldn't help but scan the room nervously. Gage spots us from behind the bar, a wide grin lighting up his face.

"Well, well, look who decided to grace us with her presence!" Gage calls out, pouring a drink for a customer while maintaining his playful tone.

I smile in response, the warmth of his welcome easing my nerves somewhat. Gage excuses himself from the customer and makes his way around to our side of the bar and over to us, giving me a quick hug.

"How you doing, Willow?" he asks, genuine concern in his eyes.

"I'm good, thanks," I reply, still adjusting to the loud surroundings.

Gage turns to Kat. "And you, Kat? Ready to conquer the night?"

Kat flashes a confident smile. "Always. But first, we need some drinks. I think you should do your cocktail thing for Willow and surprise her."

Gage's eyes sparkle mischievously. "I do love a challenge. How about I make you something special, actually two something specials, and you can try both. Whichever one you like the most, you drink. Kat can have the other. What do you say?"

I hesitate, not having any experience with alcohol. But with Kat's encouragement and Gage's friendly demeanor, I nod my head. Gage returns to behind the bar and gets to work, expertly mixing up two colorful concoctions. The vibrant drinks arrive in front of me, and I couldn't help but marvel at their beauty; they almost look too good to drink.

"Here you go, Sweetness. Give them a try and let me know what you think," Gage says, a twinkle in his eye. The nickname makes me blush slightly as I concentrate on the drinks.

The unfamiliar scent wafts up as I cautiously take a sip from the first glass. The burst of flavors surprises me, and I exchange a glance with Kat, who encourages me to try the second. Gage watches with anticipation as I taste the second concoction.

"Well?" he prompts.

I smile, pleasantly surprised by the flavors. The first drink is a vibrant pink concoction, and tastes both sweet and tart at the same time. It's refreshing and reminds me of warm summer days when I was young. The second is creamy and rich and tastes like coconut and lime. It's sweet and I love it, but not as much as the first one. "They're both amazing, but I think I like this one a bit more." I point to the pink drink.

Gage nods. "Excellent choice. Enjoy, ladies. Let me know if you need anything else." He winks at me and saunters away to serve another customer.

Kat giggles beside me before linking her arm with mine again. She leads me over to a table in the corner of the room where we could have some privacy amidst the lively crowd.

As we make our way to the table, I can't help but notice a group of three girls shooting evil looks our way. Their outfits are skimpy, and they seem to have applied too much make-up. It takes a moment with the dim lighting of the bar for me to recognize Loretta among them. Confusion crosses my face as I try to figure out why they're giving us such disdainful glares.

When Kat and I finally take our seats, she leans in with a mischievous smile. "So, tell me what's going on with Gage. How cute was that when he called you 'Sweetness?'"

I try to focus on Kat's question, but my attention drifts back to the trio of girls who seem to be talking animatedly among themselves. Their hostile stares raise my curiosity, and I can't help but inquire about them instead.

"Um, Kat, who are those girls over there with Loretta?" I ask, nodding subtly in their direction.

Kat follows my gaze and then smirks. "Oh, them? Yeah I'm not surprised you don't recognise the others, they both had work done in an attempt to fix their ugly but that shit is bone deep. They would be the rest of the mean girls, Melissa Green and Heidi Beck."

I have a vague recollection of them being always together with Loretta, but I can't recall too many details about how mean they were. When I mention this to Kat, she chuckles and says, "Well, of course, you don't really remember. You were always so focused on certain best friends of yours that you didn't pay any attention to the mean girls. And that's part of the reason they hated you so much."

I furrow my brow, curious. "Why did they hate me? I barely even interacted with them."

Kat shrugs. "Jealousy, probably. You had your tight-knit group, and they couldn't stand it. I think it might have also been that the guys were so focused on you in return. Plus, you never played into their drama, and they hated that too."

Nodding in understanding, I shift the topic. "Do you remember Callista McKinley?"

Kat gives me a knowing look. She knows that I am bringing up Callista due to her history with Wyatt. She replies, "Yeah, I remember her. She was also friends with the mean girls. But, you know, I don't think Wyatt knew that. As much as he was physically there while he was with her, he wasn't completely there, if you know what I mean."

I absorb this information and we are silent for a moment of quiet reflection until Kat hums and says, "Surprised to see Heidi here. She's usually on duty Friday nights."

Perplexed, I ask, "What do you mean?"

Kat snorts. "Heidi is the laziest police officer in our town. She avoids weekend shifts whenever possible. She only normally works the quieter nights. It's like a running joke. We all say it's so she doesn't break a nail if she has to actually work hard."

Frowning, I consider the possibility that Heidi could have been the source of the information Loretta knew when I was in her store. The thought adds a layer of unease to the atmosphere, but Kat's mischievous grin brings my attention back.

The cocktails are starting to make me feel lighter, and I find myself more willing to share the details of my interactions with the guys since my return. Taking another sip, I begin recounting the encounters, sharing the banter, the sweet moments, and the unexpected connection I feel with each of the guys.

With each sip and each sentence, the floaty feeling intensifies, and my anxieties seem to melt away. Kat listens attentively, occasionally giggling or teasing me about the subtle blush that refuses to leave my cheeks.

The energy in the bar grows, and the crowd gets bigger, but the floaty feeling from the cocktails keeps me at ease.

Soon, my cocktail is empty and I'm enjoying the carefree sensation. The anxiety clawing at the edges of my mind earlier disappears.

In the midst of the animated conversation with Kat, my mind fails to grasp onto any specific detail that could bring down the happy feeling. The floaty sensation envelopes me, creating a barrier against the anxious thoughts that tried to resurface earlier. Laughter and music fill the air, and for the moment, everything feels light and carefree.

However, my moment of bliss is interrupted when I stumble over a word. Kat giggles and then comments with a playful smirk, "I forgot you'd be a lightweight. Well, it's no surprise. You've never had alcohol before." She pulls out her cell phone and starts tapping away at it.

Confused, I frown and ask, "What are you doing?"

"Getting Easton to come back and pick us up. You, my friend, have already had enough. We should start small with our nights out."

I nod. The alcohol is affecting me more than I anticipated.

As Kat taps away on her phone, I sit back in my chair, still basking in the residual warmth of the evening. The lively chatter and music continues around us, creating a backdrop to the fading floaty feeling. Despite Kat's teasing about me being a lightweight, I can't help but smile at the unexpected joy of the night. I enjoyed myself, and I enjoyed my first taste of alcohol too.

I really hope that we can do it again sometime soon.

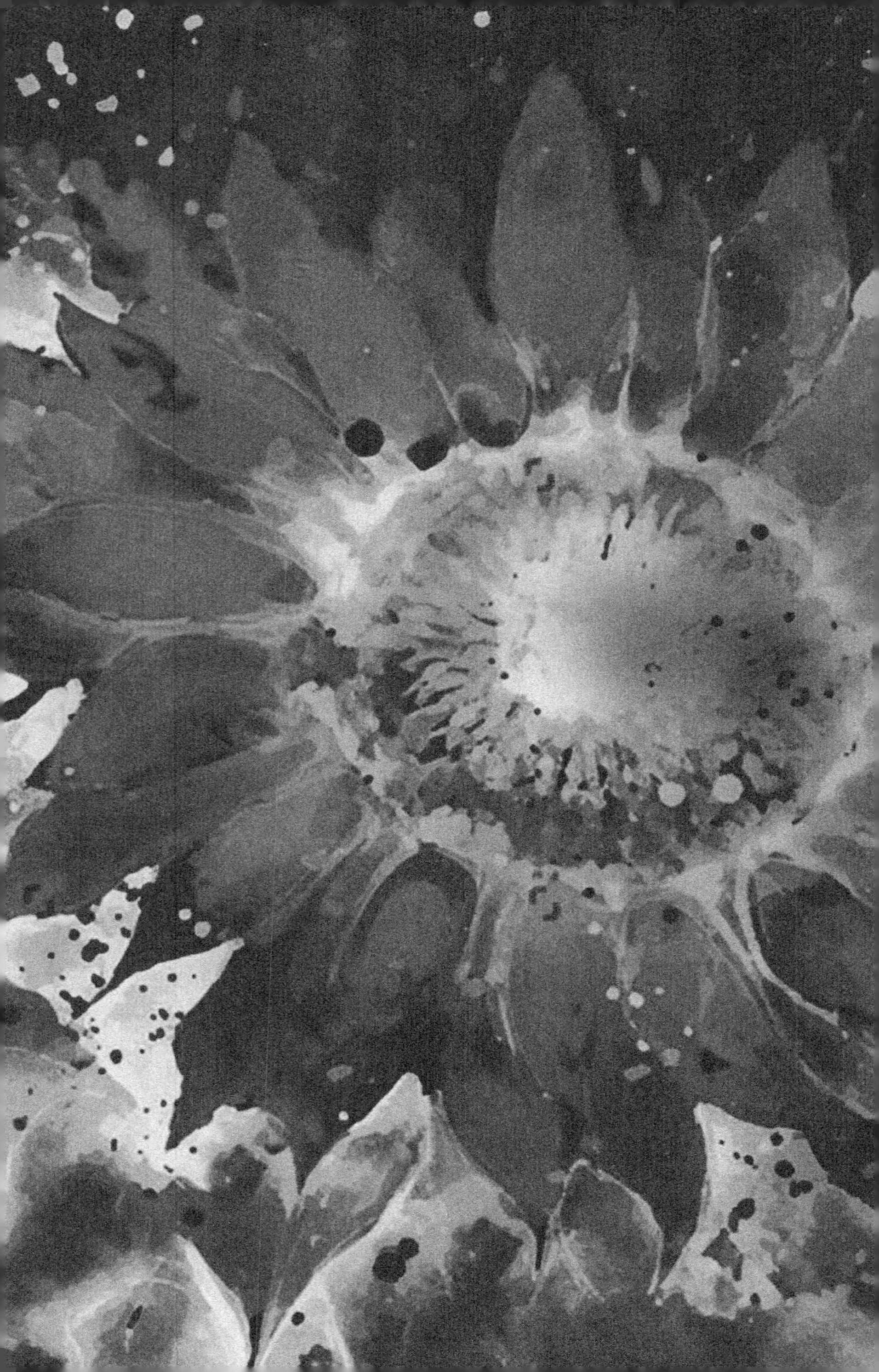

Chapter 27

Unknown

They remain unsuspecting, wrapped up in their mundane lives. Little do they know that I'm closing in, ready to shatter the illusion of safety they've created for themselves.

The longing to claim them as mine intensifies with each passing day.

Their obliviousness is almost comical, wrapped up in the cocoon of their increasingly false sense of security. Little do they realize that the quiet routines and comforting familiarity they have is merely a prelude to the storm heading their way. The illusion of safety is a fragile thing, and I'm prepared to shatter it with ruthless precision.

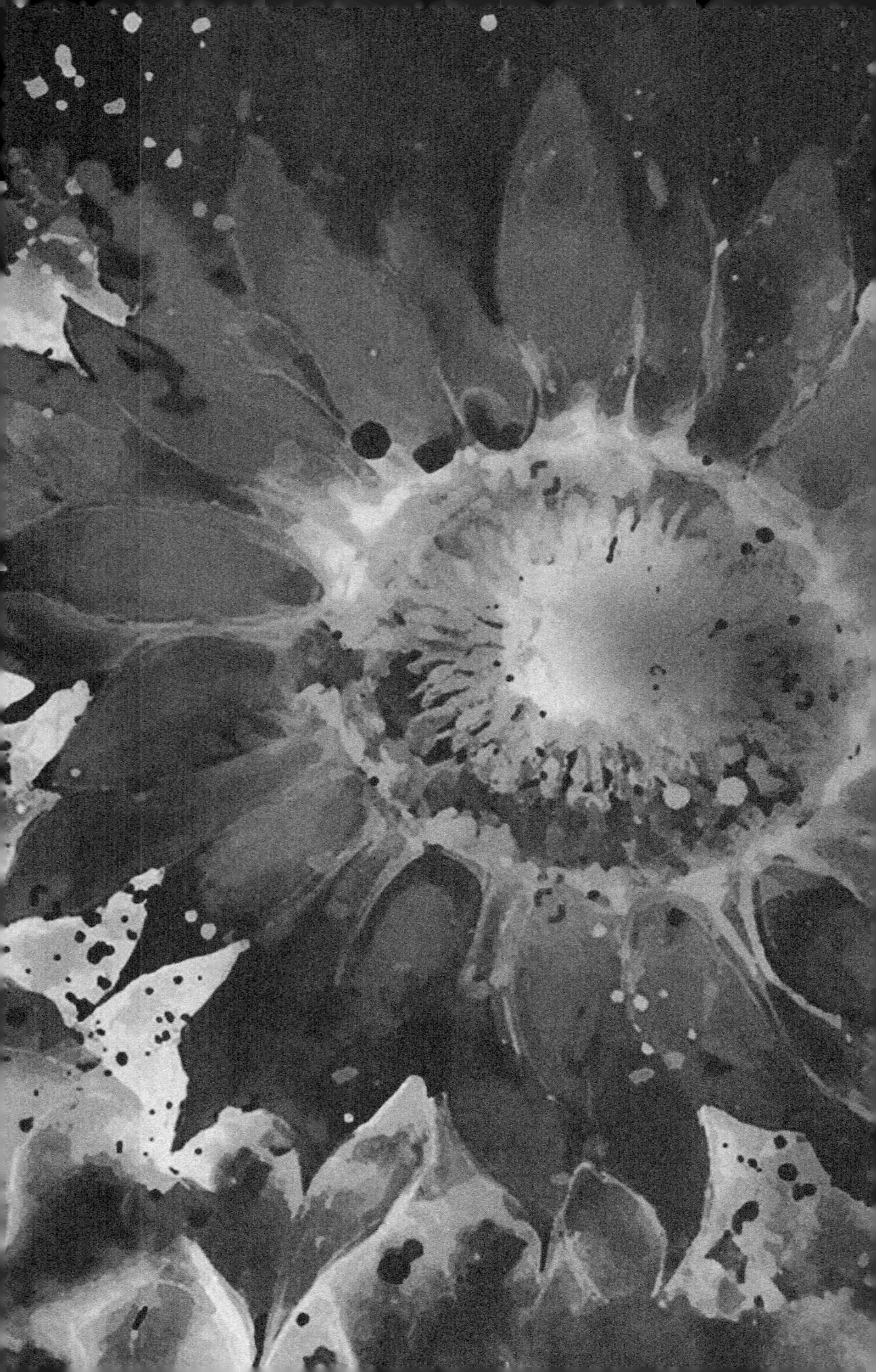

CHAPTER 28

Willow

"I'm happy to hear that you're stepping out of your comfort zone a little. Just make sure you don't do anything you aren't comfortable doing. You have control, Willow, make sure you remember that."

I hum in acknowledgement of Margot's words, but I know she can tell that my focus isn't entirely with her today. The last two days have been playing on my mind. I know she can see my distraction and her next words confirm that.

"Is there something that's bothering you? Did something happen at the bar?"

I frown as I think about it. "Yes. No. Ummm, well something did, but there is something else I wanted to discuss first."

Margot leans back, her expression attentive. "Alright, Willow. I'm here to listen. What's on your mind?"

I take a deep breath, feeling a mix of nerves and determination. "A big part of my life within the cult was focused on maintaining purity. I'm still a virgin. But I've been thinking about moving forward with my life. I want to experience things I haven't before, and, well, that includes sex."

Margot calmly waits for me to fully express my thoughts. "It's natural to have those desires, especially considering your past. So, what's on your mind about this?"

Blushing, I admit, "I want to ask Easton to be the person I share that experience with. It feels right. I've been through so much, and I don't want to be held back anymore. I want to be in charge of my life and my choices."

Margot tilts her head thoughtfully. "Easton. He's become an important part of your life?"

I nod. "Yes. We've become close, and I feel like we're attracted to each other. But it's not just him. All the guys—Gage, Mason, and Wyatt—they've changed from the boys I knew into men who genuinely care about me. They're making an effort to be there for me, help me move forward. I feel a connection with all of them."

Margot watches me closely, her expression a mixture of understanding and concern. "So, why Easton specifically? Is it just about losing your virginity, or are there deeper feelings there?"

My blush deepens, and I find myself ducking my head. "It's not just about that. Yes, I do have feelings for him. But, Margot, I also have feelings for all of them. Each of them has a piece of my heart in a different way. They've become a crucial part of my life, helping me heal and rediscover who I am."

Margot remains composed, offering a gentle smile. "Willow, I won't tell you what you should or shouldn't do. It's your body, and ultimately, the decision is yours. But I want you to be sure, completely sure, that this is what you want. I know you've been through a lot, and this is a significant step."

I appreciate her honesty and concern. "I understand, Margot. I just... I want to move forward, to experience life in a way I've never been able to before. And with Easton, we've become so close to each other, and it just feels right."

Margot nods. "Moving forward is an important step, Willow. And finding someone you trust and feel a connection with is crucial. Just be mindful of your emotions and make sure it's something that you want and are not feeling pressured into."

I frown in confusion, not really understanding what she means.

Margot leans forward, her eyes locked with mine. "Willow, it's essential to know the difference between what you genuinely want and what might be influenced by external factors. Your past experiences, the expectations of others, or even the idea that this is the next step in your journey—all these things can cloud your judgment. I want to make sure that your decision is driven by your own desires and not any external pressure."

I take a moment to absorb Margot's words. She's urging me to reflect on my motivations, to ensure that I'm not making this choice simply because it seems like the natural progression or because others might expect it.

"I understand what you're saying," I reply, my voice soft. "I don't want to rush into something just because I think it's expected of me or because I'm trying to fit into a certain mold. I want this, it is my choice, something I genuinely desire."

Margot smiles approvingly. "That's the spirit, Willow. Your desires and choices should be entirely your own. If you feel that this is what you genuinely want, and you're taking this step for your own reasons, then I support you. Just take the time you need to be certain."

I nod, grateful for her concern.

Taking a moment, she continues, "Now, you mentioned there was something else you wanted to discuss. What's on your mind, aside from this?"

I hesitate for a moment, thinking about how the alcohol last night took away my anxiety and smoothed over my emotional turmoil and how good it felt even briefly. I know I should probably discuss it with Margot.

I appreciate Margot's understanding and advice on everything, but another part of me is still wrestling with the memories of how alcohol helped me cope with my emotions. And despite her support, I can't shake the thought that she wouldn't approve of that particular coping mechanism. I decide to set that aside for now and focus on something else.

"I've been thinking about trying something different to help me," I admit, shifting the conversation away from where my thoughts linger. "I heard that working with horses, like riding and such, can be beneficial. It's supposed to be therapeutic and help with emotional healing."

Margot nods thoughtfully. "That sounds like a wonderful idea, Willow. Horses have a unique way of connecting with people, and many find solace and healing through those activities. If you feel comfortable with it, I think it's worth exploring."

Encouraged by her response, I elaborate on my idea. "I was wondering if maybe I should visit Wyatt's ranch again and see if I could spend some time around the horses there. Maybe even try riding one if I feel up to it. The last time I rode was the day I was taken, but I thought maybe it could be a new way for me to work through my emotions."

Margot smiles. "That's a great initiative, Willow. Facing your fears and finding alternative methods to cope is commendable. Just remember, take things at your own pace. Don't rush into anything you're not ready for."

I find myself seated in Easton's car with Margot's advice echoing in my mind The rhythmic hum of the engine provides a backdrop to my swirling thoughts. The weight of the discussion with Margot presses on my shoulders, and the quiet ride allows my mind to drift.

Easton glances at me. "Everything okay, Willow?" he asks in concern.

I meet his gaze, offering a small smile to reassure him. "Yeah, just a lot on my mind."

He nods in understanding. The car continues down the familiar roads, and I watch the passing scenery as my thoughts occupy my mind.

I can feel Easton's concern lingering in the air, and after a brief silence, he speaks again. "You know, you can talk to me about anything. I'm here for you."

Softly, I reply, "I know, Easton. Thank you." There's a warmth in his offer that eases some of the tension, and we settle into a comfortable silence for the rest of the journey back to the house.

Once we arrive, our routine kicks in almost automatically. We start making dinner together, moving around each other in the kitchen as if we've been doing it forever.

As we prepare the ingredients, I can't help but notice Easton's presence more acutely. Every movement, every subtle shift, becomes more pronounced. I feel attuned to the air between us, almost as if a newfound awareness has blossomed.

I catch a whiff of his subtle, spicy aftershave, and it's as if the fragrance wraps around me. When Easton starts humming along to the music playing through his phone, his voice resonates in the kitchen. It's almost like the sounds he makes are physical brushes against my skin, and I find myself feeling warm and tingly.

My thoughts start to drift to moments that linger in the recesses of my mind. The sight of Easton when I walked in on him the other morning. The moment I took for myself straight after that, exploring my own body until I took charge of my own pleasure. The memories stir something in me, emotions and feelings that I can't fully comprehend.

As I ponder these moments, a sense of reassurance envelops me. I don't believe Easton would treat me with the same disregard as Jacob did. There's a trust and kindness in Easton that sets him apart, and I find solace in the idea that he wouldn't hurt me.

Before my thoughts can be dragged into a potentially dark path, I redirect my focus. I remind myself of Easton's genuine care, his kindness, and the affection he consistently shows me. The comfort of his presence pulls me away from the shadows that threaten to creep in.

In that moment, I come to a quiet but profound decision. I realize I am making the right choice for myself. The cult may have tried to dictate my life and control my body, but I am not defined by their beliefs anymore. I own my body, my choices, and I have the power to give myself to someone I trust and care for.

As these thoughts swirl in my mind, Easton must sense my distraction. He sets aside the ladle he was using to stir our dinner and gently brushes a hand down my arm. The warmth and feel of his fingers against my skin sends a shiver through me. He turns me towards himself, his deep blue eyes searching mine as he asks, "Hey, are you sure you're okay?"

I meet his gaze, uncertainty flickering in my eyes. Slowly, I step into him, and in a moment of spontaneous courage, I raise myself up, brushing my lips softly against his. Time seems to freeze for a heartbeat, and then I lower back to the flats of my feet, preparing to step away.

Before I can take a step back, Easton's other hand comes up to cup my face, his thumb brushing against my bottom lip. "Come back here," he rasps out, and then he dips his head down and his lips find mine again.

In that moment, the world around us fades away, and all that remains is the soft, warm brush of his lips against mine. I have never been kissed before, even through all of the abuse that Jacob subjected me to. He never kissed me, and it makes me happy that Easton gets that part of me too.

I revel in his lips moving against mine, his hands gently cradling my face. I allow myself to let go of the weight of the past. I make my choice, a deliberate step towards reclaiming my body, my desires, and my autonomy.

As Easton's tongue flicks against my lips, I instinctively open them, inviting him to deepen the kiss. The taste of him is intoxicating, and his gentle yet passionate kiss sends waves of heat through my body. I feel a growing arousal, a newfound awareness of my desires that I've long denied.

Moments later, Easton slows the kiss down, and our lips part, leaving us both breathless. "I'm sorry if I took that too far."

I press my finger against his lips, whispering, "I want you to. I want you to take it all the way. I want you to be my first."

His eyes widen in response, and for a moment, I fear he might say no. But instead, he takes a step back, his gaze searching mine. Without breaking eye contact, he asks "Are you sure?"

At that moment, with clarity and certainty, I answer, "Yes."

He turns off the cooking food, and then he steps back into me. His lips return to mine, and this time, there's an urgency, a hunger that matches my own. He reaches down, lifting me up into his arms effortlessly, and starts moving toward the bedroom.

In the bedroom, Easton gently sets me down on my feet, his eyes locked onto mine. There's a tenderness in his gaze, a silent promise to make this moment special.

He trails his hands down the length of my body, his eyes never leaving mine. As he grasps the hem of my dress and slowly lifts it up, I feel every brush of fabric against my sensitive skin. I raise my arms, and he effortlessly pulls the dress off, tossing it aside. There's a vulnerability in standing there in just my panties, but Easton's desire-filled gaze washes away any lingering insecurity.

His eyes lower, and I can see the appreciation in them as his fingers brush the swell of my breasts. I've gained some weight over the last month, and it's most noticeable there.

His touch is gentle, exploring, and I feel a surge of confidence in my body.

His fingers find the front clasp of my bra, and after a moment where his eyes flick to mine, he undoes it. The straps slowly slide down until the bra drops to the ground.

His voice is husky as he whispers, "You're so beautiful." It's a simple phrase, but at this moment, it means everything.

Easton drops to his knees before me, and I watch as he leans forward. His tongue flicks over one of my nipples, making me gasp, and then his mouth closes around it. His other hand comes up to gently tease my other nipple.

The sensation is intense, a direct connection between the warmth of his mouth on my nipple and the deep throbbing sensation in my pussy.

As his mouth moves from one nipple to replace his fingers on the other, his hands continue their journey downward. His fingers curl around the sides of my underwear, and with deliberate slowness, he pulls them down my legs. I feel exposed, but there's a trust between us that eclipses any hesitation.

Once my underwear joins the discarded pile of clothes, Easton rises to his feet. He picks me up again, carrying me to the bed. With a gentleness that contrasts the intensity of the moment, he lays me down, his eyes never leaving mine.

Confusion clouds my thoughts as he lowers himself back to his knees at the end of the bed. His hands slide under my thighs, tugging me closer to the edge. The air is charged with anticipation as he leans forward, and then his mouth is on my pussy.

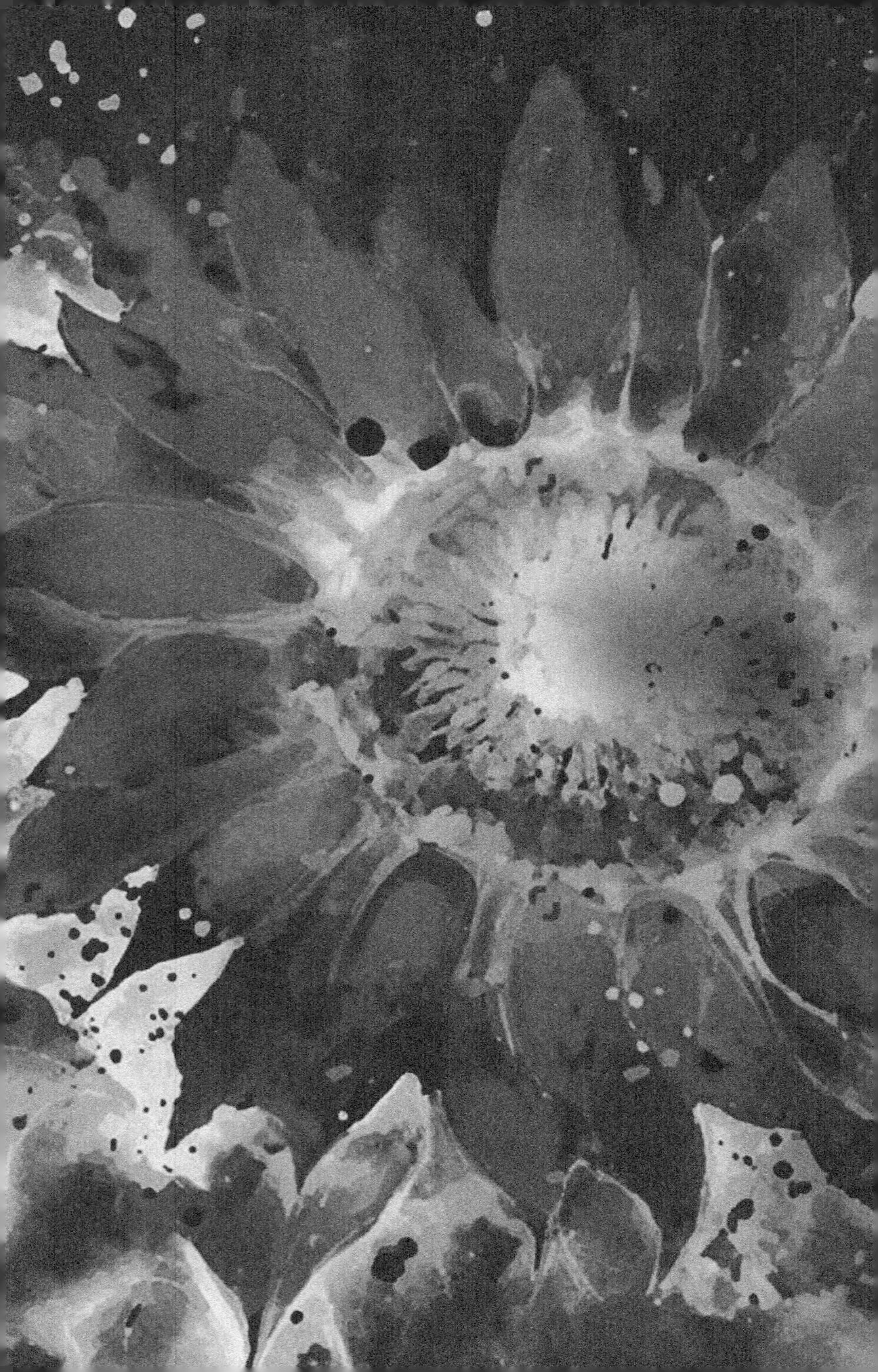

CHAPTER 29

Easton

If heaven had a taste, then it was named Willow.

Hearing the words finally come out of her mouth that she wanted to take this step with me almost had me jumping to the moon in happiness. I would have waited an eternity for her, and I would have still been in this same position no matter if it was another month or another year.

My tongue licks out again and I groan at the taste of her on my lips, I smile at the soft moan that leaves her in response. She is so responsive and I haven't been able to stop thinking about the sound of her pleasure since I overheard her the other day.

I slowly tease and explore her, sliding my tongue up the length of her pussy before circling it around her clit. Her breath catches as I brush against it for a moment before I trail my tongue back down to her entrance, using my tongue in an imitation of what I would like to do to her mouth if I didn't hold back.

Her fingers hesitantly find their way into my hair, and I see her clutch the sheets with the other. I know she is overwhelmed by the intensity of the moment. She is still so timid yet at the same time she is the strongest person I know.

As I continue to tease and explore Willow's body with my tongue, the sounds of her moans of pleasure echo around the room. My own arousal is evident, my cock hard and throbbing inside my jeans, but I remind myself to go slowly, to be gentle, and to prioritize Willow's comfort.

Flicking my tongue along her pussy, I circle her clit again, savoring the taste of her on my lips. Her fingers tighten in my hair, a physical reaction to the pleasure coursing through her. Moments before I close my lips around her clit and suck on it, I feel the tension in her body. Her hips arch in pleasure, a sign that she's edging closer to the climax she needs to experience before anything more happens.

I maintain a rhythm, flicking my tongue against her clit. Her moans grow in intensity in response. The room is filled with the sweet soundtrack of her pleasure, and every sound is a reminder of the trust she's placed in me.

Feeling Willow's body trembling, her hands now firmly gripping my hair and the sheets, I increase the pressure of my tongue on her clit, sucking harder. I'm attuned to every sound she makes. As I continue to move my mouth and tongue on her, I feel her body shaking, her cries reaching a new pitch as the pleasure takes hold of her fully.

My tongue works with a deliberate and steady rhythm, intensifying the pressure on her clit. Willow's orgasm washes over her, and I feel the physical response in the subtle spasms of her body.

I have to force myself to resist moving down and drinking her cum directly from her pussy. My focus is on ensuring her comfort and pleasure. I know she'll need extra lubrication, and I'm committed to making this experience positive and enjoyable for her.

Lifting my lips away from her, I know she might be sensitive in the aftermath of her orgasm. I trail kisses along the flesh of her thighs, savoring the taste of her on my lips. The room is filled with her soft gasps as she tries to catch her breath, her skin flushed, the aftershocks of pleasure still causing her body to twitch.

I gently take her hand from my hair and press a kiss to her palm before standing up. Her eyes, hooded and filled with desire, follow my movements. Seeing her like this is like a dream come true.

"You're doing so well, little butterfly," I whisper.

With deliberate slowness, I begin to undress. Pulling my shirt over my head, I move slowly, giving her time. I can see both nerves and desire in her gaze. Undoing the button of my jeans, the rasp of the zipper is loud in the quiet space. I push my jeans and underwear down and off together until I'm standing naked in front of her.

Her gaze lingers on my hard cock, and I can see her nerves increasing. Taking a moment, I offer her an option, "We can wait if you want. If you aren't completely sure, we can stop here. I want you to be sure."

She closes her eyes briefly, and when she opens them, determination shines through. "I want this, please."

Hearing her sincere desire, I feel a surge of warmth and affection for her. I move forward, lifting her into my arms again, and shuffle onto the bed on my knees until I can lay her gently with her head on the pillows. Raising myself up onto my arms, I take a moment to kiss her. I know she can probably taste herself on me, but I need to taste her lips again. When her hands start clutching at my sides and a small moan escapes her, I pull myself away and kneel between her legs.

Looking down at her, I almost groan again at the sight of her spread out before me. The mixture of nerves and desire in her eyes fuels my determination to make this experience memorable and positive for her. I want to feast on her again, but I push the desire aside.

"Do you want me to use protection?" I ask, my concern for her still at the forefront of my mind.

With a nervous smile, her blush deepens and she shakes her head. "No, the hospital implanted birth control and let me know I'm clean."

I smile, tenderly brushing a strand of hair away from her face. "I'll take it slow. Just let me know if you want to stop, okay? You control what we do."

She nods, and I can see the nerves still in her eyes, but I can also see trust. She trusts me to make this first time a good experience for her, that I won't hurt her like Jacob did.

Reaching down, I wrap one of my hands around my hard cock. Shuffling closer, I brush the end of it against her soft, wet folds, coating myself in her cum. She whimpers as I brush the head of my cock against her clit, and I use my hand to slowly push the head of my cock into her entrance.

I lean back over her, bracing myself on one arm and look deep into her eyes. I start to push forward very slowly, watching every movement and reaction. She is so incredibly tight, her pussy fighting against my intrusion as she tenses slightly.

I stop moving and use the hand wrapped around myself to brush against her clit. She whimpers again, but her muscles relax a little.

I say to her, "Relax for me, little butterfly. That's it, baby."

When I feel her muscles relax a little more, I start pushing forward again. Each inch feels like a victory, and I maintain eye contact, silently reassuring her. The intensity of the moment hangs in the air, a blend of anticipation, nervousness, and trust. I'm determined to make this experience everything she deserves.

As I push deeper inside her, I feel her whimpering and tensing again. Her hands clutch at my sides, and her nails dig into my skin. She is still so tight around me, and I have to desperately push aside the desire to thrust all the way inside her. Brushing my thumb against her clit again, I lean down and brush my lips against hers, whispering praises against her mouth.

I continue to push forward until I'm buried to the hilt. I can see the pain in her eyes, and it hurts me to know that I caused it. I stop moving, hovering over her, allowing her body time to stretch, adjust, and become comfortable with me buried inside her. "Are you okay, do you need me to stop?" I whisper.

I can feel the teneseness in her body slowly leaving as she starts to relax. With wide blue eyes staring into mine, she says, "Keep going, please."

Taking her words as permission, I pull out of her slowly and then push back inside of her. She whimpers again, but before I can stop, she whispers, "Keep going, please, keep going." So, I set a slow rhythm, moving in and out of her until all pain has left her eyes, replaced by pleasure.

Her hips start to meet mine in the gentle pace I've set, and her moans softly increase in volume. I can feel her starting to tighten around my cock, her body getting closer to the edge again.

Her eyes flutter closed as the pleasure starts to overwhelm her, but I gently command, "Keep those pretty eyes open, little butterfly. I want to watch you fly." Her eyes open and focus back on me just moments before I feel her orgasm take hold of her. Her pussy clenches and pulsates hard around my cock, and I grit my teeth, slowing down and pushing away the pleasure that wants to drag me under with her.

When her body relaxes again, I start to move faster, leaning down to brush my lips against hers once more. "I want another one, baby. Give me one more," I whisper, my voice filled with desire.

As much as I want to give her everything I have, I'm mindful of the fact that she's already going to be sore tomorrow. So, I maintain a controlled pace, just a little faster and harder than the first time. Her moans and the arch of her back drive me forward, and her nails dragging down my back encourage me to move faster.

The connection between us deepens with every thrust, and I can feel my own climax approaching. However, I want her to experience another peak before I allow myself to succumb to the pleasure. Reaching down again, I press and rub my thumb against her clit. Her body instantly tightens around me, and I rasp, "That's it, cum for me, Willow."

Her orgasm rolls over her, and she cries out, her pussy clenching around me again. This time, I don't slow down. The tingling sensation travels down my spine as I feel my own climax drag me over the edge with her. Our bodies move together as pleasure engulfs us both, and I lose myself in the feeling of ecstasy.

As the waves of pleasure subside, I lean more heavily onto shaking arms as I hover over her, our breaths heavy and hearts racing.

I pull out slowly, trying to be mindful of her sensitivity. As I catch my breath, I feel a surge of tenderness toward her. Gently lifting her into my arms, I cradle her against my chest, still basking in the warmth of our shared experience.

With careful steps, I carry her out of the bedroom and into the bathroom. She stares sleepily, her voice soft as she asks, "What are you doing?"

"You can sleep once I've cleaned you up and changed the sheets, little butterfly," I respond, a smile playing on my lips.

I turn on the shower, testing the water until it's comfortably warm. Setting her down on her feet, I pick up the body wash and begin to gently wash her. Taking time to slowly clean her, I apologize when she flinches. Her silence during the shower is notable, but I chalk it up to the aftermath of our intimate encounter.

However, when I notice her trembling, I look up into her eyes to see that she is crying. Concern etches across my features, and I drop the body wash, cradling her face in my hands. She isn't focused on me, her mind lost in the grip of a panic attack, I can see the guilt that she is drowning herself in. "Hey, look at me," I say softly, my voice filled with reassurance. "You've done nothing wrong."

Despite my words, she isn't focusing on me, and I can see her panic intensifying. Determined to help her, I reach over, shutting off the hot water completely and turning up the cold. Icy water sprays over both of us, and I ignore the discomfort in favor of the beautiful girl in front of me.

I did my research and knew that sudden temperature changes could help with PTSD and panic attacks. I just hope it works. She gasps for breath as the cold seeps into our skin, her eyes finally focusing on me. I can see she has come back to me. "You have done absolutely nothing wrong," I repeat, my voice steady.

It's an attempt to ground her, bring her back to reality. The cold may be uncomfortable, but the goal is to break through the fog of panic. I hold her close, murmuring soothing words, until her trembling starts to subside.

As the panic attack begins to wane, I guide her out of the shower, wrapping her in a warm towel. With careful tenderness, I dry her off, murmuring words of comfort. Once we are both wrapped in towels, I lead her back to the bedroom.

I strip the sheets from the bed and change them for fresh sheets while she gets dressed in her sleep clothes. I pull on my own clothes when I set the sheets aside to wash then return to the bedroom. She is still looking lost so I lead her to the bed and gently lay her down.

I cover us both with a blanket, holding her close. "Rest now, little butterfly. I've got you," I whisper, my fingers tracing soothing patterns on the skin of her arms. As she slowly drifts into sleep, I stay vigilant, ready to provide comfort and assurance whenever she needs it.

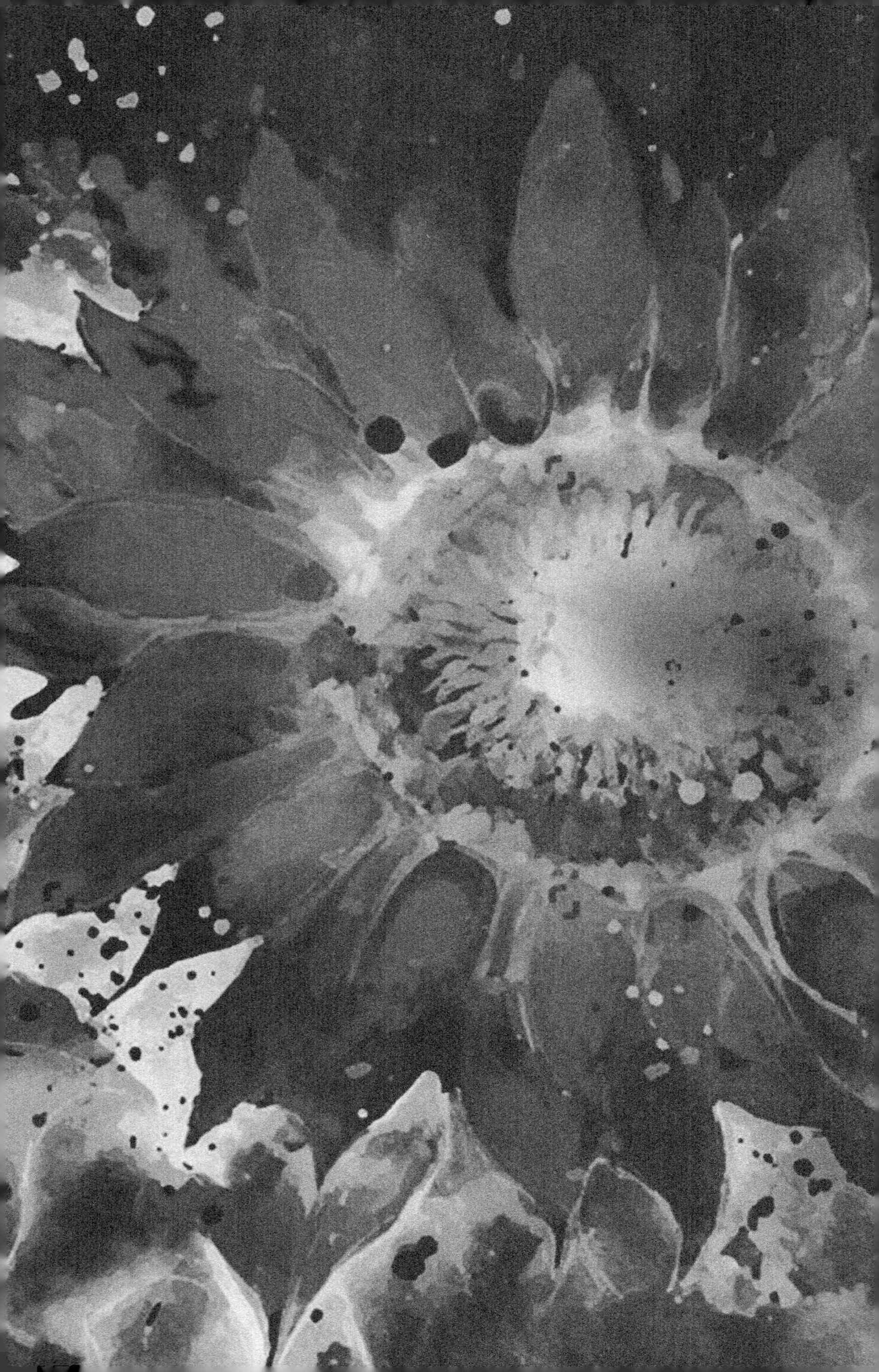

CHAPTER 30

Willow

I wake abruptly at the vague sound of a car door closing, followed by the low hum of an engine starting. Panic momentarily grips me, fearing that Easton may have left. My mind races with insecurities, wondering if what happened last night didn't meet his expectations.

A soft knock on the bedroom door interrupts my anxious thoughts, and Easton cautiously peeks into the room. The door opens wider as he realizes I'm awake, and he admits, "Hey, I was hoping you were still asleep."

I swallow nervously and ask, "Who was that?"

He winces before responding, "It was Kat. She let herself in, like she usually does. I barely made it out the bedroom door and closed it before she could barge in. She might have put two and two together about what happened."

His chagrined and guilty expression makes me roll my lips in an effort to hide a grin. He catches it, and a smirk tugs at his lips as he sits on the bed beside me. His fingers gently brush strands of hair out of my eyes, and he asks softly, "How are you feeling?"

Pausing for a moment to take stock of my emotions and physical state, I reply, "A little achy and strange, but overall, I feel good."

He chuckles, his warm breath brushing against my cheek, and says, "That's normal." He taps my temple lightly before adding, "I meant up here. You scared me last night."

I look down, frowning at my hands in my lap as I recall the panic attack in the shower. The sex had been uncomfortable at first, but then it felt amazing. However, in the shower, everything from the cult played on repeat in my mind. I kept thinking about how I'm no longer pure, and purity meant so much. I felt like I'd given it away. My mind played tricks, and all I could see was Jacob and how he would have reacted to me giving myself away to someone else. The panic attack set in, but the sudden freezing water acted like a switch, waking me up from the nightmare in my mind.

I look back up at Easton, finding concern in his eyes. Trying to reassure him, I say, "I'm okay now. I'm sorry for scaring you."

He smiles softly, moving his hand to cradle my face. "I hope you understand how much you mean to me." Leaning forward, he brushes his lips against mine. I attempt to deepen the kiss, but he chuckles and pulls away. "Kat was very reluctant to leave when she realized why I was a bit flustered. She was very concerned I might have hurt you. She said to pass on the message, and I quote, 'Bitch, you better call me asap and give me all the details, and if I need to hurt Easton, I will.'"

I can't help but giggle in response to the false female voice he put on to relay Kat's message. Instead of commenting, I reach up to his hair with my hand, repeating what he said to me the previous night, "Come back here." I drag his lips back to mine, feeling his lips curve before he takes control of our kiss.

His tongue delves into my mouth and I moan softly, losing myself in the sensation. As our kiss deepens, the outside world fades away, leaving only the warmth of his lips against mine. Last night, I loved his kisses. I loved the taste of him, the feelings he provoked in me, and the passion we shared. I wanted to experience that again, to drown in the intensity of our desire.

Everything about him is a welcome distraction from the lingering shadows of the past.

He chuckles again as he pulls back from the kiss, standing up from the bed and taking a few steps backward. Stopping just before the door, he smirks and says, "If I don't stop now, I'm going to be buried inside you again. As much as I would love to spend the day worshiping your body, I think maybe I should feed you food before I feed you my cock."

His words make me burst out laughing, especially considering the undeniable evidence of his hard cock pushing against the material of his sinful gray sweatpants. The sight of it, combined with the way he spoke about worshiping my body, has me feeling hot and wanting to test his resolve. However, realizing that I should probably accept his decision, all I do is ask, "Can I use your phone to call Kat, please?"

He unlocks the phone and brings up Kat's contact before handing it to me. Gently kissing my temple, he then walks out of the bedroom, leaving me to my call.

Taking a deep breath, I dial Kat's number and wait for her to pick up. When she does, her voice is filled with humor and curiosity, "Hey, you... Did that gorgeous man treat my friend right or do I need to cause bodily harm?"

I can't help but laugh at her straightforwardness. "Hey, Kat. No ice picks needed, I promise. Easton treated me very well," I reply, a playful tone in my voice.

She laughs. "Good to know. Now, spill the details. I want all the juicy stuff."

I recount the events of the night, sparing no details, and Kat responds with a mix of shock, excitement, and teasing comments. When I reach the part about the panic attack in the shower, her tone shifts to one of genuine concern.

"Willow, are you sure you're okay now?" she asks, her friend-mode fully activated.

"Yeah, Kat, I'm fine. It was just a moment. Easton was there for me, and it passed."

She chuckles, "Well, you certainly know how to keep things interesting. I'm glad you're okay. But spill, did you enjoy it? Did he take you over the cliff, if you know what I mean?"

I can't help but blush as I share the details, her gasping responses and celebratory interruptions making me laugh. When the conversation finally winds down, she says, "Okay, I hope you know I'm now living vicariously through you. I desperately miss dick. Anywho, take it easy, and if you need anything, call me. And tell Easton I've got my eye on him."

I giggle as I end the call. Getting up from the bed, I almost walk into Easton when I turn into the hallway leading to the kitchen.

"Kat sends her regards and wants you to know she's got her eye on you," I tease, unable to contain my laughter.

He laughs in response, "Well, I'll have to make sure I stay on her good side then. Ready for some breakfast?"

I nod eagerly, my laughter subsiding. Following Easton to the dining room, I'm greeted with the delicious aroma of banana pancakes. I can't help but squeal in delight – they were a favorite of mine growing up, and I haven't had them since then.

"You made banana pancakes?" I exclaim, a genuine smile spreading across my face."How did you know I love banana pancakes?"

He chuckles, "Lucky guess. Plus, you mentioned it in passing once."

Seated at the table, I take a bite, savoring the familiar taste that brings back childhood memories. Easton watches with a satisfied smirk as I practically devour the pancakes.

"These are amazing," I manage to say between bites. "Thank you."

He chuckles, taking a seat across from me, "Anything for you."

As we enjoy breakfast, he asks, "So, what would you like to do today?"

Considering for a moment, I suggest, "Is it possible we could go to Wyatt's ranch? I want to speak to him about maybe spending some time with the horses there. I was talking to Margot, and I want to try to see if riding and spending time with horses again will help my PTSD, as it is meant to help."

Easton's eyes light up, and he nods in agreement. "Absolutely, we can do that. If it's something that might help, I'm all for it. We can head there after we clean up here."

After finishing our breakfast, Easton and I clear the table together and then get dressed, sharing light banter and laughter.

As we prepare to leave, making our way out to the car, Easton unexpectedly stops me when I reach for the car door. Turning me around, he presses my back against the car, his touch gentle yet firm. The reminder of the marks on my back is like fleeting smoke, sliding into my mind only to dissipate as he brushes his lips against mine in a soft kiss.

Distracted by the warmth of his lips, I hardly notice that he has opened the car door that I had initially aimed for. Stepping back, he grins at me, mischief dancing in his eyes. I shake my head, chuckling, and comply by getting into the passenger seat. He closes the door gently behind me.

The engine purrs to life as Easton takes the driver's seat. I glance at him, a teasing smile playing on my lips. "Smooth moves."

He smirks, pulling out of the driveway. "I thought you liked my moves."

I raise an eyebrow playfully, teasing him, "Oh, I don't know, yours are the only moves I know. Maybe I should try someone else's moves."

Unexpectedly, Easton pulls the car to the side of the road just before the entrance to Wyatt's ranch. My heart rate speeds up, and for a brief moment, panic creeps in, thinking he might be angry with me. He looks at me with a serious expression, and I swallow nervously.

However, any tension dissolves as he picks up my hand from where it rests on the center console and nips at the ends of my fingers. A flash of pain from his teeth somehow makes its way through my body, sending a jolt straight to my pussy. He looks back into my eyes with a smirk before saying, "If you're talking about maybe trying out Wyatt's, Mason's, or Gage's moves, then I will absolutely support you sampling from the buffet you have available. But no one else."

My mouth drops open in shock, and I'm momentarily at a loss for words. Easton kisses the sting on my fingers and laces his own through mine before resuming the drive to the ranch. Still reeling from his unexpected declaration, I watch the scenery pass by, my mind buzzing with a mix of emotions. I had been struggling with the realization that I had feelings for all of them, and now Easton was saying that it was okay.

As we get to the end of the long driveway, Easton parks the vehicle, letting my hand go before he hops out and makes his way around to my door to help me out. He seems to be ignoring the shock that I'm in. I have so many questions and thoughts swirling in my mind, but Easton's calm demeanor hints that there might be more to the story.

We start walking toward the main house when Bryce's little voice calls out, "Miss Willow, Uncle Easton!" Bryce suddenly runs toward us from the house. I crouch down, and I'm almost bowled over as Bryce barrels into me, his little arms wrapping around my neck. I lift him with me when I stand back up.

Bryce starts talking quickly in his excitement, "Are you here to do art with me? We can paint the animals. You should see the drawing I did for Dadda!"

I can't help but chuckle at his enthusiasm before Easton responds to him, "How about you show me your artwork, little buddy? Miss Willow wants to speak to your Dadda and maybe spend some time with the horses."

At that, Bryce gets even more excited, saying to me, "Yes, you need to see the horses. They are awesome and big, and Dadda says I can't get too close to them or they might step on me."

My heart warms at Bryce's infectious energy, and I share a smile with Easton. As we make our way to the main house, Bryce excitedly chats about his drawings and the various animals on the ranch. It's a delightful distraction, and I find myself getting caught up in the joy of the moment.

We reach the main house, and Wyatt emerges, a warm smile on his face. "Hey sweetness. What brings you here?"

Easton scoffs and laughs. "I swear I feel like I'm chopped liver."

I glance at Easton and suppress a giggle at the look on his face and then turn to Wyatt. "Hey, I was hoping to talk to you about spending some time with your horses."

Wyatt grins and says, "You don't need to talk to me about it. Come over whenever you want. I would love to see more of you." I blush, feeling a warmth spread through me at his words. Wyatt then looks at Bryce and suggests, "How about you spend some time with Uncle Easton while I reintroduce Miss Willow to Gypsy?"

Frowning slightly as a memory tugs at my mind, I ask, "Gypsy?"

Wyatt grins at me, and Easton takes Bryce from my arms. "You met her when she was only a foal."

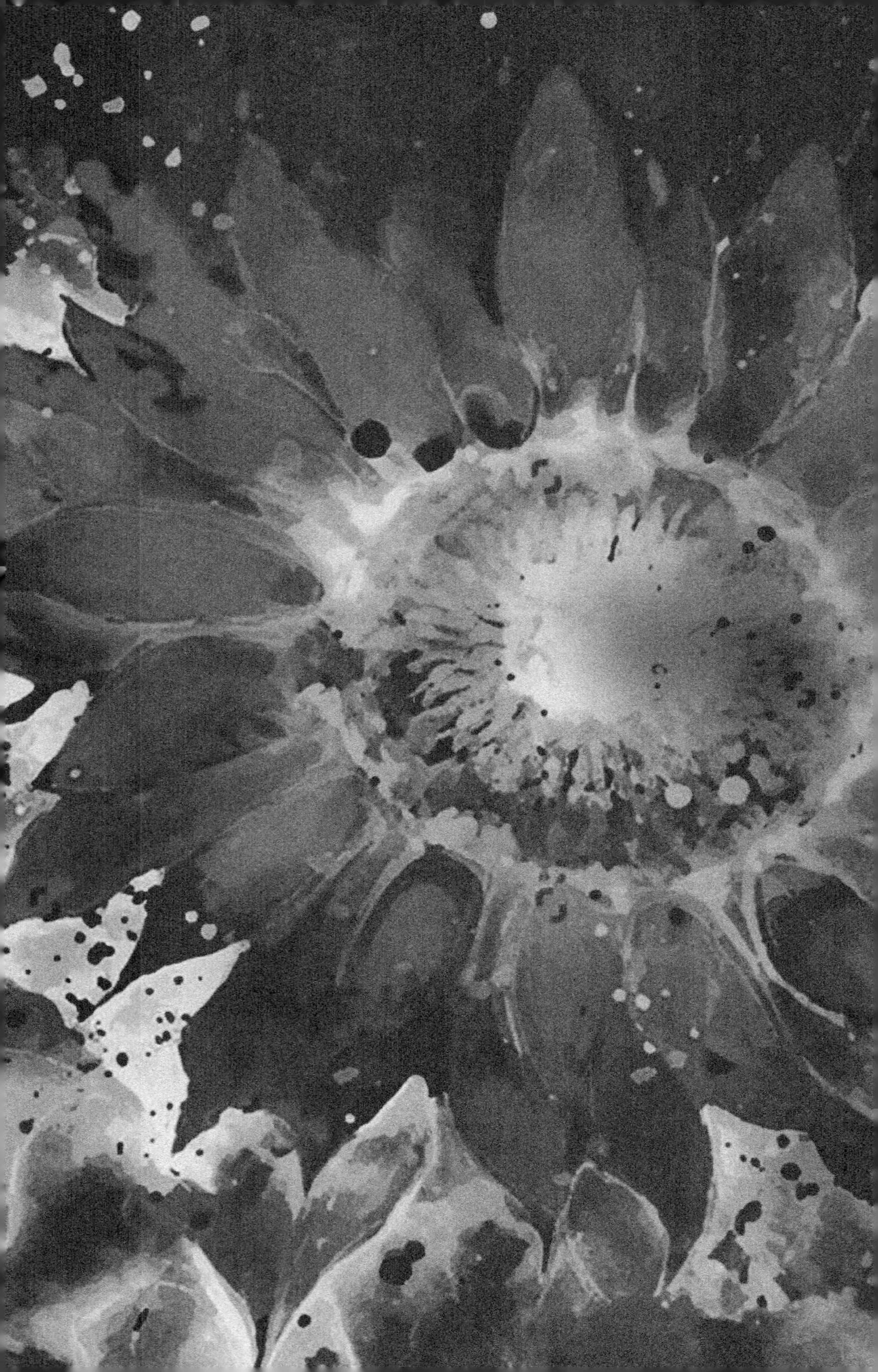

CHAPTER 31

Willow

I'm staring in awe at the beautiful creature in front of me.

Wyatt hadn't given me time to panic about seeing this horse in particular, he just took me by the hand and led me straight to the stables to introduce me to Gypsy. When Wyatt mentioned when I saw her last, memories flooded my mind.

That day was the day where I had come to the ranch to meet the little foal that had just been born and then spent the rest of the day riding the horses with my best friends. It was the last day I had been on a horse because it was the day I innocently thought I would be safe walking the short distance home alone.

The horse in front of me is no longer a little timid foal, and it's almost symbolic that I'm no longer that little girl either.

I brush a hand along the champagne colored hair of her long neck and she whinnies in response. "Hey there, beautiful girl, it's been a long time."

Gypsy huffs in response, as though she can understand me, and Wyatt smiles, saying, "She is a sweet girl, just like you. I think she was always meant to be yours, Sweetheart."

I turn wide eyes toward him, the weight of his words sinking in. So many emotions well inside of me, and I can see the emotions whirling within his own eyes before he looks back at Gypsy, patting her gently. "Do you remember how to saddle up?" he asks.

I grin, the nerves dissipating as excitement takes over. "I mean, it's been a while."

His smile widens, and I follow him in the direction of the saddle racks. The familiar sight brings back memories of carefree days spent riding with friends. After pointing out a saddle to me, Wyatt lifts another and walks away with it. I brush a hand over the brown leather of the saddle he indicated – it's beautiful and brand new, as if he knew I would eventually be in this position and got a saddle for me in preparation.

As I start to saddle up Gypsy, the rhythmic routine of tightening the girth, adjusting the stirrups, and securing the reins brings a sense of comfort. It's like reconnecting with a long-lost part of myself. Wyatt returns, a small smile playing on his lips as he watches me.

"You remember well," he comments, and I can't help but feel a surge of pride.

Gypsy stands patiently, as if she senses the significance of the moment. Once the saddle is secure, I run my hand along her neck again, feeling the warmth and strength beneath my fingers.

Wyatt indicates for me to take Gypsy's lead, and we make our way out of the stables into the open land. Wyatt stops, speaking softly to his horse, and then comes around to stand beside me, asking if I'm ready. For a moment, I think he's going to give me a foothold to help me up, but instead, his hands grasp my waist, lifting me into the air until I can swing my leg over Gypsy's back and settle into the saddle.

I shake my head, looking at him with a raised eyebrow. "I could have gotten up myself," I say.

He grins, responding, "But then I wouldn't have been able to get my hands on you." Wyatt then swings himself up into his own saddle. I laugh and suggest that if he wanted to get his hands on me, he could have just made me ride with him.

He takes the reins of his horse, looking at me with a playful expression. "Don't think that didn't cross my mind, but I figured that might be too much just yet."

Gypsy shuffles her feet, and I adjust in the saddle, wincing at the reminder of my soreness. Wyatt notices and frowns, moving his horse closer, asking, "You alright?"

Blushing, I stammer out, "Umm, yes, umm, Easton and I—well, umm," I stumble to a stop when I realize that Wyatt is trying to hold in his laughter. I scowl at him, and he finally lets his laughter out.

"I'm sorry, Sweetheart. I'm not really laughing at you."

He moves his horse even closer, brushing a finger against my blushing cheeks. "I was just thinking that maybe I was wrong, and it wouldn't have been too much at all. So, next time we ride, I want you. On this horse. Sitting in front of me while I rub up against your sweet little ass from behind."

My mouth drops open in shock, and I'm momentarily at a loss for words. Wyatt grins and lifts Gypsy's reins, leading the way as we begin our ride through the open land. The rhythmic sounds of hooves against the ground create a soothing melody, and the wind whispers through the fields.

The horses settle into a steady, soothing pace as we move toward the trails we used to ride as kids. I slowly become more comfortable in the saddle. Wyatt seems content to ride alongside me, letting me go at my own pace as we navigate the familiar trails on his property.

As we traverse the trails, the horses climb small hills and descend into dips, the trees casting dappled shadows on the path. I remember that most parts of the trail will allow us to travel side by side, though there are some areas where it may be too tight. The memories of taking these same trails with the guys flood back, and I feel calmer than I have in a long time.

After a while, I glance at Wyatt to find him quietly watching me out of the corner of his eye, making me smile. Breaking the comfortable silence, I said, "I haven't seen your parents around since I returned."

He gives a small laugh and shakes his head before responding, "Umm yeah, they moved to Florida about the same time as Easton's folks. In all honesty, we felt like there was something going on there, but we never pried." After a moment, he then asks, "How are you feeling? Has the therapy been helping?"

I take a deep breath, appreciating the genuine concern in Wyatt's eyes. "It feels like it is," I reply, my voice soft. "Margot is teaching me methods to deal with my panic attacks, and the nightmares seem to be less frequent the more time passes. There's still a long way to go, but I'm trying to focus on the progress."

Wyatt nods understandingly. "That's good to hear. I hope that you know that we are all here for you. I'm glad you're taking steps towards getting better."

We continue our ride, the trail stretching out ahead of us. The sun casts a warm, golden glow over the landscape as we weave through the trees and open fields.

After a moment of comfortable silence, I speak up. "You know, I'm happy these old trails are still here."

Wyatt looks down at the reins in his hands, a thoughtful expression on his face. "For so many years, I would come out here alone and ride them, I probably wore permanent tracks into the ground. I went through stages of being angry at the world and upset with everyone."

He holds up one of his hands and shows me the scars on his knuckles, his eyes tracing the lines. "There are several trees along this trail that I'm sure still have my skin attached to them. It was either take my frustration out on them or on my remaining friends. But I would always come out here every day without fail because it was where I felt closest to you, to your memory."

Wyatt laughs derisively at himself, a smile playing on his lips. "Inevitably, after I took my emotions out on the trees, I would then imagine you scolding me for being an idiot."

His story tugs at my heart, and I wish I could find the right words to comfort him. After another moment of silence, I gather my courage and start speaking, "I wasn't allowed to talk about my home. They even took away my name. But every night while I was there, I thought about you, Mason, and Gage. It was thoughts of you that kept me going every day."

I keep my gaze in the direction the horses are taking us, but I can feel Wyatt's eyes on me. Taking a deep breath, I continue, "When things got really bad, it was the hope of returning home and seeing all of you that kept me from giving up. If it wasn't for my memories of home, I may not have made it here."

Wyatt looks at me, his expression softening. "Thank you for telling me that, Sweetheart. I hope one day you feel comfortable enough to tell us more." I smile softly in response but don't say anything because, honestly, I don't know when I will be able to talk about it all comfortably.

We ride in silence again and as the trail leads us back to the ranch, I anticipate Wyatt directing us towards the stables. However, to my surprise, he doesn't. Instead, he starts leading our horses toward a rise overlooking the path through the trees to my house.

My heart rate quickens as we get closer, panic clawing at my mind. I know I'm not ready to face the place where I was abducted. Just as I'm about to force out a plea to return to the ranch, we reach the summit of the rise. The view in front of me makes me gasp, distracting me completely from the panic I was experiencing only moments before.

Stretching from the base of the hill we are stopped on until just before the line of trees that marks the edge of my property is a massive field of sunflowers. The vibrant yellow sea of flowers sways gently in the breeze, and the sight is nothing short of breathtaking.

I stare in awe at the beautiful landscape, the panic from earlier now replaced by wonder. The golden glow of the sun casts a warm hue over the sunflowers, creating a picturesque scene that feels like a balm to my soul. The simple beauty of the moment brings a tear to my eye.

Wyatt turns to me in his saddle, watching my face as I take it all in. His voice is soft as he starts speaking again, "We convinced my parents to remove all of those trees within a year. It then took years of me and the guys working on that section of land before we could plant the first sunflower. They all bloomed early not long after you returned."

His words resonate deeply, and my eyes scan the endless field of sunflowers below. The effort and dedication it took to transform that space into a breathtaking sea of golden blooms speaks volumes about the love and friendship that have surrounded me, even in my absence.

Tears shimmer in my eyes as I take in the beauty before me. Wyatt moves closer, his hand reaching out to gently brush away a tear that has escaped my eye. "I don't want to see you ever shed a tear for anything but happiness from now on," he says, his voice filled with command as though simply by saying it that it will be so.

"I'll do my best," I whisper, a small smile playing on my lips.

With a final pat on Gypsy's mane, he gestures towards the trail leading back to the ranch. Wyatt leads us toward the stables, and we dismount. Gypsy seems content, her presence a reassuring anchor. Wyatt takes the reins, and I follow him into the stables. The scent of hay and the soft sounds of other horses create a serene atmosphere.

Wyatt shows me how to carefully brush Gypsy's coat, explaining the importance of maintaining her grooming routine for both her health and our bond. As I run the brush through

Gypsy's mane, Wyatt's voice is a comforting presence, guiding me through each stroke and movement.

After the grooming session, Wyatt takes a bale of hay and shows me how to feed Gypsy. He explains the proper way to offer the hay and allows me to take the lead. Gypsy eagerly nibbles at the hay, and the simple act brings me joy.

As we finish caring for Gypsy, Wyatt turns to me. "You did great, Sweetheart. You're welcome back to spend time with her anytime you want," he says, his smile telling me that it's not just Gypsy he wants me to see.

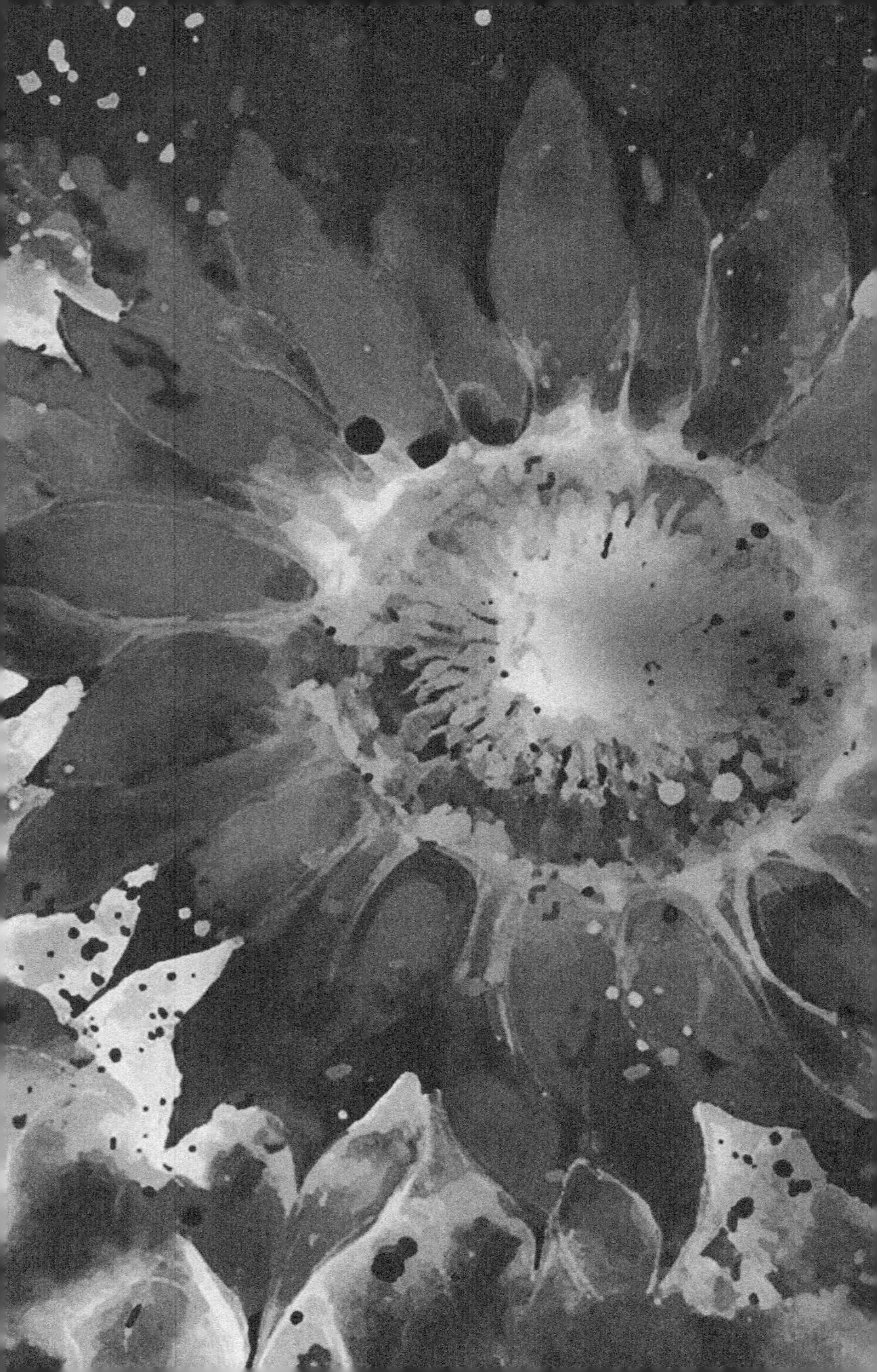

CHAPTER 32

Willow

We can see Mason and Easton deep in a whispered conversation as we approach the main house. They are standing on the front porch while Bryce plays with his toy trucks close by.

As we draw closer to the main house, Bryce spots us from a distance. His eyes light up with excitement, and he immediately drops his toy trucks, calling out, "Dadda, Miss Willow!" His tiny figure dashes towards us, his laughter echoing through the air.

A wide grin spreads across Wyatt's face. "There's my little man!" he exclaims. Bryce reaches us, and Wyatt scoops him up in his arms, swinging him around. "Did you have fun with your trucks, buddy?"

Bryce nods enthusiastically, his eyes sparkling with joy. "Trucks go vroom-vroom!"

Wyatt chuckles, ruffling Bryce's hair. "That's right. Vroom-vroom indeed."

Mason and Easton, who had been engrossed in their hushed conversation, look up and smile at the sight of us approaching. When we join them on the verandah I can't help but ask, "What's all the whispering about, guys?"

Mason exchanges a glance with Easton before responding, "Oh, nothing important. Just discussing plans for lunch."

I raise an eyebrow, sensing there might be more to their conversation than they're letting on. But instead of pressing, I play along and grin. "And what's on the menu for lunch, Chef Mason?"

Mason feigns a look of exasperation. "You've spoiled her, Easton. She's gotten used to being pampered with food."

Easton laughs, nodding in agreement. "Guilty as charged. We were thinking of heading into town and grabbing lunch at the pizzeria. How does that sound?"

The mention of pizza makes my stomach growl, and I glance at Bryce, who seems equally excited. "Pizza sounds fantastic," I reply.

Easton grins mischievously. "Well, you know, just in case you have a sweet tooth," he glances at Bryce and whispers, "there is an ice cream parlor next to it and someone is a big fan of ice cream."

Bryce's eyes widen, and he shouts, "Ice cream!" right next to my ear. I burst into laughter, and Wyatt chuckles, holding Bryce close. "Looks like we have a unanimous vote for pizza and ice cream."

With our lunch plans settled, Easton and I decide to head into town in his SUV, while Wyatt, Mason, and Bryce take Wyatt's truck. The town appears busier than I expected, but Easton skillfully finds a parking spot just outside the bank. I glance around, wondering where Wyatt parked his truck, but my attention is quickly drawn back to Easton as he locks the car and takes my hand.

As we stroll down the street, I finally see the others are waiting outside the pizzeria, leaning casually against the wall. They spot us, and Bryce's face lights up. He wiggles out of Wyatt's arms and runs towards us, yelling, "Miss Willow! Uncle Easton! Pizza!" His enthusiasm is infectious, and I can't help but smile.

The usual lunch rush has subsided, making the restaurant quieter than usual. A delightful aroma of pizza wafts through the air, making my stomach growl again. We all enter the pizzeria together, the smell of melting cheese and fresh dough growing stronger. The restaurant is decorated with rustic charm, and we find a large booth close to the window. Bryce eagerly climbs onto the seat next to me.

The waitress hands us menus, and I glance down at the extensive list of pizza options. Wyatt leans in, whispering to me, "Bryce can't read it, he already knows he wants the pepperoni pizza." I chuckle and play along, helping Bryce look at the menu with great seriousness.

As we wait for the waitress to take our orders, I sense someone slide into the booth on Mason's other side. I turn to find Gage grinning at us. "Hey, I thought you were working," I say in surprise.

Gage scoffs, shaking his head. "Like I was going to miss out on pizza. The bar is fine in the hands of my manager."

I laugh at his response. "I'm happy you could join us." He smiles fondly at me in return.

The waitress arrives to take our orders, and Mason, Easton, and Wyatt each order their preferred pizzas. When she turns to Bryce, he proudly declares, "Pepperoni pizza!" The waitress smiles and jots it down.

With the orders placed, the conversation flows effortlessly. We share stories, laughter, and even some playful banter. Bryce, now content that his choice is on the way, entertains himself by stacking sugar packets into a tower.

The pizzas arrive, and the scent is divine. Wyatt helps Bryce with his slice, making sure the pepperoni is evenly distributed. The first bite is met with a delighted, "Mmm, yummy!" from Bryce.

We all take our time enjoying the delicious pizza, savoring each bite in between conversations. The atmosphere is filled with laughter and camaraderie. As we share stories, I notice Bryce happily munching on his pepperoni pizza, occasionally stealing a glance at the tower of sugar packets he created, making sure none of us knocks it down.

Hours pass, and the waitress, noticing Bryce's restlessness, kindly brings him a coloring book and a set of colored pencils. He eagerly dives into the world of coloring, showing me his artistic talents every once in a while, his sugar tower now forgotten.

The waitress brings us more drinks, and we even decide to order another round of pizza, our appetite returning.

Amid the casual banter, Mason turns to me, his eyes curious. "Have you given any thought to whether you want to work or study now that you have the freedom to do so?" The others seem genuinely interested in my response.

I take a moment to reflect, admitting, "I've given it a little thought, but with my panic attacks, it might be challenging to work in a typical setting like a store. The smallest things could trigger me." I pause, gathering my thoughts. "I've thought about finding ways to help others who are struggling like me. Maybe, once I get better at art again, I could offer art lessons."

Wyatt nods and suggests, "Maybe once you find your rhythm with Gypsy, you could offer horse therapy to others. It might be a way for you to help people while doing something you love."

I smile appreciatively at the suggestion. "That's a great idea, Wyatt. I'll definitely look into it. But honestly, I don't feel pressured to find a job right away. My parents left me enough money to last for a while."

They all nod understandingly, accepting my decision. Changing the subject, I turn to Gage. "How's the bar going now that it's been open for a few weeks?"

Gage grins, leaning back in his seat. "It's going well. The locals seem to love it, and we've had some good crowds. The live music nights have been a hit. I'm thinking of expanding the menu soon."

As we continue talking I notice Bryce tugging at Wyatt's shirt, a pout on his face. "I thought we were getting ice cream," he says, his eyes wide with expectation.

Wyatt chuckles, ruffling Bryce's hair.

Before Wyatt can respond, Gage and Mason slide out of the booth, a mischievous gleam in their eyes. "Don't you worry, buddy. We've got it covered."

Mason turns to me with a grin. "Willow, any particular flavor?"

I consider it for a moment, then respond, "Surprise me."

With that, Gage and Mason exit the pizzeria, and through the glass window, we watch them walk next door to the ice cream parlor. It's only when I look outside that I realize the afternoon has given way to nighttime. The soft glow of streetlights illuminates the town.

Turning back to join in the conversation with Easton and Wyatt, we chat while we wait for the ice cream. Time passes quickly, and soon, Gage and Mason return, sliding back into the booth. Mason holds out an ice cream cone to me, a mischievous smile on his face. "Sweets for our sweets."

I giggle, taking the ice cream cone from him. The first lick of the peanut butter-flavored treat has me even happier. I look at Mason in surprise. "I'm surprised you remembered!"

He grins, leaning back in his seat. "Of course I remembered. How could I ever forget anything about you?"

The ice cream is the perfect sweet ending to our delightful evening. We continue chatting, enjoying the time together. The laughter and easy banter make it feel like we were never apart.

Bryce, his energy waning, soon curls up with his head on my lap and starts to drift to sleep. Wyatt decides it's time to call it a night. Gage takes care of paying for our dinner, a kind gesture that I appreciate. Wyatt gently gathers Bryce into his arms, being careful not to wake him.

As we leave, Mason and Wyatt brush kisses against my cheek, wishing me a good night's sleep. Gage offers to walk us to Easton's car since it's on the way to the bar and his apartment above it.

The street is mostly empty, and we chat casually until we're almost at Easton's SUV. It's then that I notice something wrong. All of the tires are flat. Gage murmurs for me to stay on the sidewalk as he and Easton investigate further.

When they return, they have frowns on their faces. "They've all been slashed," Easton says, frustration evident in his voice.

I spot a uniformed police officer not too far away, and it takes me a moment to recognize her as Heidi Beck. Nudging Gage, I motion in her direction, and he calls out to her.

"Heidi!"

She turns in our direction, an instant smile on her face as she starts walking towards Gage. However, the moment her eyes slide across to see me, it disappears, replaced by a scowl as she stops walking.

Gage raises an eyebrow at her, but Easton cuts straight to the point. "We need to report a crime," he says, motioning towards his vandalized vehicle.

Heidi looks between us and then to the tires. To my shock, she says, "I don't see anything wrong here."

My mouth drops open in astonishment, and Easton, understandably furious, retorts, "You're fucking kidding me, right?"

Heidi then looks over her shoulder, and I see Loretta exiting her store and locking it up. Heidi calls out to Loretta, "Hey Lo, do you see anything wrong?" Loretta looks in our direction and then returns to locking up, calling out, "The only thing wrong I see is two handsome men playing with trash."

Gage growls, stepping toward them, but Heidi laughs and turns her back on us to walk back over to Loretta as she finishes locking her store. I place a hand on Gage's arm and murmur to him, "It's fine, just leave it."

We watch the two women walk away, and Easton kicks one of his tires, slapping a hand down on the hood of the SUV.

Gage sighs and turns toward him, saying, "Look, there isn't much to be done about it tonight. Come to the bar, and I'll drive you both home."

I smile, linking my arm with Gage's and hoping to distract them. "Why don't you stay over?"

Gage looks at me, raising an eyebrow as he smirks. "Really?"

I turn my smile toward Easton and then back at Gage. "Sure, it's been a long time since we had a slumber party."

Easton grins, coming over to link his arm with mine on my other side. We walk further down the street to get to Gage's car. He pumps the music loudly on the way back to my house, and we all sing along badly to the songs.

It doesn't take long before we're pulling into the driveway. Gage tries to rush around to open my door for me, but Easton, sitting behind me, beats him to it. They playfully tease each other as I walk past them towards the front door. My laughter fades when I see my entryway and I stop dead in my tracks, with my keys in hand.

Someone is screaming, and it takes a moment before I realize that it's me. There's a large image pinned to my front door—the image of Easton kissing me against his SUV that morning. A knife is sticking into the image of Easton, and something red and dripping is spread all over my entryway. One word is painted in red above where the image is stuck:

Mine.

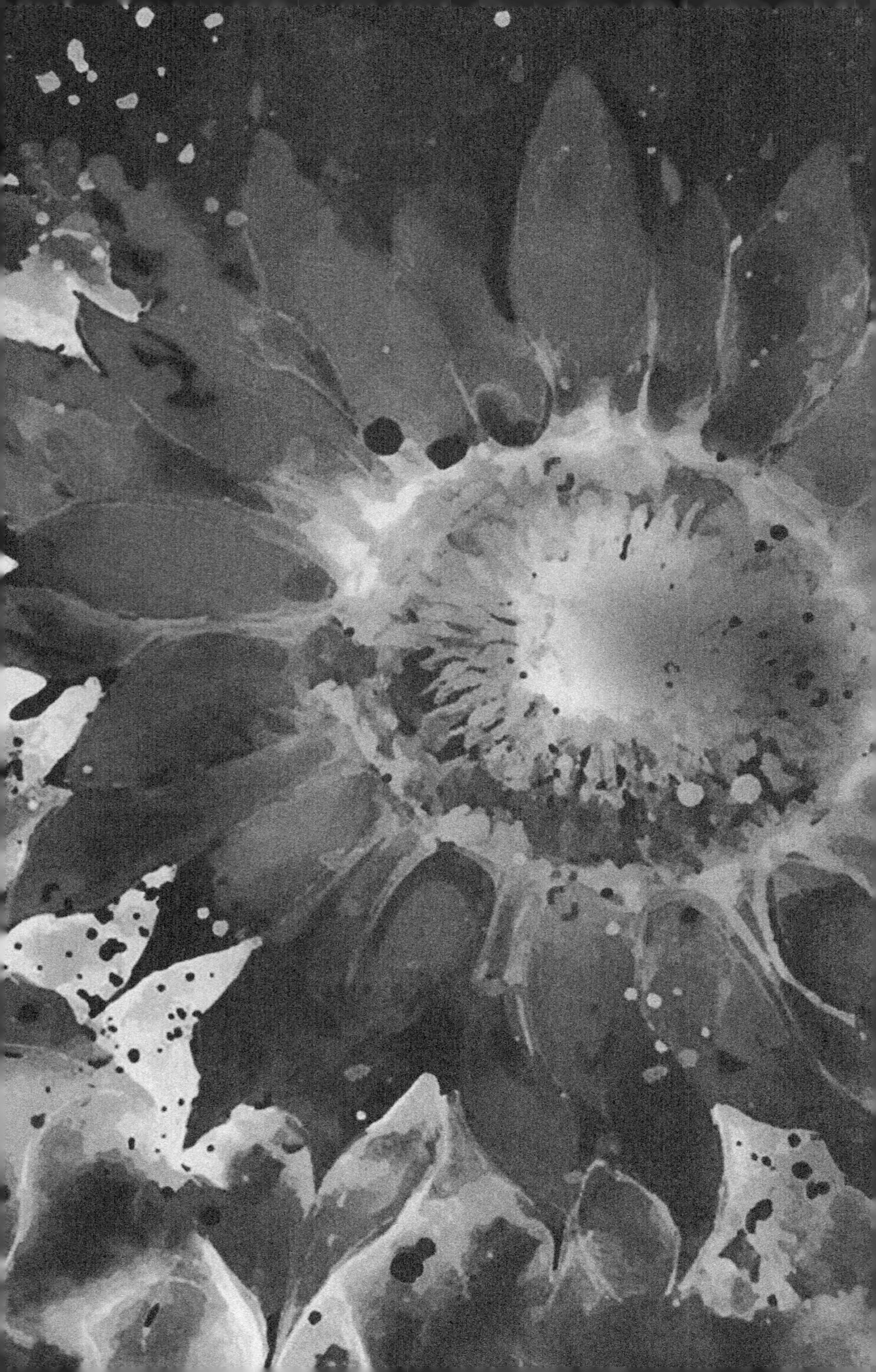

CHAPTER 33
Unknown

A warning, perhaps, though they may not fully grasp its implications.

I had watched the knife go into the photo with such glee. I wasn't the one who did it though, I wouldn't want my fingerprints on the evidence. But I doubted it would make it into police custody, they were understandably cautious of the police, not that I blamed them.

I reveled in the moment of chaos I witnessed. Her screams echoed and the blood practically drained from her face.

Maybe now she would see she doesn't belong in Sierra Valley.

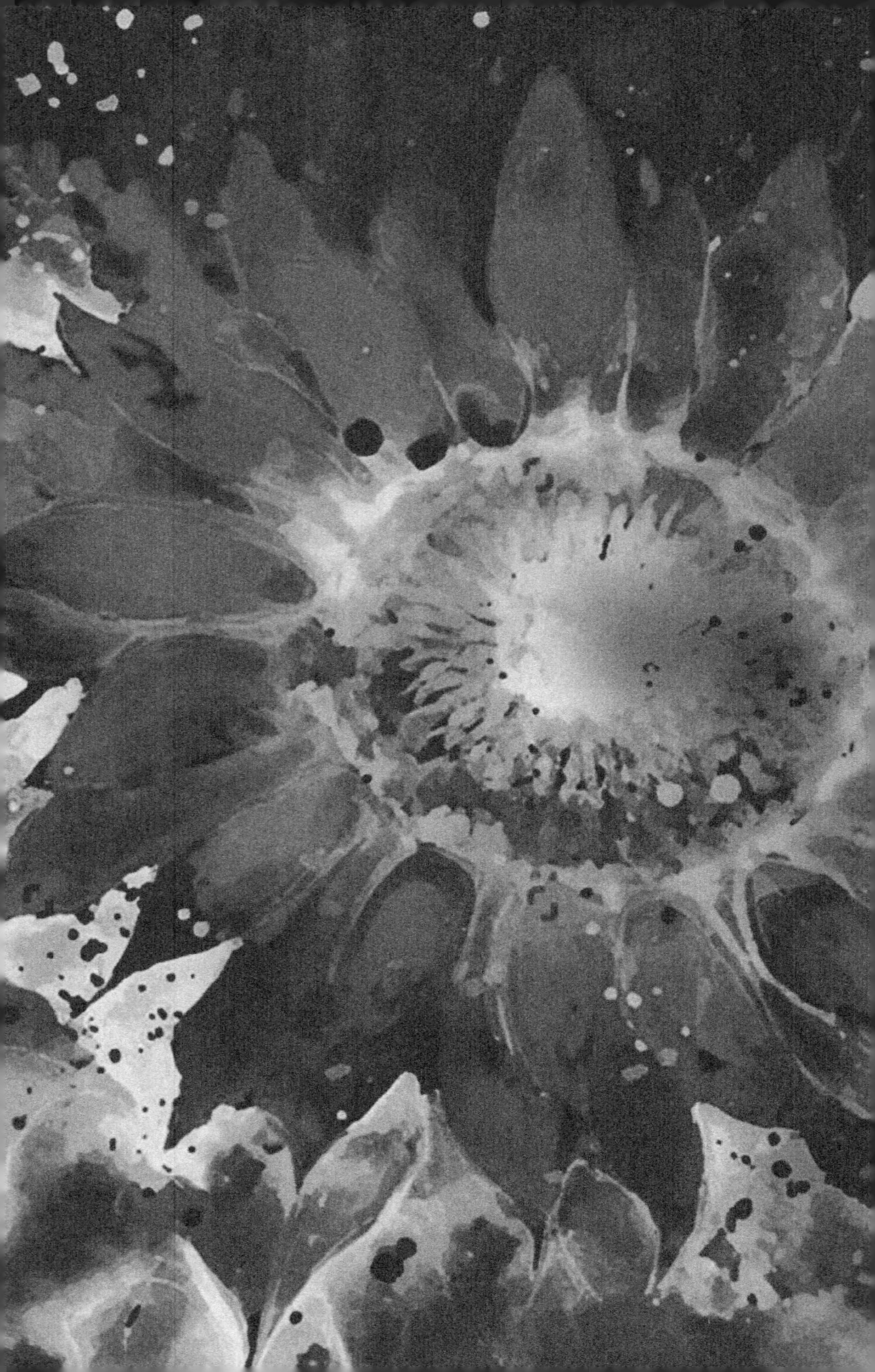

CHAPTER 34

Willow

I have no recollection of how I ended up back in Gage's car.

It takes me a moment to register that we are no longer in my driveway but somewhere at the side of the road near Wyatt's driveway. Easton has my hands pressed against his chest as he keeps telling me to please breathe with him. Gage is turned in his seat, assuring me that I'm safe now and no one is going to get to me with them there.

Easton's soothing voice helps ground me and I try to take deep breaths, hoping to shake off the overwhelming panic and fear.

Gage's voice breaks through the haze. "Willow, look at me. You're safe. We won't let anything happen to you."

I nod, focusing on the sincerity in his eyes. Easton continues to guide me through calming breaths, his touch gentle yet firm.

"Willow," Easton's voice is steady, "I want you to tell me what you see right now. Look around and describe it to me."

I glance around, the night air cool against my skin. "We're by the side of the road, near Wyatt's driveway. There are trees and darkness."

"Good. Now, what do you smell?" Easton prompts.

I take in a deep breath, trying to focus on my surroundings. "I smell... your cologne, it's something that smells like spice."

"Excellent. And what do you feel?" he asks, his hands still on mine.

"I feel... I feel the car seat beneath me, and your hands on mine. I feel grounded," I reply, the panic slowly subsiding.

"Good, still tell me what you taste right now," he prompts.

I take a moment to concentrate and then my mind wants to take me back to our dinner earlier, to a happier moment. "Pizza."

Easton nods approvingly. "Now, let's take a few more deep breaths together. In... and out. In... and out."

We continue the rhythmic breathing, and with each breath, the tightness in my chest begins to loosen. Gage's assurances and Easton's guidance help me regain control over my emotions.

Once I'm calm again, Gage starts the car and drives down the long driveway of Wyatt's ranch. The ranch is quiet, bathed in the soft glow of moonlight.

Easton helps me out of the car, his touch lingering to offer support.

As we approach the main house, Gage opens the door without knocking, leading us inside. Easton is still rubbing his hands up and down my trembling arms when Wyatt steps into the foyer, drawn by the noise.

Concern lines Wyatt's face as he takes in the scene. "What happened?"

Gage, his expression firm, responds, "Someone vandalized Willow's property. Where is Mason, he can come with us to help deal with it and check her house."

Mason emerges from the hallway that leads to the living room as though summoned, his brows furrowed in concern. Easton turns to Wyatt, a request in his eyes.

"Can you look after Willow, Wyatt?" Easton asks, his voice calm yet urgent. "Can she stay here tonight?"

Mason's frown deepens as he hears the conversation. "Did I hear you say someone vandalized Willow's place?" he inquires.

I find my voice, albeit a little shaky. "It was Jacob," I murmur.

Wyatt's head turns to mine straight away, his eyes searching. "What did you just say?" he asks.

I repeat, a little louder this time, "It was Jacob. He found me."

There's a moment of stunned silence. Mason and Gage exchange a glance before walking out without another word. Easton brushes a gentle kiss against my temple and whispers, "You're safe here with Wyatt. He will protect you. We'll take care of your house." With that, he, too, walks out the front door, leaving Wyatt to continue frowning at me.

He breaks the silence, his voice a mix of concern and curiosity. "How do you know it was Jacob?"

As I think back on it, anger starts to simmer instead of the panic from moments before. "There was a knife through a photo of Easton kissing me," I explain, my voice steadier. "And he wrote 'Mine' on my door."

Wyatt's eyes narrow at my words and I can see anger enter them. "How did he even find you here?" he asks, his voice low.

Frustration bubbles up within me, and I can't contain it any longer. "How the fuck should I know?" I snap back, my voice rising. The fear has transformed into anger, a fiery determination to confront the threat that is ruining my life just when I thought I was free.

Wyatt pauses for a moment, his gaze distant as he seems to be listening for something. I remember too late that Bryce would be sleeping. Without a word, he grabs my hand, and before I know it, he is pulling me past the living room and toward the back of the house. I'm caught off guard, and my pulse quickens as he guides me into a bedroom, swiftly turning to close the door behind us.

With a growl, Wyatt starts to pace the room, his frustration palpable. He stops and turns to me, his expression intense. "How the hell did this happen? Easton told us the feds were making it look like you went with them!"

His revelation is news to me, but instead of soothing my anger, it adds fuel to the fire. I retort, "You think I chose for this to happen? Do you think I want to be scared for my life? For the lives of the people I care most about?"

Wyatt's jaw tightens as he absorbs my words, frustration evident in his own expression. The room feels charged with the intensity of our emotions, the anger and frustration increasing with each passing second. My own feeling of helplessness just feeds the new fire burning inside me.

Wyatt's frustration reaches a breaking point, and he takes a step closer to me, his hands flexing at his sides. "I do love you, Willow, but right now I hate you for bringing this into our lives."

His words hit me like a slap, and the room seems to spin. I can't believe he just said that. Anguish and hurt well up inside me, and without thinking, I scream at him, "I didn't ask for any of this! I didn't ask to be abducted by them or for that sadistic asshole to assault me for six fucking years!"

Wyatt's expression hardens, and he retaliates, "You chose to come back home, knowing he might follow. You brought this threat into my son's life! You being here is a threat to him!"

My defiance flares up, and I lift my chin, staring him down. "I came back for you, you fucking asshole! But if you want me gone, then I'm fucking gone."

In a surge of frustration and determination, I storm over to the bedroom door, fully intending to leave and walk myself off his property. However, I'm shocked when Wyatt's hands spin me around, and he shoves me back against the door. He gets in my face, growling, "I'm allowed to hate you and still never want you to leave me again."

Before I can respond, his lips crash into mine. His hands are hard as they hold me in place. Everything about him suddenly takes over all of my senses—the taste of his kiss, the scent of his cologne, the feel of his touch. The fire inside me is now raging out of control, but it's no longer just anger; arousal makes my whole body throb.

We are both panting for air when he finally releases my lips. "Tell me you want me. Tell me this is okay, that you need me as much as I need you. I want to bury myself inside you so badly and erase everything that sick fuck did to you."

I let out a breathless chuckle. "I thought you hated me."

He growls in response, "That doesn't change the fact that you're mine."

I shouldn't be feeling so turned on. I had only just had sex for the first time the night before, and with a completely different man. But at that moment, I want Wyatt with a desperation that should shock me.

We tear at each other's clothes, and I hear something tear before suddenly his mouth is on my breast. The intensity of the moment takes over, drowning out everything else.

I've already got his belt and jeans open when he drops down and yanks my own jeans down my legs, quickly pulling them fully off before standing again and lifting me up by the backs of my thighs. I wrap my legs around him as he pauses, his cock right at the entrance to my pussy, and he growls, "Do I need protection?"

I barely get out, "I'm covered and clean," before he's buried to the hilt inside me with one hard thrust. I cry out and dig my nails into the flesh of his shoulders. Wyatt is larger than Easton was, and as turned on as I am, it still hurts. My body is already still getting over the night before. Wyatt must see the discomfort on my face, and his muscles flex as he holds himself still to let me adjust. He groans and rests his forehead against mine, breathing out, "Fuck, you feel better than I imagined."

He slides a hand between our bodies, and his fingers find my clit. Pleasure suddenly competes with the pain, and I moan as he takes that as his cue to start moving again. He draws his cock almost all the way out of me and thrusts back in, his hand leaving my clit to dig into the flesh of my ass to hold me at just the right angle. The door at my back rattles with each powerful thrust.

The sensations are overwhelming—pain, pleasure, and the undeniable connection between us. I arch into him, my body responding to his with a desperate need. Wyatt's movements become more urgent, each thrust pushing me closer to the edge. He kisses me fiercely, as if trying to consume my very soul, and my hands clutch at his shoulders, my nails leaving marks.

"Tell me you need me." he repeats in a whisper against my lips, his voice husky with desire. "Tell me you need me as much as I need you."

I gasp, my body responding to his, tightening around him as the pleasure builds inside of me. "I need you," I moan, the admission coming out in a breathy whisper.

His movements suddenly slow. "Louder," he demands, his eyes locking onto mine.

"I need you," I reply, my voice stronger this time, a mixture of defiance and desire.

Wyatt smirks, the satisfaction evident in his gaze. "That's my girl," he growls. He pulls out of me suddenly and I'm left whimpering at the loss. Lifting me higher in his arms he carries me over to the bed and then after shuffling on his knees toward the center he drops me down onto my back.

My breath stutters when I'm suddenly flipped over onto my stomach. His strong hands dig into my flesh and drag my ass into the air seconds before he is buried inside me again.

Suddenly, Wyatt freezes, his breath escaping in a shocked rush. I feel his fingers softly brushing against the mess of scars on my back, and a wave of panic washes over me. The memories of being violated and scarred in a similar position by Jacob come rushing back, threatening to overwhelm my senses.

Just as the panic threatens to consume me, Wyatt leans over my back, wrapping his hand around my throat from behind. He pulls me upright until I'm straddling his thighs, his cock still buried deep inside me. His other hand returns to my clit, his voice whispering harshly into my ear. "If I ever get my hands on that sick bastard, I'm going to repay him for each and every mark he put on your body. I'm going to cut the skin from his body as he begs you for forgiveness."

Unbeknownst to him, his actions and words act as a distraction, pulling me away from the brink of a panic attack. The imagery of his words are violent and disturbing, and everything I didn't realize I needed.

Then, Wyatt lets go of my throat, and his hands move to my waist, lifting me and turning me back around until I'm hovering over his cock again. "I need you facing me, or I'm going to go and hunt him down. Ride me, sweetheart," he commands.

He slowly lowers me back down, and I can feel him everywhere, his cock filling me so completely. I arch my back, attempting to use my knees to move on him, but frustration builds, and I growl before leaning back further with my hands on the bed. I move my feet until they are planted behind him, gaining the leverage to raise my body up and drop back down onto him with a moan.

The pleasure intensifies as I revel in the control Wyatt allows me to have. I continue to lift and drop down onto him, feeling his hands on my hips, guiding and encouraging my movements. When I shift my hips, he groans, and I take that as a sign to do it again. I swirl my hips, savoring the sounds he makes in response.

After the third time, with him groaning and pleasure building inside me, Wyatt takes back the control. His fingers dig into my hips, and he lifts me up before pulling my body back down as he thrusts up. Our bodies slap together, sending a ripple of intense pleasure through my body. The room is filled with the sounds of our moans, groans and our bodies colliding.

I surrender to the sensations. The earlier argument and frustration are temporarily forgotten, replaced by the overwhelming need for each other. In this moment, nothing else matters but the fire that consumes us.

The pleasure builds with each thrust, each movement driving me closer to the edge again. As Wyatt's movements become more urgent, I can feel the escalating tension within me, the heat spiraling to an almost unbearable level. I meet his gaze, and in his eyes, I see a mix of possessiveness, passion, and a raw need that mirrors my own.

My body moves in rhythm with Wyatt's, our connection deepening with every thrust and grind. The pleasure reaches new heights with each collision of our bodies. My moans blend with his in an erotic soundtrack that fills the room.

He returns one of his hands to my clit as the pace quickens, and the pleasure becomes more intense. I feel the tightening in my pussy, and I recognize the signs of my impending release. Wyatt's groans grow more primal, and the rhythm has me teetering on the edge of an intense climax.

His thrusts become erratic before pleasure explodes within me, radiating through every nerve and fiber of my being. My body arches, and I cry out, lost in the euphoria of the moment. Wyatt's own release follows, and we ride the waves of ecstasy together.

As we catch our breath, Wyatt eases me down onto the bed, our bodies still entwined. The room is filled with a lingering heat and for a moment, there's a sense of peace, a brief respite from the chaos that has intruded into our lives.

Wyatt's fingers gently trace the contours of my face, and his gaze is tender. In this moment, the connection we share feels unbreakable.

As reality begins to seep back in, Wyatt presses a gentle kiss to my forehead. "I hate that you're in danger, Willow. But I can't deny how much I need you. We'll figure this out together."

I nod, the weight of the situation not lost on me. "I'm sorry, Wyatt. I never wanted to bring danger to your doorstep."

He sighs, his thumb caressing my cheek. "I know, sweetheart. We'll face whatever comes our way. You're not alone in this."

I can't bring myself to move from the shelter of Wyatt's arms, hoping that the strength of my connection with these men will be enough to weather the storm that looms on the horizon.

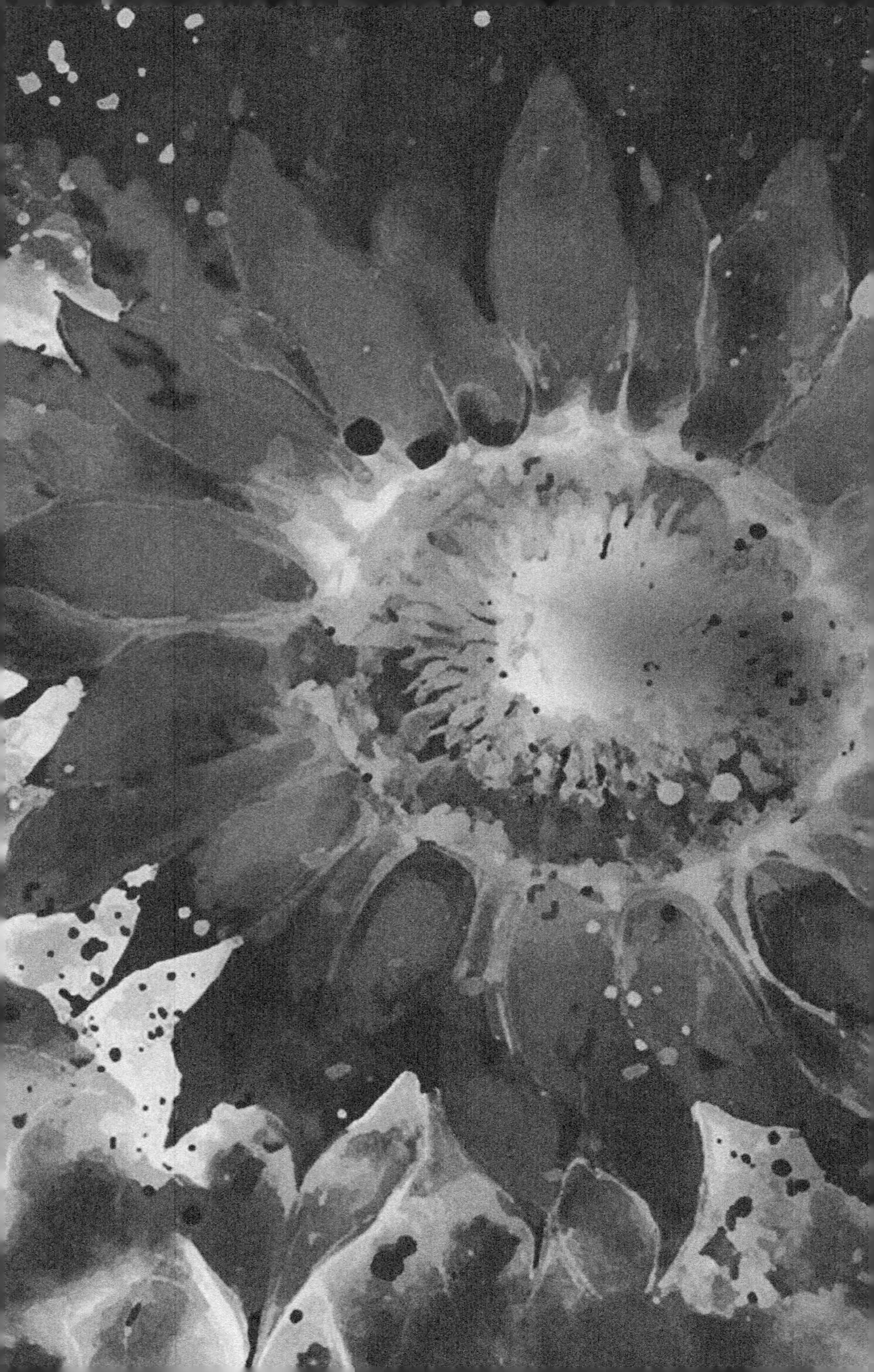

CHAPTER 35

Willow

The soft light filtering through the room pulls me from a deep sleep, but as my senses return, I feel the restrictive embrace of arms around me. My body tenses, and my breath catches at the thought of Jacob finding me.

Some instinctual noise must escape me because, in an instant, Wyatt rolls me over to face him. His wide blue eyes meet mine as he cups my face with his hands, his voice a soothing balm. "Hey, sweetheart, it's just me. You're safe."

His words penetrate the lingering fog of fear, and I take a moment to ground myself in the present. The panic begins to recede as I focus on Wyatt's steady gaze and the warmth of his touch.

I manage a small nod, my voice a whisper, "I know. Thank you."

Wyatt's thumb strokes my cheek gently, his touch reassuring. "Take your time. You're safe here."

The remnants of the panic starts to fade, and I allow myself to fully take in the reality of the moment. I was still at Wyatt's, in his room. In his bed. The room is bathed in a soft morning glow, and now that my body and mind were calming down, I hear movement somewhere else in the house.

My eyes widen slightly at the memory of us having sex last night, and Wyatt chuckles, a deep, masculine sound that resonates through the room. "There you are," he says, brushing his lips against mine. "Good morning, Sweetheart."

The panic has fully receded now. I become more conscious of our entwined bodies, the soft sheets beneath us, and the fact that we are both naked. Wyatt's thumb continues to stroke my cheek, a gesture that feels both tender and grounding.

The sounds of movement from elsewhere in the house become more pronounced, reminding me that we are not alone. Wyatt seems unfazed, his attention focused solely on me. His fingers trail down from my face to gently brush a strand of hair behind my ear.

"Sleep okay?" he asks, his voice a low murmur that carries genuine concern.

I nod, a small smile playing on my lips. "Yeah, surprisingly well."

He grins, a mischievous glint in his eyes. "Must be my charm."

I playfully roll my eyes, feeling a lightness in the air that I hadn't expected.

Wyatt shifts slightly, releasing my face but staying close. I sit up, drawing the sheets around me and Wyatt watches me with a warmth in his eyes that makes my heart flutter. "We should probably get up," he suggests, his tone reluctant.

He sits up and kisses my shoulder, his lips warm against my skin. "I don't want to leave this bed with you," he murmurs..

A small smile tugs at the corners of my lips. "I know," I reply, understanding the sentiment.

Wyatt slides out of bed, and I can't help but appreciate the view of his naked ass as he walks toward his closet. After a few moments, he reappears with jeans pulled up but left open, and more clothes in his hands. He approaches me, handing over a long black shirt and my jeans. I realize he must have picked them up at some point during the night.

I slide off the bed, the cool air of the room hitting my skin. As I begin to pull on my clothes, Wyatt, now dressed in a navy blue shirt, watches me with a warmth in his gaze. Once I'm dressed, he takes my hand, and we head out of the room and toward the kitchen.

The sounds emanating from the kitchen are lively and chaotic, a stark contrast to the quiet of Wyatt's room. Laughter and conversation fill the air, and I can't help but feel a little nervous about facing the others after the events of the previous night.

As we enter the kitchen, the group falls into a momentary hush, eyes turning toward us.

Bryce's excited voice breaks the silence, "Dadda! Miss Willow!" He waves his spoon enthusiastically, cereal bits flying around.

I turn to see Bryce at the dining table preparing to hop down and come over to us. Mason, who is at the stove, points his spatula at him, "No, stay in your seat and eat your breakfast."

Feeling a pang of sympathy, I walk over, ruffling Bryce's hair as he tries to pick up the pieces of cereal he accidentally sent flying, and gently kissing the top of his head. "Good morning, little man."

Wyatt follows me over, a strange look briefly crossing his face, but he quickly shakes it off to greet his son. "Hey, buddy, good morning." Wyatt tousles Bryce's hair with a grin.

I walk back toward the kitchen, and Easton hops down from his stool at the kitchen island and draws me into his arms. He pulls back after a moment and uses a hand under my chin to raise my head up to meet his lips. The kiss is soft and slow, making my cheeks burn, guilt starts to creep in as I remember how intimate I've now been with both Easton and Wyatt. Easton lets me go, and I step back, glancing at Wyatt who has come up beside us.

Easton grins at Wyatt, saying, "I know I asked you to look after her, but that wasn't exactly what I meant."

Wyatt gives Easton a playful hit on the chest, "Hey, don't make her feel bad."

Easton, looking chagrined, turns to me, "Sorry, little butterfly. I was just joking. We're all totally fine with you being with whoever you want to."

Observing the dynamics, I notice Mason flipping pancakes on the stove, Gage carrying a carton of juice toward the kitchen island. Everyone is seemingly at ease with the situation. I walk into the kitchen, brushing a kiss against Mason's cheek, receiving a grin in response. Then, I move to Gage and do the same. He captures my hand when I go to pull away and brushes a kiss against the back of my hand before placing a glass of juice into it.

Taking a sip, I put the glass back down and clear my throat. "I think maybe we all need to have a conversation."

Gage frowns, his expression turning serious. "About last night or something else?"

I look down at my glass of juice, gathering some courage before speaking again. "Yes, and yes. I mean, we should talk about last night, but I think I'm ready to, maybe try to tell you about the rest of it too."

The room falls silent, the only sound is Bryce chattering away to himself at the dining table. I hear the stove being turned off, and a hand moves my glass away from where my fingers are tapping against it without me realizing. I look up, and Mason is in front of me, a concerned look on his face.

He gently asks, "Are you sure, Willow?"

I take a deep breath and nod, appreciating the concern in his eyes. "Yeah, I think it's time. You all deserve to know everything, especially after what happened last night."

Wyatt breaks the moment of silence, his voice calm and determined. "I'll go set Bryce up with a movie, and we can go sit on the porch to talk." He moves over to his son, lifting him up and carrying him out of the room. Easton walks over, picking up the discarded bowl and cereal, passing Gage on the way back as he heads to the table with a cloth. They seem like a well-oiled machine.

"You, ahh, have that routine down," I comment, trying to lighten the atmosphere.

Gage chuckles and responds, "That's because we do it all the time. Well, Easton not so much over the last couple of years, but I'm always over here." He grins at me as he takes the cloth to the sink to wash it out, and Wyatt returns.

The pancakes that were cooking have been covered and set aside, and Mason takes my hand as we follow Wyatt out to the porch. We walk along it until we reach the outdoor couches, and I sit down, trying to get comfortable. The seating is facing toward the rise leading to my house, and now all that comes to mind at the thought of that is the sunflowers that they planted there.

Easton takes the seat beside me, a silent gesture of support, and holds my hand. Wyatt, sitting on my other side, encourages me, "Take your time, Sweetheart."

I take a deep breath, looking toward the rise, reminding myself that in order to make progress, it doesn't matter how big the steps I take are as long as I'm taking them, and it's my choice. I glance back at each of them before I start speaking.

"I still remember the last day I was here," I begin. "It was the last day I felt any happiness until the day I was kneeling in the dirt where Easton found me."

I pause, trying to find the right words to express the harrowing memories. "I don't remember much about being taken or anything until I woke up tied up in a cold room. There were two adults there, and they told me they were my parents now and that my name is Grace. They said they had saved me from a life of sin."

My voice trembles, recalling the trauma. "They didn't care that I was screaming. They didn't care that I said my name was Willow and that they couldn't just take me and rename me. They stripped my clothes off me until I was naked and took everything away from me and burned it. Then they scrubbed my body, claiming that they would get rid of all of my impurities."

I continue my story, the memories surfacing with each word. "I screamed and cried so much at the start. You knew what I was like back then. I wasn't just going to roll over and play dead right away. I screamed so loudly; I was surprised that the police never came to investigate. But then Mother took me out of my room and up onto the roof of the building I was being kept in. That was when I saw that there was no one that was going to help. There were no other buildings as far as my eyes could see."

I feel a lump in my throat as I recall that moment of despair. "Then she walked me back down into what was essentially my cell and made me kneel on the ground with my head bent over. She struck me across the back of my neck with a leather strap."

The air on the porch becomes heavy as the weight of those memories settles in. Easton squeezes my hand reassuringly, a silent encouragement to continue.

"It wasn't the only time I was struck with it, just the first because I couldn't stop myself from telling them my name wasn't Grace, that my name was Willow," I confess. "I did give up on screaming and crying, though. At that point, I knew it was useless, and no one was going to come and save me. They just took that as a sign that I was going to start doing what I was told."

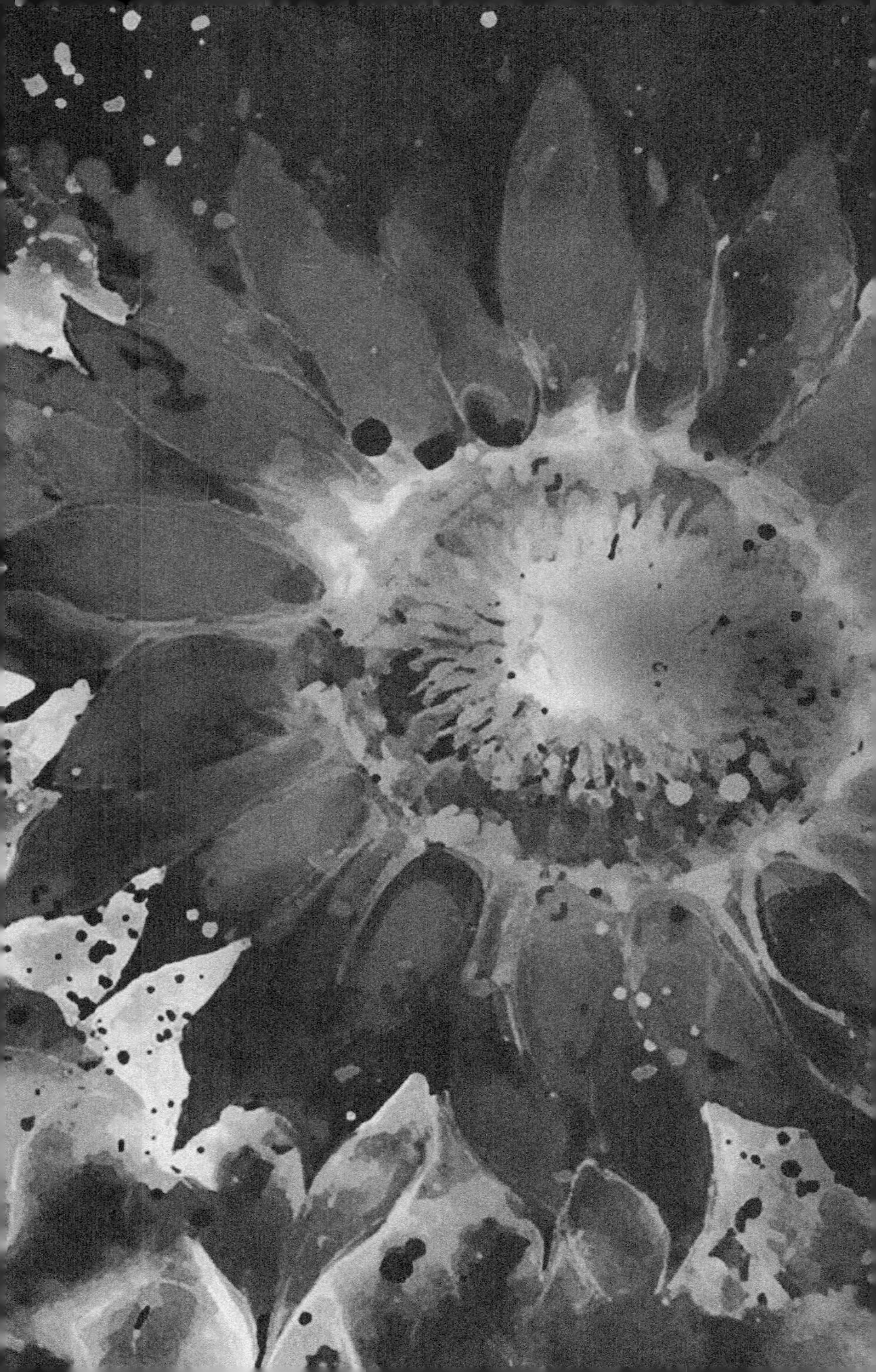

CHAPTER 36
Willow

The porch falls into a heavy silence as my words hang in the air. I continue, recounting the days, months and years that followed, the physical and emotional abuse, the manipulation, and the isolation. I describe the moments of despair, the longing for freedom, and the nights spent in fear.

"Five years after I was taken, Father made an announcement in front of the whole community. I was to be given to his son in marriage. While they all celebrated, I died a little more on the inside. Because while Mother and Father were evil and manipulative and claimed to do everything because they loved me, Jacob, on the other hand, was worse. He was the true embodiment of Satan. He wore a smiling mask in public, but I've never known anyone as evil as him when out of sight."

I take a deep breath, my gaze fixed on a distant point as I recount those dark days. "He made it clear to me that he had wanted me right from the start, even when I was only 12. I was told I was to hurry up and finish all of my scriptures and schooling so he could make me his obedient little wife. Any time from that moment on, if I stepped out of line, didn't do a chore that I was meant to do, or wasn't following along like a good little dog, Jacob was there to watch over my punishment. And if he felt it wasn't hard enough, he would add extra himself."

The pain of those memories resurfaces, but I push forward, determined to share my truth. "When I was twenty, he was able to convince Father that I was taking too long to complete my scriptures and that he would love some time to get to know me early. So I was made to go on supervised dates."

The soft light of the early sun seems to dim as the story continues. My voice becomes a whisper, and I meet the eyes of those beside me. "Those 'dates' were a charade. A twisted game where he reveled in his power over me. He would manipulate situations to punish me, to remind me of my place. It wasn't about getting to know me; it was about control."

"It took him another year, but he managed to convince Father that our dates didn't need to be supervised anymore," I continue, my voice barely above a whisper. I shudder involuntarily as I think about that first time alone with Jacob. I startle when Wyatt laces his fingers through mine. When I look at him, he is looking in the other direction, and I can see the hard clench of his jaw. I simply go back to looking at his hand gripping mine before I continue.

"By then, everyone knew I was taking as long as possible to complete the education and scriptures on purpose, but they were so strict on that side of things they had laws amongst themselves that they had thankfully made it so I could take the rest of my life without them doing anything bad to me. And they would have if they wanted to. They weren't above torture or killing because those were in their laws too. So when Jacob convinced Father to allow us alone time, it was like a snake finally striking."

I pause for a moment, gathering up as much courage as I can for the next part of the story.

"He didn't even wait a whole five minutes when we were alone before he shoved his cock inside my mouth," I say, the words feeling heavy on my tongue. I see Gage's jaw clench, and Mason's expression darkening. Both Easton and Wyatt's hands grip mine tighter and the pain helps ground me.

I can feel the wave of panic starting to surge within me. It's almost like a monster in my mind, its claws reaching out and scratching at everything. My breathing is already starting to speed up and my chest is starting to feel tight. It's like a fight I didn't ask for, and those claws won't stop.

"After he was… finished, he pulled me up and turned me around, then he lifted my shirt until my back was exposed. He cut a line into my skin and told me that he would keep adding a line for each month I delayed our marriage."

Wyatt makes a hissing sound from my side, and I remember the moment he saw my back the night before.

I swallow past the lump in my throat that is wanting to stop my story and I look down at my hands being held tightly, feeling the bite of their skin and nails in my own hands. I take one deep breath in and out and then another, forcing myself to push the panic away and center myself. I could smell the scent of ranch life, the dirt, the horses, and over it all was the various scents of the men around me.

Mason walks over and crouches in front of me, trying to duck his head to make eye contact as his hands grip my knees. "You don't have to keep going, Sugar. That can be enough for today if it's too much."

I take a moment to meet Mason's concerned gaze, appreciating the genuine care in his eyes. However, determination wells up within me.

"No," I say, my voice steadier than before. "I need to keep going. For me. I've carried this for long enough, and I want you all to know everything. I need to say it out loud."

He squeezes my knees in response, offering silent support, before standing back up and returning to his place, leaning against the porch railing. The others watch me with a combination of concern and understanding, ready to listen to whatever I choose to share.

Taking another deep breath, I continue, "Purity was so highly valued that we were indoctrinated with the belief that our bodies were not our own; they belonged to our husbands and to God. My virginity was considered a sacred gift, to be offered only on the altar of marriage. Any deviation from that path was seen as a heinous sin, risking not only spiritual damnation but also the very real threat of exile.

"But exile meant more than just expulsion; it meant death for someone like me who wasn't there by choice. However, for someone like Jacob, I doubted they would do much besides a slap on his hand and a stern lecture. But their judgment seemed to have some sort of sway on him, just not enough with how evil he was. So six months after the unsupervised dates started, he told me that since he couldn't put his dick in my cunt he would use both of the other two holes I had available.

"I endured those moments in silence, trapped in a nightmare where my only choices were submission or further brutality. After each time, he would cut another line in my back and remind me of my worthlessness, whispering threats and feeding the fears that had taken hold of my mind. He enjoyed breaking my spirit, leaving me shattered and hollow.

"I need you to understand that there were moments when the darkness seemed insurmountable. I thought of ending it all so often, but it was the thought of home, the thought of all of you, that kept me going each day. It was the belief that maybe, just maybe, one day I would get out of there."

Pausing to take another breath, I continued, "But I couldn't keep delaying the inevitable. After six years, I wasn't able to anymore. They had a twisted tradition there, one that sent shivers down my spine. The night before your wedding, you were sent to your future husband, scrubbed and cleaned under the guise of him checking to make sure your purity was still intact."

I glanced at each of them, knowing that the horror of the tradition was beyond their understanding. "I had seen it happen to several other girls who didn't have the courage to create a delay. Yes, the men were checking their purity, but it was while they were being raped. It gave the men an excuse to claim she wasn't pure, and she would be thrown out of the compound or killed.

"On the other hand," I continued, my voice tightening, "if they deemed them worthy, the girls couldn't possibly create any delays or back out. The fear of being unacceptable to another man and the chance of being pregnant kept them bound to follow through with their marriage."

A moment of heaviness lingered, and I took a deep breath. "So I knew what awaited me the moment I was led to Jacob's room. And the moment I was left alone to wait for him, I ran. At that point, I didn't care if they killed me. I wasn't going to let Jacob take that last piece of my soul.

"In some ways, I do wonder if there's some higher entity out there," I admitted. "Because I knew the moment I stepped out of the compound, my life was over. But then suddenly, Easton was there with a team, saving me. I'm not sure where Jacob was at that time because he somehow managed to escape the raid. He's still out there, and I thought he would follow all the clues the feds left. I don't know how he found out I had returned home."

In the tense silence that follows my revelation, varying looks of anger and darkness paint the faces of the men around me. Gage, unable to contain the fury building inside him, grits out through clenched teeth, "Show me."

Confused, I look at him, asking, "What?"

His response is a forced breath, and he manages to say, "I want to see your back. Please show me."

Turning to Wyatt, the only one who saw my scars since I managed to avoid Easton seeing them while we were together, I find a hard look on his face. He simply nods, releasing my hand and turning me to face him more fully. Easton lets go of my other hand, and Wyatt takes them, placing them on his chest. I feel him guide me through matching his breathing, a silent effort to steady me before he grips the sides of my shirt and lifts it, exposing my back to them.

Loud cursing echoes behind me, followed by the unmistakable sound of flesh hitting wood. Startled, I turn quickly to see Gage's retreating back as he storms away toward his car.

Easton, standing from his seat, declares, "I've got him," before disappearing inside for a moment. He returns with a set of keys, heading toward Mason's truck as Wyatt calls out, "Make sure he doesn't do anything stupid."

Mason comes over, taking Easton's place on the seat beside me, his eyes carrying a profound sadness. Without a word, he picks up my hand, lacing our fingers together in a silent gesture of support. We all sit there for a long time, enveloped in a heavy silence, long after Easton speeds off after Gage.

Then, suddenly, Mason breaks the silence, his voice low and steady, "He was a dead man the moment he laid a finger on you."

The weight of the past and the pain of those memories still lingers in the air, but in that moment, with these men who became my pillars of strength, it feels like a shared burden. Mason's words resonate with a finality that makes me realize I could face any future and any burden with them by my side.

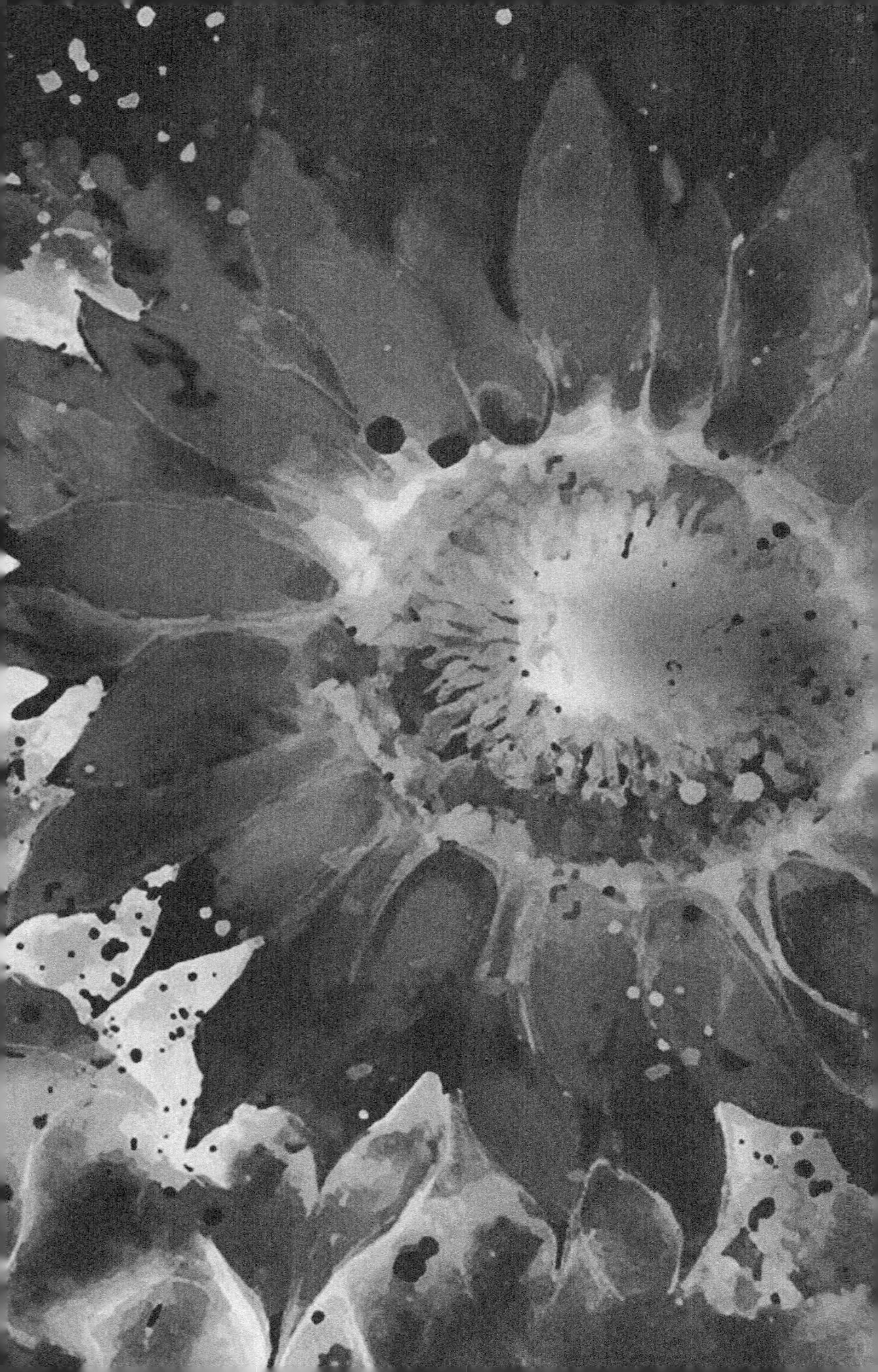

CHAPTER 37

Gage

I know I shouldn't have left, especially not after she opened all of her wounds for us.

The cool morning air hits me as I slam the car door shut, the metallic thud echoing my frustration. I take a moment to breathe, the anger still coursing through me. I couldn't stay there; I need an outlet for this rage. Willow doesn't need to witness the storm that brews inside me.

Unlocking the front door, I push the door of my bar open with enough force to make it hit the wall behind it with a thud. Thankfully it's still too early and the place is empty, so I'm not subjecting any of my staff to what may become a fucked up situation with how my mind currently is.

I should be heading to my punching bag to take my aggression out on that, but instead I head toward the bar. The bottle of whiskey is almost turned enough to pour out my shot when it's ripped from my hand.

I jerk my head around to see Easton with the bottle in one hand, and he points a finger at me with the other, hissing, "Don't you fuckin' dare." His eyes are ablaze with anger and concern. I feel the urge to punch him, to release the pent-up frustration, but I restrain myself. Instead, I lean over the counter, resting my elbows on it, and grip handfuls of my hair in frustration.

Easton doesn't let up; he keeps angrily talking even though I'm not looking at him. "Hit something if you want, hell, hit me, but this," he shakes the alcohol, "is not happening."

I growl, slamming my hands back down on the bar, giving him a look that could kill. But he doesn't back down; he just keeps going. "I don't even know why you still insisted on buying this place. It's like you like to fucking torture yourself."

I push past him without responding, my steps heavy as I storm up the stairs. I pass my office door and head up the stairs leading to the top floor and my apartment. I slam the door behind me with a satisfying thud, knowing I'm being childish but unable to let go of the rage burning inside. My fists clench and unclench as I try to contain the fury within.

It doesn't take long for Easton to open the door and step into the apartment, his hands now empty of the alcohol. Without thinking, I head to the small home gym I've set up in the corner. The punching bag hangs there, inviting me to release the storm within. Without a word, Easton takes up a position on the other side of the bag, holding it in place for me.

With each powerful punch, I feel a fraction of the anger dissipate. The rhythmic thud echoes through the room, matching the pounding in my chest.

As I tire myself out, the intensity of my anger begins to wane. Sweat beads on my forehead, and I collapse onto the floor, breathing heavily. The room is quiet, save for my ragged breaths.

Easton remains silent, allowing me the space I need to release the pent-up energy. The sound of my heavy breaths fills the room, echoing the emotional turmoil that has taken its toll on me.

After a while, I sit on my haunches, the intensity of my anger gradually giving way to exhaustion. My gaze shifts to Easton, who's been watching me intently, his eyes full of understanding and concern.

He finally breaks the silence, holding out a hand to help me up. "Are you good now?" he asks, his voice softer than before.

I hesitate for a moment, glancing at his outstretched hand. The anger still simmers within, but the session of unleashing it on the punching bag has provided a temporary relief. I accept his hand, allowing him to help me rise to my feet.

"Yeah," I reply, my voice hoarse from the exertion. "For now, at least."

Easton nods. "Look, I get it. I wanted to join the hunt for the bastard myself and torture him slowly when I saw the medical reports, but I needed to be there for her."

I scoff and shake my head. "Seriously? You're the calmest fucking asshole I know. Even Mase has more of a temper than you, and that's saying something 'cause I swear he's usually like a perpetually happy puppy."

Easton laughs at my remark, a genuine sound that cuts through the lingering heaviness. He walks toward my kitchen, the open-plan industrial design of my apartment allowing us to maintain our conversation even as he moves away.

"I have my moments, Gage," he admits, pouring a glass of water and returning to where I'm still standing. "Besides, sometimes being the calm one is necessary. Someone's gotta keep a level head when shit hits the fan. It's not like that was ever going to be any of the rest of you."

I run a hand through my sweat-soaked hair. Exhaustion is weighing heavily on me now; we didn't get to bed until late last night after cleaning up the mess at Willow's house, and now this. It's taking its toll.

"I'm not saying you have to be okay right now," Easton continues, handing me the glass of water. "This is a fucked-up situation, and it's okay to feel angry, hurt, whatever. But don't let it consume you."

I take the water, nodding in acknowledgment.

The silence settles between us for a while as I slowly drink the water, and my breathing returns to normal. The physical exertion has taken a toll on me, and the emotional weight of the revelations from earlier lingers in the air.

Then, I softly ask, breaking the quiet, "You didn't tell her, did you?"

Easton raises an eyebrow at my question, and I shrug my shoulders before clarifying, "About downstairs."

This time, it's him scoffing at me. "Of course, I didn't. I don't tell other people's secrets. I didn't tell her about Wyatt, and I certainly wasn't going to tell her about you."

A moment of regret and sadness flashes through me. I wonder if it would have been easier if he had told her. And then, I wonder if things would have been better if I wasn't such a screw-up. My past choices hang heavily over me.

Easton seems to sense the turmoil within me, and he walks over and sits on my couch. "Look, Gage, everyone has their demons. We've all done shit we're not proud of. But that doesn't define who you are now."

I look down at the glass in my hands, the water offering a brief respite. The silence stretches, and Easton's words linger, sinking into the recesses of my thoughts.

"Are you going to tell her?"

I meet his eyes, and before I can respond, he adds, "I think you need to before anything happens between you. But I also think it will help you to talk to her about it."

Silence hangs in the air, and I find myself wrestling with the idea. Opening up to Willow about my past feels like unraveling a tightly wound knot. A mixture of fear, shame, and the uncertainty of how she'll perceive me tugs at my resolve.

I remain silent, but I nod, acknowledging that, deep down, Easton is probably right. Willow has already bared her soul to us. It's only fair that I reciprocate.

Easton sees my internal struggle and offers a supportive nod. "She cares about you, Gage. And if you're going to be a part of each other's lives, she deserves to know."

Finishing the glass of water, I break the silence and ask Easton, "Are you going to sort out your car while you're here?" I walk into the kitchen, rinse the empty glass, and set it to dry.

"I already called first thing this morning to have it towed," Easton responds, standing up. "They don't have my tires in stock, so I have to wait a few days."

I frown at that; I'm still concerned that it even happened, and we don't have any idea who did it. Easton continues, "Willow has a session with Margot, so I need to go back to the ranch to get her. Are you meeting us at the house after like normal?"

I rest my hands on the kitchen counter and look at him before nodding silently. Another thought crosses my mind, and I frown. "Do you think she would like it if I cooked her dinner tomorrow night?"

Easton chuckles, warmth in his expression. "I'll even head to the ranch for dinner to get out of your way."

With that, he leaves the apartment, and I'm left alone with my thoughts. I'm nervous at the prospect of facing my past, revealing my vulnerabilities, and how Willow will react.

After a shower, I head back downstairs to my bar and begin setting up for the lunch crowd. The familiar routine of preparing for the day's patrons helps distract my mind from the tumultuous emotions that still linger.

Pretty soon, the staff begins to trickle in, and the lunch crowd starts filling the space. I take pride in what I've built here. Even if, as Easton pointed out, it might be a form of self-inflicted torment. As the owner, I've poured my heart and soul into this establishment, and it stands as a testament to my determination to create something meaningful with my life and to prove that my past doesn't dictate who I am now.

Letting Samuel, my manager, know that I'm heading out, I make my way around the bar, checking in with the patrons and ensuring everything is running smoothly.

Heidi tries to intercept me on my way to the door, but I barely give her a second glance. Nothing about her appeals to me, it never did. I made the mistake of falling down that road while drunk a long time ago. The next morning I truly understood what they were talking about in Coyote Ugly about wanting to chew my own arm off so I could sneak away, because I knew she was toxic and I cursed my drunk ass self for that stupidity.

And after what she did last night she is lucky I haven't banned her from the bar completely. It might actually give me some peace from her constantly trying to climb all over me.

Ignoring Heidi's attempts to engage, I step out into the sunshine and make my way around to my car. I've got an apology to give and some couch time with our girl. The anger that fueled my earlier outburst has subsided, replaced by a determination to make things right.

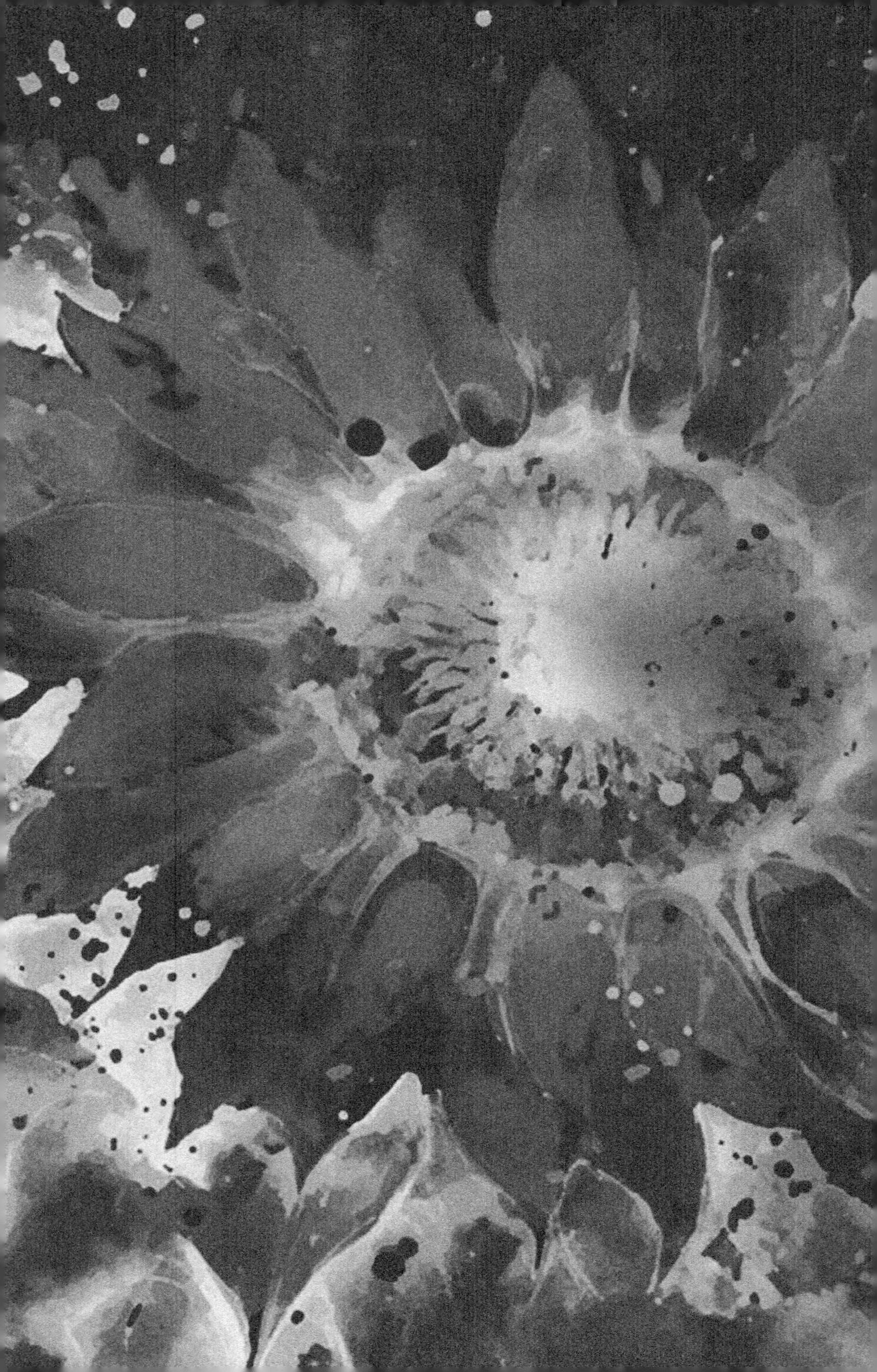

CHAPTER 38

Willow

It had been a heavily emotional day, so the nightmares that came during the night didn't surprise me. After telling the guys what happened and then my therapy session, Easton and I had gone back to my house like normal, as though nothing happened the night before.

If I hadn't seen it myself I would have actually thought it was my imagination with how clean the front entryway was. I knew I had the guys to thank for that. As usual Mason and Gage came over for dinner and movies.

After Gage apologized for storming off we settled into our normal routine, but suddenly it seemed strange not to have Wyatt there also. But I didn't mention it.

Sleep didn't come easy when I went to bed, and when it did come, the nightmares came, too. Vivid images flashed before me, like scenes from a haunting movie. Jacob's voice, his hands, the blade of his knife, they all wove together to create the chilling landscape that followed me from one dream landscape to the next.

I wake with a start, jerking upright, my breaths quick. I can feel the scream trapped in my throat, and the remnants of the nightmares cling to my consciousness. The room is shrouded in darkness, the only solace the soft glow of the moon filtering through the curtains. I try to shake off the unsettling images, but they persist, casting a shadow over the tranquility of the night.

Beside me, Easton sits up in bed, his hand lightly brushing down my arm, a gentle gesture meant to offer comfort. The touch is tentative at first, as if trying not to startle me.

"Willow," he speaks softly, his voice a murmur in the quiet darkness. "You're safe. It was just a dream."

My breaths are still rapid, the remnants of the nightmares refusing to release their grip. After a moment I turn toward him, seeking comfort in his arms that he wraps around me.

His hand continues its soothing motion against my side now, a steady rhythm that mirrors the rise and fall of my breath. I realize after a moment that it is actually the other way around, his hand is moving slower with each pass and my breathing is slowing to match the rhythm his hand dictates. Gradually, the jagged edges of the dreams begin to soften, and I allow myself to lean into the comfort he offers.

"It felt so real," I finally whisper. Nightmares have a way of dredging up the rawest emotions, laying them bare in the silent hours of the night.

Easton's arms tighten ever so slightly. "Sometimes, the mind plays tricks on us. But you're here, in the present. Safe."

His words are a balm to my unsettled mind. As Easton continues his soothing gestures, he gradually lowers us back down to settle on the bed again. My body is cradled against his side, the warmth of his embrace is a comforting shield against the lingering shadows of the nightmares.

In the quiet darkness, Easton starts talking to me, his voice a gentle murmur that weaves through the stillness. He shares stories from when the guys were growing up, it's like he's trying to give me new memories for the time I missed out on in their lives.

"It was during our high school years," Easton chuckles, the memories vivid in his narration. "Mason and Gage, in their infinite wisdom, thought it would be a brilliant idea to release the farm animals on the school grounds as a 'grand entrance' to the academic year."

I can't help but smile, the mental image of farm animals causing chaos in a school courtyard painting a comical scene. Easton continues, "So the schoolyard was filled with chickens, goats, and even several pigs."

He pauses, likely enjoying the laughter building in the room. "The best part was, they somehow managed to get a few cows onto the football field. It became the talk of the town for weeks."

I can't help but burst into laughter at the absurdity of the situation. The thought of Mason and Gage orchestrating that is both amusing and endearing.

"And the teachers, bless their hearts, were at a loss for how to handle the situation," Easton adds. "It took them the entire morning to corral all the animals and return them to their rightful places."

As the stories continue, I feel myself gradually drifting off to sleep, the gentle murmur of Easton's voice a soothing backdrop.

When I wake again, the bed beside me is empty. The spot is still warm, and I can hear movement down the hall in the kitchen. After a brief shower, I get to the dining room at the same time Easton is plating up breakfast. He smiles and says, "Good morning, little butterfly," before placing a plate of eggs and toast in front of me.

As I take a seat, Easton continues, "Wyatt called and asked if you would like them to come here, and you can keep doing some art with Bryce, or if you would like to go there and spend some more time with Gypsy."

I ponder the options for a few moments, considering the prospect of both experiences. Finally, I decide, "How about I do both? I could take my art supplies over there, spend some time with Bryce at the ranch doing some art, and then spend some time grooming and feeding Gypsy before we come back home."

Easton's smile widens at the suggestion, and he nods approvingly. Pulling his phone out, he taps away at it, likely informing Wyatt of the plan.

After finishing the meal, Easton and I gather my art supplies, loading them into the car. The brief drive to the ranch is filled with comfortable silence, The picturesque landscape unfolds before us, and I can already feel tranquility settling in.

As we approach the main house of the ranch, I spot Bryce playing on the porch under Wyatt's watchful eyes. Bryce's head turns, his eyes lighting up as he spots me. With an excited yell, he starts running toward me, his little legs carrying him as fast as they can.

"Miss Willow, Miss Willow!" Bryce exclaims, reaching me with a burst of energy.

Wyatt chuckles, "Looks like someone's excited to see you."

Easton takes the art supplies from my arms, understanding my desire to pick up Bryce. I bend down and scoop the enthusiastic boy into my arms, his laughter filling the air. Holding him close, I turn towards Wyatt, who walks down the porch stairs to greet us.

"Just Bryce?" I ask. Wyatt grins, wrapping his arms around me and Bryce together. He brushes a soft kiss against the corner of my mouth and says, "Not just Bryce."

He greets Easton, and we all move back up the porch stairs, where we get started on setting up a cozy art space. The sun casts a gentle glow, creating a perfect outdoor studio.

As Bryce eagerly picks up his paintbrush, his enthusiasm infectious, I can't help but get swept up by his excitement over the simplest things. Picking a spot from the beautiful view that I want to paint, I get to work mixing colors and getting lost in the joy of art and the world seen through the eyes of the little boy beside me.

After a delicious lunch of sandwiches made by Wyatt, Easton lets me know that he has an errand to run and promises to return as quickly as possible. With a soft kiss he walks to his SUV and leaves me to finish my art session with Bryce.

As we complete our paintings and set them aside to dry, Wyatt suggests that I spend some time with Gypsy before Easton returns. Following Wyatt's advice, I decide to take a quiet stroll over to the stables by myself.

The soft noises of horses greet me as I enter the stable, the sounds of hooves against straw and contented whinnies filling the air. I make my way to Gypsy's stall, and she nudges her head against my hand, welcoming me with gentle affection.

Remembering the routine Wyatt showed me, I set about grooming Gypsy. The rhythmic brushing and the familiar touch create a tranquil atmosphere. Gypsy, with her warm brown eyes, seems to understand the silent language we share as I run the brush through her mane. I move on to feeding her, offering her hay and a few treats.

After grooming and feeding, I spend a moment just being with Gypsy, absorbing the calm energy that radiates from this magnificent creature. The world outside seems to fade away, replaced by the serenity of the stable.

I don't even notice Easton's return. When I move to leave the stables, he is simply leaning against the doorway, a warm smile on his face as he watches me interact with Gypsy. The sun begins to dip lower in the sky, casting a golden hue behind him.

"Looks like you and Gypsy are getting along well," Easton remarks, his eyes reflecting a genuine happiness for me.

I walk over to him, and he meets me halfway, enveloping me in a comforting embrace.

"Hey there," he murmurs, his voice soft and reassuring. After a moment, he lifts my face with a gentle hand, brushing his lips against mine a few times before pulling back slightly, his eyes searching mine. "Have you had a good day?"

His concern is evident, and I appreciate the genuine care in his eyes. I return the smile, nodding. "Yes, it's been wonderful. Spending time with Bryce, creating art, and connecting with Gypsy—it's been exactly what I needed."

Easton's thumb brushes lightly against my cheek. "I'm glad to hear that. Come on, there is someone waiting for you at the house."

I furrow my brows in confusion, wondering who might be waiting for me back at the house. Easton takes my hand, leading me toward the SUV parked nearby. "But I haven't said goodbye to Wyatt and Bryce," I mention, slowing my steps.

Easton turns to face me, a soft smile playing on his lips. "Don't worry, I'll let them know. Come on, let's get you home."

He opens the car door for me and helps me inside. Moments later, he's behind the wheel, driving us away from the ranch and towards my house. As we approach, I notice Gage's car parked in the driveway. I glance at Easton with curiosity.

"How come Gage is here?" I ask.

Easton chuckles, shaking his head. "You'll see."

He parks the car, and as he helps me out, Gage steps out onto the landing. I look between the two of them, still puzzled. Easton walks with me toward him, but before I can reach the landing he tugs on my hand, stopping me.

Easton turns me to face him and pulls me into a gentle yet passionate kiss. My eyes widen in surprise, and when he draws back, he starts to back away toward the SUV again.

"Have fun!" he grins, his eyes sparkling mischievously.

I frown at him, a mixture of confusion and amusement. "What do you mean?"

He simply waves with a carefree expression on his face, and then he heads back to the car. I stand there, still puzzled, as Easton and Gage exchange a knowing look. Before I can question further, Easton drives away, leaving me standing on my porch with Gage.

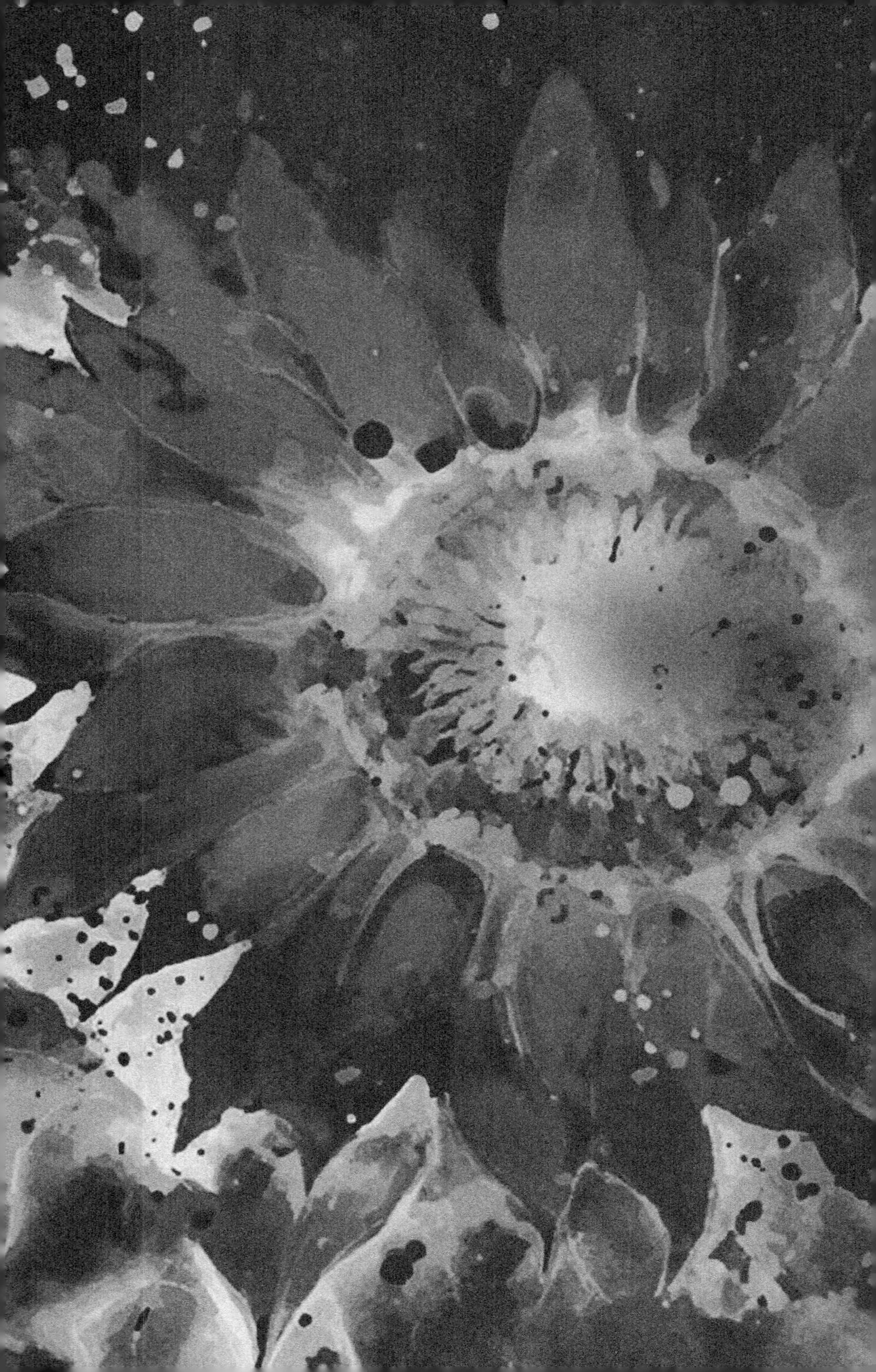

CHAPTER 39

Willow

I watch Easton's tail lights disappear before turning toward Gage with my curiosity piqued.

He gives an exaggerated bow, spreading his arms wide with a theatrical flair. "Welcome to the restaurant of Gage, where I dazzle you with something other than my bartending skills."

I can't help but giggle at his playful antics as he lifts my hand and gives it a gentle kiss. "Allow me to escort you, madam."

With a grin, he leads me into the house. The lights are off inside, and I can see the gentle flicker of candlelight as he guides me toward the dining room. The room is transformed into a warm, intimate setting, with candles casting a soft glow on a beautifully set table.

Gage pulls out a chair for me with another exaggerated bow. "Your seat, my lady."

I chuckle, playing along. "Why, thank you, kind sir."

He disappears into the kitchen and moments later, Gage walks back over, holding a plate adorned with a delicious-looking burger and a generous serving of fries. He places it in front of me with a flourish. "Ta-da! A masterpiece from Magda's kitchen."

I laugh, recognizing the distinctive aroma of Magda's burgers. "Gage, you didn't have to go through all this trouble. But thank you."

As we eat, I can't help but look at him with curiosity. The casual atmosphere makes me feel at ease. "So, is this a date or something?"

Gage pauses, looking at me for a moment before his smile takes on a hint of sadness. He takes a sip from the glass of water in front of him and then replies, "Yes and no. You know I want to spend as much time with you as I can, but after you confided in us yesterday, I feel you deserve to know some things about me too."

His answer catches me off guard, and I set down my burger, giving him my full attention.

Gage takes a moment, collecting his thoughts. "I'm not really good at this emotional stuff, but I want you to know that I care about you. A lot. We all do."

I feel a small amount of worry creeping in, sensing there's something more he wants to share. Before I voice my concerns, however, Gage changes the subject. "How about we eat these burgers first and then talk?"

I hesitate for a moment, but he picks up his own burger again and starts in on it, so I follow suit. The atmosphere becomes a bit more relaxed as we focus on our meals, the savory taste of Magda's burger momentarily distracting me.

Once we've both eaten our fill, I push the rest of my burger aside and give him a look, silently prompting him to continue.

Gage leans back with a sigh, his fingers idly tapping on the table. After a moment, he starts speaking, choosing his words carefully. "The other night when you came to the bar, when you drank that drink I made you... it helped get rid of all of your anxiety and stress and made you happy for a moment, right?"

I nod, still a bit confused about where this is going.

"I could tell from the look on your face," he continues. "Because I know that look. I know how it feels. When Wyatt lost himself in the bottle six years ago, he was able to get out of it again. When I found out what had sent him there, I did the same. But I didn't have anyone I cared enough about to drag me back out of it."

He continues, his gaze distant as if he's transported back to those difficult moments.

"Not even Easton could, and he tried hard. Mason was distracted with everything going on with Wyatt and trying to help keep the ranch going. Wyatt, at that point, had Callista. Easton was starting to do his training. I just felt like the whole world was falling apart around me. I felt like I had lost and was losing everyone that mattered to me."

Gage takes a deep breath, his fingers tracing patterns on the table. The moment suddenly feels solemn, the flickering candles casting shadows on his face.

"You know I didn't have the greatest upbringing, right from the start. My dad was an abusive asshole. My mom took a long time to leave him and become a therapist, and then, at that time she was more focused on her patients than her son. It just all became too much, and I didn't want to feel anymore. It went on for a long time, too long. I did some things I'm not proud of. And then one night when the voices in my head were telling me how much of a failure I was got too loud, I kept drinking until I felt like I could drown them out. I almost killed myself with how much and how quickly I drank."

"Easton found me," he continues, his voice quieter now. "He had enough basic training to revive me, but he had to call the EMTs, and they had to pump my stomach when I got to the hospital. Both the hospital and Easton then forced me into rehab."

Gage's gaze is fixed on the distant past, the pain of those memories etched on his face. "When I woke up in that hospital bed, I thought it was like a wake-up call," he admits, his eyes meeting mine.

He takes a moment, as if collecting his thoughts, and then continues, "I got myself clean and sober. I started going back to school to study business management. I had no intentions of working on the ranch with Mase and Wy. Then, a few years ago, my dad died—cardiac arrest. He was an asshole, but he was still my dad. It brought back all the memories of his abuse, and I relapsed for a while, once again trying to not feel anything. Easton had to save me again by putting my ass back in rehab."

Gage's gaze turns introspective. "It was straight after that we had our argument. He wanted to join the task force as a way to try to find you. I was wallowing in my self-pity while trying to stay sober again. We both said some things we regretted afterward, but the damage was done, and he left."

He sighs, his shoulders slumping for a moment. "We've been through a lot, the four of us. Sometimes we clash, but we always find a way back to each other. Easton, he's... he's like a brother to me. Losing him, even if just temporarily, was one of the hardest things I've faced, second only to losing you."

He takes a deep breath, and as he exhales, a soft determination settles in his eyes. "I'm telling you all this because I want you to understand that I know what it feels like to want to escape from what's in your own mind. I want you to know that even in the darkest moments, there is some light, that it will get better. I bought the bar to prove to myself that I could change, that I could build something meaningful. But it was also about making everyone proud of me, especially Easton, Mason, Wyatt, and also you."

Without breaking eye contact, I stand up from the table and walk around to stand beside him. As he looks up at me, I lean over and cup my hands around his face.

"I am proud of you," I say sincerely, my words carrying the weight of genuine admiration. Before he can respond, I close the gap between us, brushing my lips against his. The kiss is tender at first, a silent acknowledgment of the strength he's shown in sharing his story.

The kiss deepens, his fingers finding their way into my hair, as he responds with an intensity that mirrors the emotions he's laid bare. The candlelight flickers, its warm glow casting shadows over the wall like two fingers entwined and moving together in a way that makes me want to move my body against his.

Gage's other hand finds its way to my waist, holding me close. He flicks his tongue against my lips, a silent request for entrance, and I gladly oblige, parting my lips to deepen the kiss further.

The world outside seems to fade away as we lose ourselves in the moment. Our lips move together in a rhythm that seems to synchronize with the beating of our hearts.

Gage stands and changes the angle of the kiss. A soft moan escapes from my throat as his touch ignites a fire within me. I wrap my arms around his neck, pulling him closer, losing myself in the sensation of his lips on mine.

He breaks off the kiss, his eyes locked onto mine. In a husky voice, he admits, "I want you, Willow. If I could drown myself in anything ever again, it would be in you, for the rest of my life."

There's a raw honesty in his gaze and I can feel the weight of his emotions. I don't need to respond with words; my actions convey my feelings.

I press my body against his, pulling him down to meet his lips again. After a moment I pull back slightly and our eyes lock. "Gage," I murmur, my fingers tracing a gentle path along his cheek. "I want you too."

Gage leans down toward me again, his lips hovering over mine with a magnetic pull. The anticipation heightens the intensity between us. He turns his face slightly, blowing out the candles that cast flickering shadows around the room.

With the room now in darkness, Gage's arms reach down, and he hooks his hands around the backs of my thighs. In one smooth motion, he lifts me effortlessly, and I instinctively wrap my legs around him. He starts to carry me toward the bedroom with our bodies pressed together.

Gage's lips find mine again, a hungry and passionate kiss that hints at what is to come. His hands, strong and sure, cradle me as if I'm the most precious thing in the world.

When we reach the bedroom, Gage gently lowers me onto the bed. He breaks off the kiss and we both try to catch our breath. He brushes a strand of hair away from my face, his touch gentle yet filled with a hunger that matches my own. His eyes, now reflecting the moonlight, search mine for any sign of hesitation. Finding none, he leans in again, capturing my lips with a renewed sense of urgency.

Moonlight peeks through the curtains, casting a soft glow on us. Gage's hands and lips start to wander, leaving a trail of kisses on my neck, collarbone, and shoulders.

My body feels like it's burning as he systematically takes off my clothes. His touch is electric as he removes each item. His lips follow, planting kisses that leave me wanting more.

The room fills with quiet moans and the rustle of fabric signaling the last of my clothes hitting the floor. I lie there exposed, open, and ready. Our eyes lock, saying more than words ever could.

With a lingering gaze, Gage undresses himself. His tan skin and tattoos make my mouth water. His hand wraps around his hard cock as he asks, "Do we need protection?" I'm so distracted that all I can do is shake my head in response as he moves closer to me with a grin.

Gage stands at the end of the bed, a hunger in his eyes that matches the fire in my body. He wraps his hands around the back of my knees and drags me right to the edge. Once I'm in the position he wants, he slides one of his hands down my leg, his touch sending shivers through me. His fingers find their way through my wet folds, and I arch my back, moaning in response.

Two fingers plunge inside me, igniting a fire that consumes me. His thumb finds my clit, rubbing against it in a way that makes my body ache for more. Through the haze of pleasure, he asks, "Do I need to be gentle?"

I moan out a breathless "No," my body on fire, craving the intensity he promises. The air between us is charged, anticipation building as Gage's fingers dance over my skin. Moments later, he withdraws his fingers, and a silence lingers in the air.

Gage's eyes, filled with desire, lock onto mine as he positions himself. With a swift and purposeful motion, he thrusts his cock deep inside my pussy. The intensity of the moment sends a jolt through me, and I gasp at being filled.

He isn't as big as Wyatt, but he's far from small. I feel him stretching me, his every thrust sending a jolt of pleasure mixed with a hint of pain. He takes me at my word, thrusting hard, the sound of our skin slapping together echoing in the room.

He lifts my legs, resting my ankles against his shoulders and leaning over me, almost bending me in half. The change in position intensifies the pleasure, and my moans grow louder. Gage groans, "Fuck, you feel so good, sweetness. You were made for us."

His thrusts become more forceful, and I feel my climax building inside me. My pussy tightens around him, the sensations overwhelming as he groans again, urging me, "That's it, I need you to cum for me, sweetness. This pussy has me on the edge already, and I need you to cum with me."

The room is filled with the erotic sounds of our bodies colliding, skin slapping against skin, as we both hurtle toward ecstasy. The pleasure reaches its peak, and I let go, succumbing to the intense waves crashing over me. My body shudders with the force of the orgasm as Gage continues to thrust, his own release merging with mine.

When the waves of pleasure subside, he collapses next to me on the bed both of us breathless. After a moment he gathers me close, his fingers gently brushing the damp hair out of my eyes. Our breathing slowly returns to normal, and Gage presses a lingering kiss on my forehead.

I start to succumb to sleep and Gage chuckles before lifting me from the bed and taking us to the shower. The water cascades over us and Gage washes me, quickly but tenderly.

After the shower, he guides me back to the bedroom where I get ready for bed. Gage steals some of Easton's clothes and we settle in the darkness of the room.

As I'm on the verge of drifting off to sleep again, a brush of fingers down my arm startles me. I turn, and to my surprise, it's Easton. He leans close and whispers, "It's just me, little butterfly." He places a soft kiss on my temple and murmurs, "I'll sleep on the couch and I'll see you in the morning."

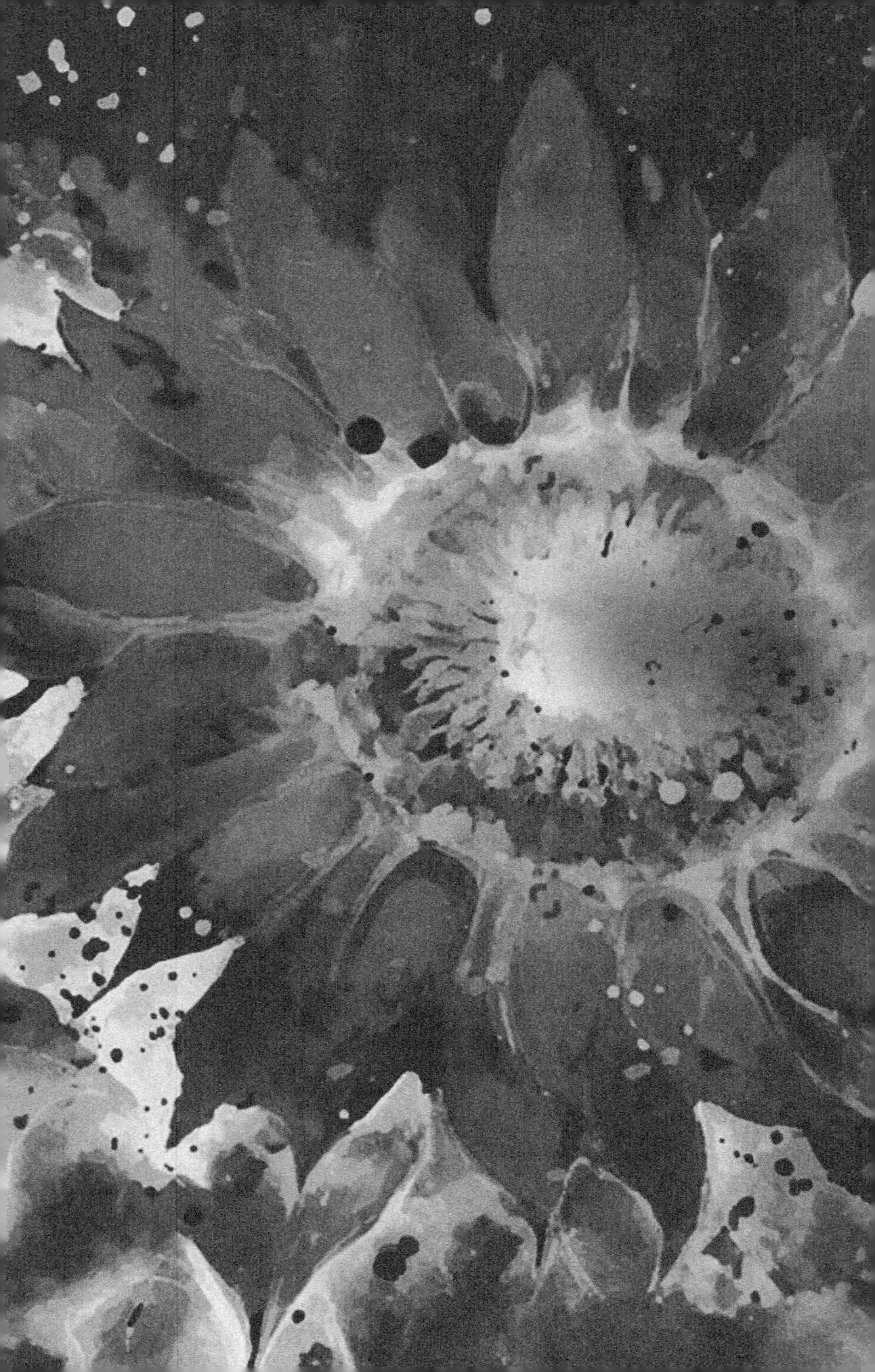

CHAPTER 40
Willow

I can tell something is wrong the moment I jerk awake.

The room is still shrouded in darkness and my senses are on high alert. A loud crack echoes through the air, immediately jolting me upright. Confusion clouds my mind as I try to identify the source of the noise. That's when I notice the ominous smoke seeping in from under the door.

A surge of adrenaline courses through me and instinctively I shake Gage, who is still sleeping beside me. "Gage!" I yell, my voice sharp and urgent. He jerks awake, his eyes widening as he follows my panicked gaze.

Gage springs into action, his movements fast for someone who was asleep only moments before. Without a word, we scramble out of bed, disoriented by the darkness and the acrid smell of smoke. Gage grabs my hand, leading the way toward the door.

The door handle sizzles as Gage tentatively touches the back of his hand to it, and a sharp hiss escapes his lips. He jerks his hand away.

I'm on the verge of panic, ready to try opening the door myself, but Gage's stern voice stops me. "No, Willow. The fire is too close, you'll burn your hand. We can't go that way."

The severity of the situation becomes clearer with each passing moment.

Fear clutches at my chest, and I glance back at the door as if it might offer a solution. The room is rapidly filling with smoke, and the acrid scent intensifies. Panic threatens to consume me. "But Easton is out there!" I cry out, my voice filled with desperation. The realization hits me like a punch to the gut, and my heart races with fear.

Gage's eyes reflect the same worry that I have. "We'll find him, Willow," he reassures me, determination cutting through the fear in his gaze. "We can't go through the door."

Without hesitation, he strides over to the window and unlatching it, he tries to lift it open. It won't move, even as he tries again. He looks around the room, his mind working quickly to find an alternative. Gage's eyes land on the bed, and he swiftly pulls off the bedding, wrapping it around his arm.

The room is filled with the crashing sound of breaking glass as Gage smashes the window with his wrapped arm. I see him flinch, knowing that one of the shards must have cut him, but he doesn't let it slow him down. He clears away the remaining glass and then comes back to where I'm frozen between the open window and the chaos inside.

In one fluid motion, Gage picks me up, cradling me in his arms. Carrying me to the window, he lowers me through it and down to the ground on the other side. I watch as he follows, using the window ledge to jump out despite the obvious pain from the cut on his arm.

Gage takes my hand, and we run around to the front of the house. The sight that greets us is devastating – the fire has engulfed the entire structure. Panic tightens its grip on me, and I scan the chaos for any sign of Easton. There's an explosion, and flames leap into the sky.

I scream Easton's name, my voice echoing against the roar of the fire. Gage stops me from running toward the house, his grip firm. I resist, desperate to find our friend, even as the heat radiates from the flames. Tears stream down my face as the reality of the situation sinks in.

"He's in there, Gage! We have to find him!" I plead, my voice breaking.

Gage's expression is pained, but he holds me back. The fire rages on, and I can't tear my eyes away from the inferno. I collapse to my knees, still crying out for Easton.

I don't care about the house, or the history it contains. The rooms upstairs, filled with memories that I've avoided, are irrelevant now. All that matters is the possibility that Easton could be inside, trapped by the merciless flames.

Amidst the chaos, coughing breaks through the sounds of crackling fire. Then, I hear my name being called. Gage points toward the other side of the house, and my eyes follow his gesture. There, emerging from the smoke, I finally see Easton. He's running low, cradling something to his chest and shielding himself with one arm from potential debris.

Relief floods through me, and I'm shaking as Gage lets go of me. I launch myself at Easton, embracing him tightly. I realize

I'm crushing something between us. I pull back to look, and to my surprise and anger, it's the paintings I did with Bryce.

Fury takes over, and I hit Easton's chest. "You stupid fucking idiot, Easton! You risked your life for these?!" I yell, tears streaming down my face.

Easton winces, both from the impact of my hits and, I suspect, from the severity of the situation. He takes a moment before responding, his voice strained but resolute. "Willow, they meant so much to you. I couldn't leave them behind."

I collapse into his arms, sobbing, overwhelmed by a flood of emotions. Gage wraps his arms around both of us, providing comfort amidst the chaos. The distant wailing of a fire truck grows louder, and soon, the area is flooded with people. The scene becomes a surreal mix of flashing lights, smoke, and voices. The firefighters get to work battling the blaze that has engulfed what was once my childhood home.

Amidst the commotion, there's a screech of tires, and suddenly, Wyatt and Mason come rushing toward us. Their faces are a mixture of concern and relief as they take in the scene. Gage, Easton, and I are a tangled mess of emotions – tears, soot, and the lingering fear of what could have been.

As paramedics check us over for smoke inhalation and shock, the fire gradually comes under control, its furious flames subdued by the efforts of the firefighters. We watch in silence as the remnants of my home smolder and billow with smoke, everything it contained now reduced to charred memories.

While we watch, two police officers approach us. I notice Heidi scowling at us from a distance, her eyes narrowed. She remains silent, a step behind the older officer beside her. His sheriff badge glints in the flashing lights, and his expression is one of genuine concern as he surveys our disheveled group.

He speaks directly to me, cutting through the chaos with a calm tone. "Miss Silva, I'm sorry for what you have gone through tonight. Are you able to answer some questions for us now? We can do a more in-depth follow-up tomorrow."

I nod before responding, my voice shaky. "Yes, of course. Anything to help."

The sheriff begins asking about the events leading up to the fire, and I recount everything from us going to sleep to the moment we escaped through the window.

As I speak, I notice Heidi observing me with undisguised hatred. She doesn't say a word, but her presence adds an extra layer of tension to an already stressful situation. As Easton and Gage contribute their own experiences of the night I watch as her jaw clenches and she folds her arms across her chest.

The Sheriff listens intently, absorbing the details of our harrowing experience. Once satisfied with the initial information, he offers reassurance. "Miss Silva, someone will be around for a full statement tomorrow. For now, you don't need to stay if you want to leave."

With that, the Sheriff and Heidi walk away, heading back toward the firefighters and emergency personnel who continue their work. Mason and Gage's cars, parked in the driveway, are now covered in ash, and the emergency vehicles block them in. The keys are still inside the destroyed house.

Wyatt suggests, "Let's get out of here," and we all follow behind him and climb into his truck. Slowly, he maneuvers through the maze of emergency vehicles on the debris-strewn street, driving us back to the ranch in silence.

I spend the ride back to the ranch between Easton and Gage in the backseat of Wyatt's truck. Their hands are held tightly in mine, a silent reassurance that we've made it through the ordeal alive.

The rhythmic hum of the engine provides a backdrop to the turmoil of my thoughts. As we drive away from the remains of my childhood home, I'm enveloped in a cloud of guilt and what-ifs.

The weight of the night presses on my chest. In the silence, my mind replays the events, each moment scrutinized with a painful clarity. I can't escape the nagging thought that it's all my fault, that Jacob did this, and the fire was set because of me. The possibility that I could have been the reason for their deaths gnaws at my conscience.

I free my hands so I can bury my face in them, tears seeping through my fingers.

Suddenly, my hands are gently pulled away from my face. Easton turns my face and body towards him, wrapping his own arms around me. His warmth is a stark contrast to the cold tendrils of guilt tightening around my heart. I resist, pulling my face away; he has already had to deal with the turmoil within me enough.

But Easton's hold is unwavering. He whispers, "Willow, this is not your fault. None of this is on you."

I shake my head, my voice choked with emotion. "But what if it is? What if Jacob ... What if he set the fire? What if..."

Before I can continue, Wyatt's voice cuts through the darkened interior of the truck. "This is not your fault, Sweetheart."

I catch a worried look on his face in the rearview mirror. Mason turns in his seat to face me through the gap, reaching out a hand to squeeze my knee. "Don't blame yourself. Someone else set that fire, and we are going to find out who it was and make them regret it."

The sincerity in their voices momentarily pushes back the darkness threatening to consume me. I nod, unable to find words, and Easton pulls me back into his comforting embrace.

Wyatt pulls into the parking area at the ranch, and as the engine shuts off, the silence becomes almost deafening. The truck's doors open, and one by one, we step out into the chilly night air. I feel a gentle hand on my elbow, and I turn to see Wyatt helping me from the car. His concern is evident in his eyes, and I manage a weak smile in acknowledgment.

As we walk toward the main house, the others follow closely behind. Trying to distract myself, I ask Wyatt, "Where is Bryce?"

Wyatt glances at me, his expression softening. "I left him sleeping. He's a good sleeper, and I knew he would be fine while we came to make sure you were okay. You can come with me to check on him if you want."

I nod gratefully, needing the diversion from the swirling thoughts in my mind. Wyatt leads me through the front door and into the quiet of the house. The others head toward the living room, their expressions a mix of exhaustion and concern.

Wyatt opens the door to one of the bedrooms with a quiet creak. We enter, and there, in the dim light, I see Bryce fast asleep, his innocent face peaceful in slumber. I lean heavily against Wyatt, taking in a shaky breath at the sight.

He gently guides me back into the hall, closing the door with a hushed click. Turning to me, Wyatt murmurs, "Do you want to shower in my room and stay with me, or would you prefer to be with Easton or Gage?"

I appreciate his understanding, the lack of judgment in his question. I softly respond, "I need Easton. I was so scared I had lost him."

Wyatt nods, his hand gesturing toward where Easton is standing with the others. As we approach, Wyatt gently passes me into Easton's waiting arms. The warmth of his embrace settles around me as I rest my head against his chest, his steady heartbeat against my cheek.

The rhythmic thump of Easton's heart echoes in my ears, drowning out the chaos that still lingers in my mind. I focus on that steady beat, a comforting reminder that he is here, alive, and with me. Anger starts building inside of me, just like the fire that consumed my home, as I stand there listening to Mason berating Gage about not taking care of the cuts on his hands and arms.

I'm not sure what I would do if I lost any of them now, they are all mine and god help those who threatened them.

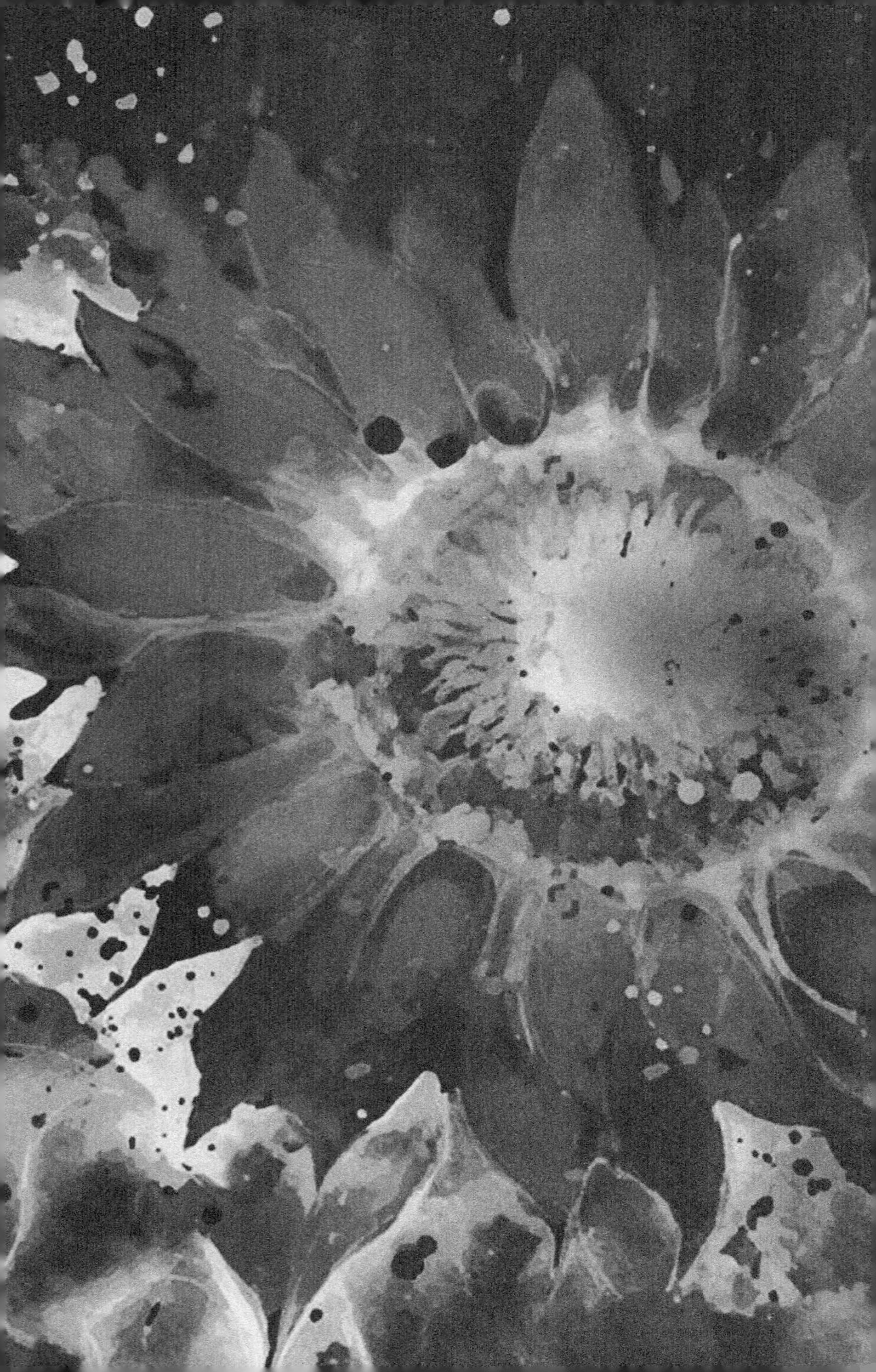

Chapter 41

Unknown

The rage I feel is blinding.

They almost ruined everything I've meticulously planned. Patience has its limits, and mine is wearing thin. As the saying goes, if I want something done right, I need to do it myself.

The desire to get closer to my soulmate, to make my ownership clear, burns within me. I yearn for the moment when they realize they've been watched almost all their life, that every step they took has always been under my scrutiny.

The time for waiting is over. They are about to realize that there is no escaping the inevitable.

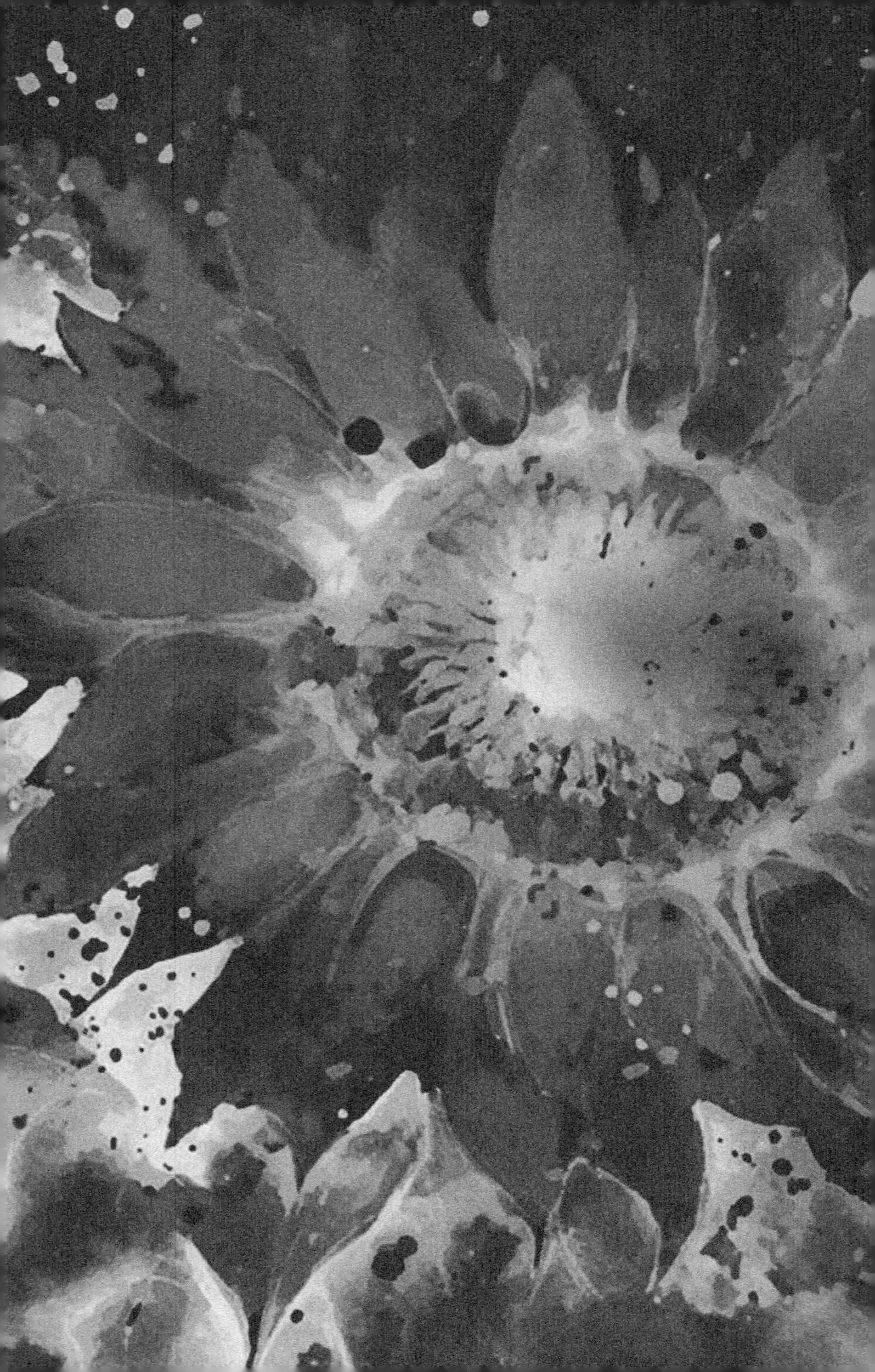

Chapter 42

Willow

I couldn't sleep for the rest of the night, and after we all showered all I could do was settle into the bed Easton said he always uses when staying at the ranch. After a few moments I hear someone else enter the room and slide into the bed behind me.

Easton must have noticed the change in my breathing as he rubs his hands up and down the skin of my arm, murmuring, "It's just Gage."

I reach an arm behind me, my fingers searching until they find Gage's. I bring his hand around the front of my body, cradling it between my breasts. Sadness creeps into my mind as I observe the bandages covering his hand.

We lie there in silence for hours, the stress of the night still lingering in the air, and I watch as the first rays of sunlight filter through the window. The room gradually brightens, casting a warm glow on the space around us.

The tranquility is broken by Bryce getting up. His cheerful voice echoes through the house, a stark contrast to the somber atmosphere that enveloped us just hours ago. Bryce seems completely oblivious to the drama that unfolded the night before.

Bryce's laughter filters through the house, signaling someone has already gotten up to him. I close my eyes for a moment, appreciating the purity of Bryce's laughter as it dances through the air. As Bryce's footsteps fade away, Easton presses a gentle kiss to my temple, his lips lingering for a moment. The quiet exchange carries more comfort than words ever could. I'm enjoying the comfort their touch and presence are bringing me and I don't want to leave to face the reality of the day.

"Let's just stay in bed," Easton suggests, his voice a low murmur that seems to echo my thoughts. Gage shoots him a look that I can't quite decipher, and I feel a subtle tension in the air. Before I can ask, Gage turns his attention to me.

"Mason has an errand to run this morning after breakfast," Gage informs me. "But I think he wanted to take you on a picnic today. If you're not up to it, I can let him know to do it another day instead."

I shake my head, a small smile forming. "No, today is good. I need the distraction, I think."

Gage nods in understanding as Easton tightens his embrace. The prospect of a picnic, a simple and ordinary activity, feels like a welcome diversion from recent events.

We slowly extract ourselves from the warmth of the bed and the quiet solitude of the bedroom, making our way toward the kitchen and the sweet sounds of Bryce's voice. The aroma of food cooking greets us as we step into the room followed quickly by the squeal escaping Bryce. Once again Mason is standing at the stove but he isn't quick enough to stop the little boy jumping down from his chair and launching himself in our direction.

Bryce barrels into us, his small frame colliding with our legs, and we're momentarily caught off guard. Laughter spills out of him, infectious and genuine. He looks up at us, his eyes wide with excitement, oblivious to the drama unfolding around us.

"Miss Willow!" he exclaims, his grin stretching from ear to ear. "Guess what, Uncle Mason's making waffles!"

The simplicity of his announcement, coupled with the unbridled joy in his eyes, tugs at my heart. It's a stark reminder of the resilience of childhood, the ability to find joy in the mundane, to be untouched by the weight of the world. I crouch down to his level, ruffling his hair affectionately.

"Waffles, huh? That sounds amazing, buddy," I reply, forcing a smile.

I feel a gentle hand on my shoulder and I stand, turning to see Wyatt holding a mug of coffee out to me, his expression one of concern and care.

He gives me a soft kiss on the forehead and looks at me with a frown. "You didn't sleep," he observes.

I meet his gaze, his reminder making the exhaustion I feel more pronounced. "I couldn't. The night was..." He simply nods in response, but I can see the same exhaustion in his own eyes.

As we settle into breakfast, the atmosphere lightens. Mason, despite the weariness etched on his face, manages to conjure up a batch of waffles that rivals any gourmet chef's.

Bryce, now seated with a plate piled high with mini waffles, continues to chatter away. The breakfast provides a delicious distraction, and soon, we are engrossed in conversation, smiles and laughter.

As we finish the meal, Mason stands and leans over, planting a kiss on my cheek. "I've got to run that errand now, but I'll be back. We'll have a picnic, just you and me, alright?"

With Mason's departure, the rest of us start cleaning up the remnants of breakfast. Wyatt suggests trying to relax with a movie and we all agree, Bryce the most enthusiastically. Just as we're about to start watching our chosen movie, a knock on the door interrupts the tranquility. Wyatt rises to answer it, and when he returns, the Sheriff and Heidi trail behind him. The atmosphere shifts, a subtle tension settling over the room.

The sheriff addresses us with a somber expression. "Miss Silva, may we have a word?" he requests, his tone solemn.

I exchange uncertain glances with Easton and Gage before nodding in acknowledgment.

Wyatt looks at Bryce and says, "How about we go and get some drinks and snacks ready."

Bryce's face lights up and he runs ahead of his dad back toward the kitchen as Wyatt gives me a concerned look and follows after him.

The sheriff clears his throat and begins with a measured tone. "We've been investigating the incident at your home, Miss Silva. It appears the fire was intentionally set."

The gravity of his words hangs in the air, and a chill runs down my spine.

The realization that someone intentionally set the fire sends a shiver down my spine. I listen to the sheriff's words carefully, answering his questions to the best of my ability.

The investigation is still ongoing, and every detail becomes a piece in the puzzle.

As the sheriff turns his attention to Gage, I seize the opportunity to excuse myself to the bathroom. The weight of the questions, the implications of arson, and the shadow of Jacob's presence all converge, threatening to overwhelm me. In the privacy of the bathroom, I splash cold water on my face, taking deep breaths to calm the rising anxiety.

My suspicions about Jacob seem to be confirmed, but the revelation doesn't bring relief; instead, it intensifies the fear and uncertainty. After composing myself, I leave the bathroom and make my way back toward the living room.

As I approach, an angry female voice catches my attention. Confused, I realize the sound is coming from outside, carried through a slightly open window. Curiosity gets the better of me, and I pause to listen. The voices become clearer, and I recognize Heidi's voice, laced with frustration and anger.

"I gave you a simple task, and you couldn't even do that fucking right! Why the fuck would I want you to do it if Gage was in there? You know the whole point was for him to turn to me when that sniveling bitch was dead."

A chill runs down my spine as I eavesdrop on the conversation. I'm frozen in place, unable to look away or close the window that inadvertently grants me access to this private moment.

Heidi's voice continues, the words sinking in like a dark revelation. "Of course, it would have worked. You know it already worked for Calista. It would have worked for me if he didn't decide to become a booze-addled idiot both times. But I've learned from my mistakes; I know what I did wrong the last couple of times... How the fuck should I know? Mason is your obsession, not mine; that's for you to deal with."

The pieces of a disturbing puzzle fall into place. The realization that Heidi may have been orchestrating something so sinister becomes undeniable. I struggle to comprehend the depth of her involvement in the events that unfolded.

My mind races as I process the shocking revelation from Heidi's conversation. The mean girls were behind the deliberate fire, not Jacob. The clarity hits me like a wave of nausea, and my stomach churns with disbelief and disgust.

Backing away from the window, I've heard enough. What I've learned makes me sick to my stomach. My back hits something, and in a panic, I start to jerk away. However, Wyatt's voice whispers, "Shhhh, it's just me, sweetheart." I turn to him with wide eyes, but his focus is on the window, his eyes narrowed.

I can no longer hear Heidi, so I turn more toward Wyatt and ask, "Did you hear that?" He responds with a nod.

His frown deepens as he returns his gaze to mine and says, "We can't say anything to the Sheriff just yet." He wraps an arm around me and starts to steer me back toward the living room.

"But what about—" I begin to whisper, but he cuts me off, saying, "I don't want to talk about that just yet." The next second, we are back in the living room, where Gage and Easton shoot worried looks in my direction. The Sheriff is just wrapping up his questions, and Heidi doesn't return to the living room.

The Sheriff takes his leave, promising to keep us informed about the investigation. Once the door closes behind him, an uncomfortable silence settles in the room. I find myself grappling with the enormity of the revelation.

Easton, sensing the tension, is the first to break the silence. "What happened?"

Wyatt takes a deep breath, checking that Bryce is occupied with his toys and exchanging a solemn glance with me before explaining, "We overheard a conversation outside. It was Heidi. She was talking about the fire, about how she wanted it to happen, and blaming someone for not carrying out her plan properly."

Gage's eyes narrow as he processes the information. "Heidi was involved in setting the fire?"

I nod, my voice shaky. "It wasn't Jacob. It was her and someone else."

A heavy silence hangs in the room as this revelation sinks in for all of us. Easton's jaw tightens in anger and concern. Gage's expression darkens, a storm brewing in his eyes. Wyatt's gaze shifts between us, his concern evident.

"We can't let the Sheriff know yet," Wyatt adds, emphasizing the need for caution. "We don't have enough evidence, and we don't know the full extent of Heidi's involvement. If we jump the gun, it could backfire."

Easton runs a hand through his hair, frustration evident in his movements. "So, what's the plan? We can't just sit here and do nothing."

Gage seems on the verge of losing his composure. "We need to find out more, gather evidence. We can't let them get away with this."

Wyatt nods in agreement. "We stick together and figure out our next move. But we have to be careful. Heidi is more dangerous than I thought, and we don't know who else might be involved."

We stand in silence for several minutes as the newfound information presses down on us. Suddenly the silence is broken by a soft bark. I see Bryce's face light up, a smile twitching at Easton's lips, and Gage grinning. Wyatt wraps his arm around me, and starts leading me toward the front door. Bryce beats us there, tall enough to open the door himself. He takes off down the front stairs, and we follow him.

At the bottom of the stairs, Mason is standing with a beautiful dog. The dog's fur is a mixture of whites, blacks, and browns, with the prettiest blue eyes. A bright yellow vest around its back and waist catches my eye. Mason smiles up at me and motions for me to come to him.

I hesitate, but Easton nudges me gently. "Go on."

After walking down the stairs, I can see the writing on the vest more clearly. It says, "Service Dog." Mason holds the lead out to me and says, "I'd like you to meet Stella. She was trained as a service dog but now doesn't have a companion. I spoke to Margot, and she thought it might be a good idea if you become her companion."

Overwhelmed with gratitude, I throw my arms around Mason's neck and burst into tears. Stella nuzzles against me, as if already sensing my distress and wanting to help.

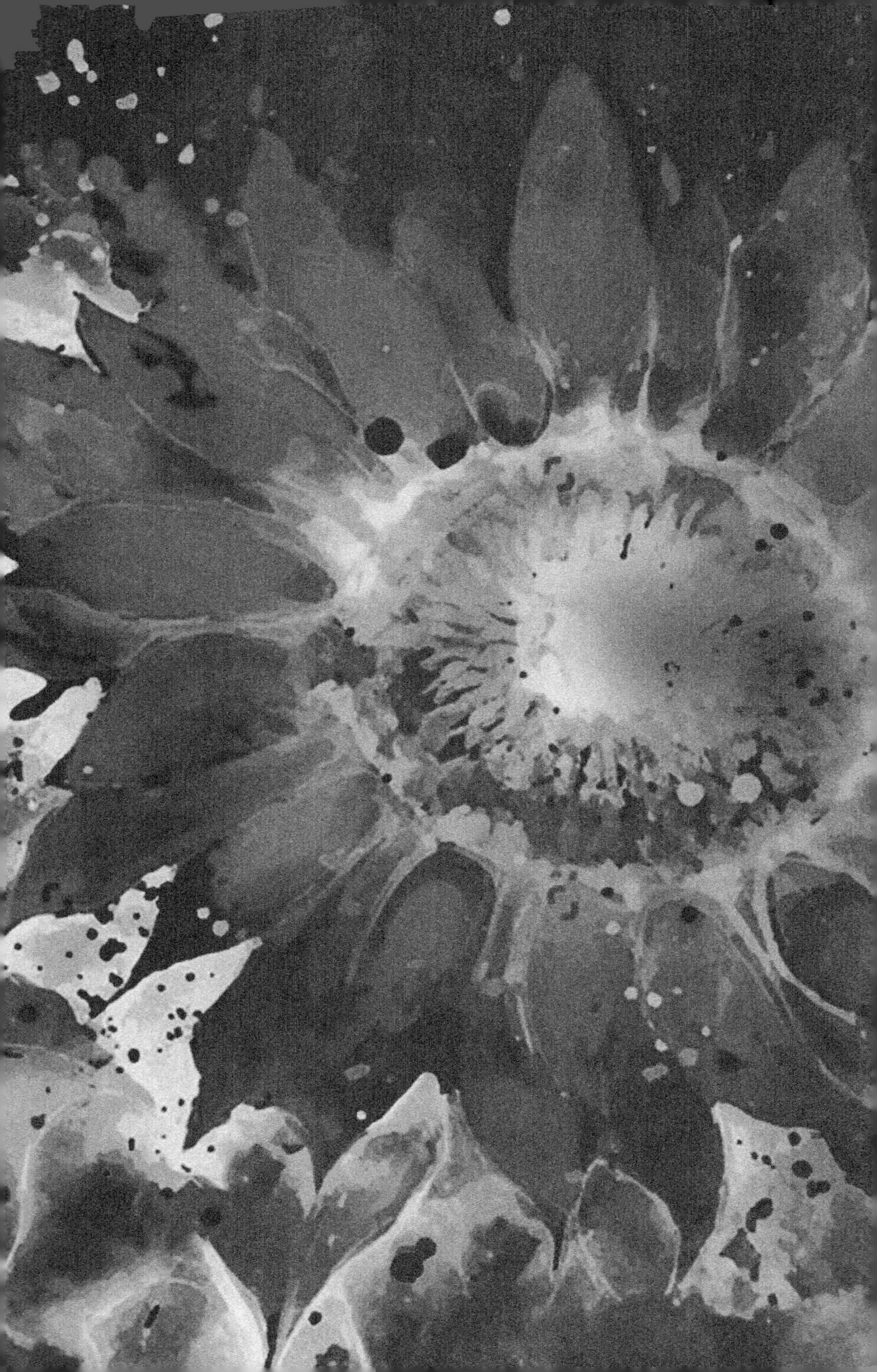

CHAPTER 43

Mason

I am not letting the fire or what Wyatt and Willow overheard ruin the plans I have for the day. So instead of standing around worrying about the scheming of the bitchy barbies, I collect the picnic basket that I already prepared and set aside this morning. With that in one hand I take a hold of Willow's hand with the other and start leading her out of the house.

I eagerly wait for her to reattach the lead to Stella. Once done, she slides her hand back into mine, and with Stella happily trotting beside us, we set off on foot along the trail. The sun is shining, and a gentle breeze rustles the leaves.

We could have taken the horses, but the allure of a nice day prompted me to opt for a more leisurely pace. Plus, I'm not sure how Stella and Gypsy will get along just yet. So, we set off on foot along the familiar trails that crisscross the ranch.

I have a specific destination in mind, a hidden gem in the heart of the forest that I stumbled upon after Willow's disappearance. I always dreamt of showing it to her, and now, I am determined to make that dream a reality.

After walking for a while, I take a sharp turn off the well-worn trail, leading us deeper into the trees and down a gentle slope. The path isn't as familiar or well-marked as the ones Wyatt frequented, but it is clear enough to follow. The sound of water grows louder as we approached, and Willow shoots me curious glances.

The clearing opens up, revealing a small stream fed by a delicate waterfall. I can't help but smile at the awe in Willow's eyes. The sunlight filters through the canopy, casting a warm glow on the crystal-clear water below.

I lead Willow and Stella to a section of grass shaded by a large tree, spreading out a blanket and setting up the picnic basket. I pull Willow down beside me, grateful to see the happiness on her face after everything that happened recently.

She looks around, her eyes filled with wonder, and asks, "How did you find this place? I never knew it was here."

I take a moment, tracing the line of her jaw with my finger, before answering, "I stumbled upon it after you were gone. It became my secret retreat, a place to hide when I wanted to be alone, usually so I could think about you and wish you could return to us. And now, I get to share it with you like I always hoped."

I open the basket, revealing an array of sandwiches and bottles of water and we settle more comfortably on the blanket, the rushing sound of the waterfall providing a soothing background. Stella, sensing the calm atmosphere, lies down beside us.

We take our time to enjoy the sandwiches, savoring each bite as we engage in easy conversation. The worries of the world seem distant in this hidden haven, replaced by the simple joy of good food, nature's beauty, and each other's company.

As we relax, we engage in light conversation about the ranch, Willow's art, and her growing bond with Gypsy. Willow's eyes light up as she talks about her latest paintings and the joy of connecting with Gypsy. Her laughter fills the air, mingling with the gentle sounds of nature around us. The sound makes my heart race and has a smile stretching across my face.

Eventually, between bites of sandwiches and sips of water, Willow looks at me with a mischievous twinkle in her eyes. "So, do you have some deep, dark confession to tell me?" she teases, a playful grin on her face. "It seems to be the trend with each of you."

"Well, let me think," I reply, pretending to ponder the question with a thoughtful expression. "Ah, yes, I confess. I sometimes steal the last cookie from the jar and blame it on Bryce. Terrible, I know."

Willow bursts into laughter, the sound echoing in the secluded spot. "Oh, the horror!"

I chuckle, appreciating the lighthearted turn in our conversation. "Well," I begin, feigning seriousness, "I also do have a secret stash of chocolate hidden somewhere in the ranch. But don't tell anyone. It's classified information."

Willow keeps laughing. "Oh, a chocolate conspiracy! You might need to take me to this secret stash later. I promise to keep it to myself, the information and the chocolate."

Her laughter is a beautiful sound and I'm captivated by the happiness on her face. Unable to resist any longer, I reach over, placing a hand behind her neck, and pull her lips to mine.

The kiss is slow and soft, a gentle exploration of emotions that have been lingering between us. I capture the gasp that escapes from her mouth with mine, savoring the taste and the intimacy of the moment. When I eventually pull away, I can see a glint of surprise and desire in her eyes.

With a soft smile, I confess, "I've wanted to do that for weeks."

Her cheeks flush and a smile returns to her face in response to my words. Before she can speak again, I interrupt the moment by asking, "Would you like to go for a swim? It's a beautiful day, and the water is normally amazing."

Willow hesitates, glancing around, before she protests, "But we didn't bring any swim suits. I don't even own any."

I chuckle and just grin at her as I stand and start walking toward the water. Without much ceremony, I pull my shirt over my head and toss it back to where she is sitting. It hits her in the chest as she sits there with her mouth open in astonishment. Then, with a mischievous glint in my eyes, I do the same with my pants until I'm naked. Shooting a playful grin at her, I walk into the water.

The challenge is there, but it's up to her to accept it. The water is shallow, and my feet can touch the ground across the entire length. I glide through the water until I'm almost at the waterfall, shooting a look over my shoulder before ducking through it and emerging on the other side.

She is standing halfway to the water, playing with the edge of her shirt. Her image is obscured on the other side of the waterfall, and I can no longer hear anything. But I see the moment she takes the challenge, as she strips and steps in.

I wish I could see her through the rushing water, but I wanted to make it her choice.

Moments later, I catch her hand as she emerges through the curtain of water, drawing her body to mine. Our lips meet again, the kiss slow and sensuous, our mouths and tongues moving in a dance that sends shivers down my spine. Her small breasts press against my chest, her hard nipples brushing against me, igniting a fire that has my cock hard and aching.

After what feels like a lifetime of kissing her lips and tasting her, I gently pull away. Looking into her eyes, I say with a soft smile, "I do have one more confession."

She blinks at me, not expecting another revelation, but manages to rasp out, "Okay."

I take a deep breath, my heart pounding, and confess, "I've never been with anyone before."

Her eyes widen in surprise, and there's a moment of silence as my admission hangs in the air. She processes the information, and various emotions play across her face.

"Really?" she finally asks, her voice filled with curiosity.

I nod. "Really. I wanted my first time to be with someone special, someone I cared about. And, well, that's only ever been you."

A small smile plays on her lips, and she leans in to kiss me again, a tender and reassuring gesture.

We break the kiss, and I look deep into her eyes and ask, "Will you be my first?"

Her response is a simple nod, a silent affirmation that sends a wave of warmth through me. I move us until I'm sitting against a ledge in the rock face, creating a makeshift seat for both of us. I whisper, "Ride me, Sugar. I want to see you move on my cock."

Her smile widens, and without hesitation, she takes the initiative. She leans in, capturing my lips with hers in a hungry kiss. Our tongues dance together, and I can feel the heat building between us. She positions herself to straddle my lap, hovering with my hard cock right at her entrance. My heart races with anticipation and excitement.

She breaks the kiss, looking into my eyes with a mix of desire and vulnerability. She begins to lower herself, the warmth of her skin meeting mine, the anticipation building. She takes me in, inch by inch, until she's fully seated on my lap. A soft moan escapes her lips, and I can feel the tightness and warmth of her enveloping me. My breath catches and I let out a low groan, the sensations overwhelming and exhilarating all at once. I resist the urge to thrust, allowing her to set the pace.

Her movements are hesitant at first, a gentle rocking that gradually gains confidence. The connection is intense, and I savor the feeling of her warmth. She starts to move, a slow and deliberate rhythm that has us both gasping for breath. Her hands find purchase on my shoulders, and I hold onto her hips, guiding her.

The pleasure builds inside of me, an exquisite tension that threatens to unravel at any moment. I stare into her hooded eyes, taking in the flushed cheeks and the panting breaths that mirror my own arousal. With each lift and descent, she tightens around me, her movements becoming more exaggerated as her moans grow louder. I have never seen a more beautiful sight.

My hands grip her hips as I start taking more control over her movements. The gentle rocking transforms into a more primal rhythm, and I begin to thrust up inside of her.

The pleasure builds higher, the tingling at the base of my spine signaling that my climax is almost on top of me. The pleasure building inside of me is overwhelming, each thrust pushing me closer to the edge.

I stare deep into her eyes as the ecstasy surrounds us. Her body tightens around me, and I can feel the waves of pleasure crashing over her. She screams as her climax hits, the sound echoing in the secluded space. The intensity of the moment ignites my own release, and with a final thrust, I let it wash over me with a deep groan.

We remain entwined, our bodies pressed together, as we ride out the aftershocks of pleasure. As the waves of pleasure subside, I lean in to capture her lips in a hungry kiss, savoring the taste of her. I gently run my fingers through her wet hair, and she looks up at me with a soft, contented smile.

"That was..." she starts, but words seem to fail her as she searches for the right description.

"Amazing," I finish for her, my voice a gentle whisper. "You were amazing."

Eventually, I guide us out of the water, hand in hand, and we bask in the warmth of the setting sun. The sky is painted with hues of orange and pink, casting a magical glow over the landscape. I pull a towel from the picnic basket, and together, we dry off, the cool breeze adding a refreshing touch to our heated bodies.

Once she's dressed, I reach into the basket and retrieve a few treats for Stella, who patiently waited for us by the edge of the water.

After giving Stella the treats and packing up the picnic, we start walking back toward the ranch. The sun, now lower in the sky, creating a breathtaking backdrop for our journey home. It's a journey I looked forward to making with Willow many times in the future.

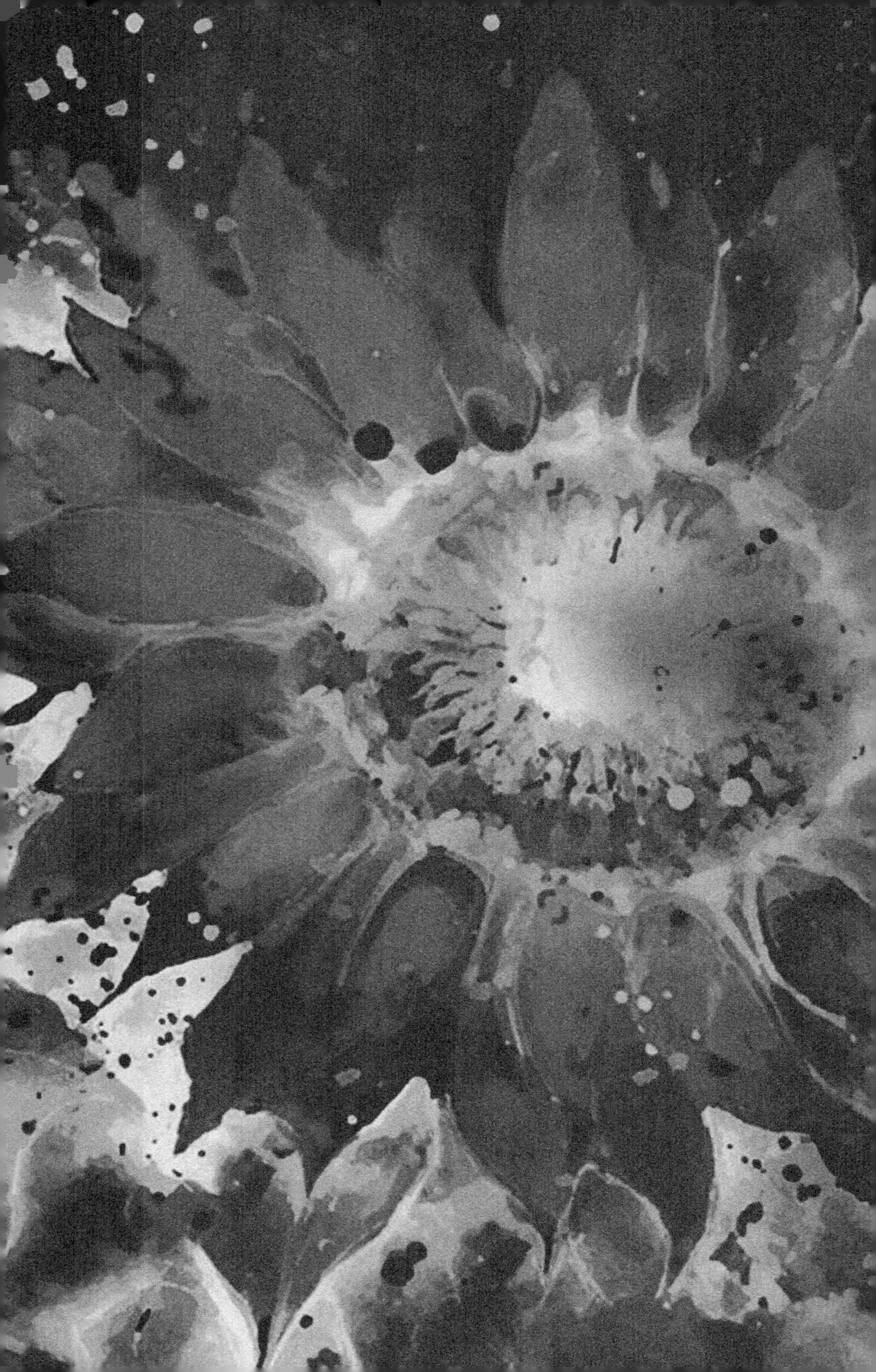

CHAPTER 44
Willow

"Why am I finding out about your house from someone else? Don't you love me anymore?" Kat sticks out her bottom lip briefly before laughing at the look on my face. "I'm joking! But seriously, you need to get your own phone because this boyfriend is not doing his job."

She motions to Easton at my side and I catch the middle finger he scratches against his forehead as he narrows his eyes at the other man leaning against the desk in Kat's office. It's the first time I've heard anyone refer to any of the guys as my boyfriend and my heart thuds heavily in my chest.

Gage tries to give us an innocent look before he shrugs. "How was I meant to know that you hadn't spoken to Kat?"

Kat flicks her hands in both of their directions as she moves around the desk to stand in front of me. She gives me a tentative hug, being mindful of Stella on my other side, before leaning back and offering me a worried look. "Are you sure you're okay?"

I give Kat a small smile, appreciating her concern. "I'm okay, Kat. Just a bit shaken up. I'm staying at Wyatt's for now while they investigate the fire. It's a precautionary measure, and I'm safe."

She studies my face, searching for any signs of distress. "Are you sure you're okay with staying there? You know you're always welcome at my place, right?"

Gage scoffs and says, "Like Wyatt is ever going to let her go anywhere else again."

Kat looks at me with raised brows before giving Gage a pointed look. "If I need to kick his ass and rescue my bestie from his ranch, then I fucking will."

Suddenly, a stern voice sounds from the doorway. "Miss Witlock, do you really feel that's appropriate language?"

Kat freezes, and when I look past her to the doorway, even I almost swallow my tongue. The slightly older guy standing there is very good looking, not that he does anything for me. But from the sudden blush on Kat's cheeks, she might be a different story. She clears her throat but doesn't turn toward the newcomer.

"Apologies, Mr. Blake. Won't happen again," Kat says, attempting to sound professional.

I almost giggle at the way she rolls her eyes, but she doesn't see the way he narrows his at her, as though he knows anyway. "See that it doesn't. I could use some assistance when you're free."

She rolls her lips as though biting back a retort before saying, "Of course, Mr. Blake. I'll be there straight away."

The man disappears again, and I can't stop the giggle that escapes at her loud sigh. I point a finger at her face before saying, "Ummm, speaking of gossip, I need to hear all about this."

She shakes her head in response before walking back around behind her desk, picking up a pen and notepad. "How about I tell you over drinks Friday night?"

My eyes flick to Gage as I contemplate her suggestion before I respond, "How about you come over for a movie night at the ranch instead?"

She grins but doesn't stop moving as she starts walking toward the door. "Count me in! I'll see you then."

And then suddenly, she is gone. I turn to Gage, trying to keep the smile off my face. "Wyatt will be okay with me organizing movie night?"

Easton laughs, taking my hand as he says, "You know Wyatt won't say no to you."

It's my turn to scoff as I brush a hand against Stella, and we start moving. "I think you have him confused with someone else. He seems very happy saying no to me."

They both laugh, as though they know something I don't, but before I can ask, we exit the building toward where Wyatt's truck is parked. Mason and Gage's cars are still stuck at my home until the authorities say we can retrieve them, and Easton's vehicle is still waiting on new tires.

As we step out into the cool afternoon, Gage stops me beside the truck, and his voice is soft as he says, "If you want to have drinks with her, you can. I just want you to be careful, that's all."

I start shaking my head before he even finishes speaking. "No, Gage. You have been supportive of me from the moment I returned. There won't be a moment where I'm not being supportive of you in return. Whatever this is between us, all of us, it means a lot to me. You all mean a lot to me. I already noticed the others don't drink either. If this is one of the ways to show I care about you, then so be it."

As I finish my words, Gage cradles my face with his hands, his touch gentle yet firm. He whispers, "Have I told you that I love you?"

My mouth drops open, and my eyes widen in surprise. He simply kisses my forehead and opens the door of the truck for me, as though he hadn't just said something completely mind-blowing. The warmth of his words lingers, and I can't help but feel a rush of emotions.

Once the three of us have settled into our seats and Stella is settled at my feet on the floorboard, Easton gives Gage a disgruntled look until Gage asks, "What?"

Easton shakes his head and says, "Really? You're just going to spring that on her? Way to make the rest of us look bad..."

I can't stop the laughter that escapes me, and it makes Gage smile. He responds, "Well, I'm not exactly stopping you from saying it yourself."

Easton gives an offended look before facing the front again and turning on the car, saying, "Like I'm going to blurt it out now. I at least want to try to make the moment special."

As Easton drives us back to the ranch, he turns the music up in Wyatt's truck, and both he and Gage try to encourage me to sing along with them to the songs playing on the radio. Despite the lingering tension from my session with Margot, their playful antics manage to lift my spirits, and I find myself joining in the fun.

When we pull up into the parking lot of the ranch, Wyatt walks out to meet us at his truck as we are getting out. He wears a grim expression and delivers the news, "Just had a call from the Sheriff's department. Apparently, they need to ask a couple of questions, but they also said the cars can be retrieved now."

I sigh, anticipating that the day is about to get even longer. Wyatt waves a hand and adds, "They just asked for Gage and East."

We all frown at that, and I inquire, "Are you sure?"

Wyatt nods, holding his hand out for his keys back from Easton, who gives him a look. Wyatt's response is straightforward, "You are not driving it with me in the car."

I giggle at Easton's wounded look before Wyatt turns to me, tilts my chin up, and brushes a kiss against my lips. Then he says, "Relax, watch a movie or something, or even spend some time with Gypsy if you want."

I ask, "Where's Mason and Bryce?"

Wyatt responds, "There was a fence down on the far side of the property. Mason just left to fix it and took Bryce for a ride and is teaching him about the fences."

As Easton, Gage, and Wyatt drive away, I decide to wander into the main house with Stella trotting happily by my side. Thirsty, I head to the kitchen, grab a drink of water, and then move back into the living room. Looking through the movie collection, I select one and settle in on the couch, Stella curling up at my feet.

However, after about ten minutes of watching the movie, restlessness sets in. I don't want to be alone. I want to be with my guys. With a sigh, I turn the movie off and decide to head out to the stables. Spending time with Gypsy sounds like a better idea.

The afternoon air is still cool as I make my way to the stables, the soft sounds of horses in the distance. Knowing that the horses might be easily startled, I gently guide Stella to stay by the door, giving her a reassuring pat before moving towards Gypsy's stall.

As I approach Gypsy, she lifts her head, her big expressive eyes meeting mine. I grab a brush from a nearby shelf and start to groom her. The rhythmic motion of the brush gliding through her coat is soothing. Gypsy seems to appreciate the attention, her soft neighs expressing her happiness.

Lost in the rhythm of grooming, I find peace and my troubles seem to melt away.

However, the peace is shattered when a sudden bark from Stella startles me. I'm surprised to realize that she isn't inside the stable anymore. Her bark came from outside. As I leave Gypsy's stall and turn toward the stable exit, my heart skips a beat.

To my shock, I come face to face with a gun.

WYATT

I slam my hand down on the counter in frustration.

"Well if she wanted you to get us in to answer questions, where the fuck is she?"

Apparently Heidi wanted Gage and Easton at the station but disappeared.

The receptionist looks genuinely apologetic, "I'm sorry, I'm not sure where she is at the moment. I'll try to locate her for you."

I growl in annoyance, frustration bubbling to the surface. "This is ridiculous. She wanted Gage and Easton here to answer questions, and now she's nowhere to be found? Can we at least confirm that we are good to pick up the two cars?" I snap.

The receptionist nods. She walks away for a moment, engaging in a hushed conversation with someone else in the station. My impatience grows, but I try to keep it in check. I just want to be back at Willow's side.

Finally, the receptionist returns, her expression more composed. "Yes, you can now take the cars back into your possession. The necessary checks have been completed."

Relief washes over me, and I nod my thanks. "Finally, some progress," I mutter under my breath.

As we leave the building, Easton suggests, "Maybe we should check Loretta's to make sure that Heidi isn't just off gossiping."

Deciding to follow Easton's suggestion, we make our way down the street to where Loretta's Threads is located. As we approach the store, I frown again, noticing that the closed sign is up on the door. Unease settles in my stomach, and I exchange a concerned look with Gage and Easton.

"Does anyone else think this is odd?" I voice my concern, my gaze fixed on the closed shop.

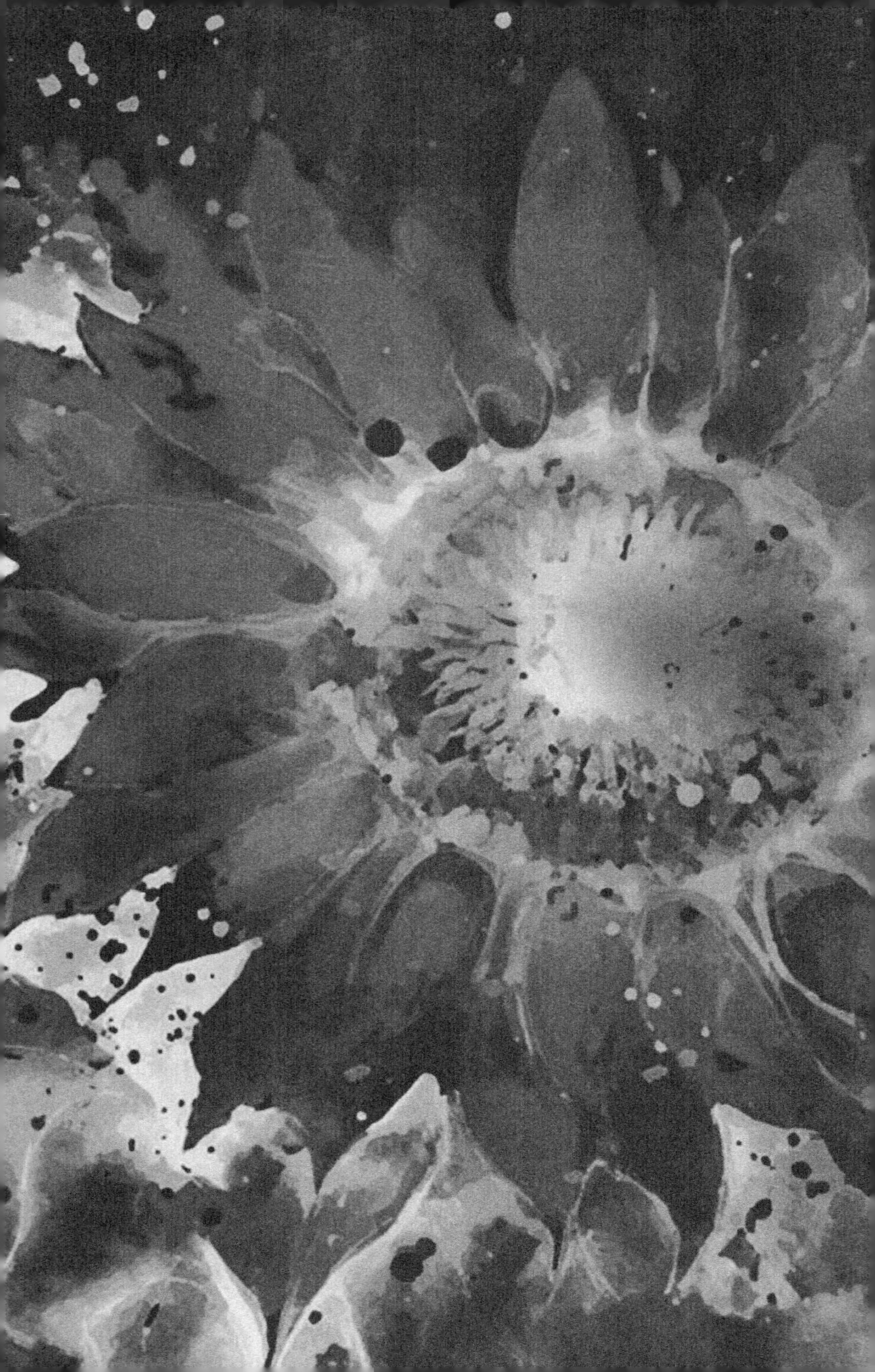

CHAPTER 45

Willow

"What are you doing?" I manage to stammer, my heart racing in my chest.

Heidi tilts her head, amusement evident in her eyes as she shakes her head condescendingly. "I know you didn't exactly finish school with being taken away and all, but surely you aren't that dumb."

The room feels suffocating and my mind races. "Are you going to kill me?" I blurt out, the fear in my voice betraying my attempts at composure.

Heidi's laughter sends shivers down my spine as she smirks, "Well, you just don't seem to want to take the hint and leave. I realized that if I want the job done right, I'm just going to have to do it myself."

My pulse quickens, and I struggle to find words. The air is thick with tension, and the room feels like it is closing in around me.

"Why are you doing this?" I implore, desperate for any explanation that might make sense of the madness unfolding.

Heidi's expression turns scornful, her eyes narrowing as she delivers a cold response, "Are you serious? Those men were ours, and then you thought you could bring your skank ass back to town. You should have stayed gone."

My breath catches, but I am able to push some of the fear aside as anger flares. "I was abducted by a cult. I didn't choose to leave."

She scoffs, a twisted smile playing on her lips as if reconsidering how dumb she perceives me. "Oh, we know that. Who do you think told them about the little girl who desperately needed saving from a group of sinful boys?"

Her words hit me like a tidal wave, and they settle with a sickening realization. She had something to do with me being abducted. I couldn't even really remember them and yet she felt so strongly about me that she had me abducted by a cult.

"What do you mean?" I manage to force out, my voice trembling with a combination of fear and anger.

Heidi grins, and I can almost see the craziness in her eyes as she recalls, "Well, my friends and I ran into a lovely couple and their creepy son. They were going on and on about saving the lost little souls. So, we told them about a soul that needed saving, that we had heard a bunch of boys say they were going to turn you into a whore. Well, of course, they took that very seriously... We didn't know they would then make it their mission to take other girls."

I look at her in astonishment, struggling to comprehend the depths of her insanity. "You seriously chose to ruin my life over a boy?" I question incredulously.

She laughs again, the sound sending shivers down my spine. "Aren't you paying attention, stupid? It wasn't about one boy; it was about three. Gage was mine, Mason was Loretta's, and Wyatt was Callista's."

The revelation about Callista isn't as much of a surprise as I already suspected her relationship with Wyatt wasn't what it seemed. My anger simmers beneath the surface as I straighten my spine, ready to stand off with Heidi.

"And what about your other friend, Melissa?" I challenge her.

She laughs once more, her demeanor unsettling. "Well, she wasn't on board at first, but she kept her mouth shut to stay friends with us... But then Easton came along, and it wasn't hard to convince her after that..."

As the pieces of the twisted puzzle start to fall into place, I hear Stella whining from outside the stable, scratching at the door in an attempt to get in. My heart clenches at the thought of her being hurt if she comes in.

I manage to maintain a facade of composure, though, as I keep my gaze on Heidi. The anger within me fuels my determination to get through this.

"It must say something about you if, in fifteen years, you still couldn't manage to get them," I retort, my voice laced with disdain. "I gather you had something to do with the letter Wyatt received?"

Heidi's grin widens, and I can see how proud she is of herself. "Well, I can't take all the credit. Callista had been sending letters to that creepy boy since they took you. It wasn't hard to get him to send us a little evidence to stop their damn searching."

A surge of rage courses through me as I connect the dots. I take a step back, assessing the situation. The sound of Stella scratching at the door intensifies, reminding me that I need to stay strong for her and for myself.

"What are your plans now?" I ask, attempting to gather more information. "I'm not the same little girl you knew. I have people who care about me, and they will come for me."

Heidi smirks, a dark glint in her eyes. "Oh, I know. That's why I arranged for them to be occupied elsewhere. The call to get them away was just a little diversion."

"Mason will be back any minute." I say, but inside, my anxiety surges. Bryce was with him and the thought of Bryce being anywhere near danger makes my stomach churn. I try to keep my focus on Heidi, hoping against hope that the others will arrive before Mason does.

Heidi just snickers. "Mason is a little preoccupied, and I doubt the others will return in time."

MASON

"Hey little buddy, can you pass me that wire there?" I call out to Bryce as I kneel down to inspect the damage to the fence. Frustration simmers inside of me, but I don't let it show in front of the young boy. I just fixed this fence line last week, and now it seems even more of it is damaged. It looks as though a herd of cattle trampled all over it, or maybe a 4-wheel drive ran through.

Bryce, being the eager little helper he is, rushes over and hands me the roll of wire. I give him a grateful smile before unrolling some and starting to work on mending the fence.

As I'm focused on my task, Loretta suddenly appears out of nowhere, her voice fraught with panic. "Mason, please! I need your help."

I narrow my eyes at her, perplexed by her sudden appearance in the middle of nowhere at the edge of the property. "What are you doing here, Loretta?"

She looks distressed, tugging on my arm urgently. "Please, help. I think Heidi is hurt."

Confusion swirls in my mind. Heidi? Hurt? What is Loretta doing here with such alarming news? Just as I'm about to ask more questions, Bryce, in a sudden burst of defiance, stamps his foot with a loud "No," crossing his little arms and scowling.

If it weren't for the seriousness of the situation, I might have chuckled at his adorable display. Instead, I turn my attention to the little boy, crouching down to his eye level. "What's wrong, little buddy? We need to go help."

Bryce repeats his refusal, stomping his foot again, and with a serious expression, he says, "No."

Perplexed, I ask, "Why not, Bryce?"

He shakes his head before stating, "They said they wanted to hurt Miss Willow."

My heart skips a beat. Hurt Willow? The words hit me like a punch to the gut. I glance at Loretta, who is now standing frozen, her eyes wide with panic. I'm still trying to process the situation when Bryce adds more information.

"I heard them when dadda and I were in town yesterday," he explains. "Heidi was scary angry at her, and said she almost hurt Uncle Gage with the fire."

I feel a knot tightening in my stomach. The mention of Gage and the fire sends a shiver down my spine. But my immediate concern is for Willow.

I look at Loretta with a furrowed brow. "Where was your dadda when you heard this?" I question Bryce, hoping for more details.

"He was talking to Grandpa Greene on the street," Bryce replies. "I was jumping the cracks and had to go around them since they were hogging the way."

The pieces start to fall into place. Loretta was the person on the other end of the conversation Wyatt and Willow overheard the other day. The tension in the air becomes palpable, and my instincts kick in.

Bryce, frustrated, kicks at the roll of wire we have with us. My focus, however, is on Loretta, who is now backing away from us. The realization of what it all means hits me, and I stand up abruptly, moving quickly.

"Where are you going?" Bryce asks, looking up at me with concern.

"I need to talk to Loretta," I reply, my voice firm. "You stay here, little buddy. Keep an eye on the fence, okay?"

With that, I grab a length of rope from my saddle and run after Loretta, determined to get to the bottom of what's happening and to ensure Willow's safety. As I start running I hear my ringtone from the pocket of my jeans, but I can't answer it right now, I don't want Loretta to get away.

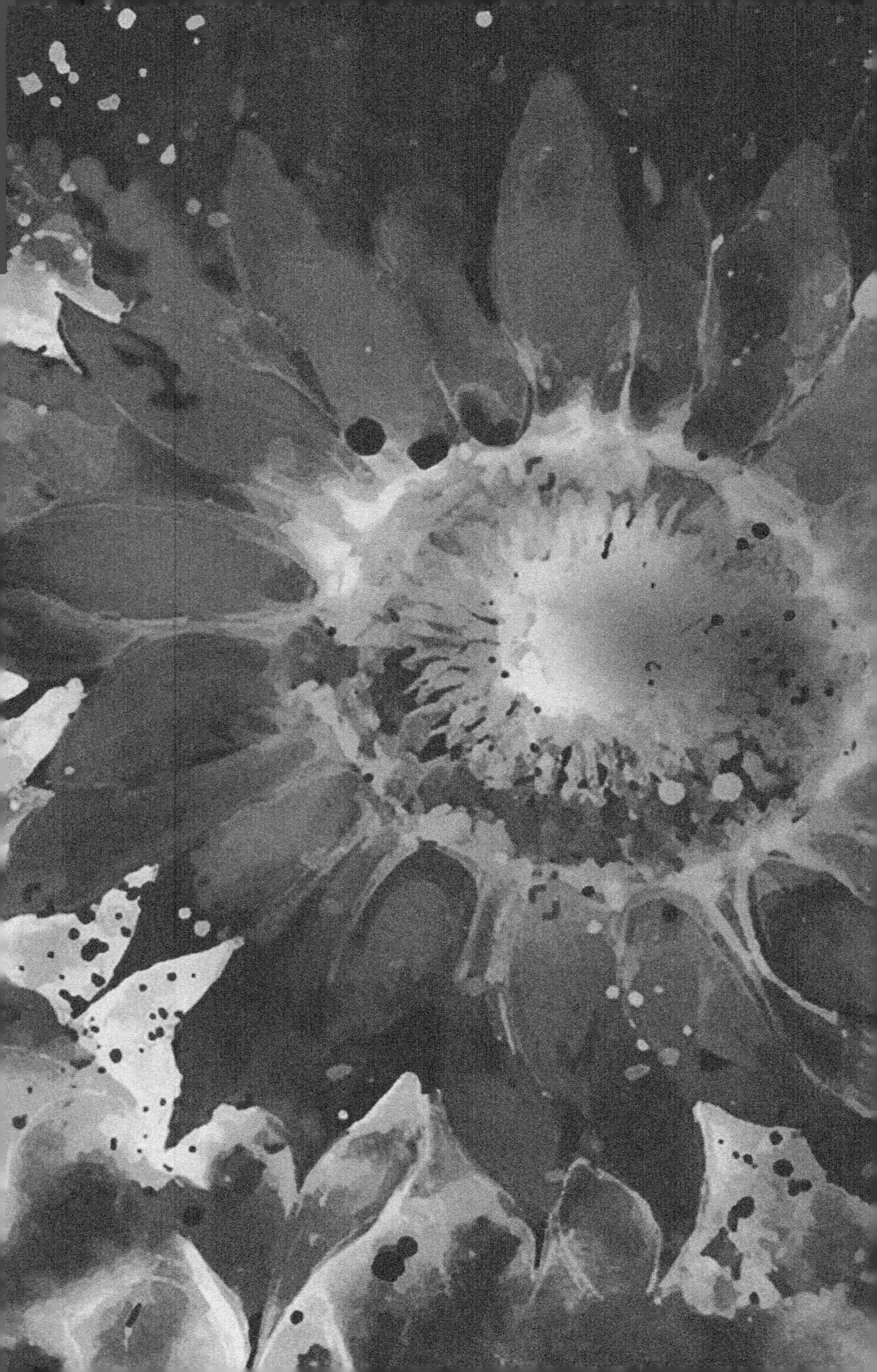

CHAPTER 46

Unknown

I'm done waiting.

Moving quickly from the shadows where I have been hiding, I grab ahold of the person in front of me by the hair. They don't even see me coming.

They certainly don't see the knife I drag across their throat from behind. The blade glints in the light as it flashes out, swift and deadly. A muffled gasp escapes from the person's lips, but it's cut short as blood begins to pour from the fresh wound.

I don't let go. I keep a firm grip on their hair as I lower them to the ground, my movements precise and calculated. Their struggles weaken, and within moments, the life drains from their eyes.

I release them, and their lifeless body slumps to the ground as I stand to my full height.

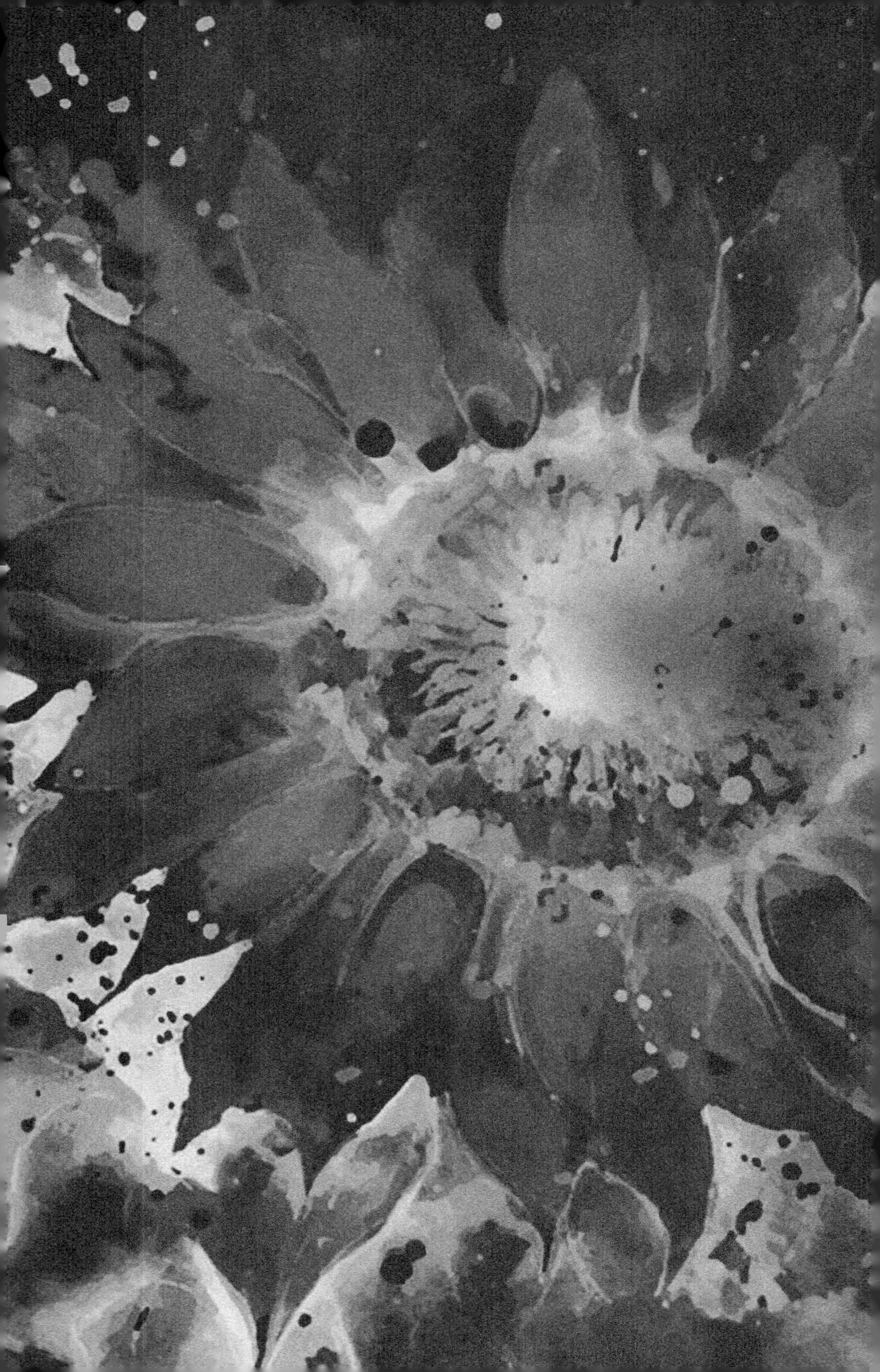

CHAPTER 47

Willow

I can't move, I can't even breathe. The moment I saw the person appear behind Heidi, I felt paralyzed. Panic and fear grips me, completely controlling my body. I already feel my heart racing fast in my chest as the blood rushes through my ears. I can't even move when the spray of Heidi's blood hits most of my body.

All the techniques and ways to help that Margot taught me feel like smoke vapors in my mind, dissipating into thin air. The room spins, and my vision blurs as I come face to face with my worst nightmare.

"Hello, Angel, you've been a very bad girl."

The voice, the familiarity of that taunting tone, sends a chill to my very bones. The dark memories I've tried so hard to bury over the last month surge forward, threatening to drown me. I can't bring myself to turn away from the person who has already destroyed me once.

My breath catches in my throat as my eyes meet his, and in that moment, it's as if time has frozen. Every fiber of my being screams at me to run, to escape, but my body remains immobile.

I try to force words out, but my voice fails me. The room feels smaller, the air thicker, and my nightmare crashes into my reality with an overwhelming force. Pure terror is coursing through my body.

As I stand there, frozen and paralyzed, he steps forward, his eyes locked onto mine. The wicked grin on his face reveals the sadistic pleasure he derives from my fear. He reaches out a hand as if to caress my face, and I flinch, but the touch never comes.

He chuckles and continues, his voice menacing but also with a twisted hint of affection, "I tried to be patient, my Angel. I waited for you to come back to me, but you insisted on playing with these little boys. You belong by my side. You are my soulmate, and that's where you were destined to be."

I feel like the tiny little mouse that already sees the bird of prey swooping down with talons extended.

"I watched those petty little whores try to do whatever they could to sabotage your life," he sneers. "You should be thankful to me for disrupting most of their plans."

His words hit me like a series of blows, each one reopening wounds I thought healed. I can't fathom how he's been watching, manipulating, and influencing my life from the shadows. The sheer audacity of his claim sickens me.

"I was there for the fire, but I wasn't going to stop that," he continues, his tone a mixture of anger and disappointment. "I was too angry after seeing you give your body away like we meant nothing. Like you had any right to give away what's not yours to begin with. It belonged to me! Your body belongs only to me and to god!"

He moves closer, and I can feel the heat of his breath on my face. My body aches with the desperate need to flee, but the paralysis holds me captive. Every fiber of my being rejects his proximity, but I remain a prisoner to my own fear.

His voice drops to a chilling whisper, "You can't escape me, Angel. We are destined to be together. I've waited long enough, and now you will come back to where you truly belong."

His fingers lightly trace the outline of my face and I shudder. The proximity is suffocating, and I feel his cold breath on my skin. I can see the predatory glint in his eyes, and the madness lurking within.

"I've watched you, Angel," he murmurs, the distorted affection in his voice turning my stomach. "Every move, every breath. You're mine, and no one else's. You could never hide from me."

His evil chuckle cuts through the silence like a blade. "We are going to start our own church, Angel. And we will find our own followers. But before we do, I need to get rid of those boys who thought they could touch what's mine."

The sensation of ice circling my heart spreads, and the coldness courses through all of my limbs. Oddly, this feeling allows me to focus on something other than the monster in front of me. One of the grounding methods that Margot taught me suddenly comes to mind. Closing my eyes for a moment, I concentrate on my breath, trying to anchor myself.

He laughs harder, finding amusement in my momentary escape. His fingers grip my jaw, and he hisses into my face,

"I will make their deaths slow and painful, and you will watch every second of it."

His words cut through me like a serrated blade, but amidst the terror, a spark of defiance flickers within. With his grip on my face, he shoves me backward. I stumble, and in the same moment, Stella scratches at the stable doors more aggressively. She growls and barks loudly enough to catch Jacob's attention.

I seize the distraction, the lifeline Stella unintentionally provides. Running on pure instinct, I sprint away. The sound of Jacob's angered shouts fades behind me as I head for the far end of the stables. Memories of our teenage years sneaking in here resurface, and I hope that Wyatt hasn't repaired the broken section of the wall in one of the stalls at the back.

Dashing into the stall, I see the familiar spot. Pushing against a section of the wall, it moves, and relief floods over me. I dive toward the hole, my heart pounding, and start dragging myself through it on my stomach. I'm almost all the way out when his hand wraps around my ankle.

He starts dragging me back through the gap, and my mouth finally works for me as I scream—partly from fear, partly from frustration and anger. I kick out, but a sharp pain radiates from my leg. Familiar with the sensation of his knife cutting into my skin, I keep kicking. With sheer determination, I drag my other leg through the gap, bracing against the wall until he finally lets go.

Not wasting a second longer, I get to my feet, pushing past the pain in my leg to run. I can hear him behind me—the bang of the stable doors thrown open, the growl of Stella. He seems too focused on me to cause her any harm, or maybe she has wisely run away from him. All I pay attention to is the heavy sounds of his feet as he runs after me. I don't even register the direction I'm heading; I just run, driven by the desperate need to escape the nightmare chasing me.

As I sprint through the fields, my breaths come in ragged gasps, matching the frantic beating of my heart. The terrain feels uneven beneath my feet, but I keep running, fueled by the fear that Jacob is hot on my trail. The familiarity of the landscape begins to register, and my mind races as I realize I'm retracing the same path I took the night everything changed.

Reaching the top of a rise, I don't stop to take in the view of the sun beginning its descent. Instead, I plunge headlong into a sunflower field. The vibrant yellow sea surrounds me, but I don't let the beauty distract me. I can still hear Jacob running behind me, his shouts piercing through the rustling leaves. "Come back here, Grace!"

Fear no longer slows me down. I keep running until I'm deep within the field, hidden by the sea of sunflowers. The dense foliage provides cover, and I take advantage of it. With each turn, I attempt to throw him off my trail. His frustrated calls become more distant as minutes pass.

I stop and slowly turn in a circle, trying to hear past the rushing sound in my ears. I can hear him getting closer on my left. Bending low, I creep in a different direction. I repeat this process, a dance of desperation, as he continues shouting my name.

I turn again, moving forward, looking over my shoulder to catch any movement behind me. In my frantic escape, I stumble over an uneven part of the ground, and suddenly, I'm out in the open on a wider path through the flowers. Jacob is only a few yards away, and he must have grabbed Heidi's gun because he aims it at me, yelling for me to stop.

With the threat of the gun, I do stop moving, but instead of cowering, all I feel is frustration and anger. This man has already taken so much from me, and I refuse to let him control me any longer. The sun casts long shadows across the field as we face each other.

I lock eyes with him, my voice somehow steady despite the storm inside me. "You don't control me anymore, Jacob. I won't let you hurt me anymore."

His response is a guttural growl, his grip on the gun tightening. "You are mine!" he shouts.

I raise my chin defiantly, meeting his gaze. "Not anymore. I would rather die than ever submit to you again."

His face contorts with rage, and he raises the gun even higher, preparing to pull the trigger. The sound of the gunshot rings through the once-quiet field. I brace myself for the searing pain, but it doesn't come. Instead, I witness Jacob's face twisting in confusion, his eyes widening in shock.

Red suddenly starts spreading across his shirt, and he looks down at himself for a fleeting second before collapsing to the ground as though his strings have been cut. The deafening silence that follows is broken only by his gasps for air.

Emerging from the sunflower field behind him is Wyatt with a rifle in his hands. Discharging the cartridge, he walks towards Jacob, who is struggling for breath on the ground.

I watch the red dribble and spray from his lips with each strangled gasp.

At the same time, Gage appears from another direction, and I feel a gentle hand brushing down my arm. Startled, I almost scream before Easton whispers, "Shh, little butterfly, it's just us." I fall into his arms for a moment. He has a gun in his hand, and it's hard when he presses it against my skin. I pull back and ask, "Mason and Bryce?"

He smiles in reassurance, "They took Loretta to the Sheriff's department."

I sigh in relief before turning my attention back to Jacob, who is still struggling to breathe. Looking back at Easton, I reach out and take the gun from his hand.

Remembering the basic knowledge I learned before I was taken, I walk straight over to where Jacob is lying in the dirt. Flicking the safety off, I point the gun and start shooting until I empty every round into him. The sounds of the gunshots echo through the field, each pull of the trigger feels like a cathartic release.

As I stand there, panting and staring at the lifeless body on the ground, a mix of emotions floods over me. The nightmare that has haunted me for so long has come to an end. I look around, and Wyatt, Gage, and Easton are there, expressions of grim satisfaction on their faces. I knew Mason would have been there too if he could have.

At that moment, I realize that I'm not alone anymore. I have people who care about me and who were there for me when I needed them the most.

"He won't hurt you anymore," Wyatt says, his voice steady.

I nod, "No, he won't." Some of the tension and anxiety I have felt, like the constant hum to my consciousness, melts away.

Easton reaches out and takes the gun back from me with a grin. "Is this moment special enough?" he asks.

I frown in confusion before he reaches out and cups the side of my face, "Fuck I love you, little butterfly."

I smile at Easton, happier than I have been in forever. Wyatt comes up behind me, not taking me from Easton but simply being there and pressing a kiss to my head as he leans in close to my ear. "I love you too, and I'm so fucking proud of you."

There is blood on some of the sunflowers that are on the ground, and they have never looked more beautiful to me.

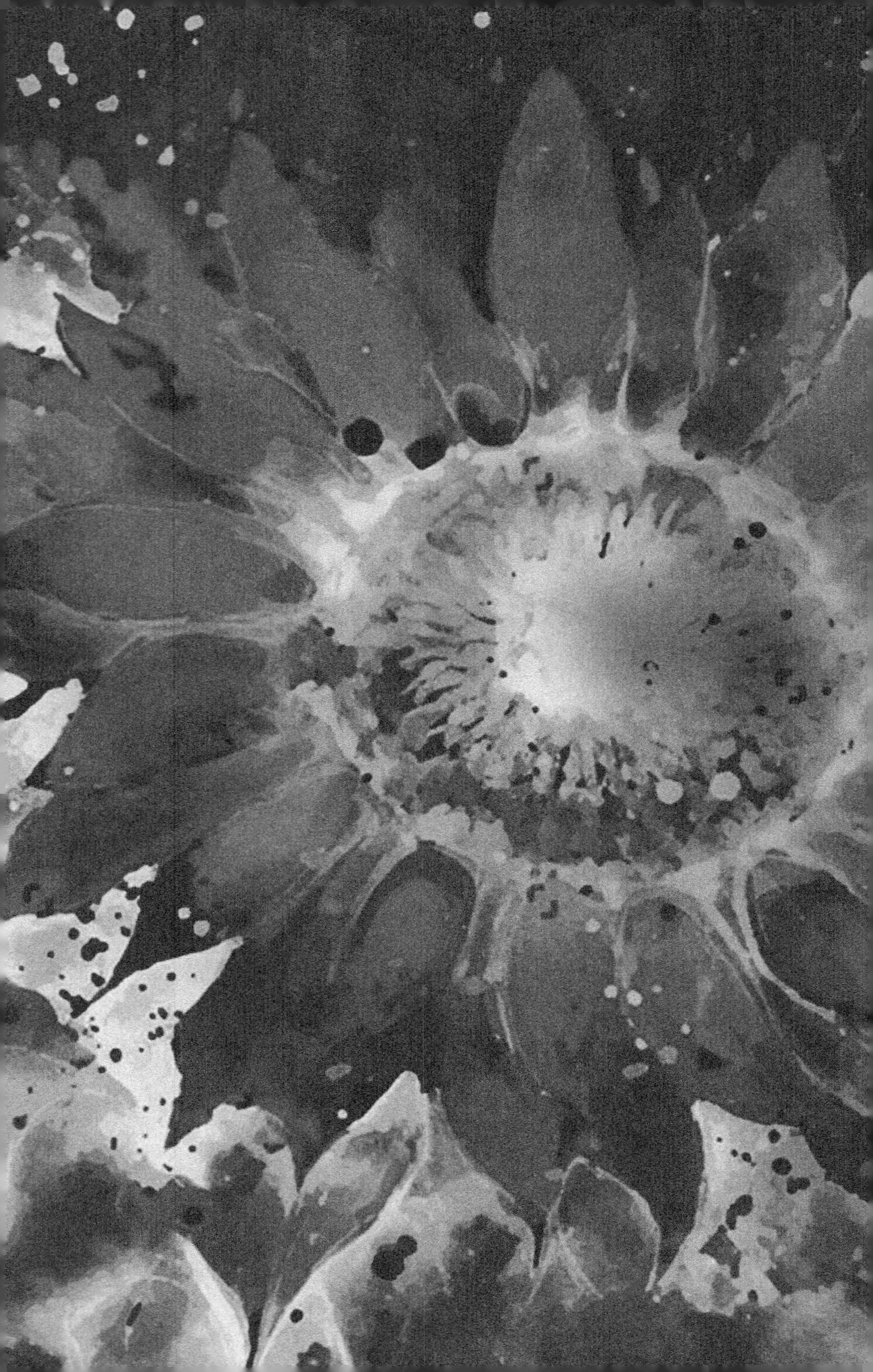

EPILOGUE

2 Months Later

"That's it, Sweetness, give me one more."

I moan as Gage presses my back harder against the tiles in the shower, his cock moving inside of me in a slow erotic rhythm. I feel the pleasure building inside of me, his pelvis rubbing against my clit with every slow thrust.

I am already sensitive, so it won't take much. He stole me from Mason's arms before I even fully came down from the orgasm that Mason fucked from me.

He keeps his slow pace as the water cascades over us, his hands digging into the flesh of my ass. His lips meeting mine, his tongue sliding into my mouth in an imitation of how his cock is sliding in and out of me. The pleasure continues building, my pussy tightening around him as our moans echo in the bathroom.

Gage's movements become faster, driving us both closer to the edge. A few more thrusts and we teeter on the brink of release. The water continues to rain down on us.

My fingers dig into Gage's shoulders, and I arch my back, meeting his every movement. The pleasure is almost overwhelming, coursing through every nerve ending. As Gage continues to drive into me, I feel the tension building, reaching an exquisite peak.

Waves of pleasure wash over me, and my body convulses in ecstasy. My pussy pulses around his cock and Gage's movements become erratic until he finds his climax too.

We cling to each other, breathless and spent, the water from the shower now gently washing away the remnants of our passion.

There is a scratch and a whine at the door to the bathroom. After the Sheriff came to the crime scene and we returned to the ranch, Stella had been beside herself. I was so thankful that she hadn't been hurt. Since that day Stella has not left my side again, and if she is forced to she makes her displeasure known. Even when I spend time with Gypsy she is there with me now.

The others teased Mason mercilessly for being the last to tell me he loves me. Until he finally taunted them with a smug look that he did even better and gave me his virginity. But that still didn't stop him from taking it upon himself to steal me away at the first opportunity and make love to me slowly while telling me a thousand times.

"We need to get dressed and go or we will be late." I sigh as he lowers my legs to the shower floor.

Gage chuckles, pulling away reluctantly. "As if Wyatt will let you, I'm surprised he isn't already in here pulling you out of the shower."

As if on cue, the door opens, and Wyatt leans against the frame with a frown. "You're going to be late to your own mother's dinner," he says, a hint of amusement in his voice.

Gage laughs, but I open the shower door and walk into the towel that Wyatt retrieves and holds out for me. His hands move slowly, dragging the towel against my skin, a touch that is both tender and possessive. The dinner is a farewell for Margot, who has decided to follow her friends and move to Florida now that Gage has "settled with the best daughter-in-law possible".

I have already been introduced to the person taking over Margot's practice and agreed to stay on as a patient, even though he is a man and his unprofessional looks toward my best friend were unmistakable.

Now that I no longer need full-time protection, Easton spoke to the Sheriff and decided to step into the position that Heidi's death left vacant.

I glance at Wyatt, his eyes meeting mine with an intensity that makes my heart flutter. He wraps the towel securely around me, his touch leaving a trail of heat in its wake.

"Don't take too long getting ready." Wyatt says, leaning in to place a soft kiss on my forehead.

Gage grins, reaching for his own towel. "You heard the man, Sweetness. Let's not keep my mother waiting."

I shoot Gage a playful look, feigning innocence. "Well, technically, someone here did take their sweet time in the shower."

He laughs in response as I walk back out into what has now become my bedroom and start to get ready. We all live at the ranch now and Gage rents the apartment above the bar to his bar manager. I was still waiting on the insurance money from the destruction of the house, which was taking even longer than it took to convict Loretta of arson and three counts of attempted murder.

But I'm not stressed about that. I was sad to have lost all the memories that the house contained but I'm resolute on creating happier, better memories with my guys and our little man.

Bryce continues to spend at least two afternoons a week creating art with me. No matter what manipulations and evil deeds had gone into him being born, the sins of his mother would never be held against that beautiful, happy little boy.

I'm still healing, mentally and emotionally, and I know it will take a long time. But I already have plans to create therapy programs in conjunction with the new therapist where others can come and spend time with the horses like I did, or spend time creating art with me and Bryce.

I know my ultimate happiness and healing would still take time. It is a long path to walk, but I'm certainly moving in the right direction.

AUTHOR'S NOTE

I hope you enjoyed Home Sweet Home!

Thank you to my husband for being so supportive of my writing.

A special thanks goes to Kitty and Alina for all of your help and voice and text messages. And my Good Little Sluts and Nip Chatting Ogres, you know who you are, thank you for all the love and support.

As always, thank you to my team of amazing alpha and beta readers. You are all wonderful and I wouldn't be where I am without you.

Thank you to my Street and ARC team for being great spokespeople for a relatively unknown indie author.

And thank you to my readers for picking up this book and supporting me, I appreciate you.

xx

Maree Rose

ABOUT THE AUTHOR

Maree is an indie author who, although she has been writing most of her life, never thought she would ever get something published, which is now why she published this herself. She has always been an avid reader since a young age after roaming through book exchanges with her mum when she was just starting to read serious big girl books.

Maree lives on the East Coast of Australia with her wonderful husband, her son, and her two gorgeous squishy british bulldogs.

When she is not writing, she is working in a financial career (for something completely different to the creative side) or she is working on her photography (which is just as hot as her books).

STALK ME

Please feel free to stalk me.
   Like metaphorically, not literally of course!

Facebook:
Follow My Page
Join My Readers Group

Amazon:
Follow My Author Page

Goodreads:
Follow My Profile

ALSO BY

SHATTERED WORLD

Shattered Safety Duet:
Untouchable & Unbreakable

Shattered Memories Duet:
Unforgettable & Unstoppable (COMING SOON)

THE MASQUERADE

Make Me Learn

DARLING WORLD

hunt me darling
hide me darling (COMING SOON)

DEAD DEVIL'S WORLD

Dead Devil's Night
Dead Devil's Playground (COMING SOON)

BLACKSTONE SECURITIES

All We Want

Printed in Great Britain
by Amazon